Inside
MARI
3

Shuzo Oshimi

contents

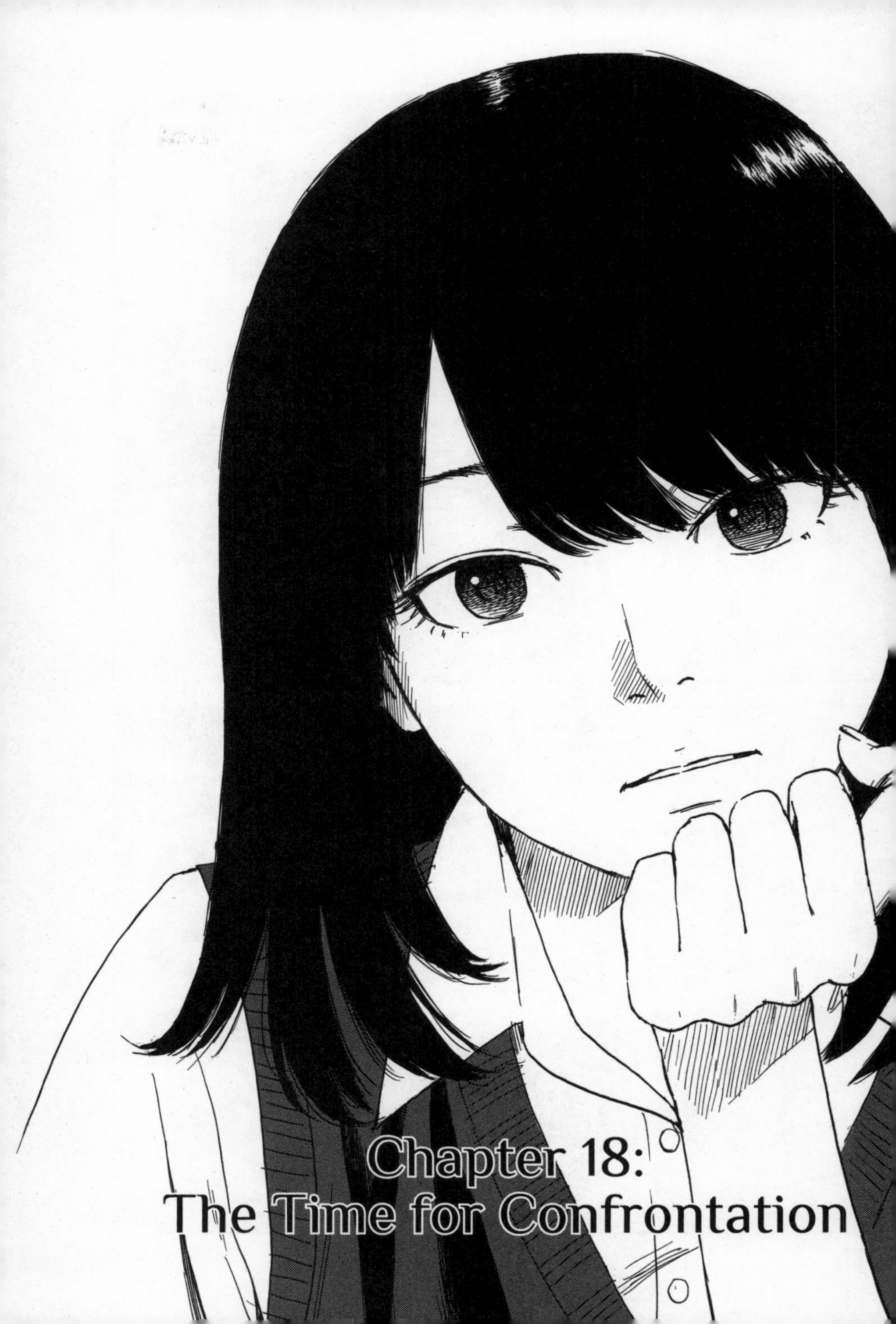
Chapter 18:
The Time for Confrontation

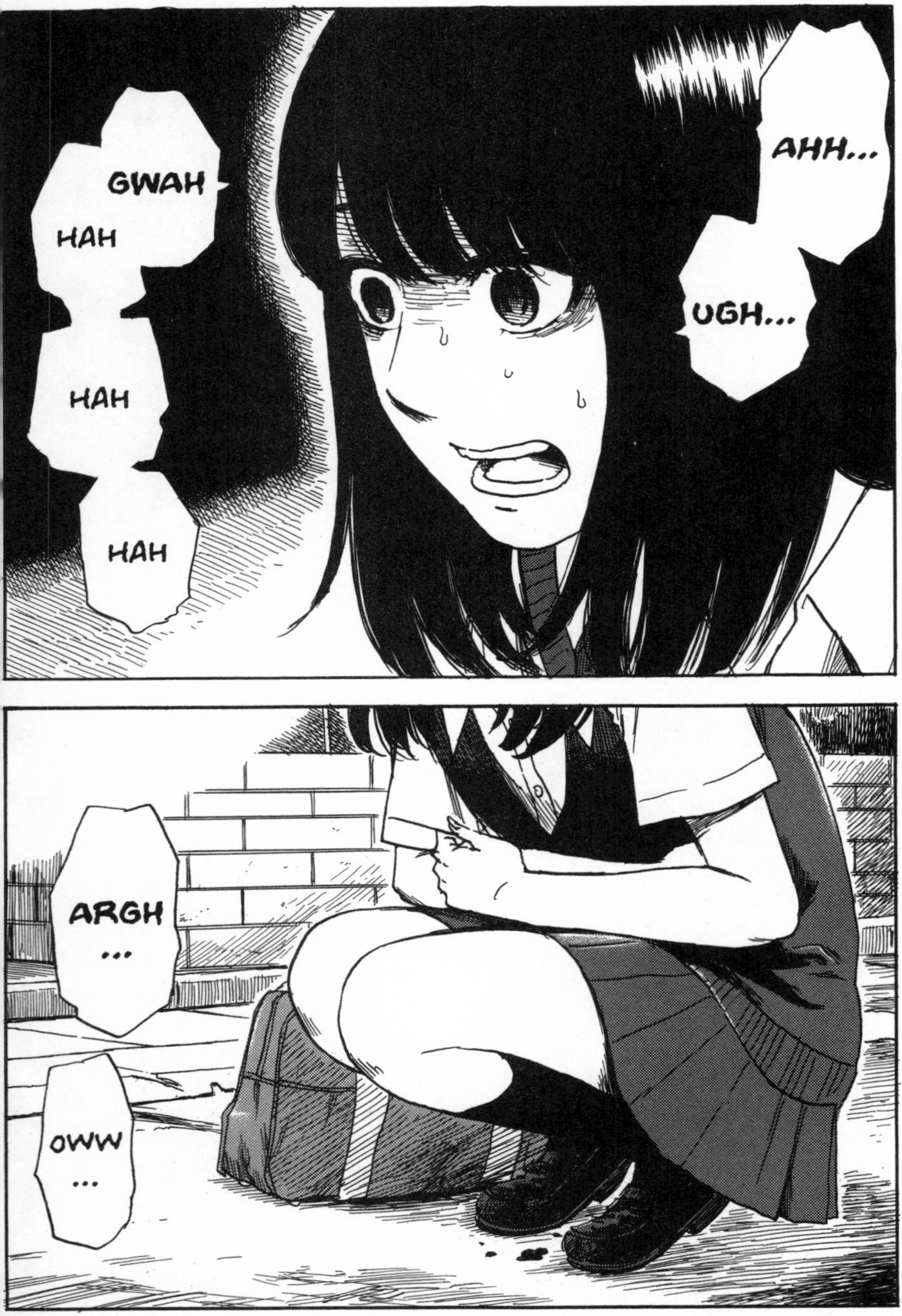
AHH...
UGH...
GWAH
HAH
HAH
HAH
ARGH ...
OWW ...

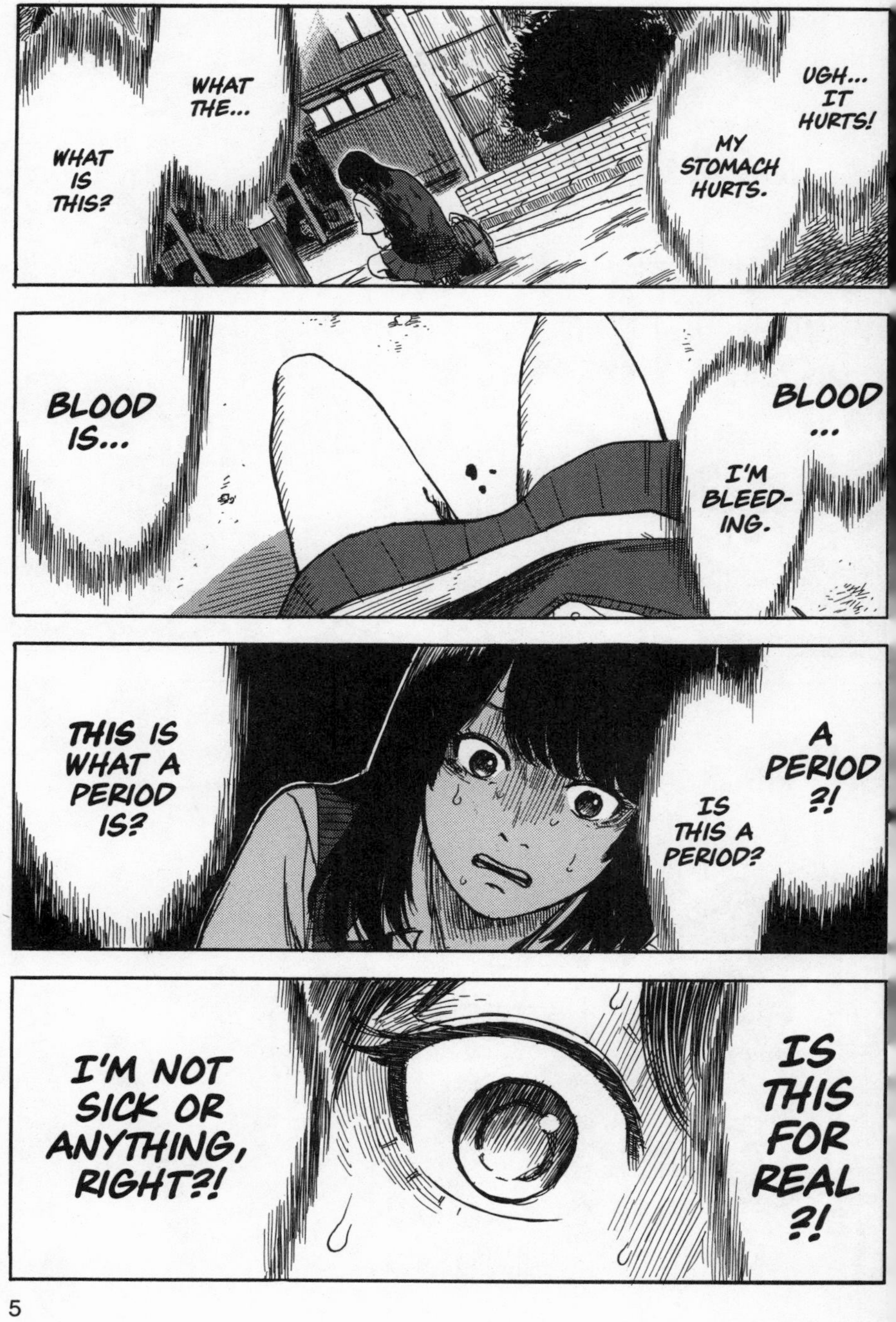
UGH... IT HURTS!
MY STOMACH HURTS.
WHAT THE...
WHAT IS THIS?
BLOOD...
I'M BLEEDING.
BLOOD IS...
A PERIOD?!
IS THIS A PERIOD?
THIS IS WHAT A PERIOD IS?
IS THIS FOR REAL?!
I'M NOT SICK OR ANYTHING, RIGHT?!

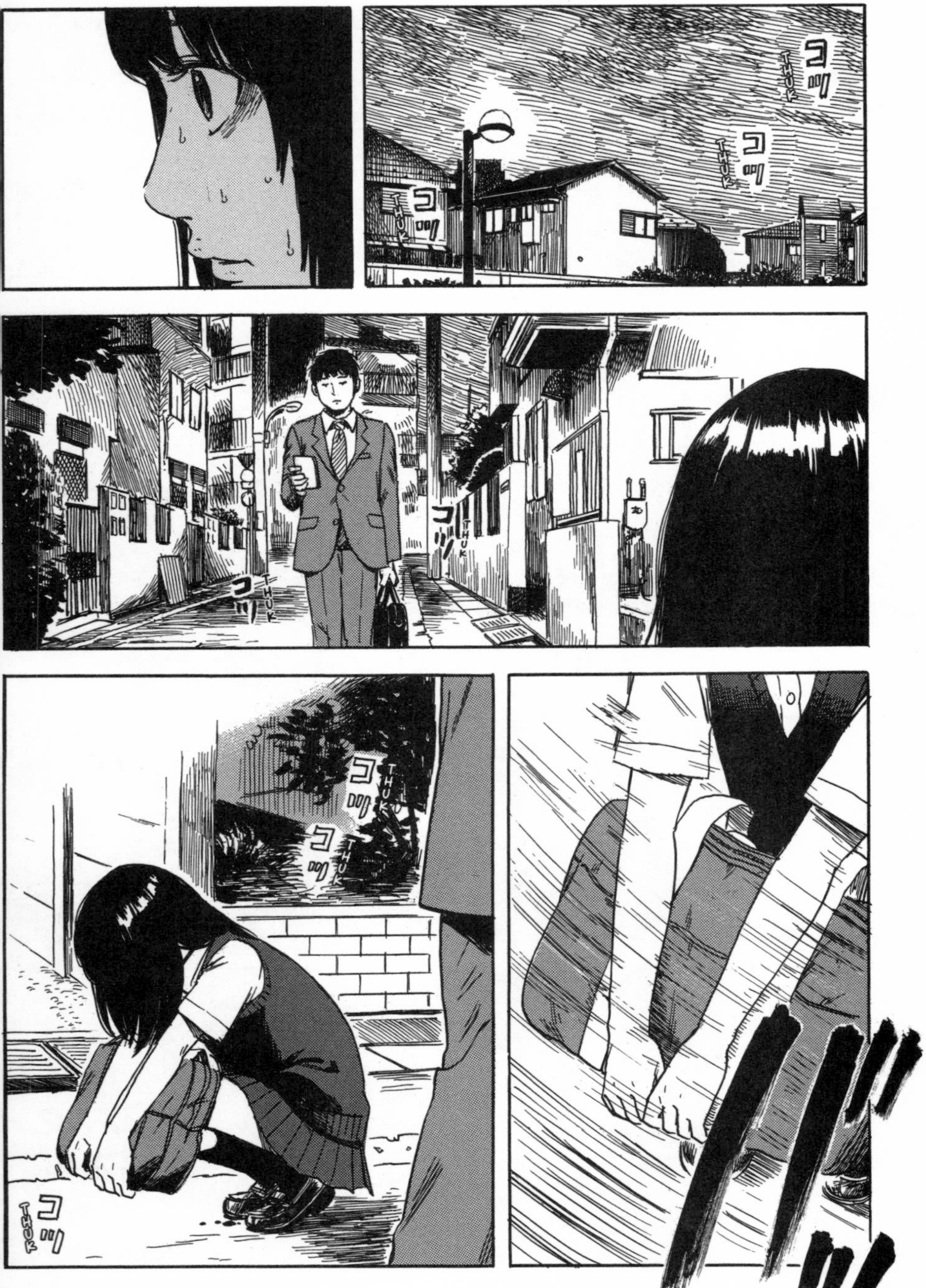
コッ THUK
コッ THUK
コッ THUK
コッ THUK
コッ THUK
ギュッ CLUTCH
コッ THUK
コッ THUK
コッ THUK

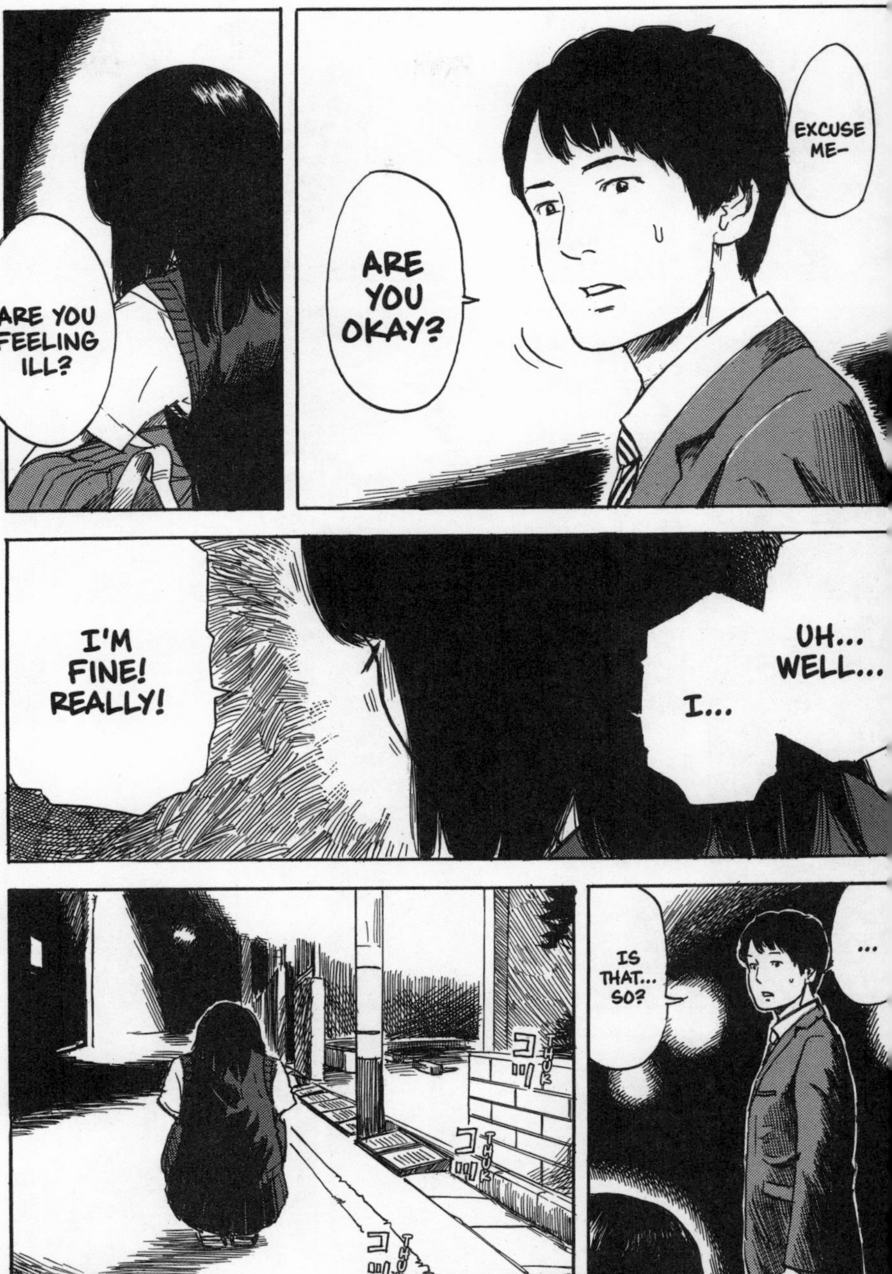
EXCUSE ME-
ARE YOU OKAY?
ARE YOU FEELING ILL?
UH... WELL...
I...
I'M FINE! REALLY!
...
IS THAT... SO?
コッ THUK
コッ THUK
コッ THUK

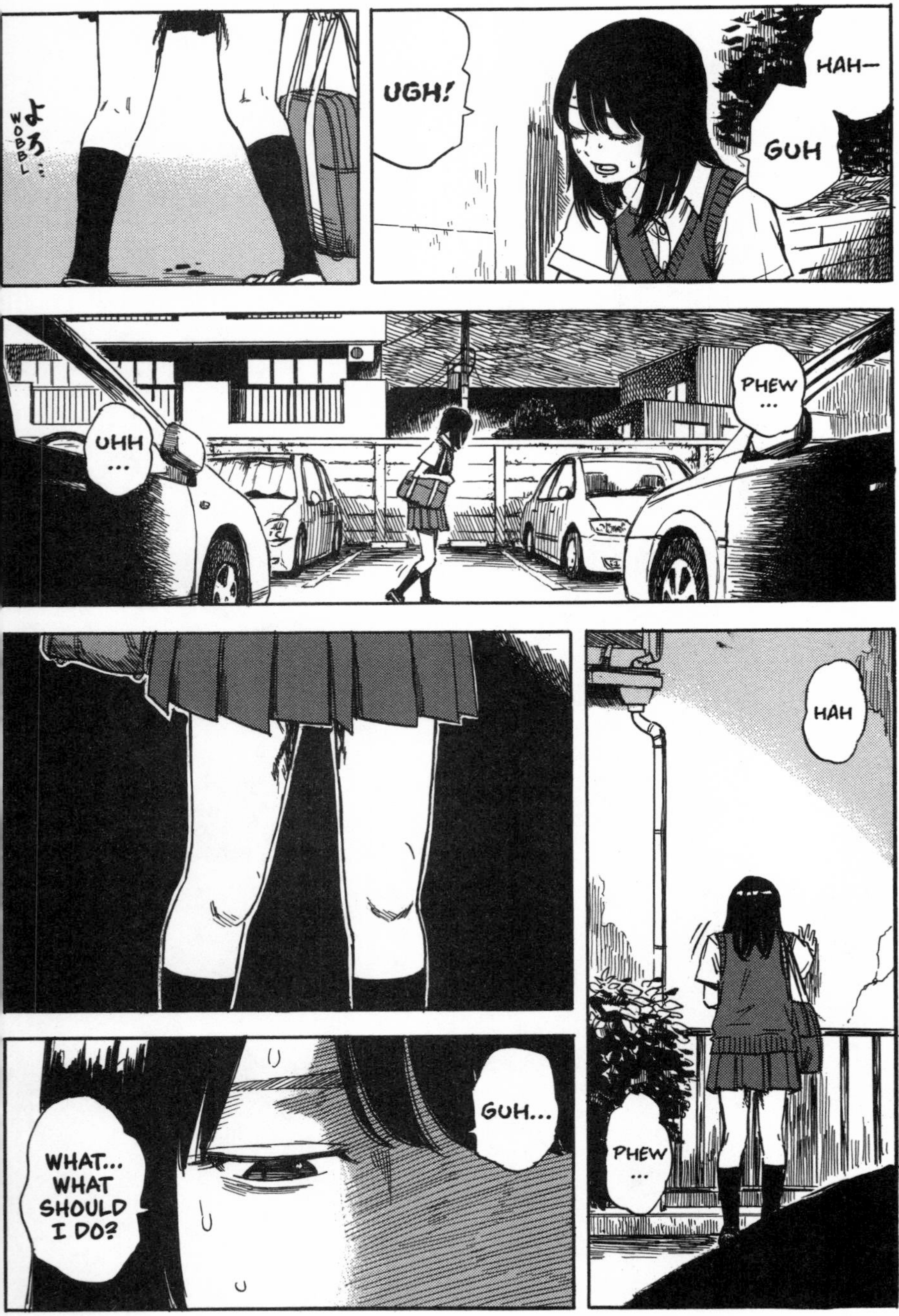
HAH—
GUH
UGH!
よろ
WOBBL
PHEW ...
UHH ...
HAH
PHEW ...
GUH...
WHAT... WHAT SHOULD I DO?

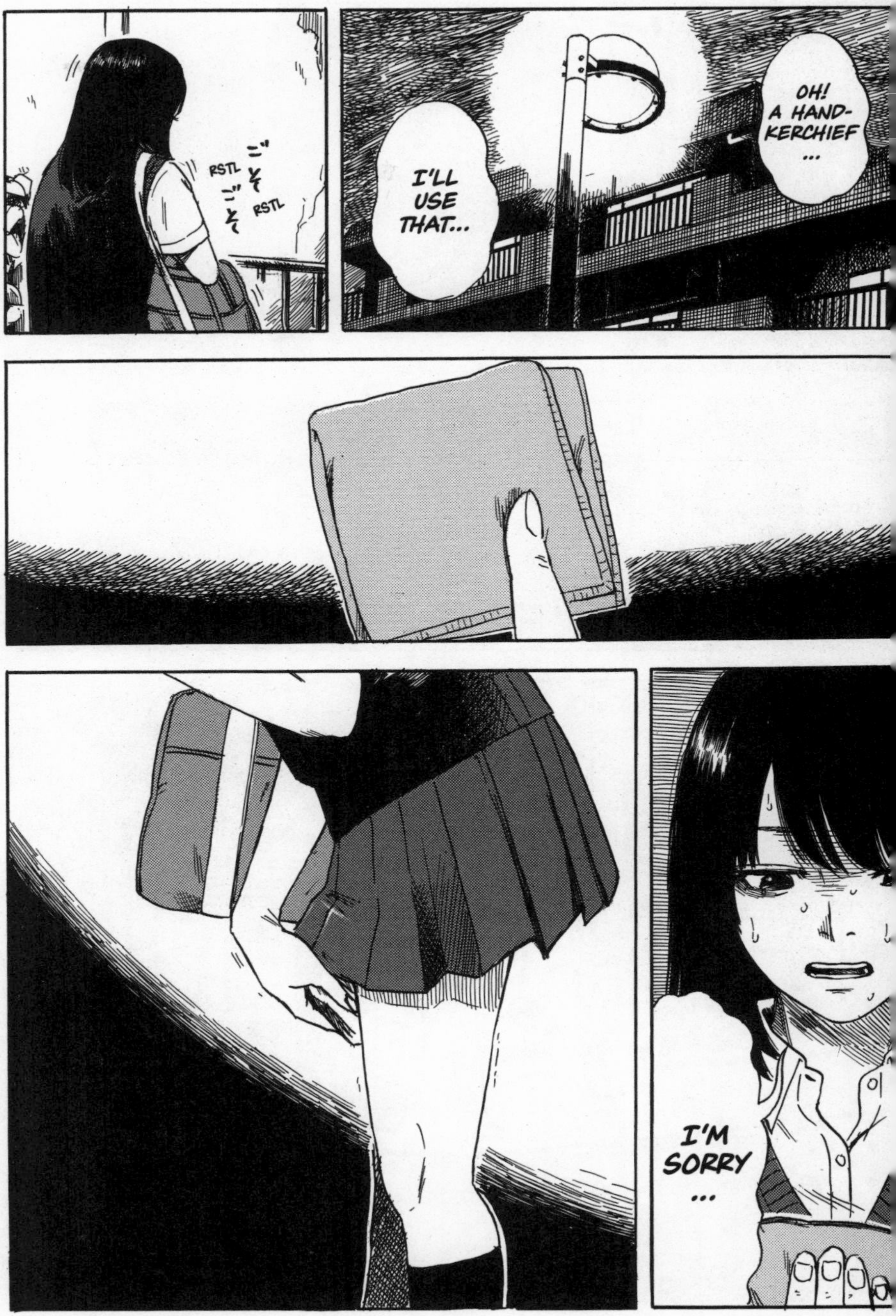
OH! A HAND-KERCHIEF ...
I'LL USE THAT...
ごそごそ
RSTL RSTL
I'M SORRY ...

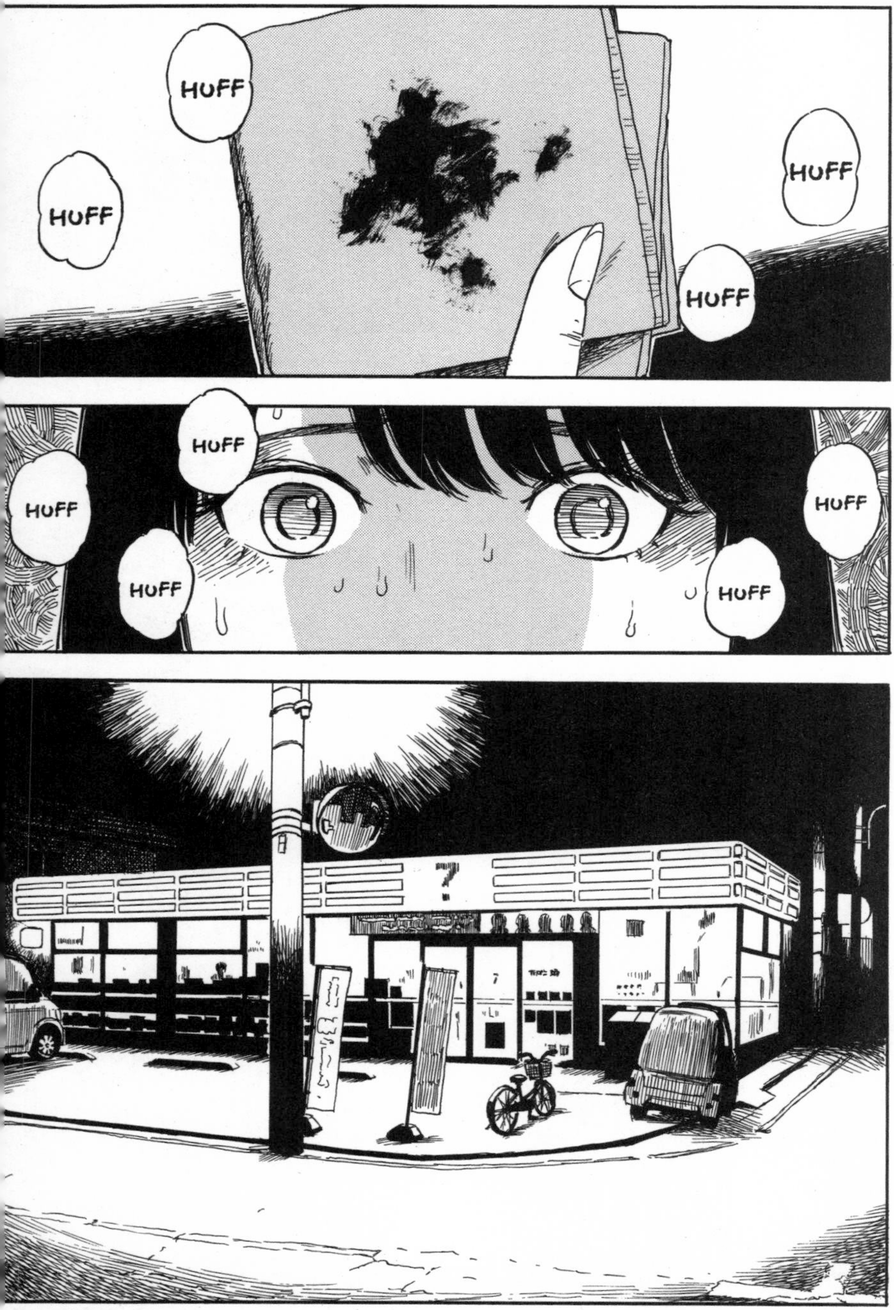
HUFF
HUFF
HUFF
HUFF
HUFF
HUFF
HUFF
HUFF
HUFF
HUFF

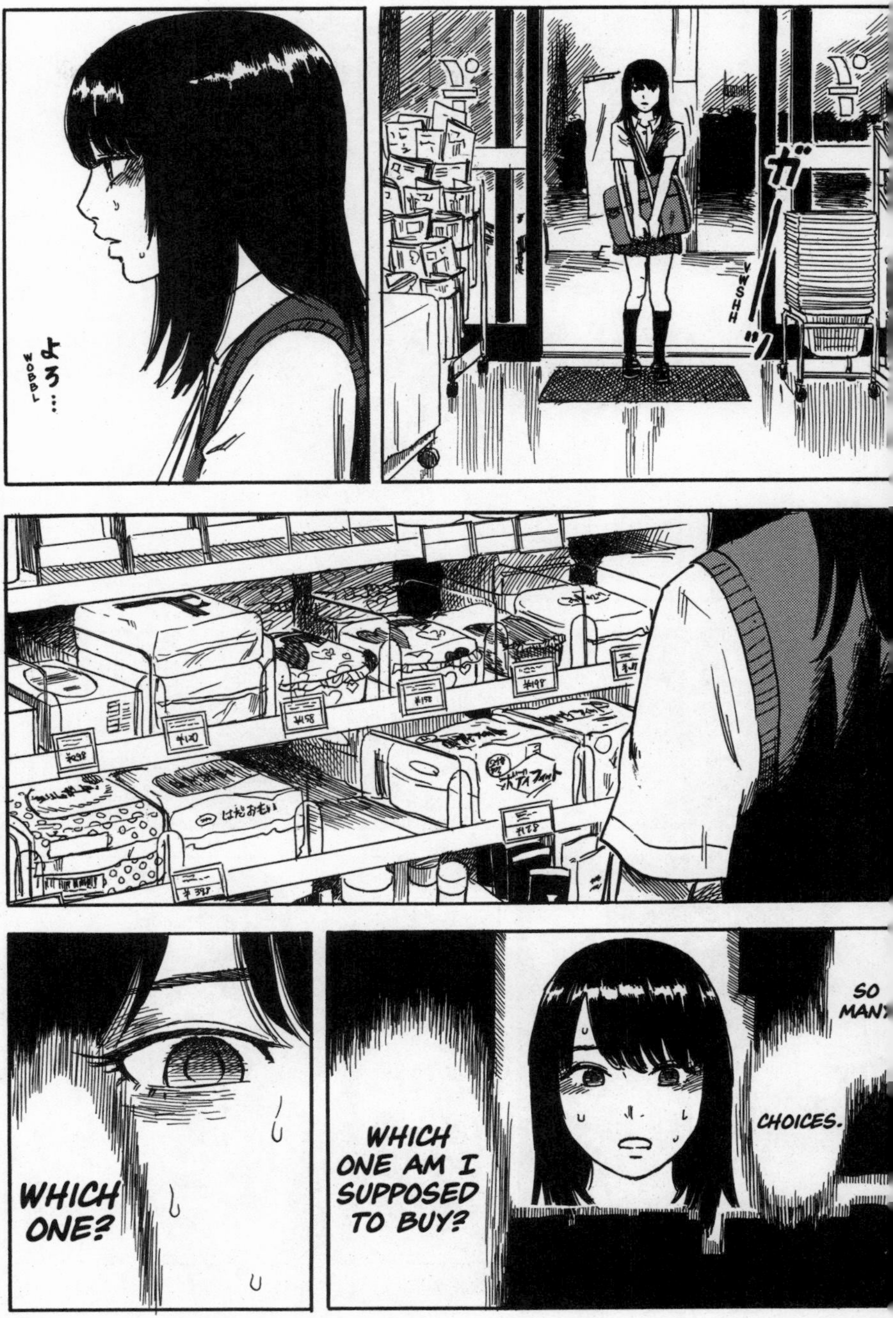
ガ
VWSHH
よろ…
WOBBL
SO
MAN
CHOICES.
WHICH ONE AM I SUPPOSED TO BUY?
WHICH ONE?

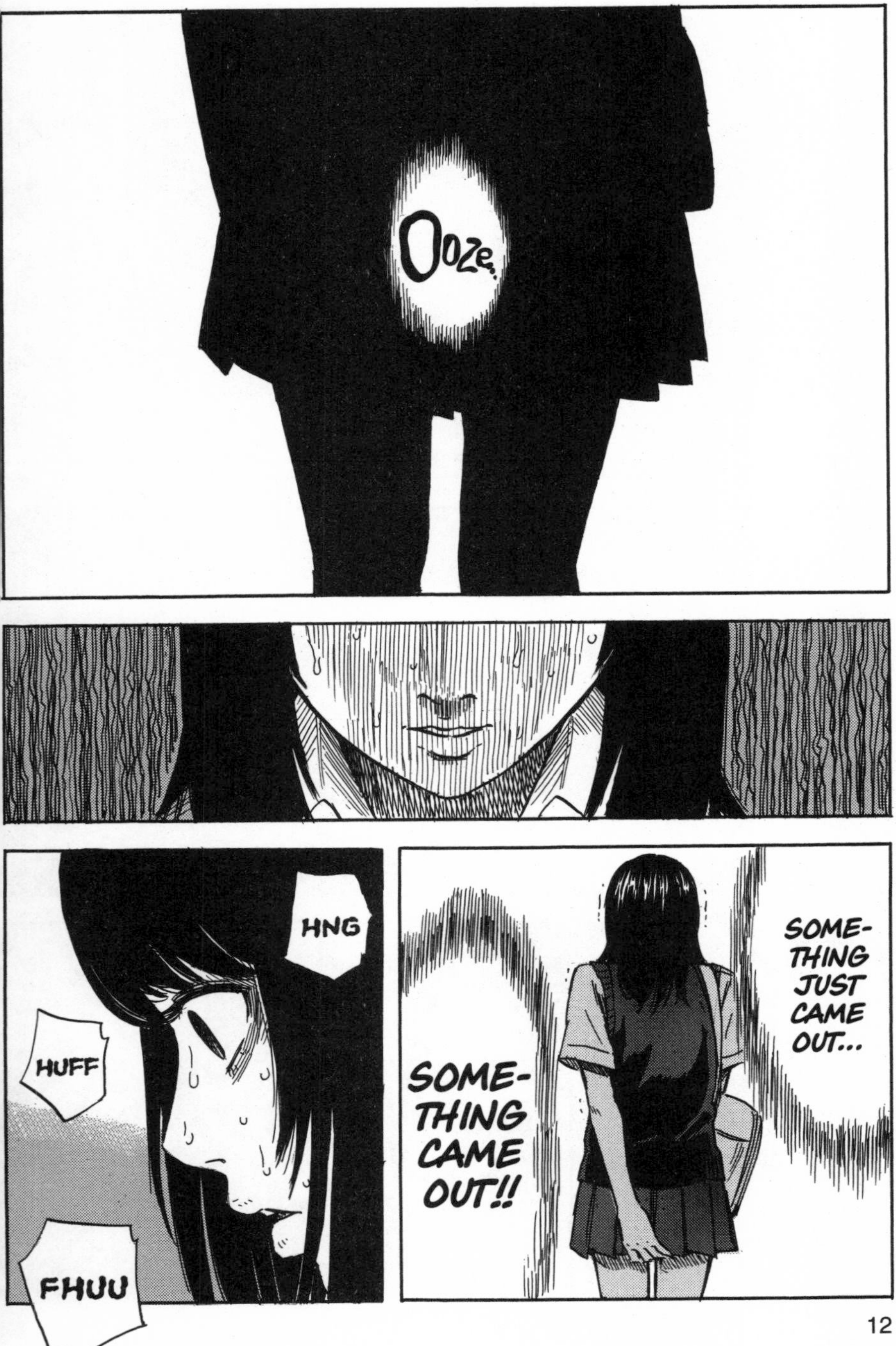
Ooze..
SOME-THING JUST CAME OUT...
SOME-THING CAME OUT!!
HNG
HUFF
FHUU

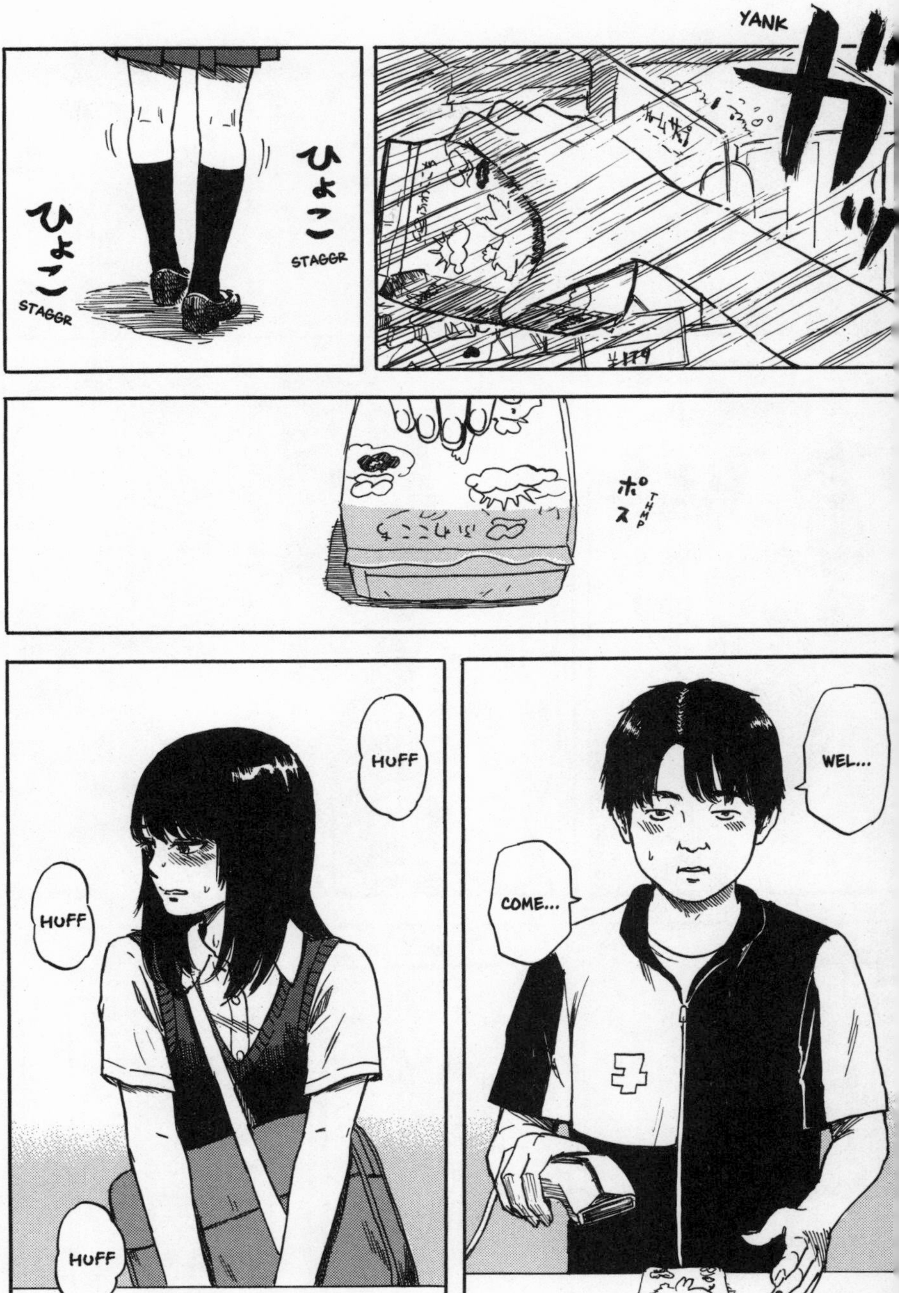
ガッ
YANK
ひょこ
STAGGR
ひょこ
STAGGR
ポス
THMP
WEL...
COME...
HUFF
HUFF
HUFF

UM...

THAT'LL BE 178 YEN.

ガサ...

PLEASE...

LET ME USE YOUR RESTROOM.

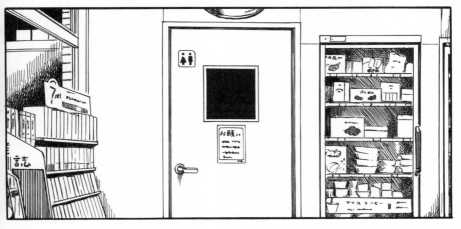

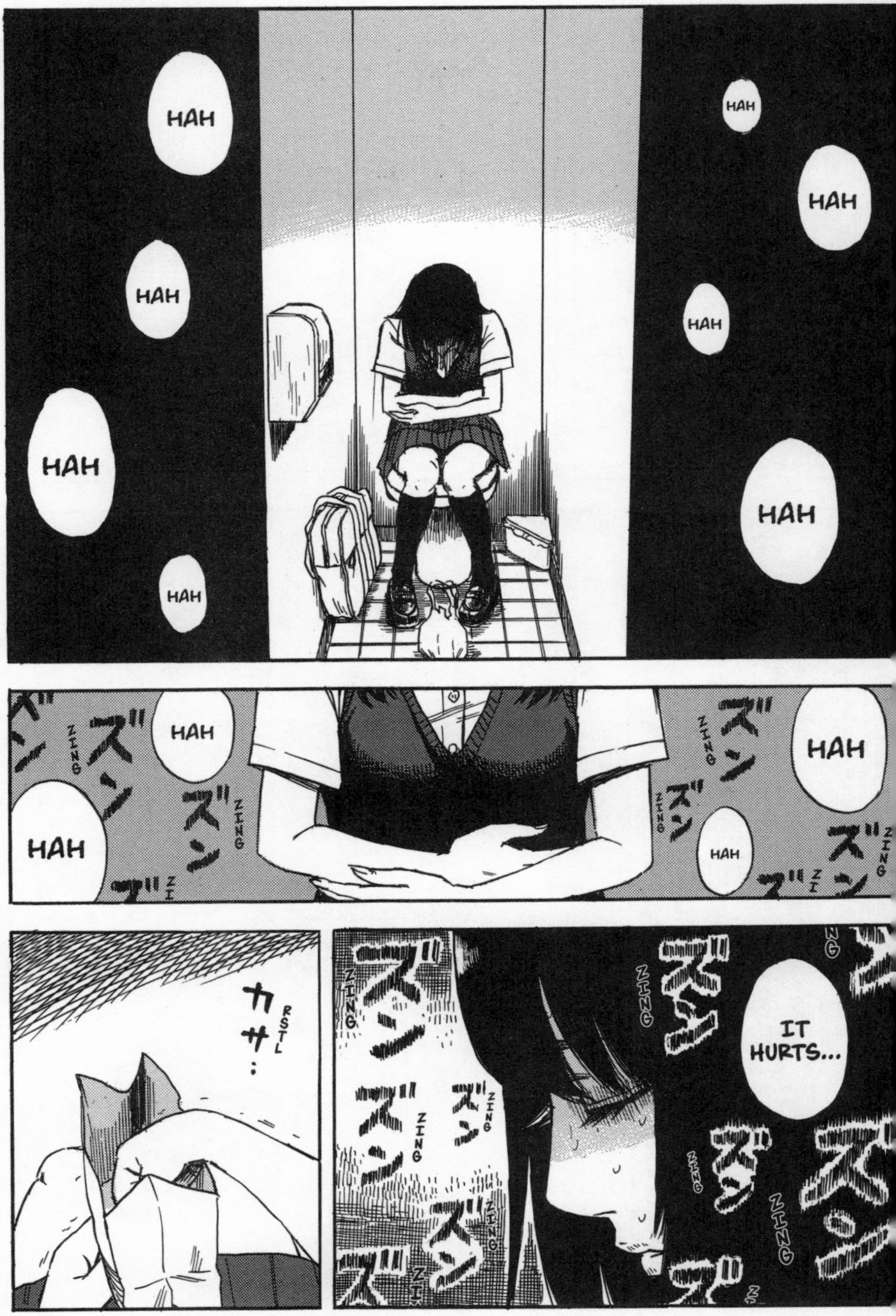
HAH
HAH
HAH
HAH
HAH
HAH
HAH
HAH
ズン
ZING
HAH
ズン
ZING
HAH
ズン
ZING
ズ
ZI
ズン
ZING
HAH
ズン
ZING
ズン
ZING
ズ
ZI
HAH
ズン
ZING
ZING
ズン
ZING
IT HURTS...
ズン
ZING
ズン
ZING
ズ
ZI
ズン
ZING
ズン
ZING
ズン
ZING
ズン
ZING
ズン
ZING
ズ
ZI
カサ:
RSTL

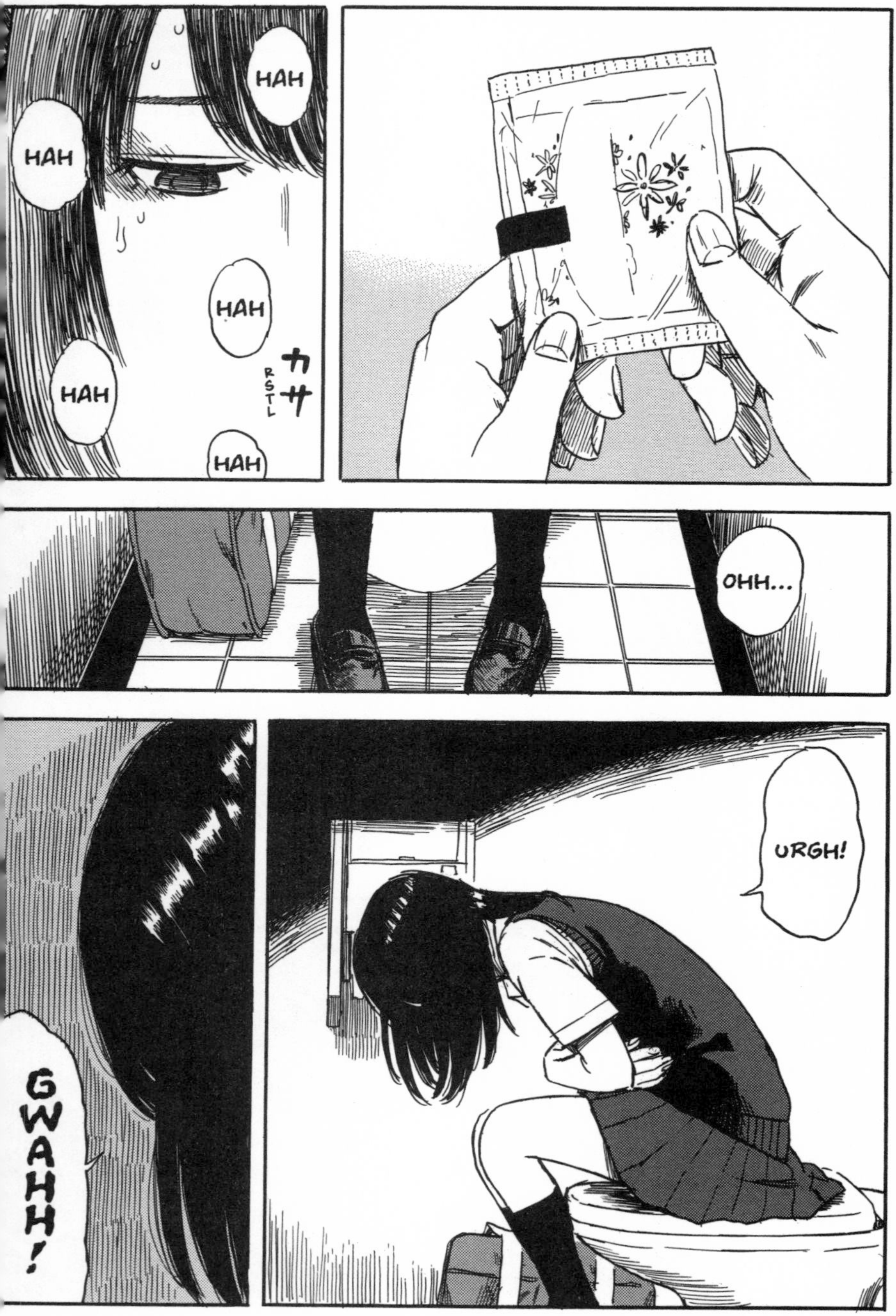
HAH
HAH
HAH
RSTL
HAH
HAH
OHH...
URGH!
GWAHH!

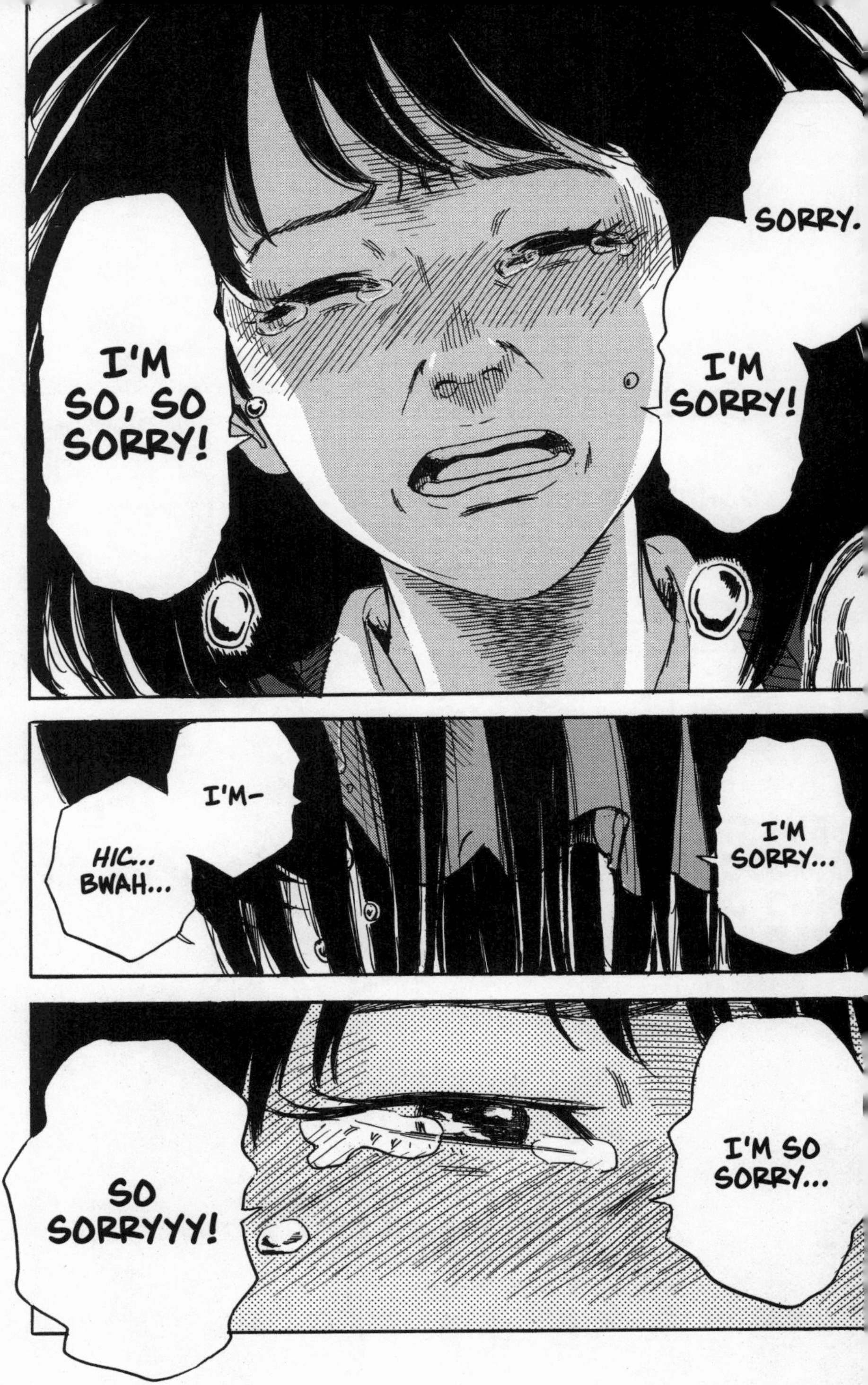
SORRY.
I'M SORRY!
I'M SO, SO SORRY!
I'M SORRY...
I'M-
HIC... BWAH...
I'M SO SORRY...
SO SORRYYY!

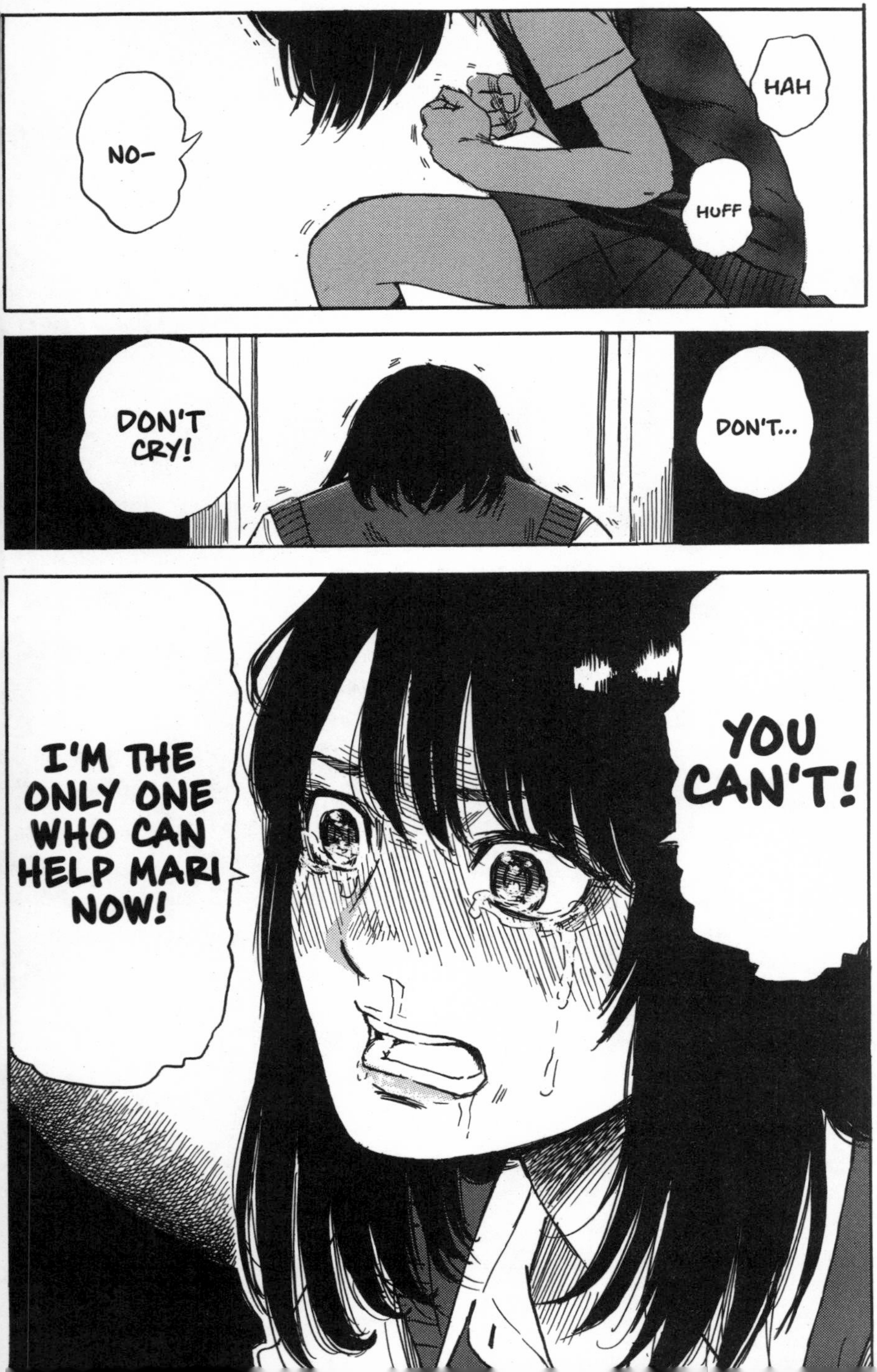
HAH
HUFF
NO-
DON'T...
DON'T CRY!
YOU CAN'T!
I'M THE ONLY ONE WHO CAN HELP MARI NOW!

SHFF
HUFF
HUFF
HAH
HAH
SHFF
HUFF
HAH

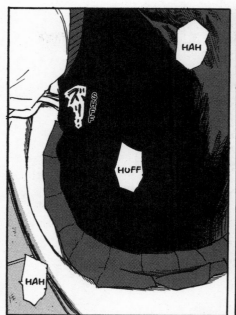

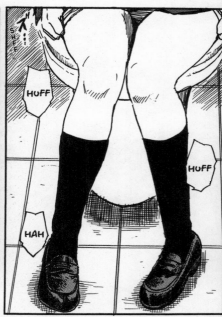

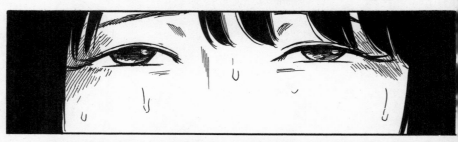

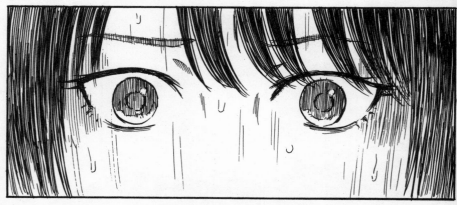

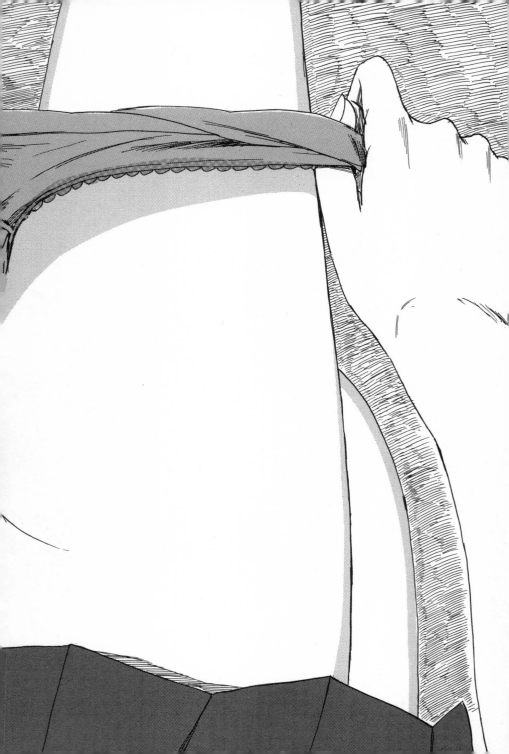

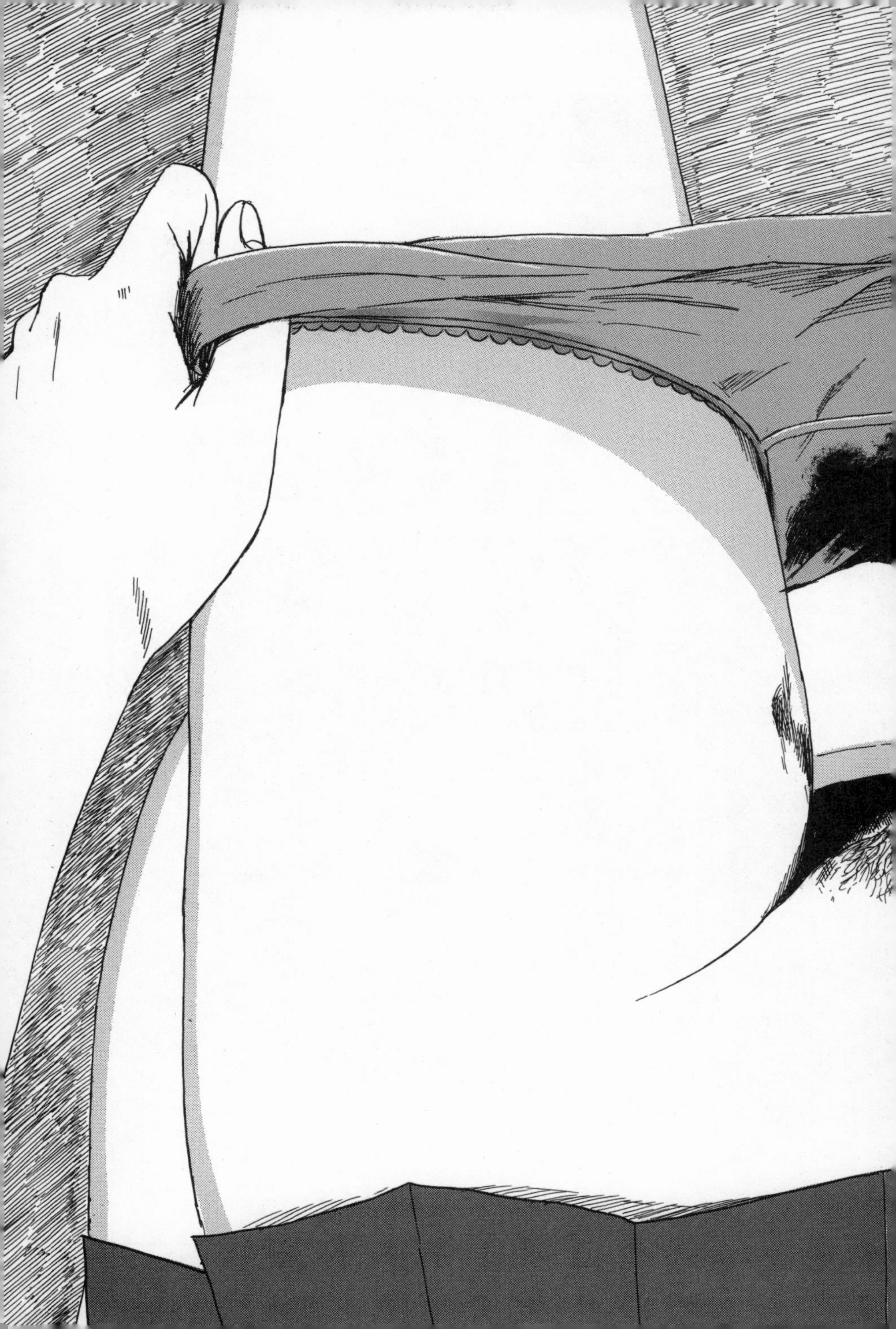

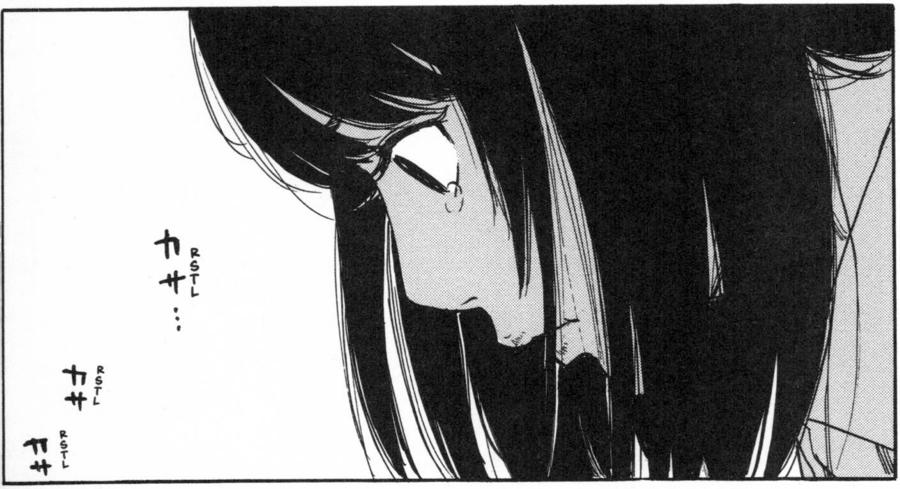
カサ…
RSTL
カサ
RSTL
カサ
RSTL

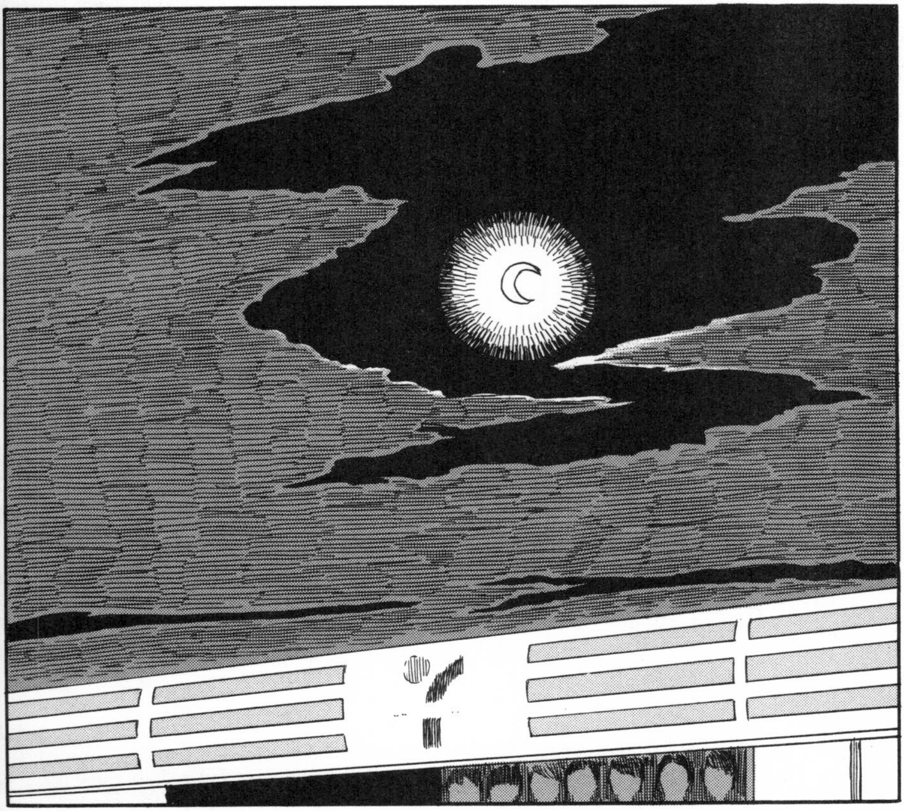

Chapter 19: Mari's Modern Life

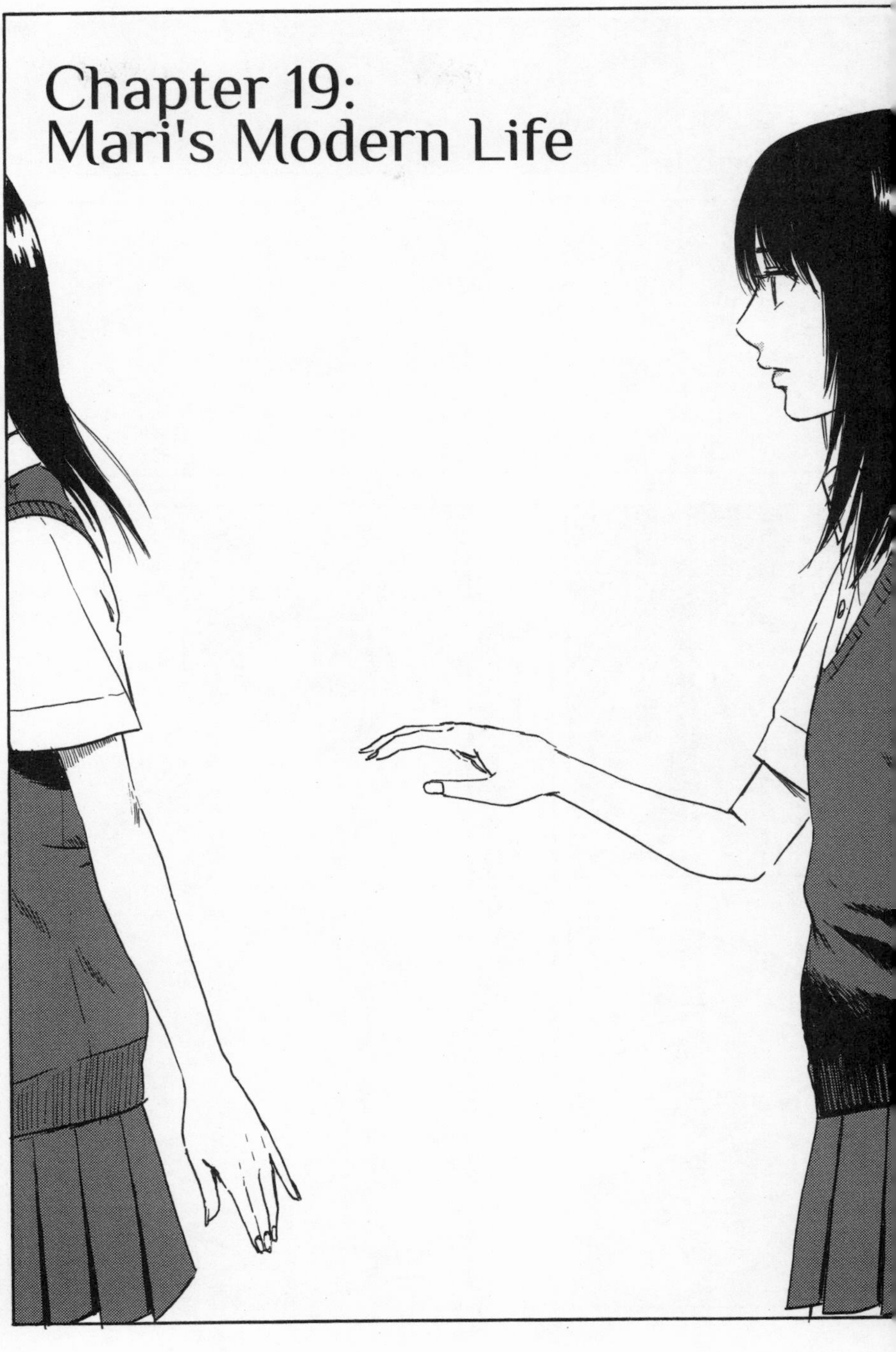

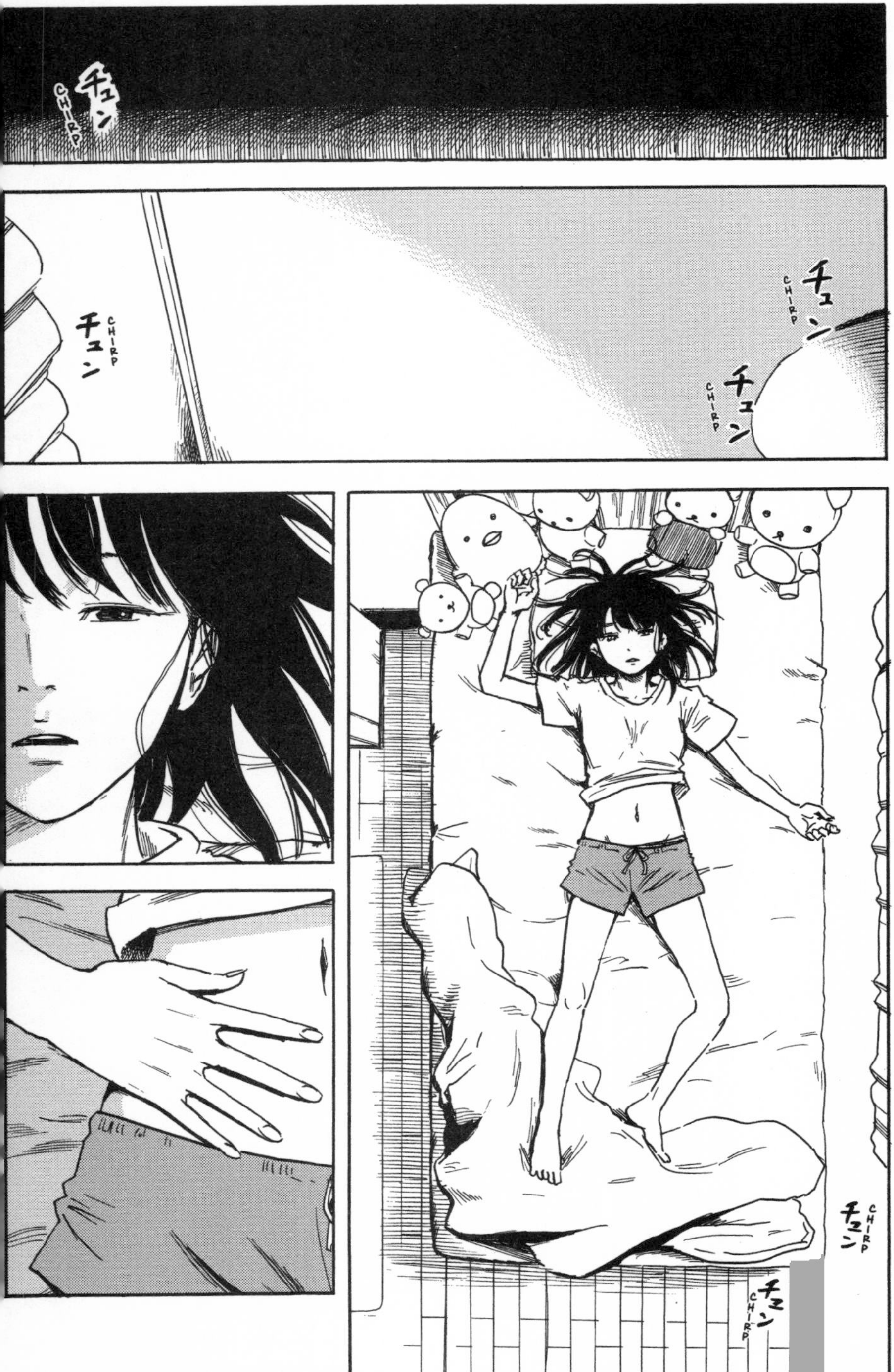
チュン CHIRP
チュン CHIRP
チュン CHIRP
チュン CHIRP
チュン CHIRP
チュン CHIRP

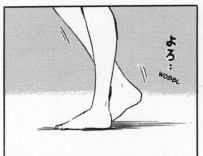

よろ…
WOBBL

ズリ…
SHFF

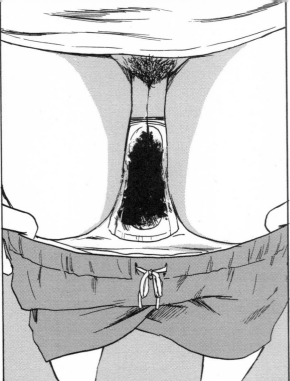

くしゃ
KSHH

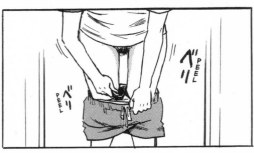

ベリ
PEEL

ベリ
PEEL

カサ
SKFF

ペリ

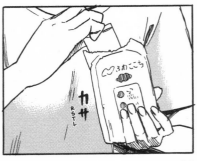

カサ
RSTL

～ふわごこち

26

しゅる
SHOOM

ガラ
RTTL

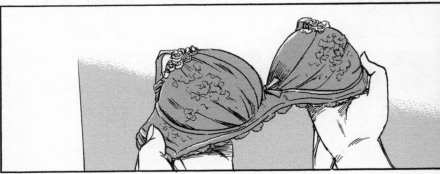

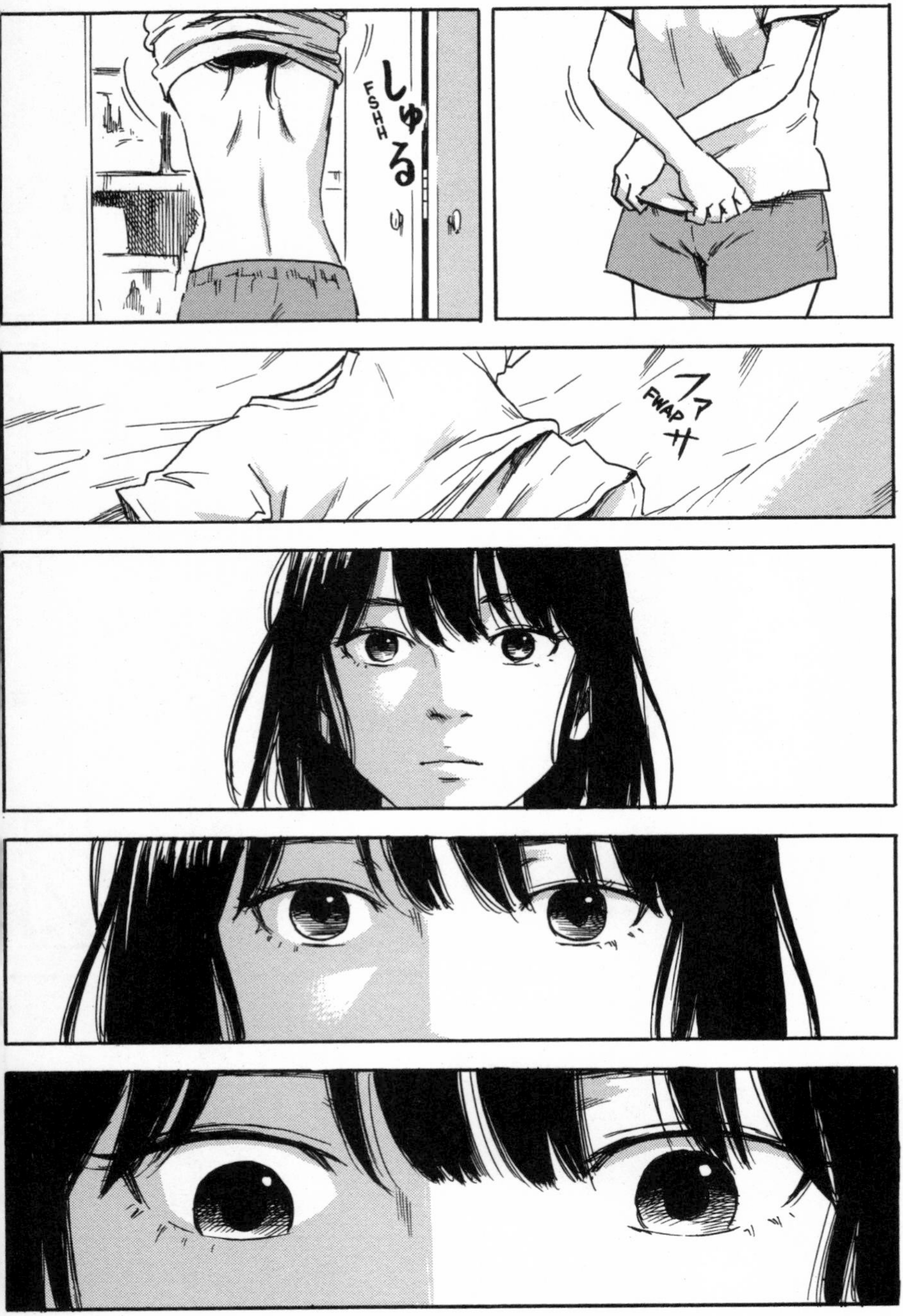
しゅる
FSHH
ファサ
FWAP

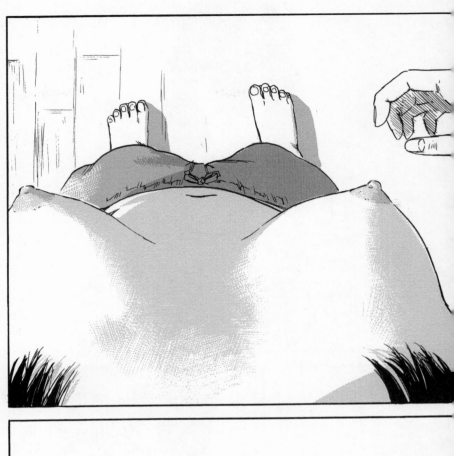

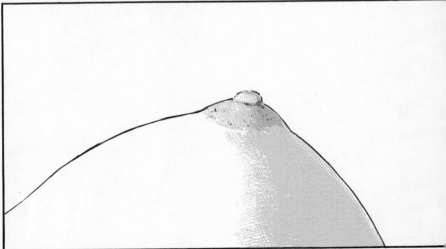

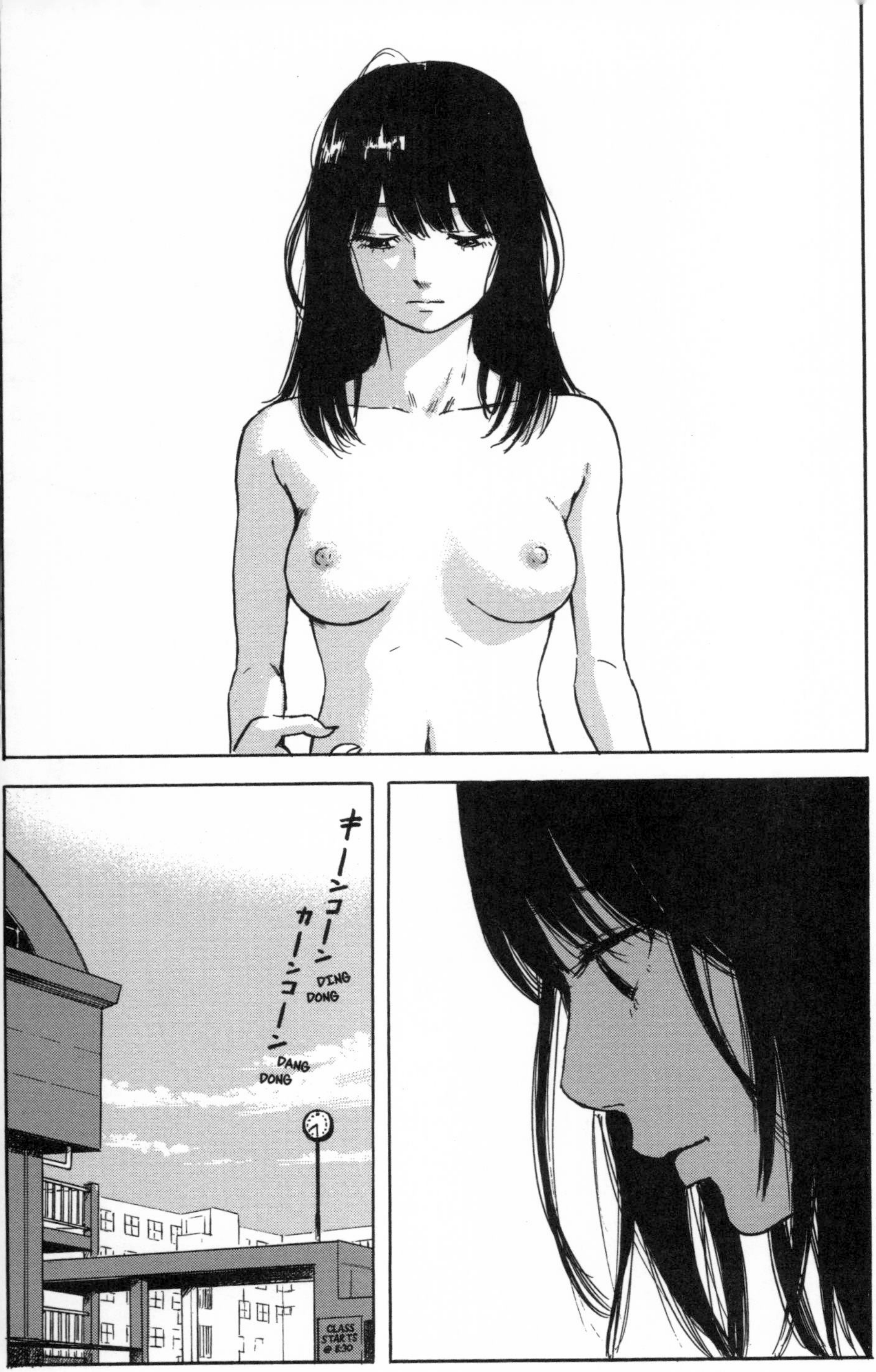
キーンコーン
DING DONG
カーンコーン
DANG DONG
CLASS STARTS @ 8:30

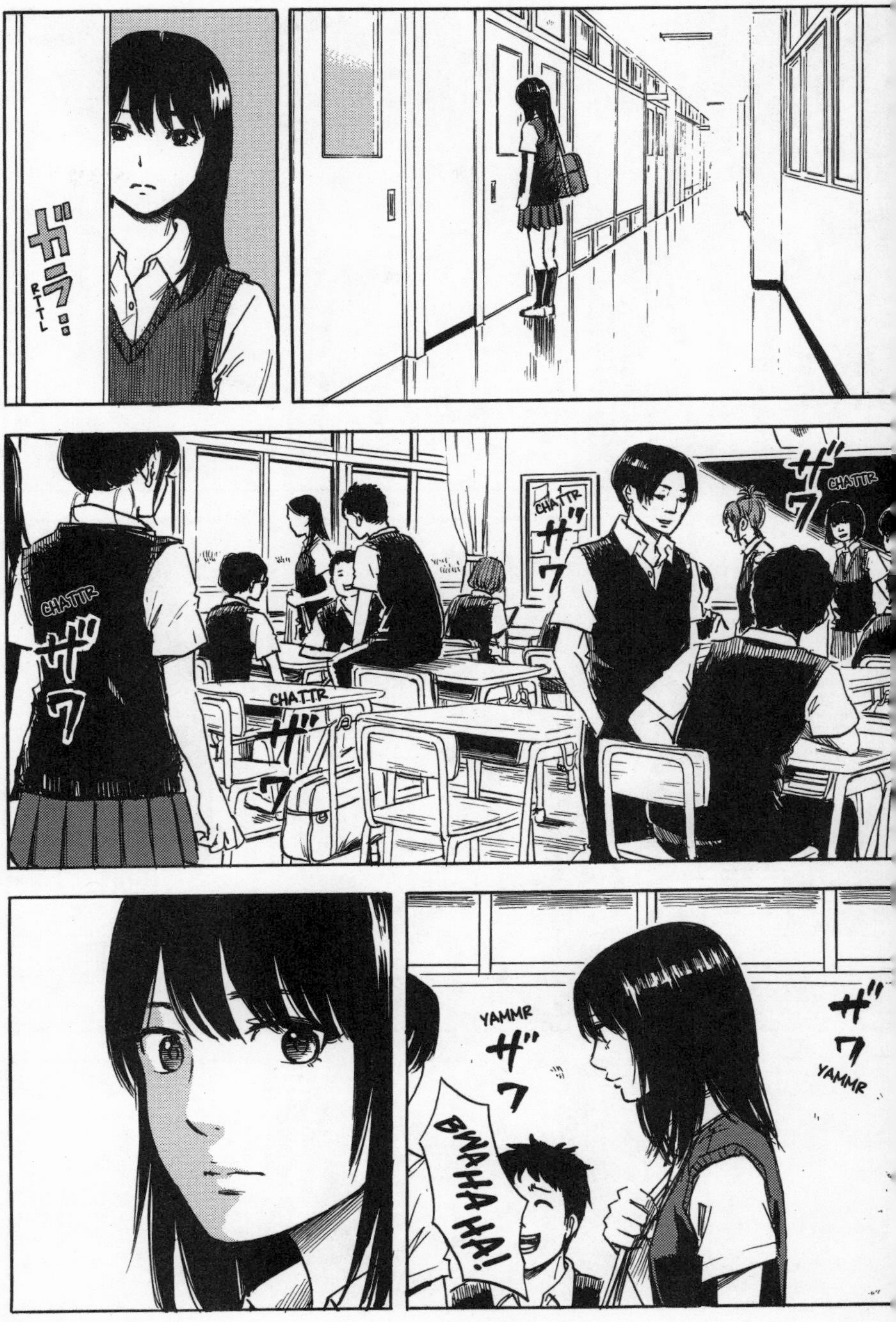
ガラ
RTTL
ザワ
CHATTR
CHATTR
ザワ
CHATTR
ザワ
CHATTR
ザワ
ザワ
YAMMR
YAMMR
ザワ
BWAHAHA!

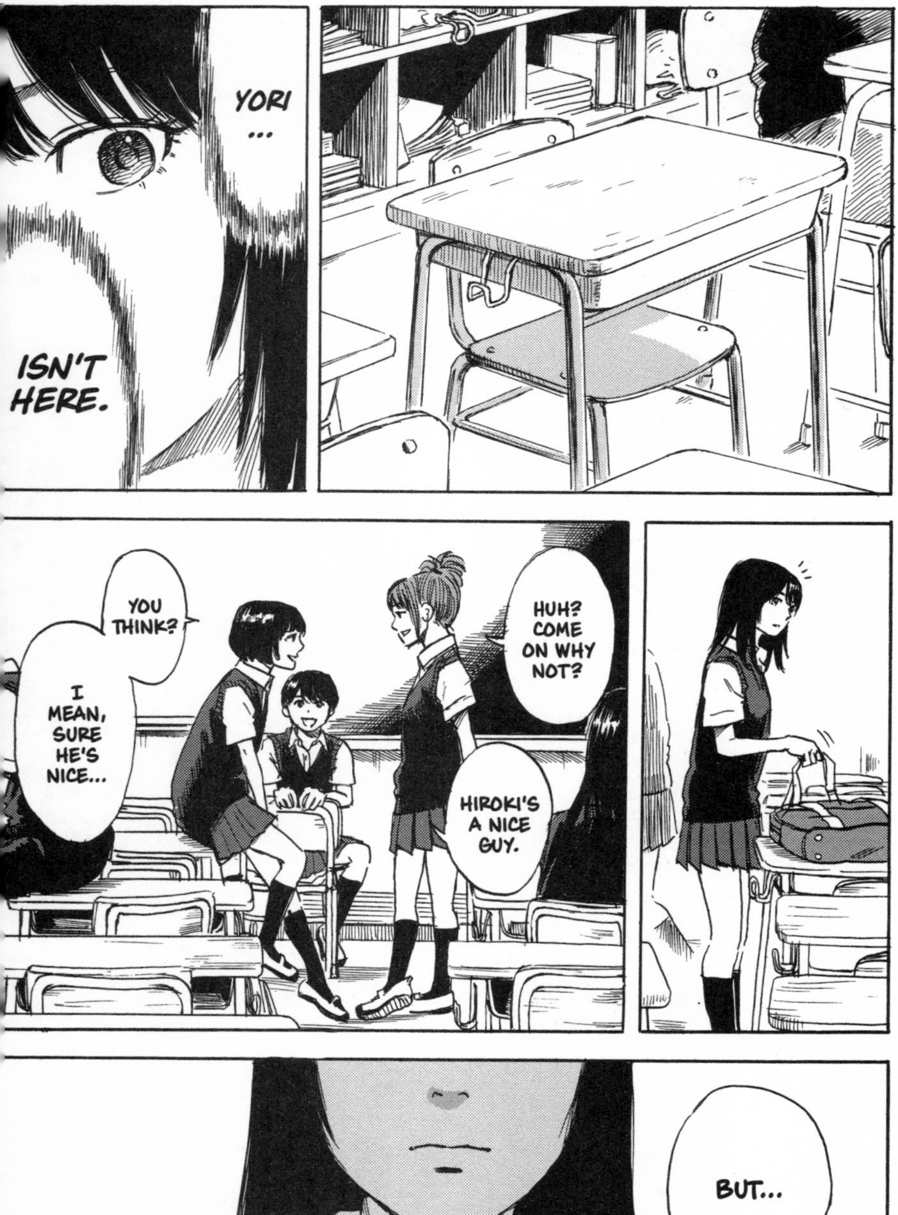
YORI ...
ISN'T HERE.
HUH? COME ON WHY NOT?
HIROKI'S A NICE GUY.
YOU THINK?
I MEAN, SURE HE'S NICE...
BUT...

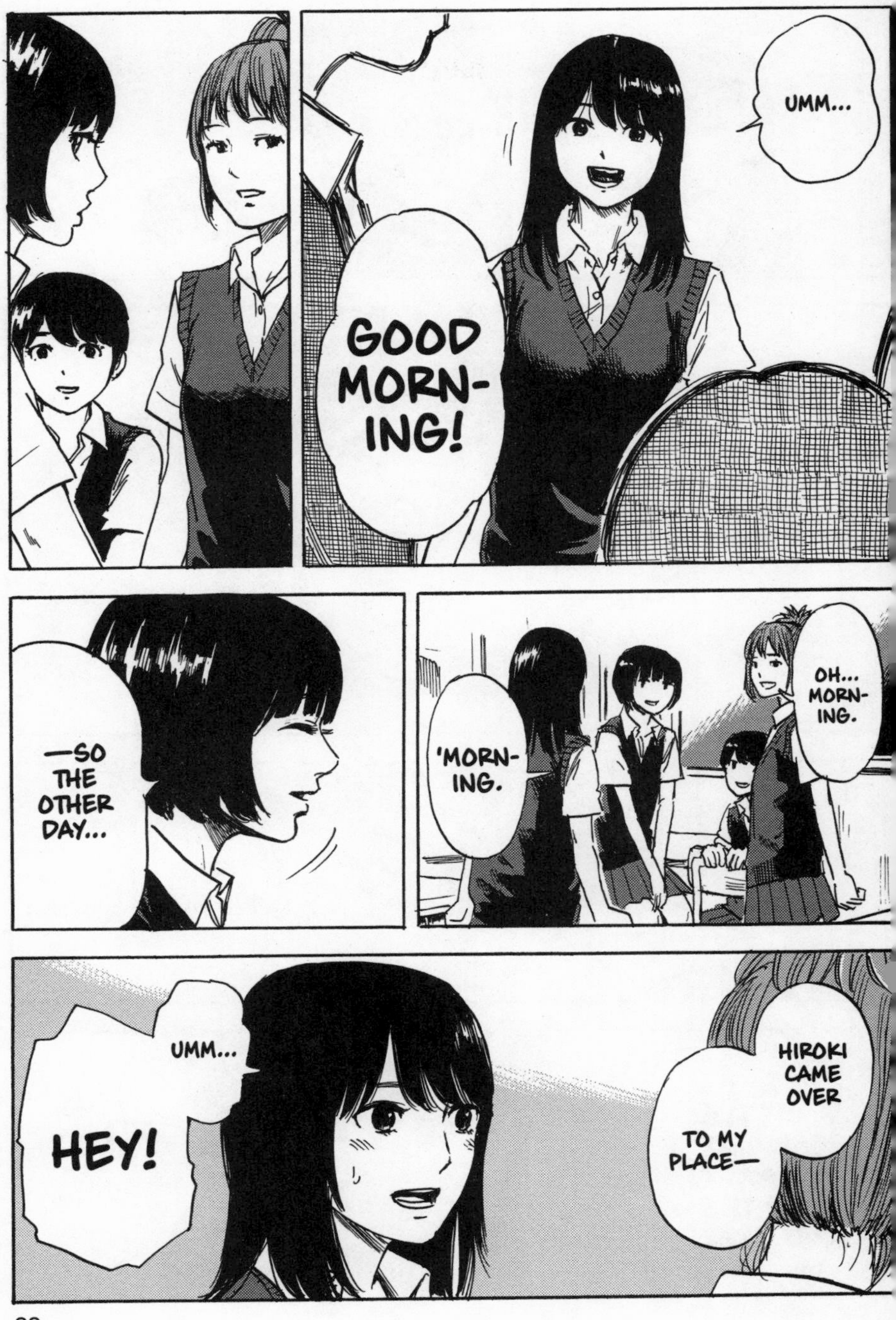
UMM...
GOOD MORN-ING!
OH... MORN-ING.
'MORN-ING.
—SO THE OTHER DAY...
HIROKI CAME OVER
TO MY PLACE—
UMM...
HEY!

HUH?
OH...
I-I'M SORRY ...
ABOUT YESTER-DAY.
SORRY?
FOR WHAT?
AH! WELL... I MEAN...
I GOT A LITTLE CARRIED AWAY... WITH THE KARAOKE...

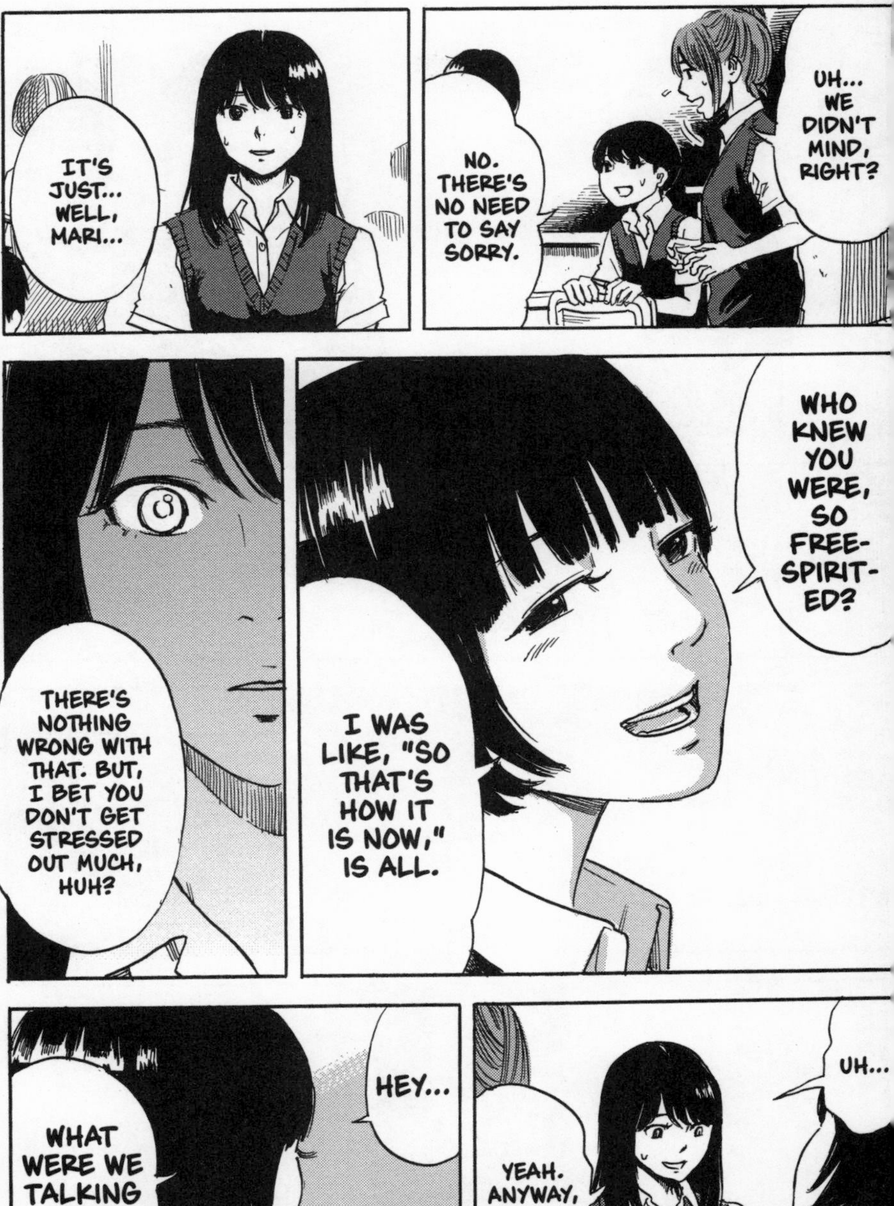
UH... WE DIDN'T MIND, RIGHT?
NO. THERE'S NO NEED TO SAY SORRY.
IT'S JUST... WELL, MARI...
WHO KNEW YOU WERE, SO FREE-SPIRITED?
I WAS LIKE, "SO THAT'S HOW IT IS NOW," IS ALL.
THERE'S NOTHING WRONG WITH THAT. BUT, I BET YOU DON'T GET STRESSED OUT MUCH, HUH?
UH...
YEAH. ANYWAY, I'M SORRY...
HEY...
WHAT WERE WE TALKING ABOUT AGAIN?

OH,
YEAH—
SO,
HIROKI...

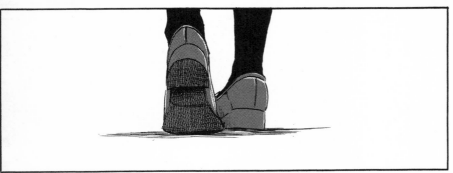

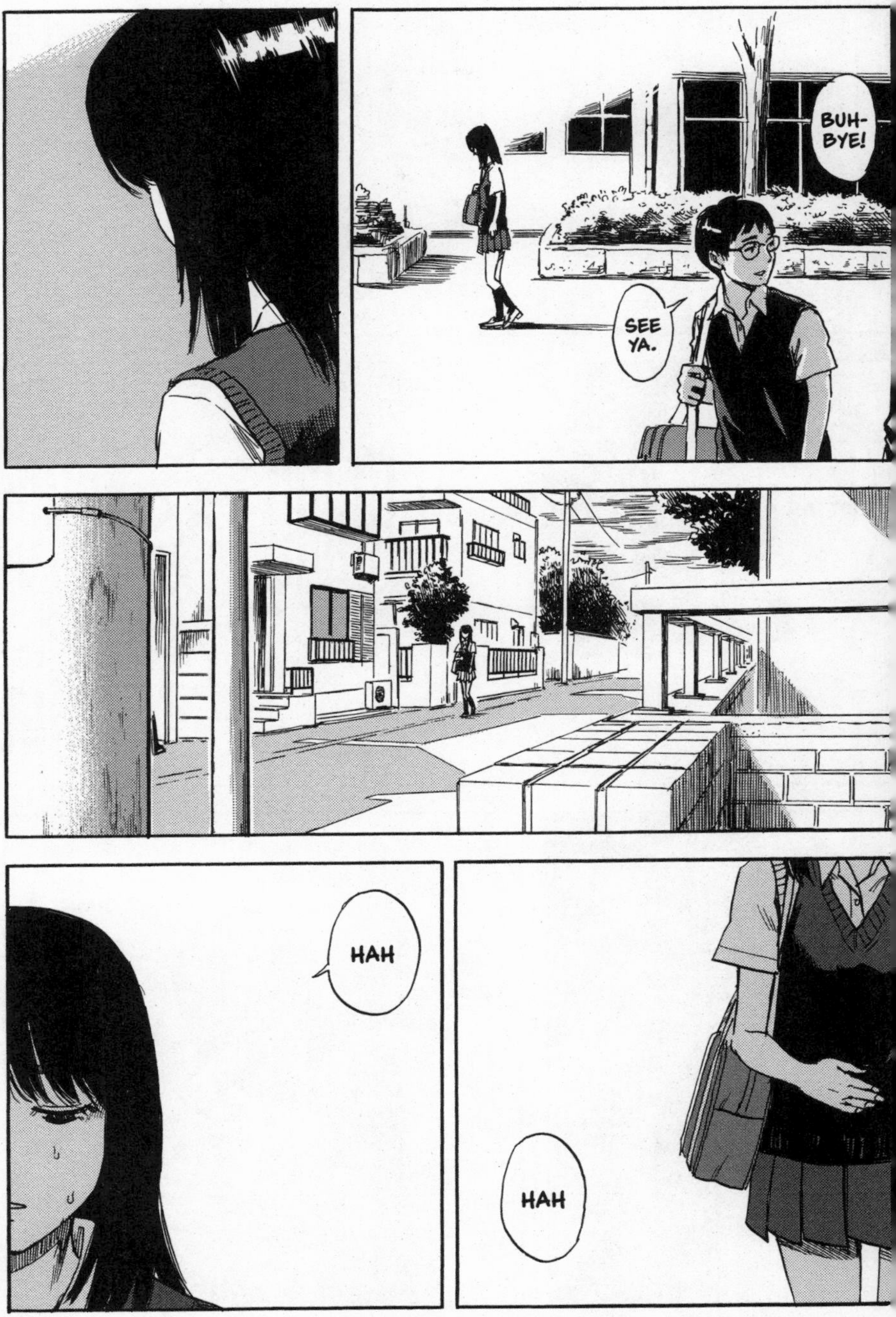
BUH-BYE!
SEE YA.
HAH
HAH

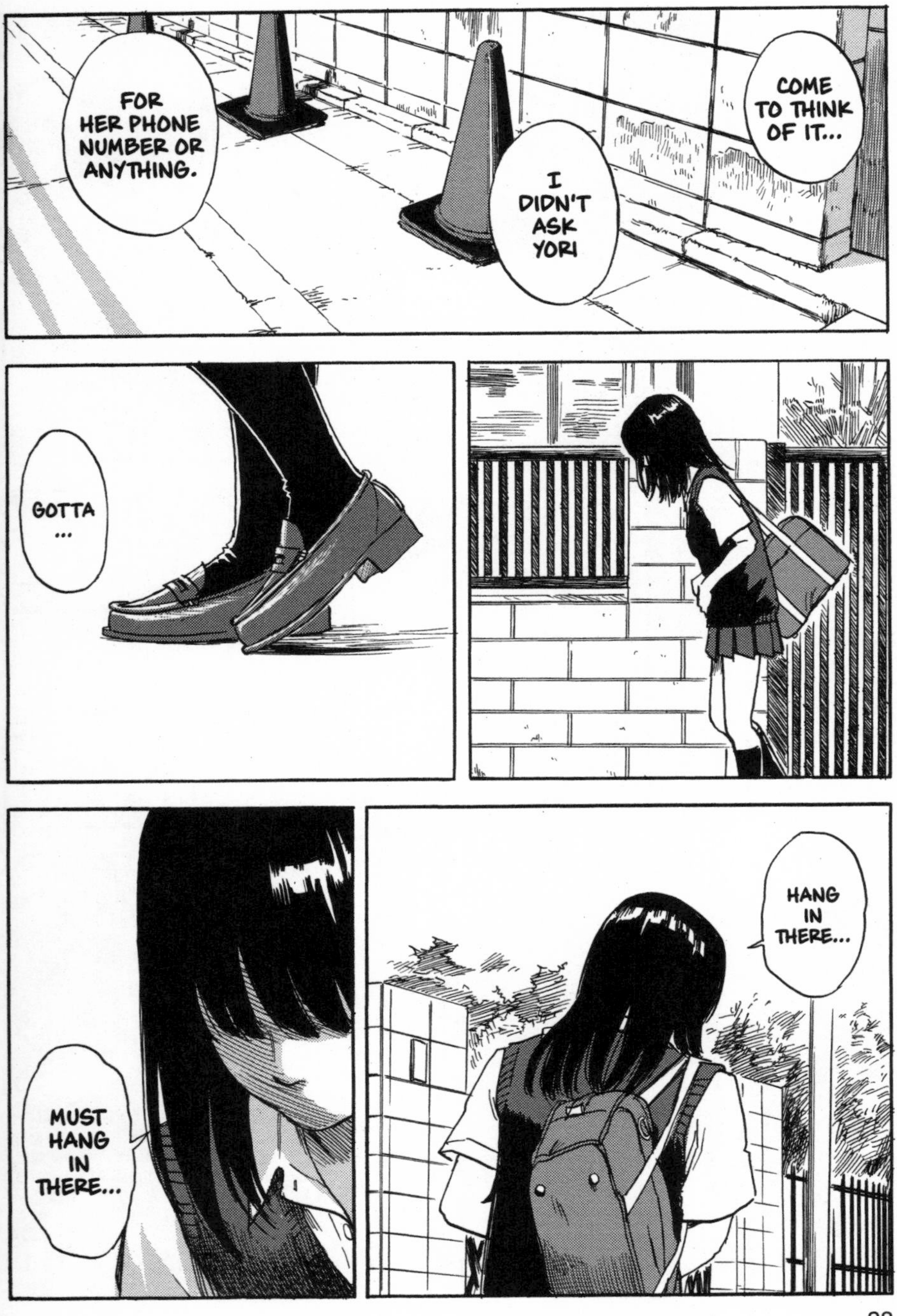
COME TO THINK OF IT...
I DIDN'T ASK YORI
FOR HER PHONE NUMBER OR ANYTHING.
GOTTA ...
HANG IN THERE...
MUST HANG IN THERE...

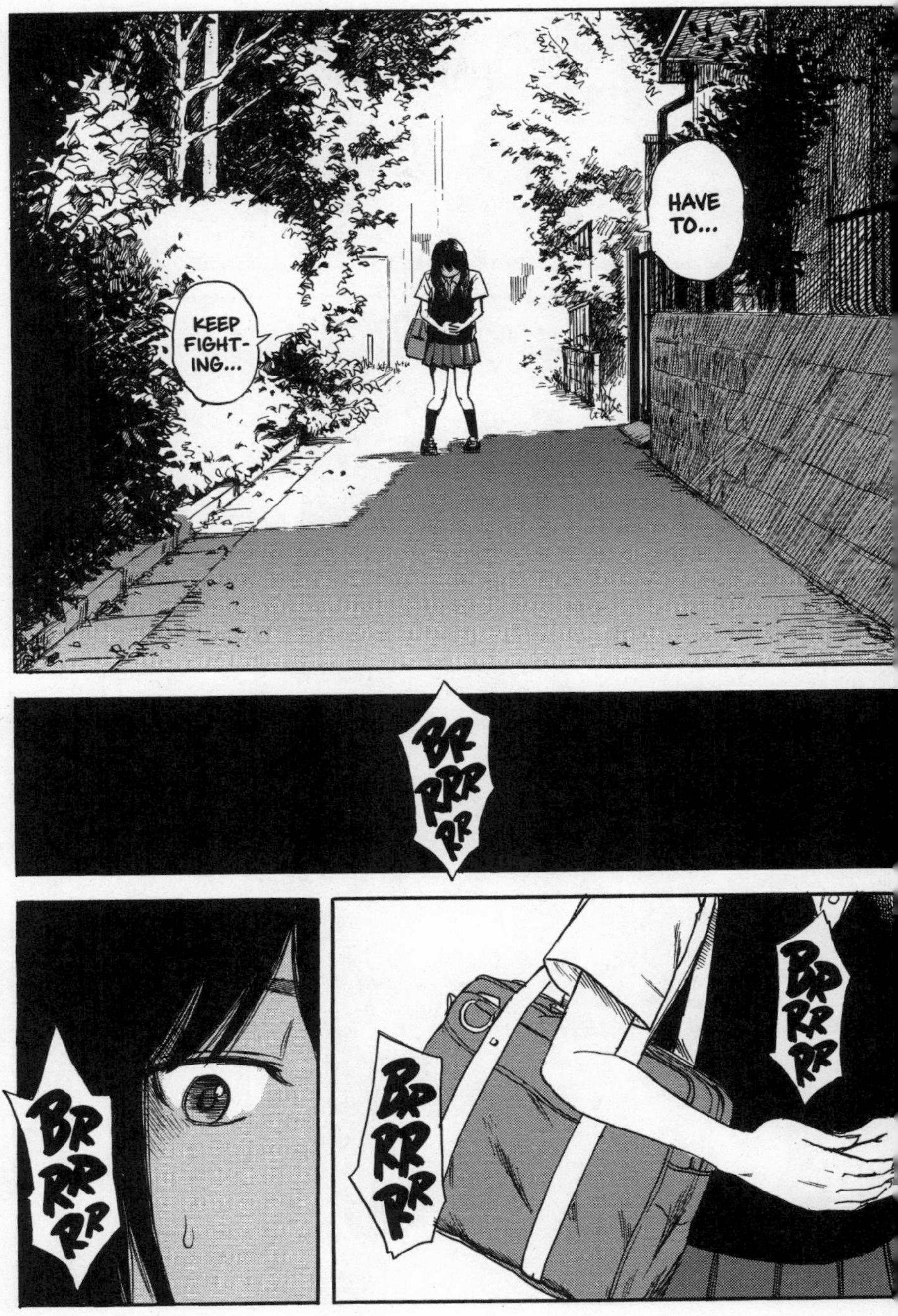
HAVE TO...
KEEP FIGHT-ING...
BRRRRRR
BRRRRR
BRRRRR
BRRRRR

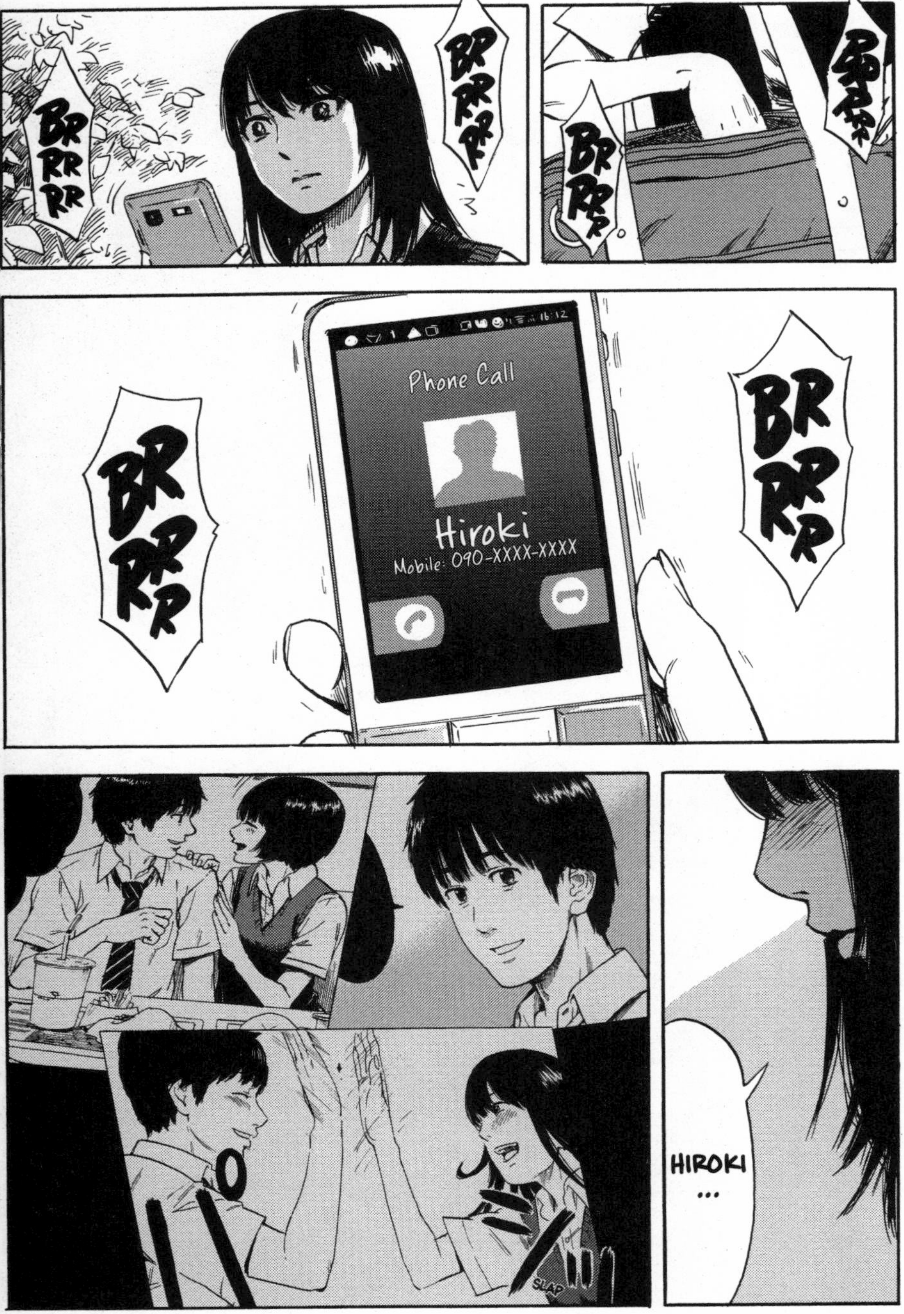

BRRRR
BRRRRRR
BRRRR
BRRRRR
Phone Call
Hiroki
Mobile: 090-XXXX-XXXX
BRRRRR
HIROKI ...
SLAP

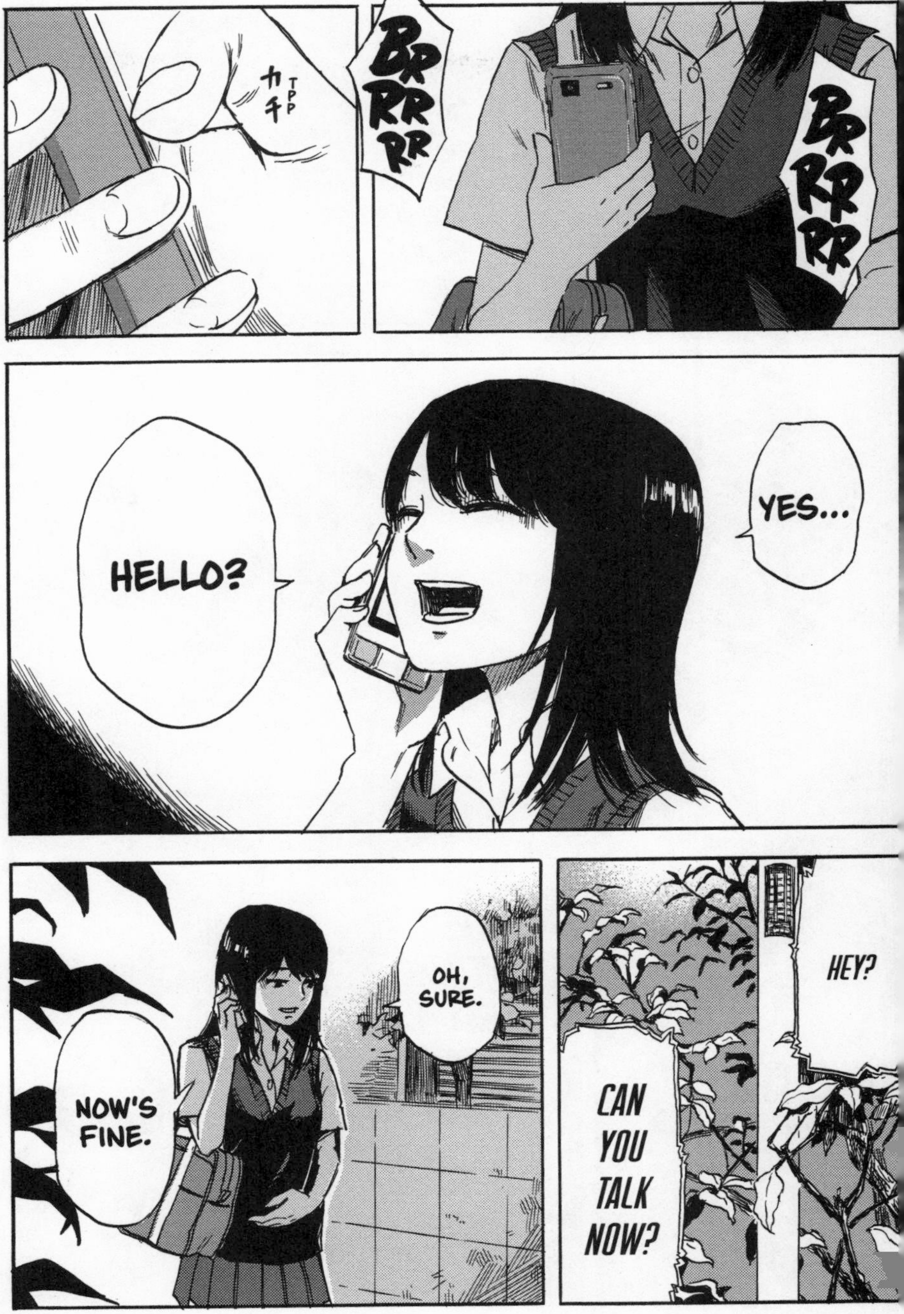
BRRRRR
BRRRRR
カチ TPP
YES...
HELLO?
HEY?
CAN YOU TALK NOW?
OH, SURE.
NOW'S FINE.

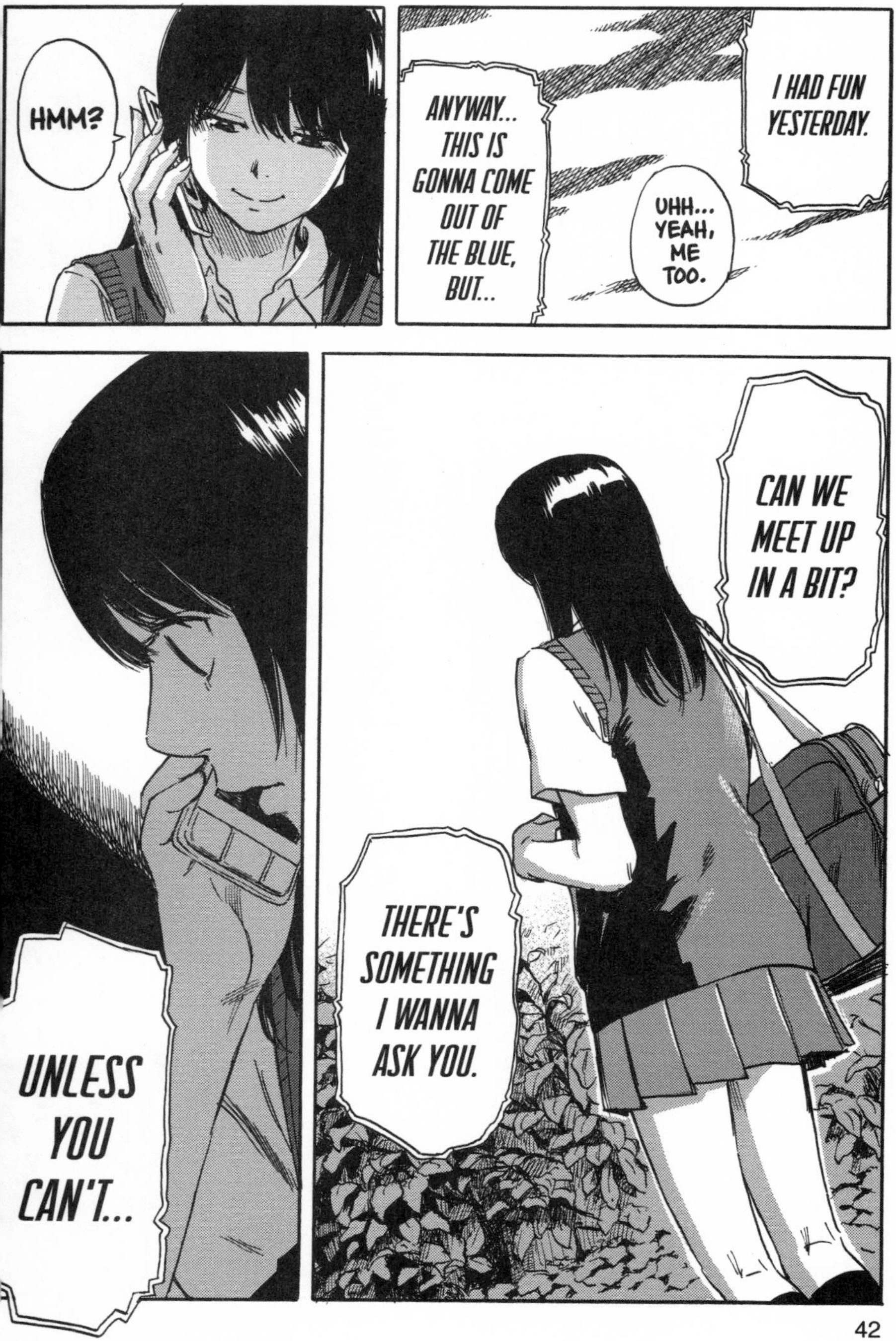
I HAD FUN YESTERDAY.
UHH... YEAH, ME TOO.
ANYWAY... THIS IS GONNA COME OUT OF THE BLUE, BUT...
HMM?
CAN WE MEET UP IN A BIT?
THERE'S SOMETHING I WANNA ASK YOU.
UNLESS YOU CAN'T...

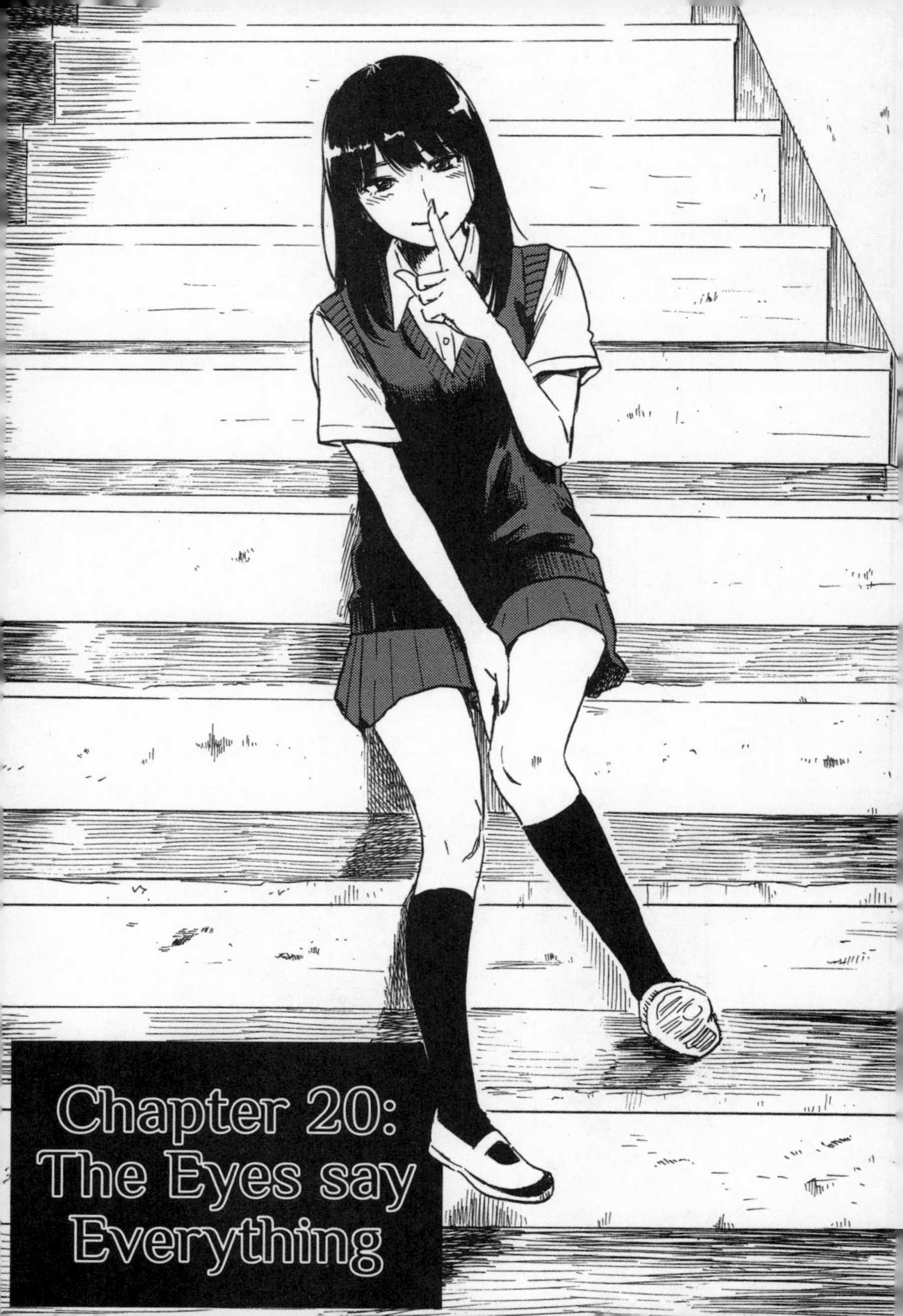
Chapter 20:
The Eyes say
Everything

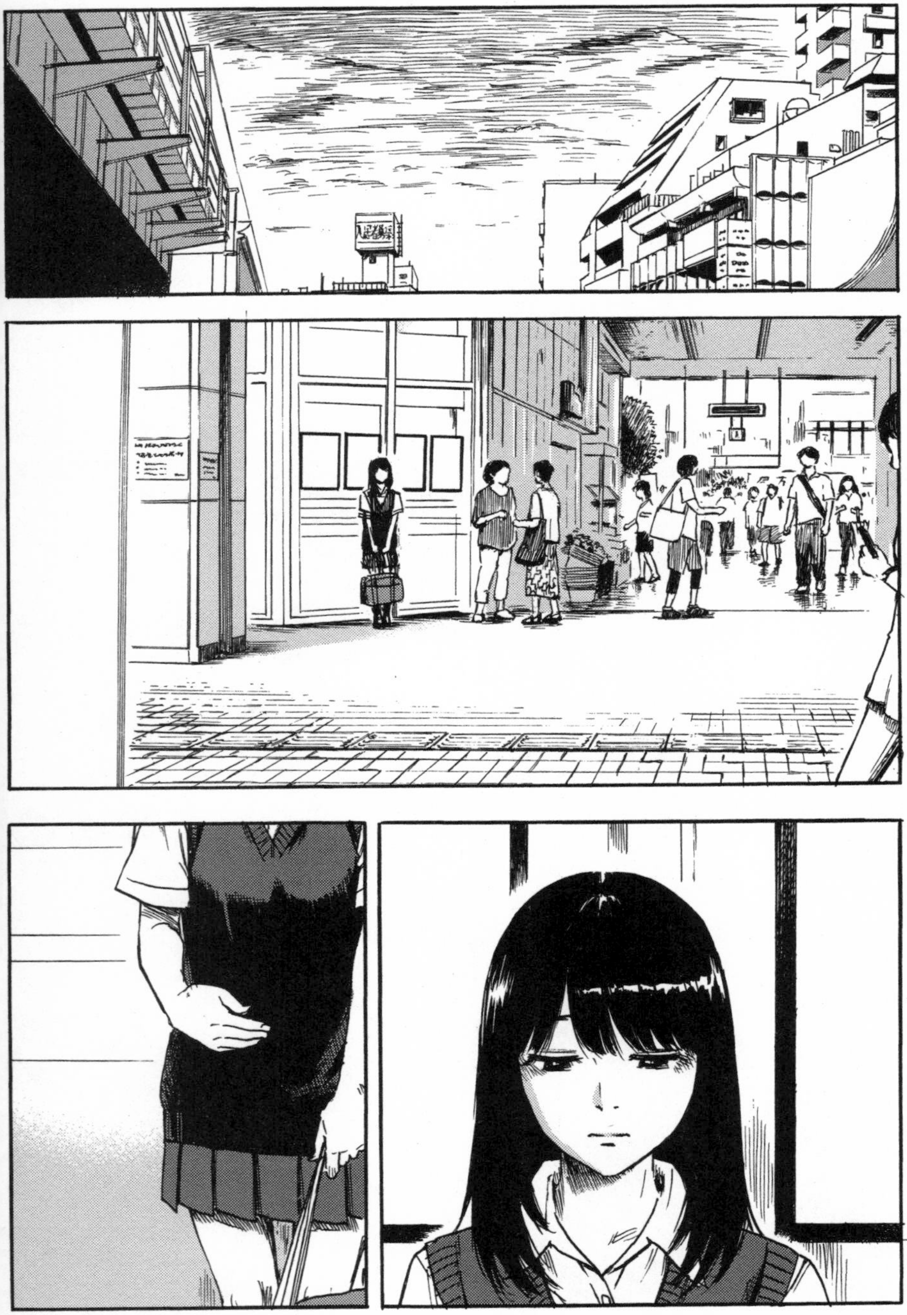

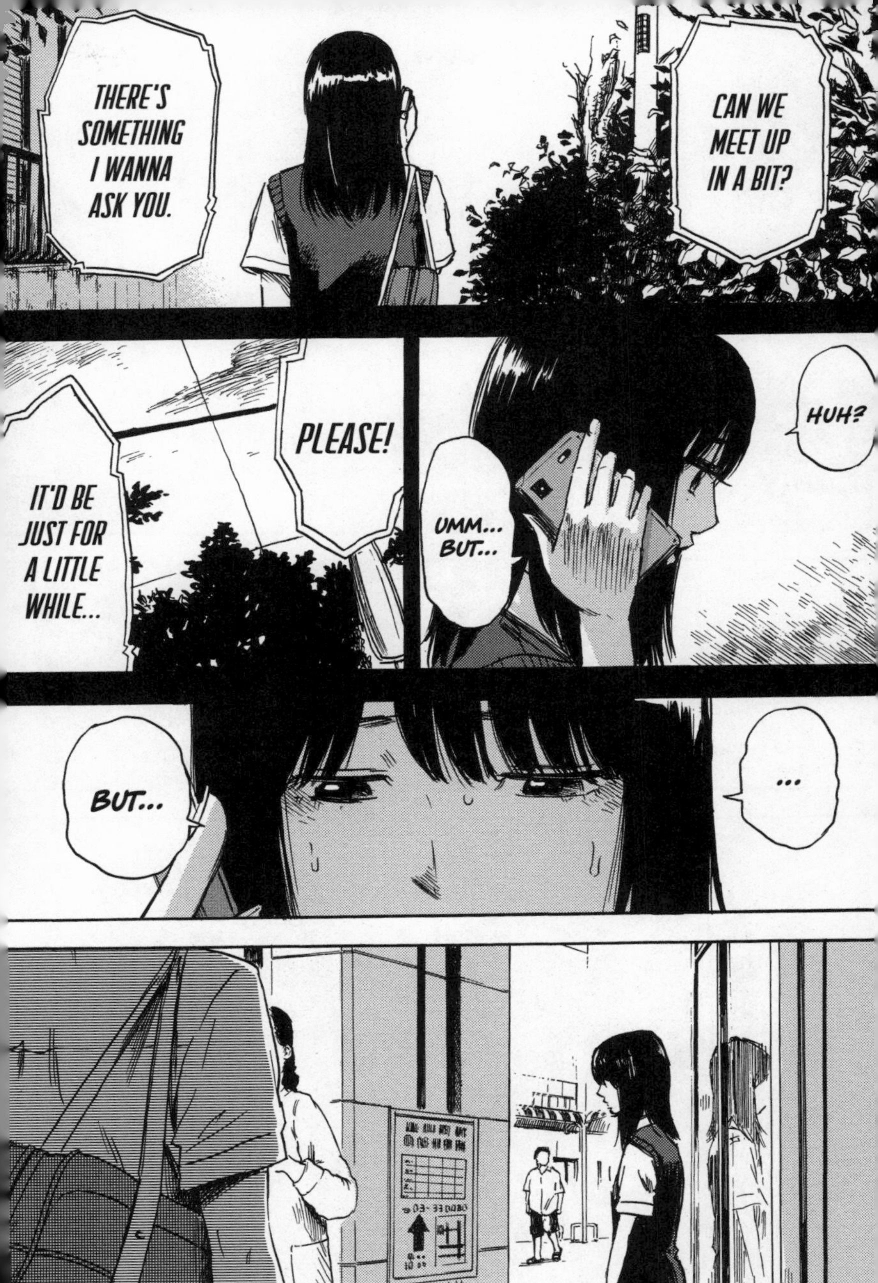
CAN WE MEET UP IN A BIT?
THERE'S SOMETHING I WANNA ASK YOU.
HUH?
UMM... BUT...
PLEASE!
IT'D BE JUST FOR A LITTLE WHILE...
...
BUT...

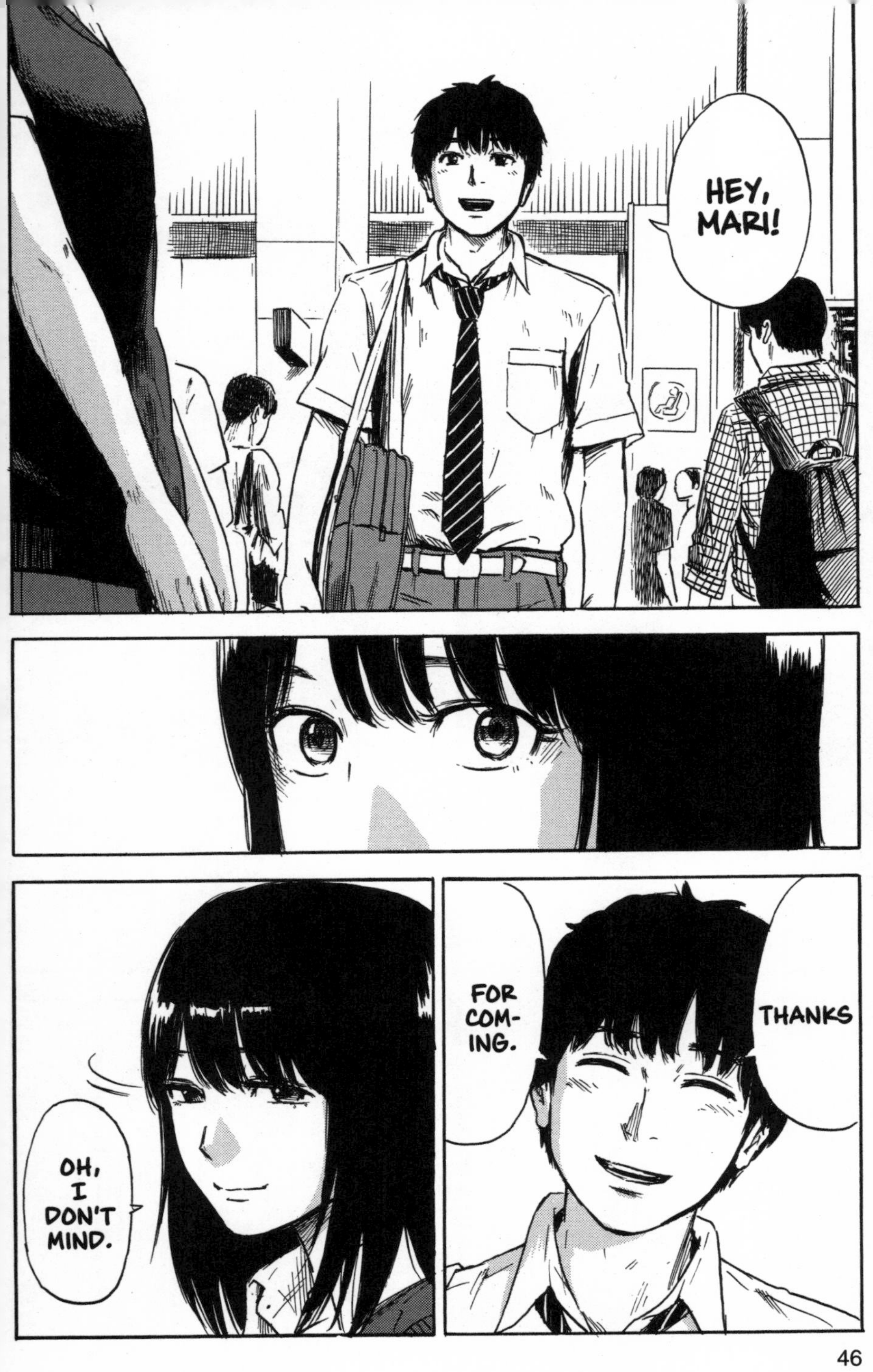
HEY, MARI!
THANKS
FOR COM-ING.
OH, I DON'T MIND.

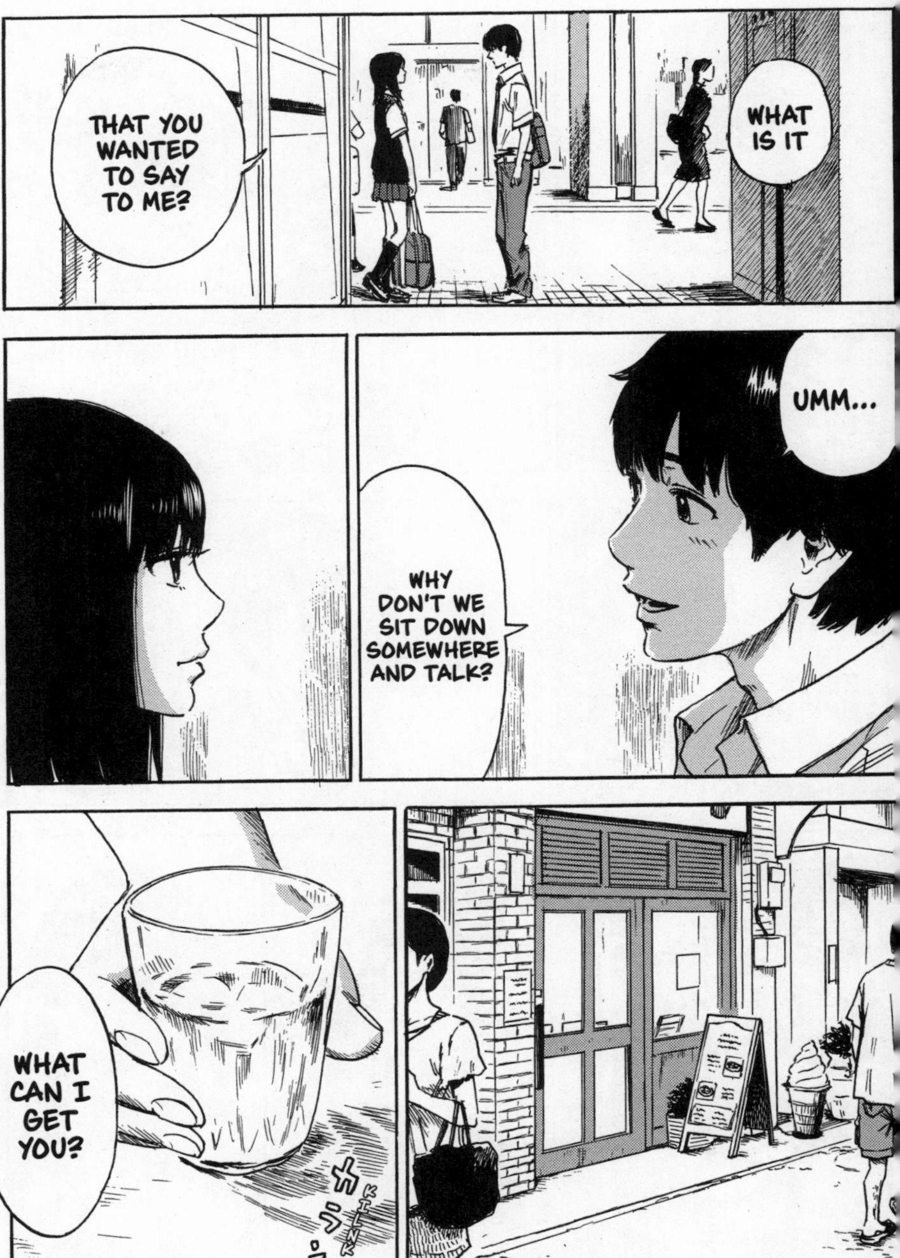
WHAT IS IT
THAT YOU WANTED TO SAY TO ME?
UMM...
WHY DON'T WE SIT DOWN SOMEWHERE AND TALK?
WHAT CAN I GET YOU?
KLINK

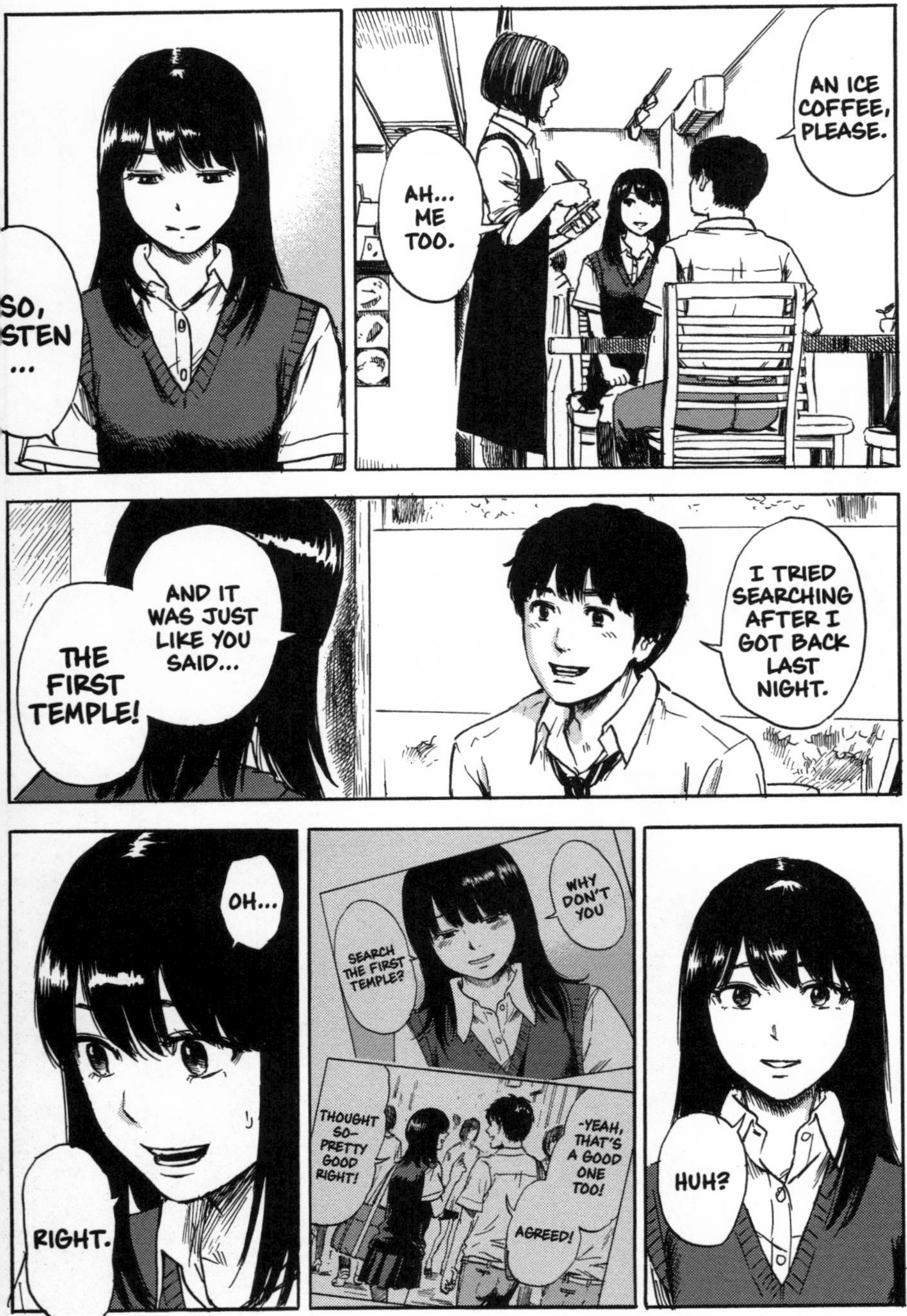
AN ICE COFFEE, PLEASE.
AH... ME TOO.
SO, STEN ...
I TRIED SEARCHING AFTER I GOT BACK LAST NIGHT.
AND IT WAS JUST LIKE YOU SAID...
THE FIRST TEMPLE!
HUH?
WHY DON'T YOU
SEARCH THE FIRST TEMPLE?
-YEAH, THAT'S A GOOD ONE TOO!
AGREED!
THOUGHT SO- PRETTY GOOD RIGHT!
OH...
RIGHT.

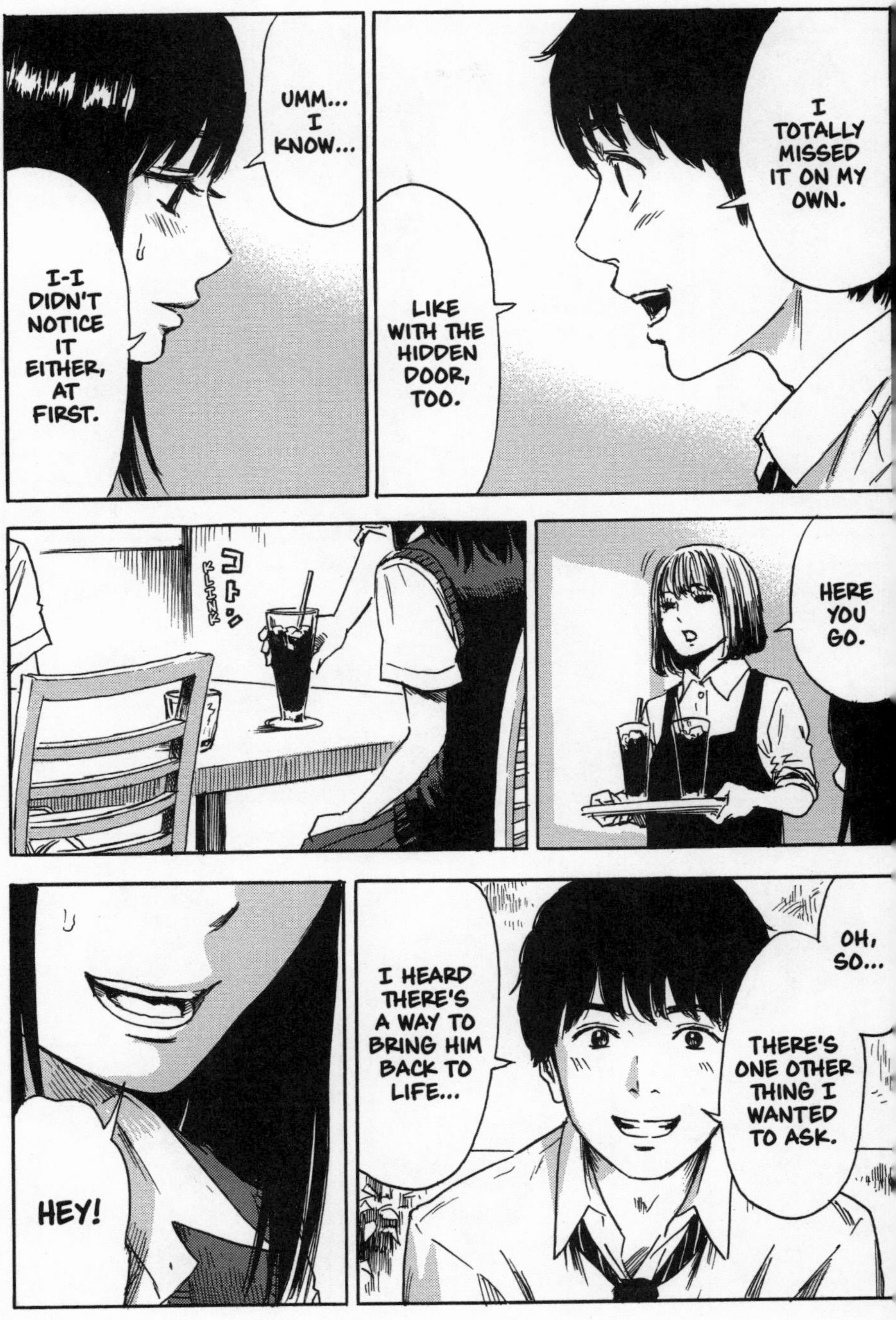
I TOTALLY MISSED IT ON MY OWN.
LIKE WITH THE HIDDEN DOOR, TOO.
UMM... I KNOW...
I-I DIDN'T NOTICE IT EITHER, AT FIRST.
HERE YOU GO.
コト。
KLINK
OH, SO...
THERE'S ONE OTHER THING I WANTED TO ASK.
I HEARD THERE'S A WAY TO BRING HIM BACK TO LIFE...
HEY!

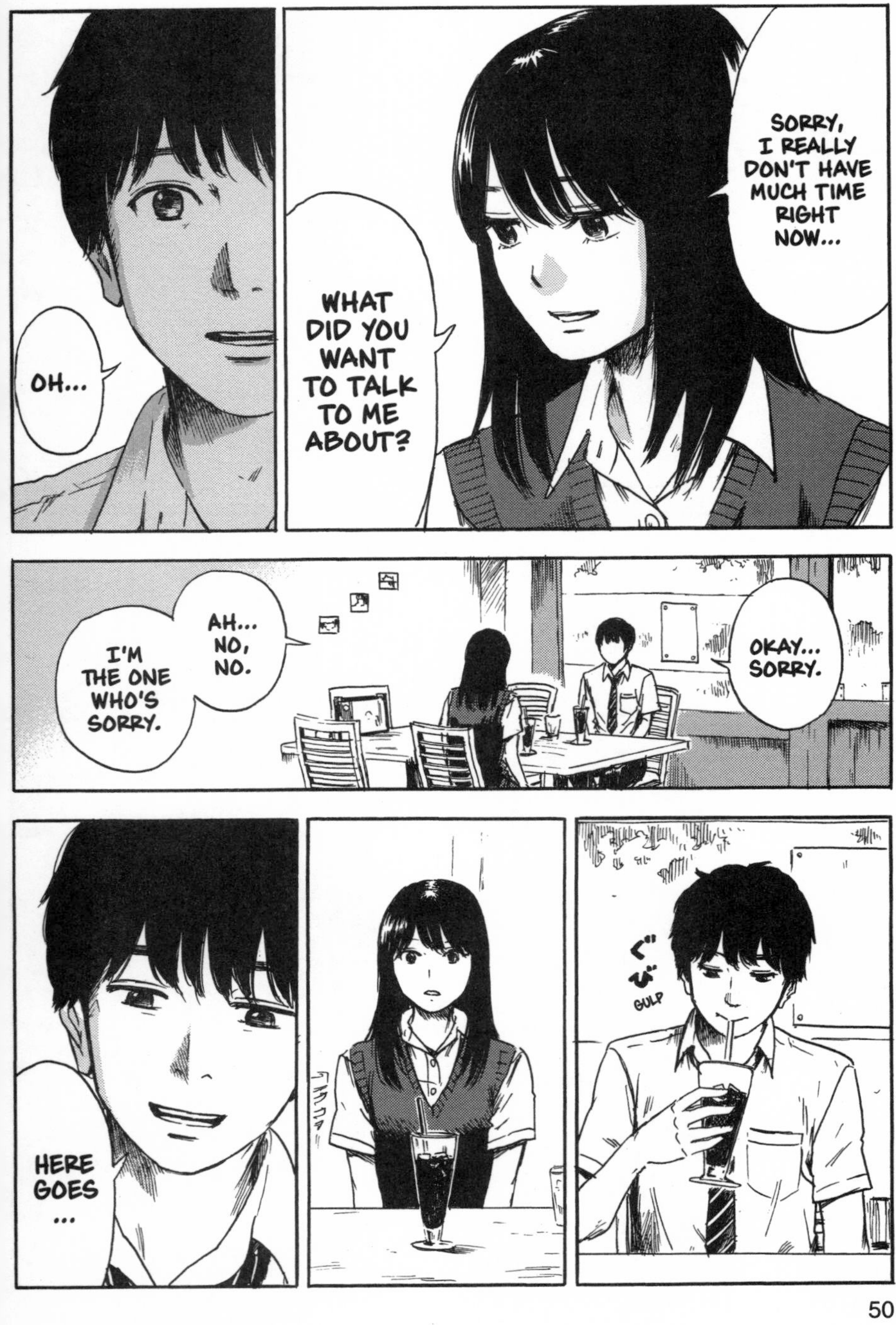
SORRY, I REALLY DON'T HAVE MUCH TIME RIGHT NOW...
WHAT DID YOU WANT TO TALK TO ME ABOUT?
OH...
OKAY... SORRY.
AH... NO, NO.
I'M THE ONE WHO'S SORRY.
ぐび
GULP
HERE GOES ...

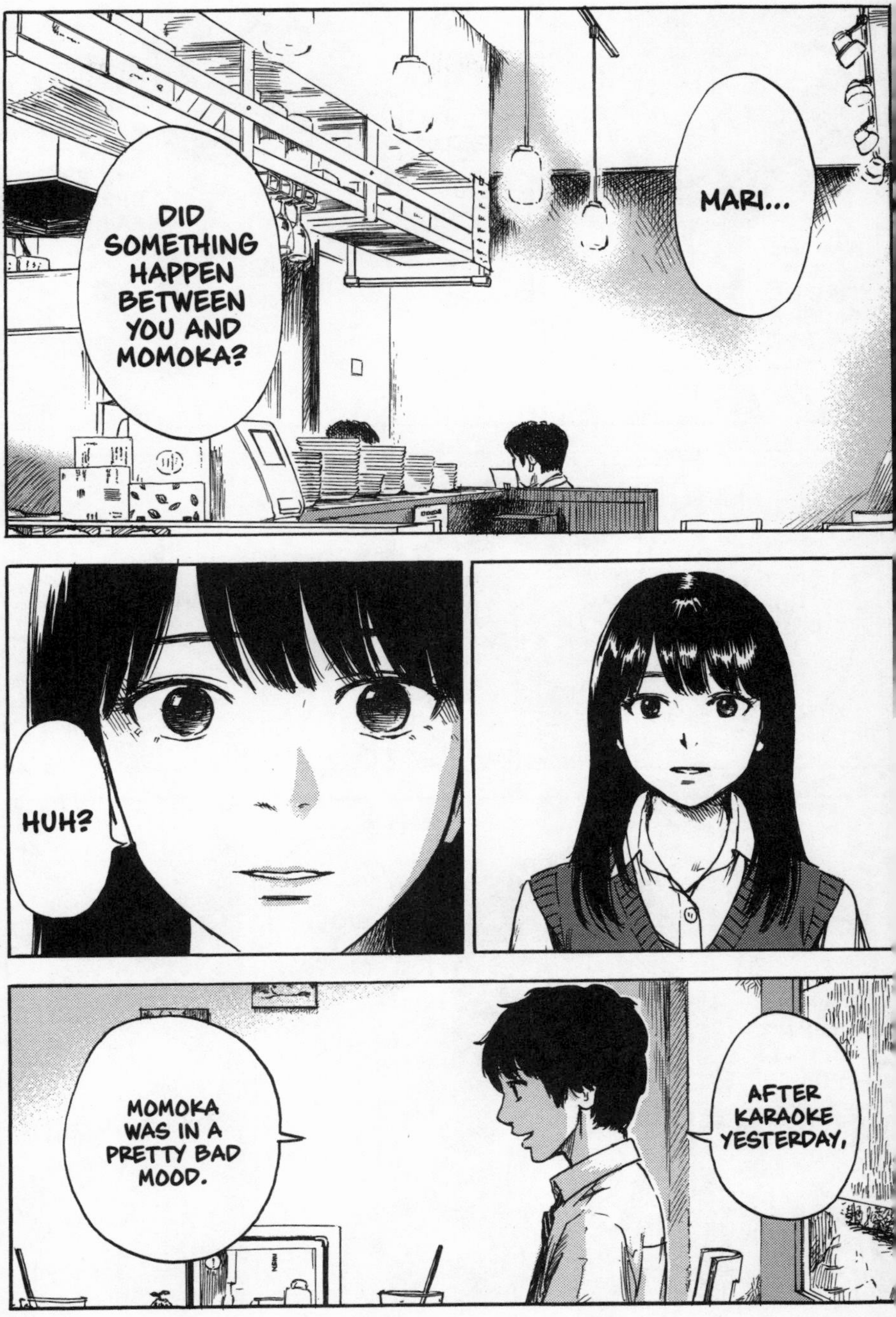
MARI...
DID SOMETHING HAPPEN BETWEEN YOU AND MOMOKA?
HUH?
AFTER KARAOKE YESTERDAY,
MOMOKA WAS IN A PRETTY BAD MOOD.

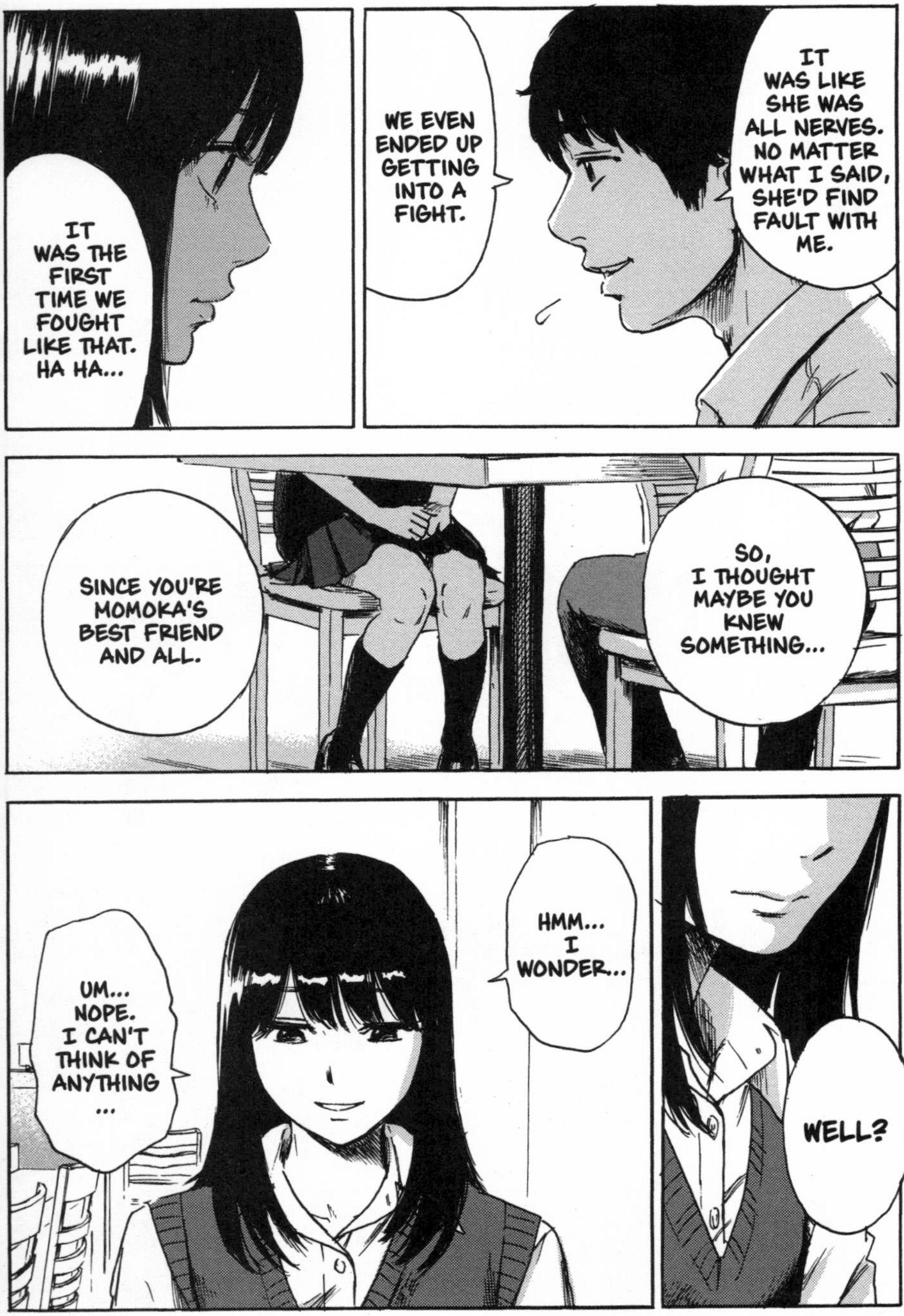
IT WAS LIKE SHE WAS ALL NERVES. NO MATTER WHAT I SAID, SHE'D FIND FAULT WITH ME.
WE EVEN ENDED UP GETTING INTO A FIGHT.
IT WAS THE FIRST TIME WE FOUGHT LIKE THAT. HA HA...
SO, I THOUGHT MAYBE YOU KNEW SOMETHING...
SINCE YOU'RE MOMOKA'S BEST FRIEND AND ALL.
WELL?
HMM... I WONDER...
UM... NOPE. I CAN'T THINK OF ANYTHING ...

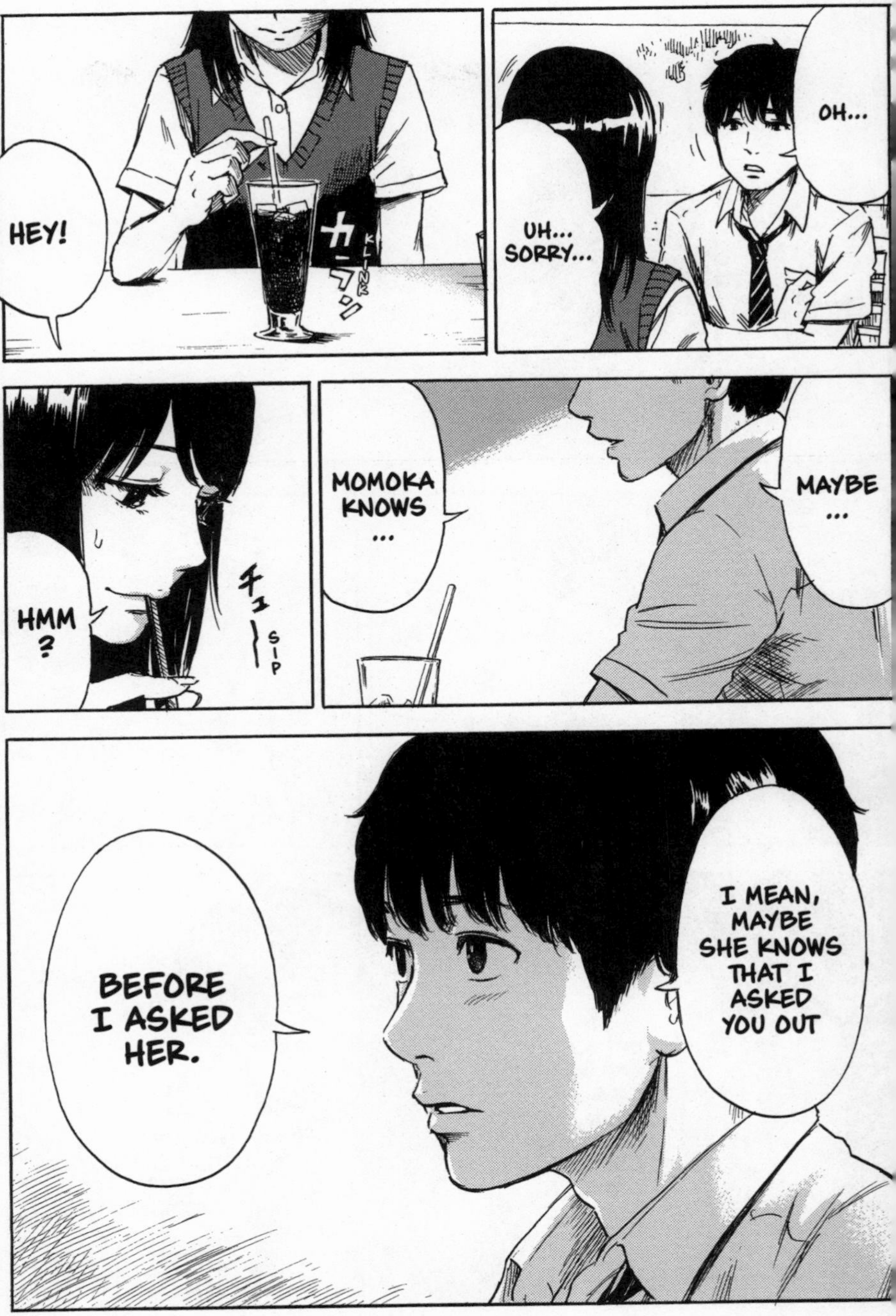
OH...
UH... SORRY...
HEY!
カーン
KLINK
MAYBE ...
MOMOKA KNOWS ...
チュー
SIP
HMM ?
I MEAN, MAYBE SHE KNOWS THAT I ASKED YOU OUT
BEFORE I ASKED HER.

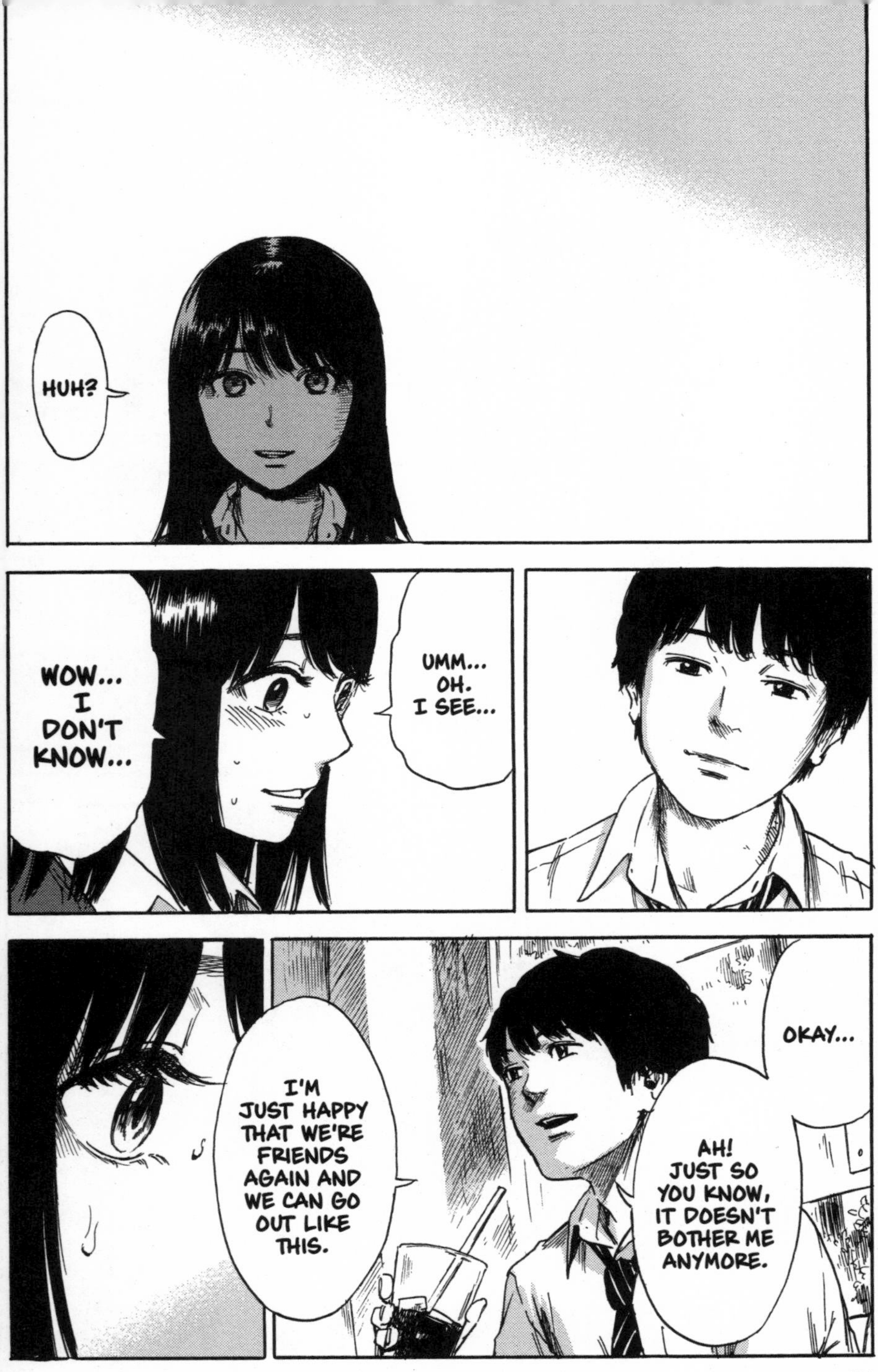
HUH?
UMM... OH. I SEE...
WOW... I DON'T KNOW...
OKAY...
AH! JUST SO YOU KNOW, IT DOESN'T BOTHER ME ANYMORE.
I'M JUST HAPPY THAT WE'RE FRIENDS AGAIN AND WE CAN GO OUT LIKE THIS.

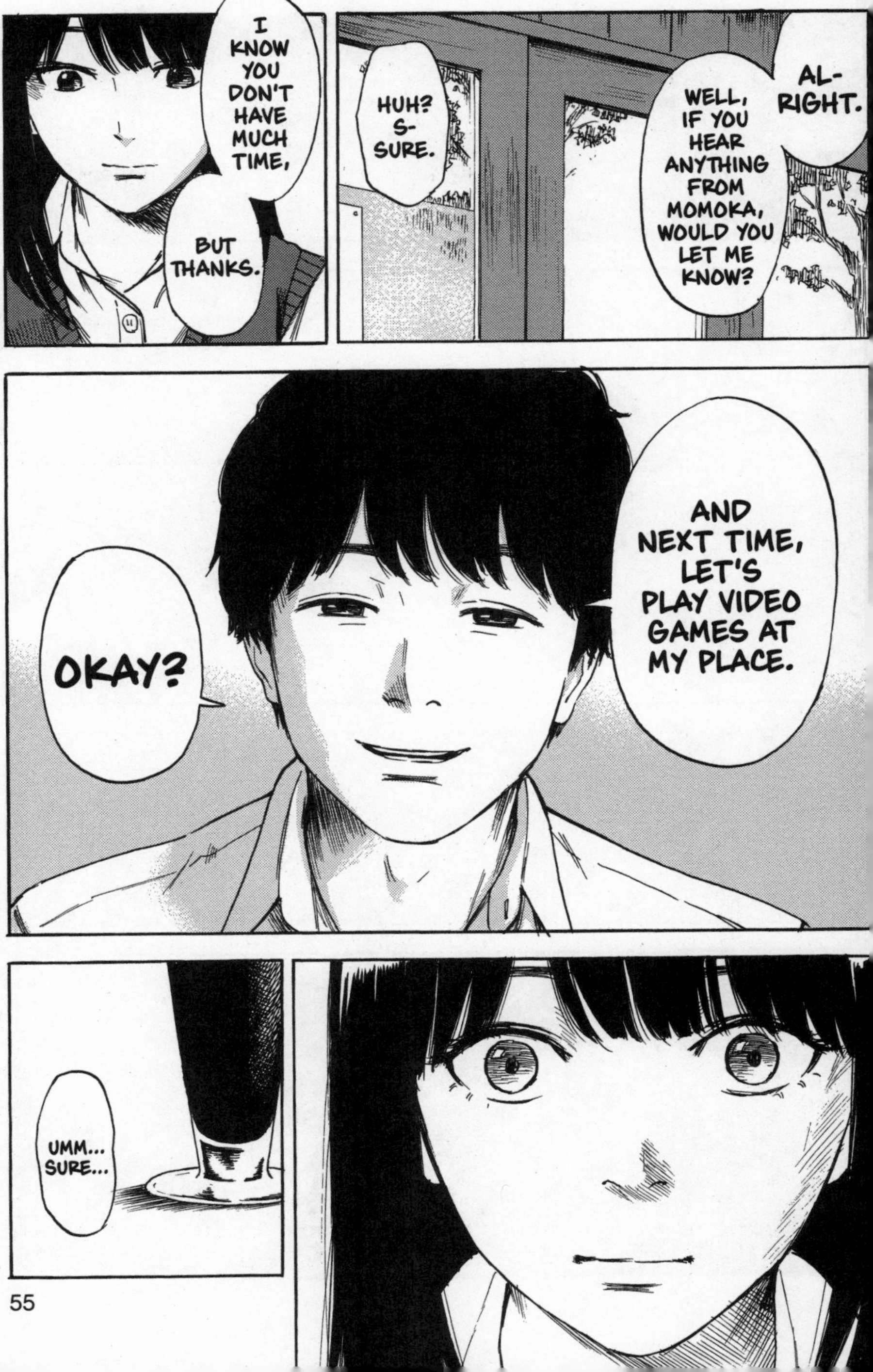
AL-RIGHT.
WELL, IF YOU HEAR ANYTHING FROM MOMOKA, WOULD YOU LET ME KNOW?
HUH? S-SURE.
I KNOW YOU DON'T HAVE MUCH TIME,
BUT THANKS.
AND NEXT TIME, LET'S PLAY VIDEO GAMES AT MY PLACE.
OKAY?
UMM... SURE...

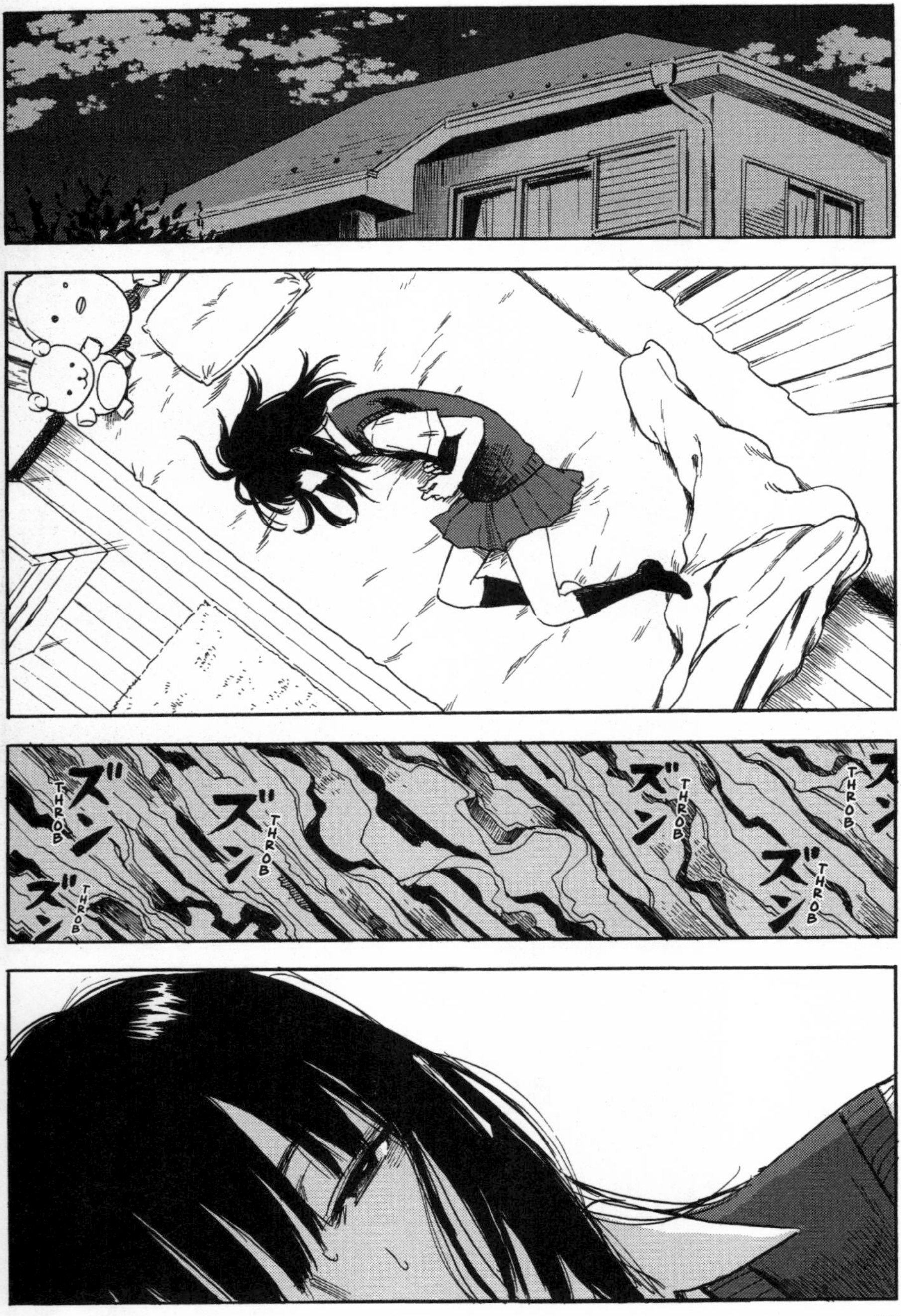
ズン
THROB
ズン
THROB
ズン
THROB
ズン
THROB
ズン
THROB
ズン
THROB

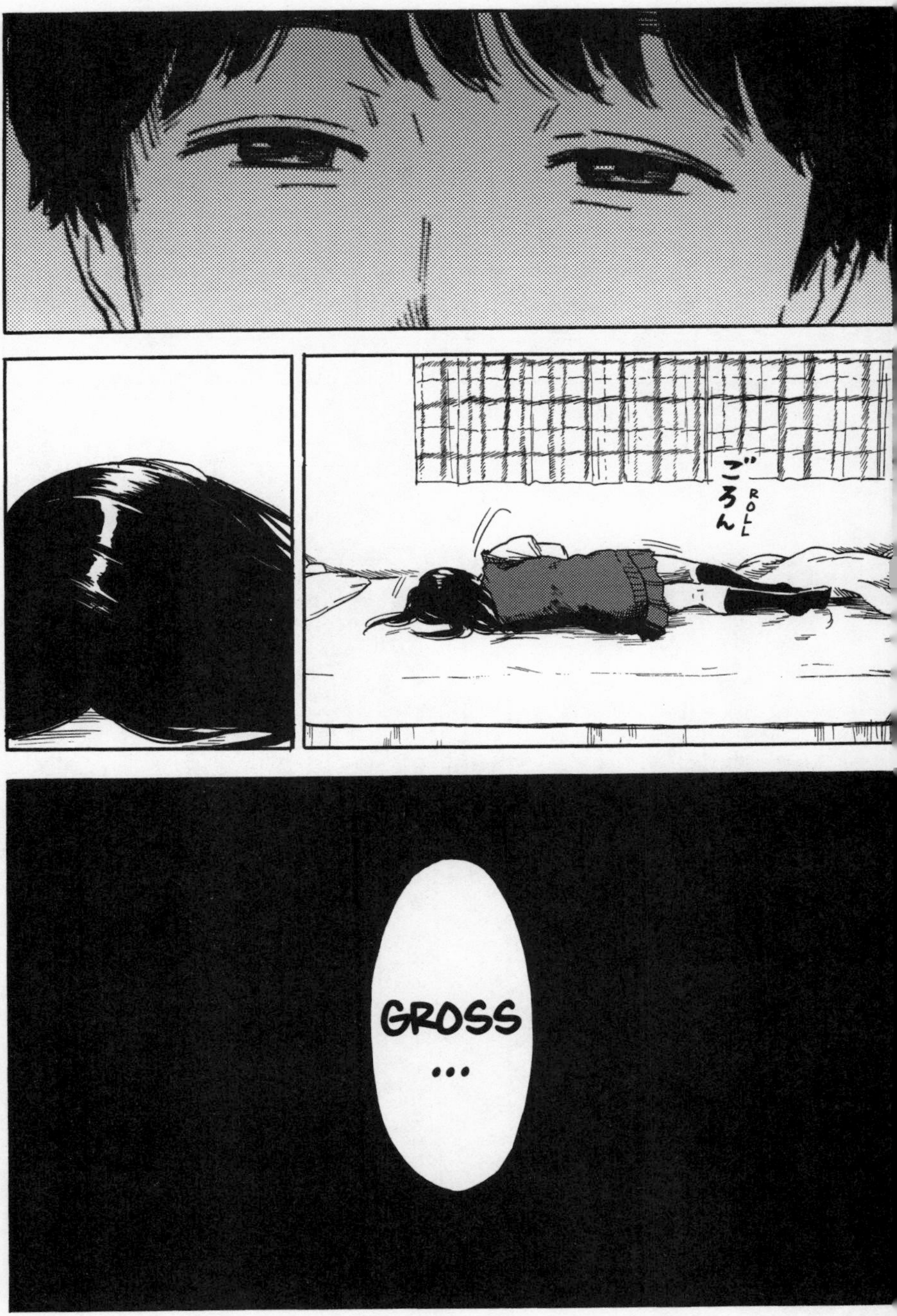
ごろん
ROLL
GROSS
...

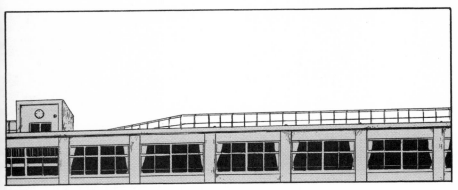

MORN-
ING!

HEY!
MORNING!

RATTL
ガ
ラ
ラ

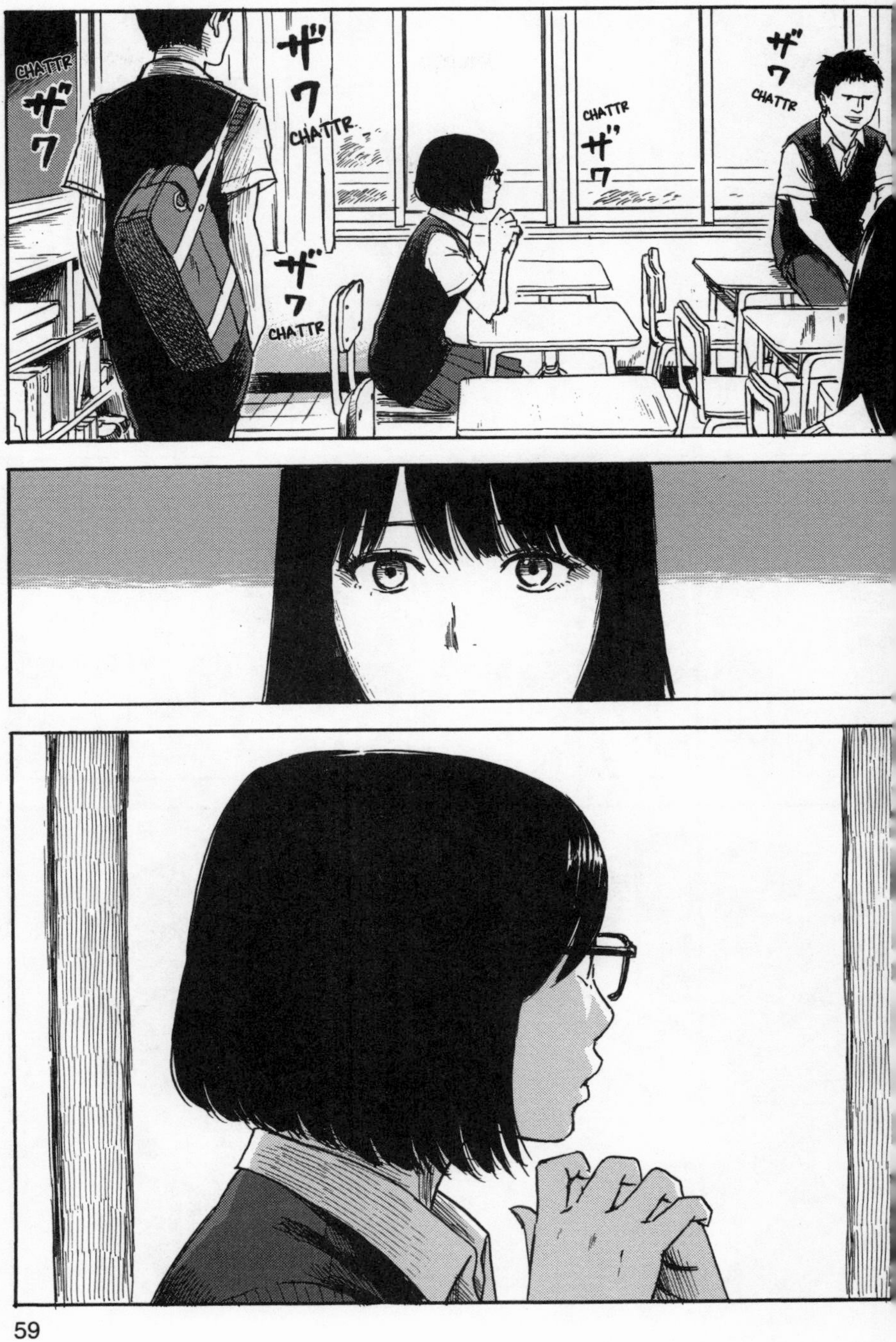
ザワ
CHATTR
CHATTR
ザワ
ザワ
CHATTR
ザワ
CHATTR
CHATTR
ザワ

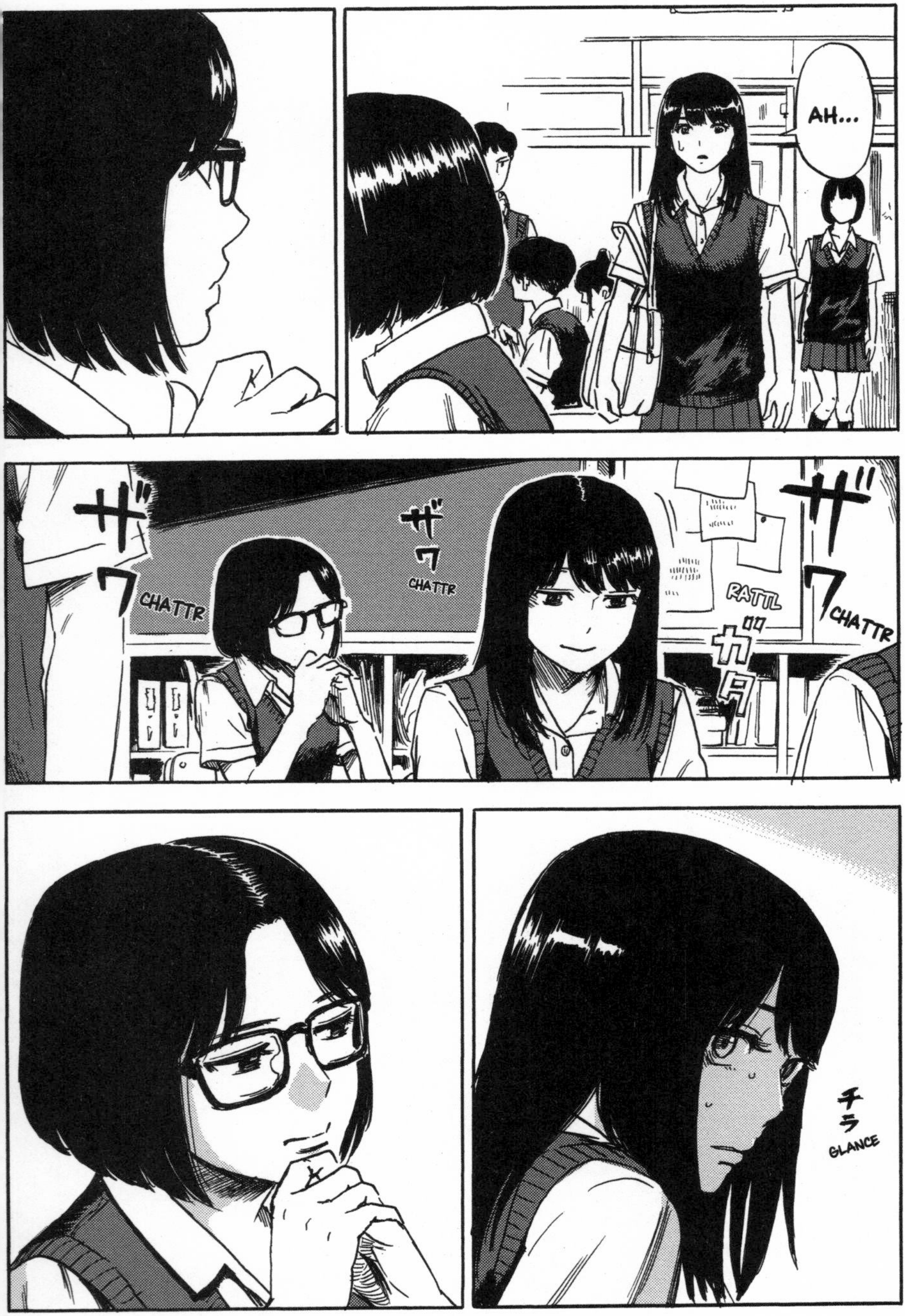
AH...
ザワ
CHATTR
ガタ
RATTL
ザワ
CHATTR
ザワ
CHATTR
チラ
GLANCE

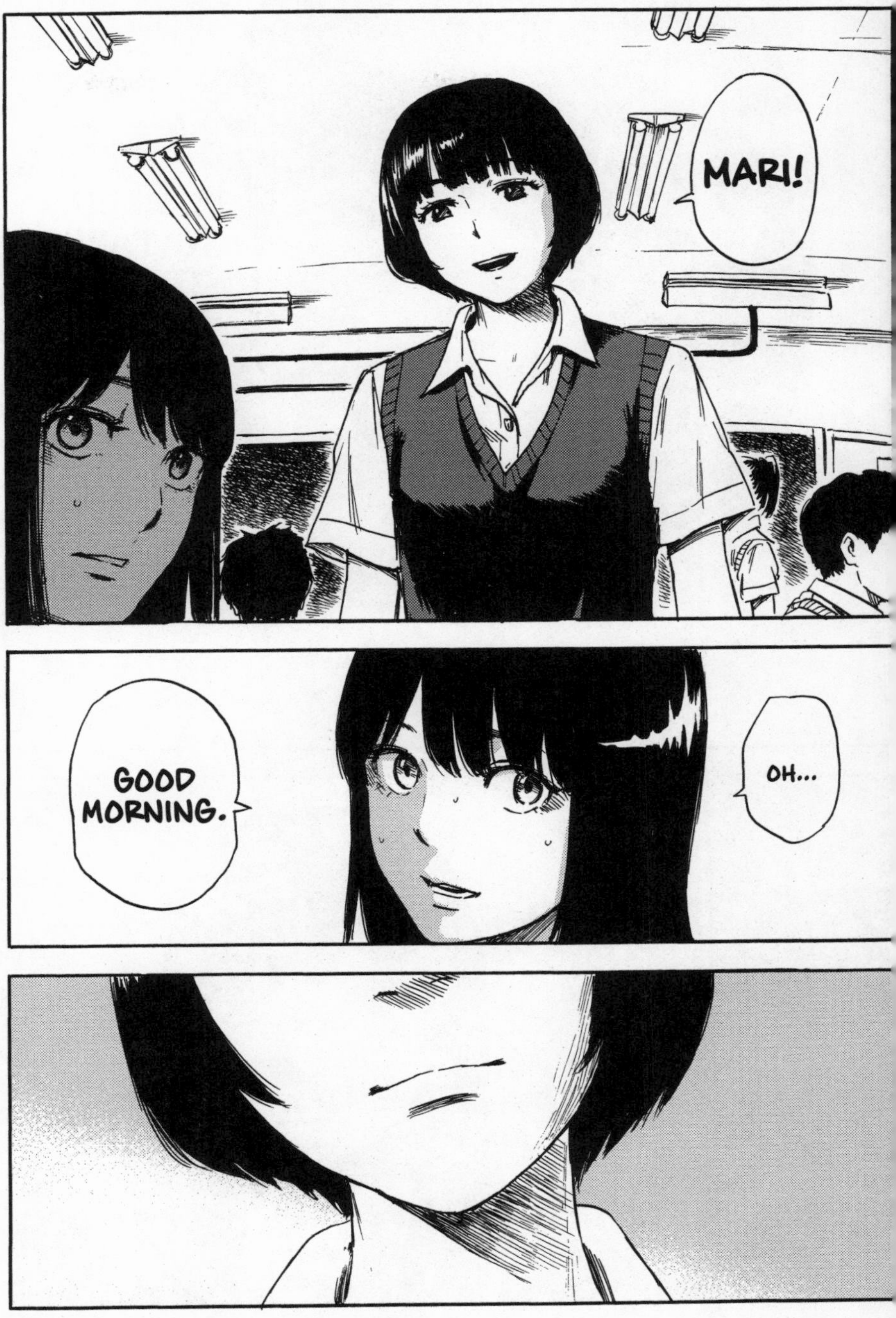
MARI!
OH...
GOOD MORNING.

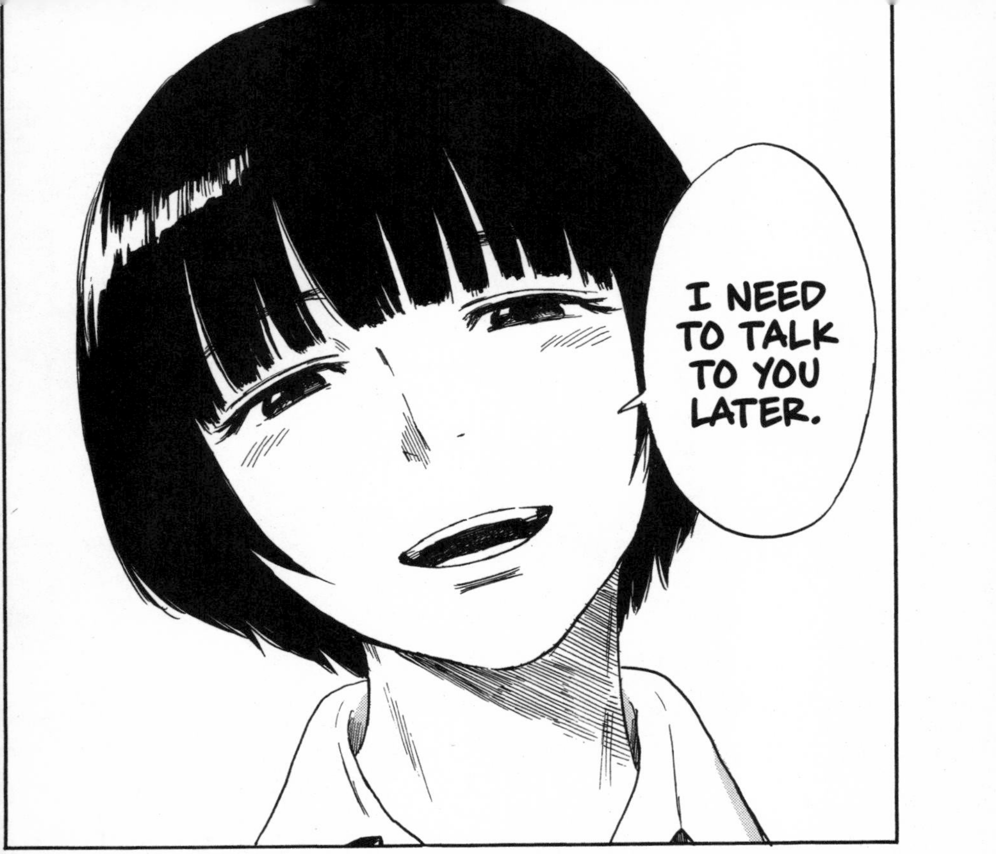
I NEED TO TALK TO YOU LATER.
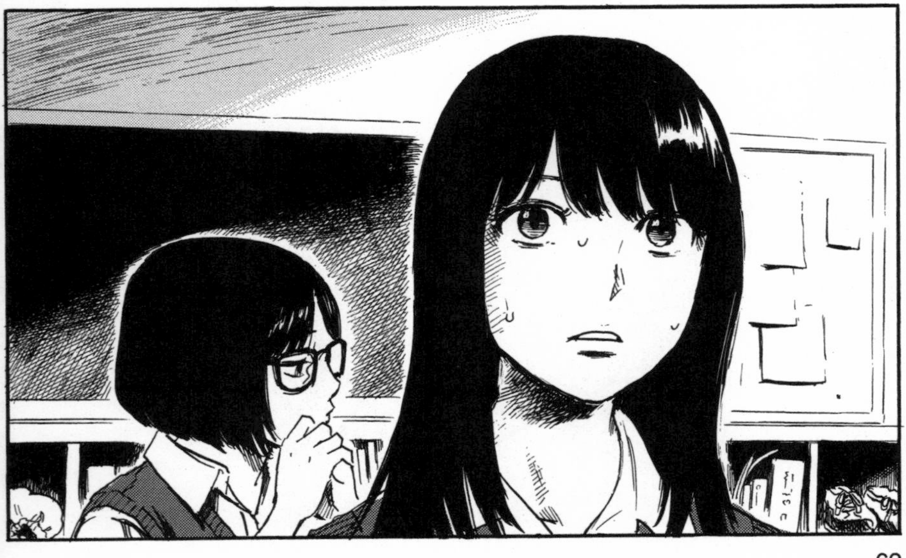

Chapter 21: Banished by the Girls' Club

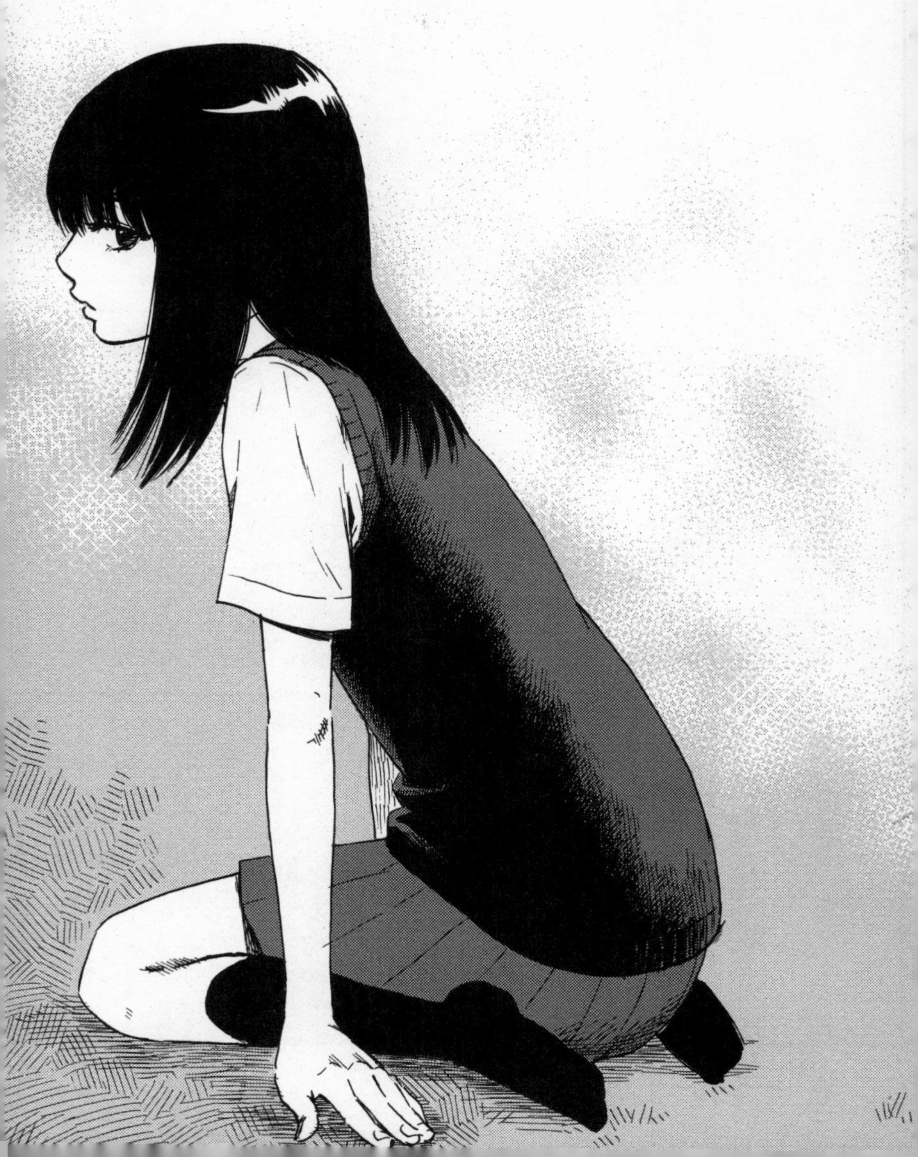

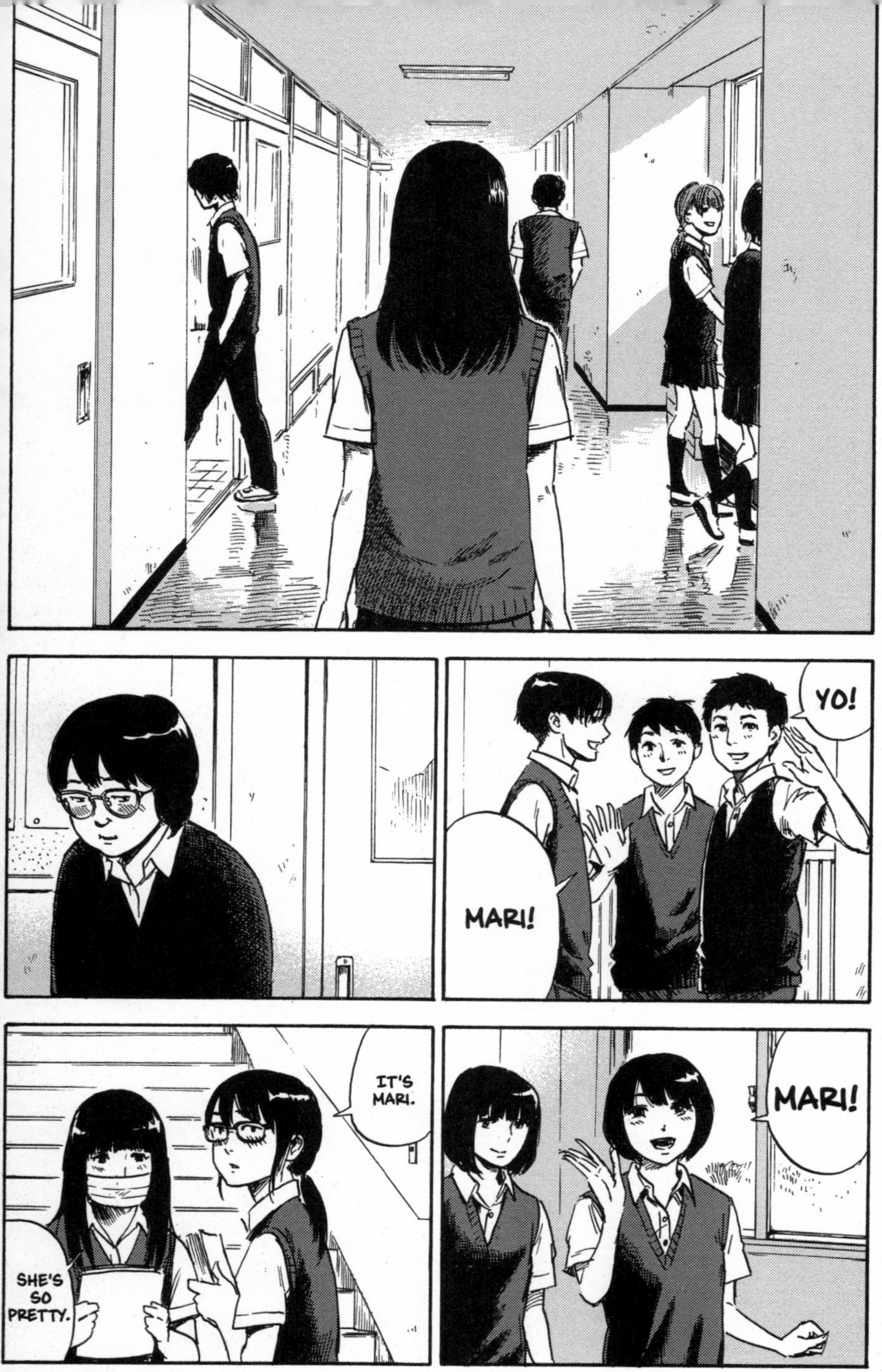
YO!
MARI!
MARI!
IT'S MARI.
SHE'S SO PRETTY.

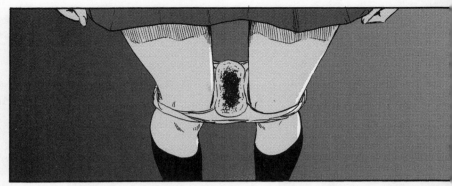

HUH? THAT'S WEIRD!

RIGHT?

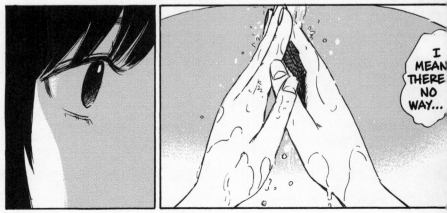

I MEAN THERE NO WAY...

KYA
HA
HA

I
KNOW
...

YOU
REALLY
CAN'T
THO...

キィ
KREAK

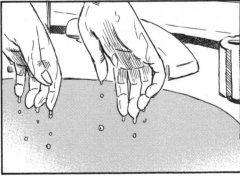

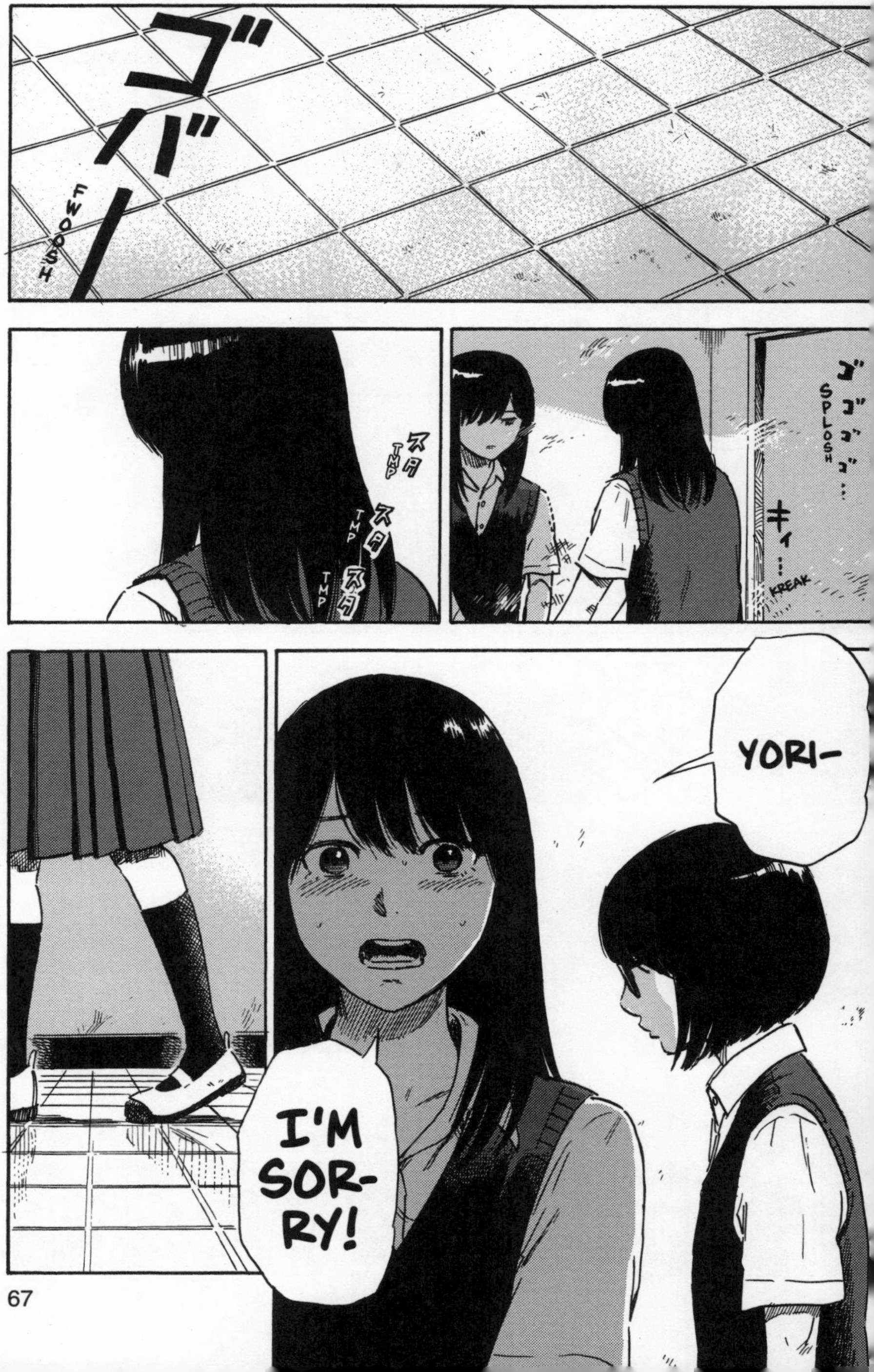
ゴバー
FWOOSH
ゴゴゴゴ…
SPLOSH
キィ…
KREAK
スタ
TMP
スタ
TMP
スタ
TMP
YORI-
I'M SORRY!

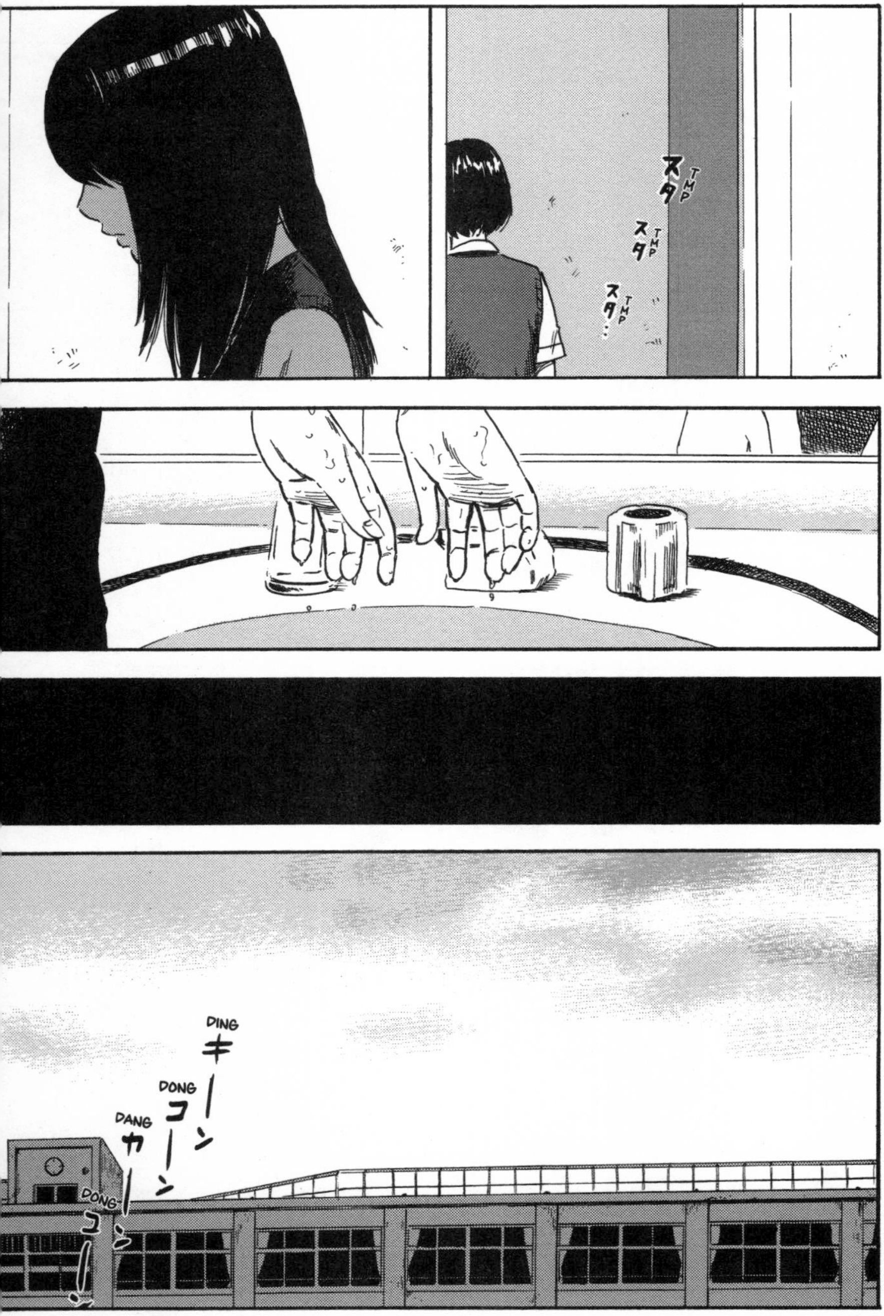
スタ TMP
スタ TMP
スタ… TMP
DING キーン
DONG コーン
DANG カーン
DONG コーン!!

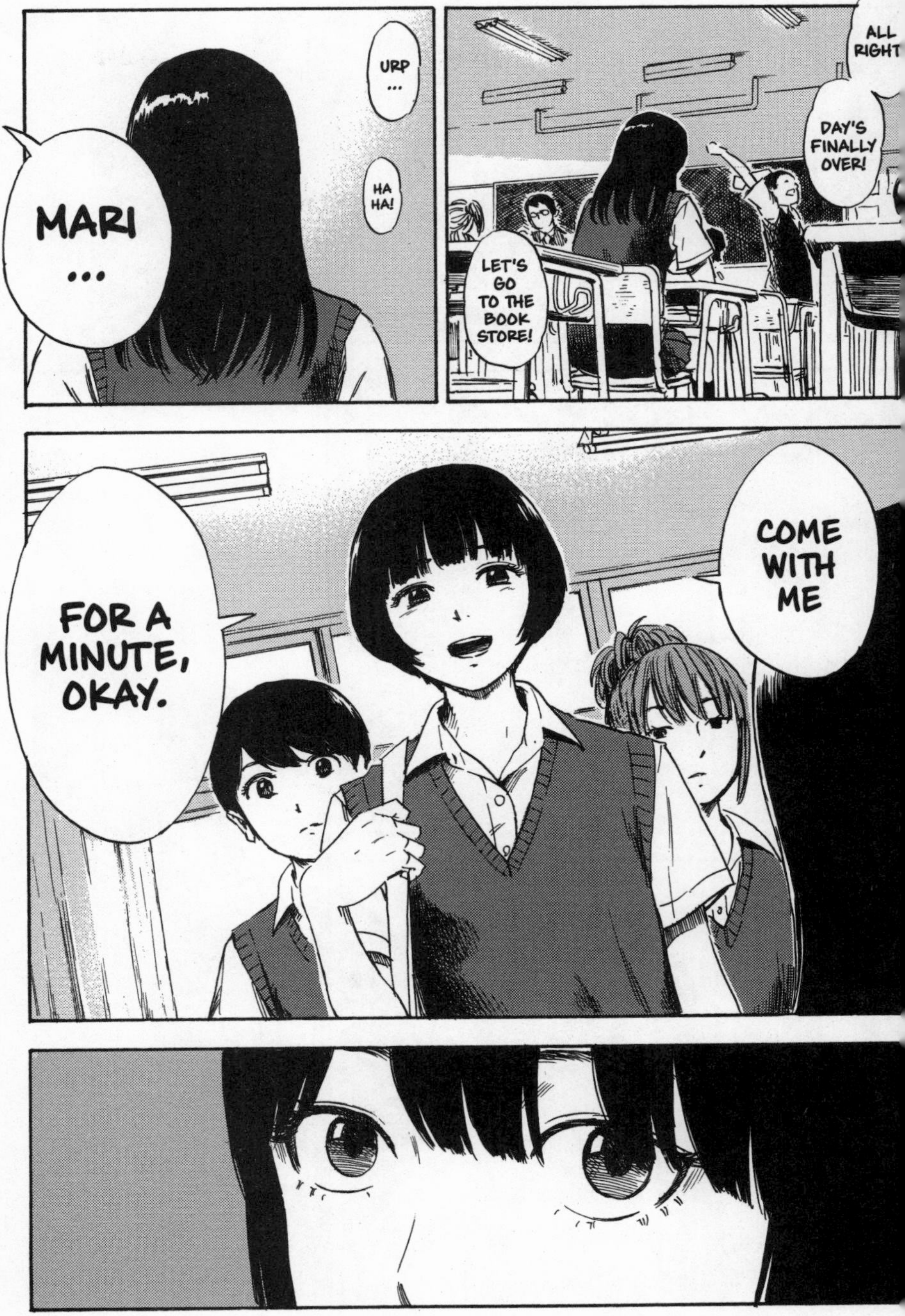
ALL RIGHT
DAY'S FINALLY OVER!
LET'S GO TO THE BOOK STORE!
URP ...
HA HA!
MARI ...
COME WITH ME
FOR A MINUTE, OKAY.

RATTL

WHAT
IS IT?

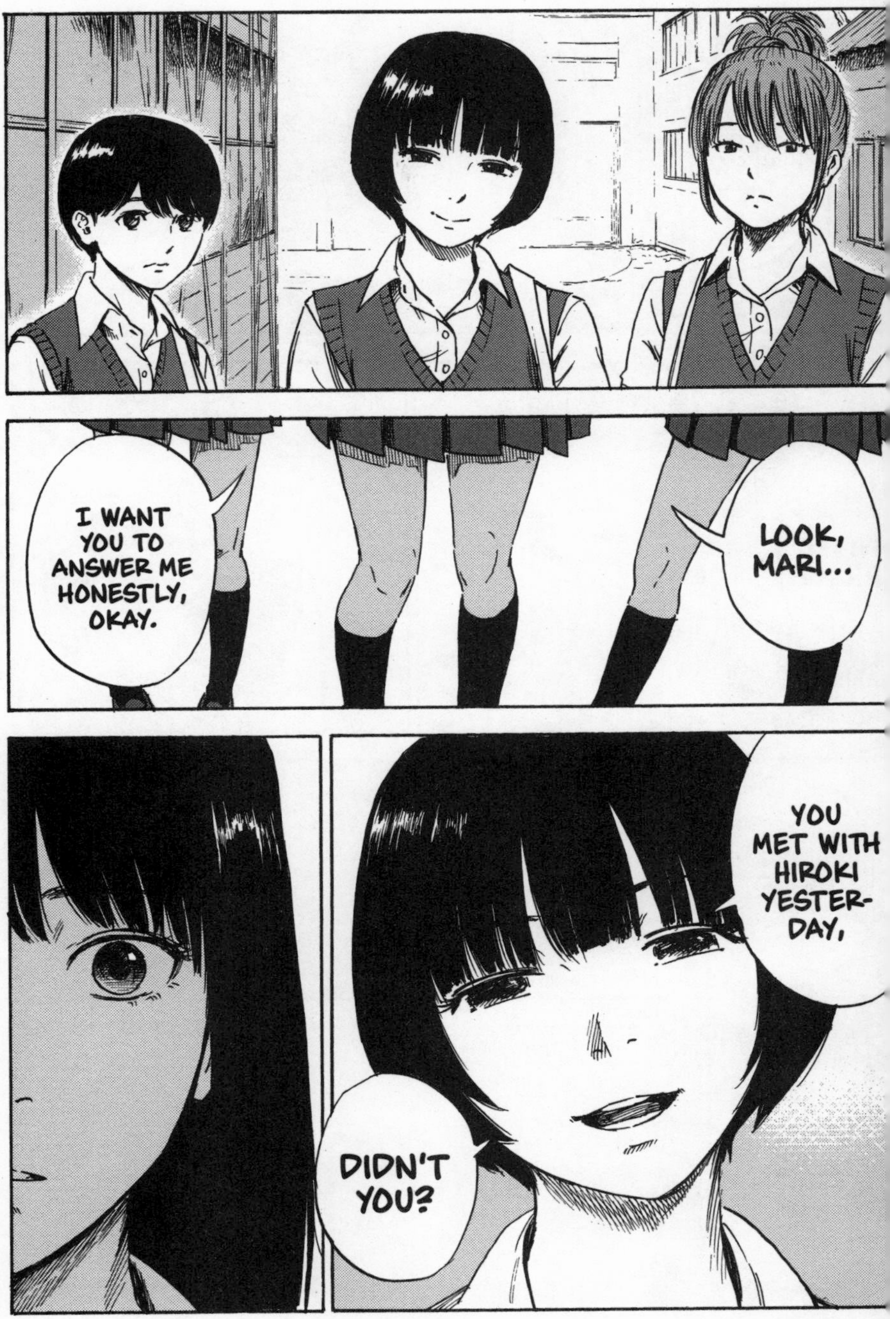
LOOK, MARI...
I WANT YOU TO ANSWER ME HONESTLY, OKAY.
YOU MET WITH HIROKI YESTER-DAY,
DIDN'T YOU?

WE DID MEET, BUT—

UM...

YES.

WHO...

INVITED WHOM?

UM... HE DID.

HIROKI CALLED ME.

OH...

HUH?

AND WHERE TO?

UH-HUH...

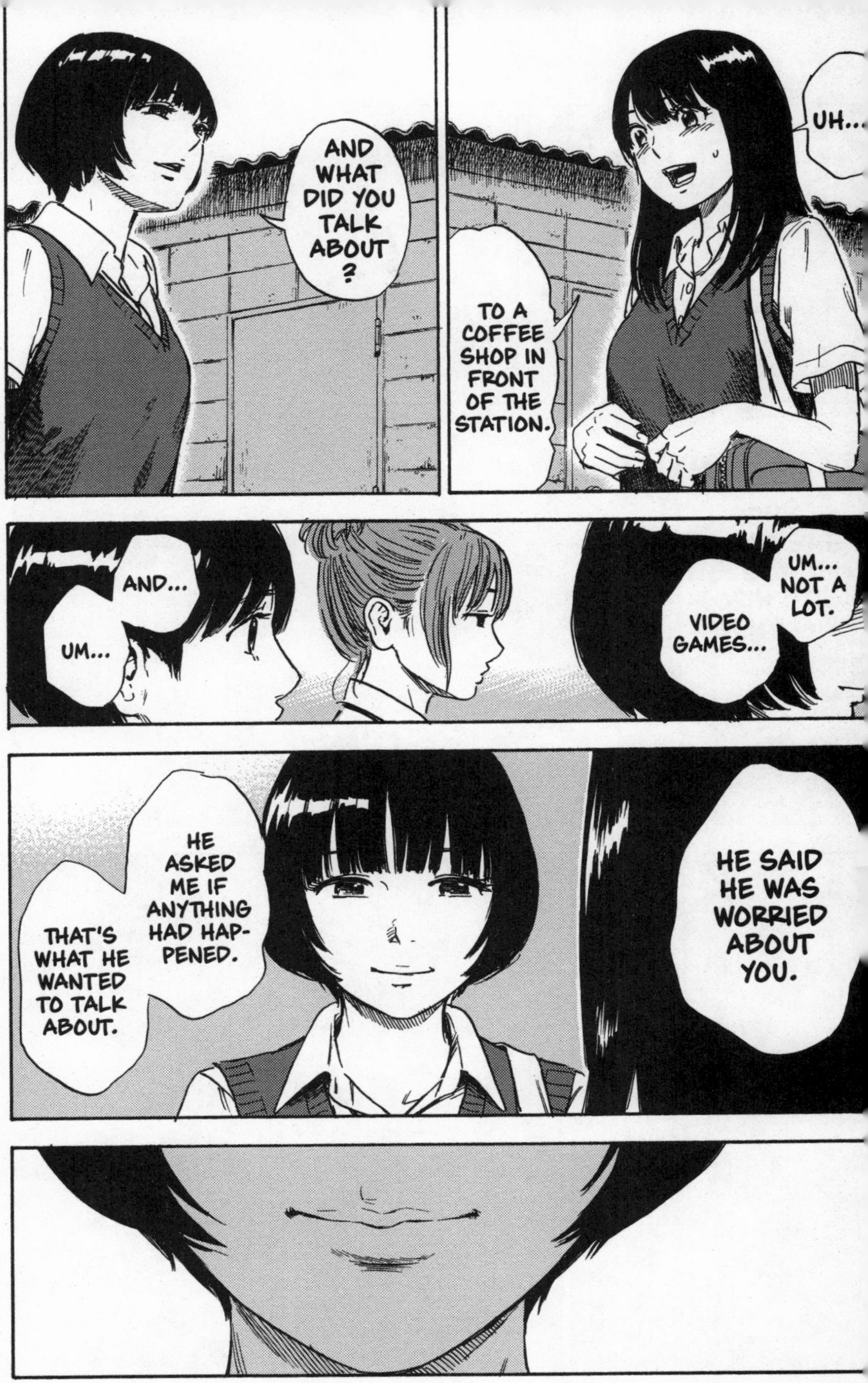
UH...
TO A COFFEE SHOP IN FRONT OF THE STATION.
AND WHAT DID YOU TALK ABOUT?
UM... NOT A LOT.
VIDEO GAMES...
AND...
UM...
HE SAID HE WAS WORRIED ABOUT YOU.
HE ASKED ME IF ANYTHING HAD HAP-PENED.
THAT'S WHAT HE WANTED TO TALK ABOUT.

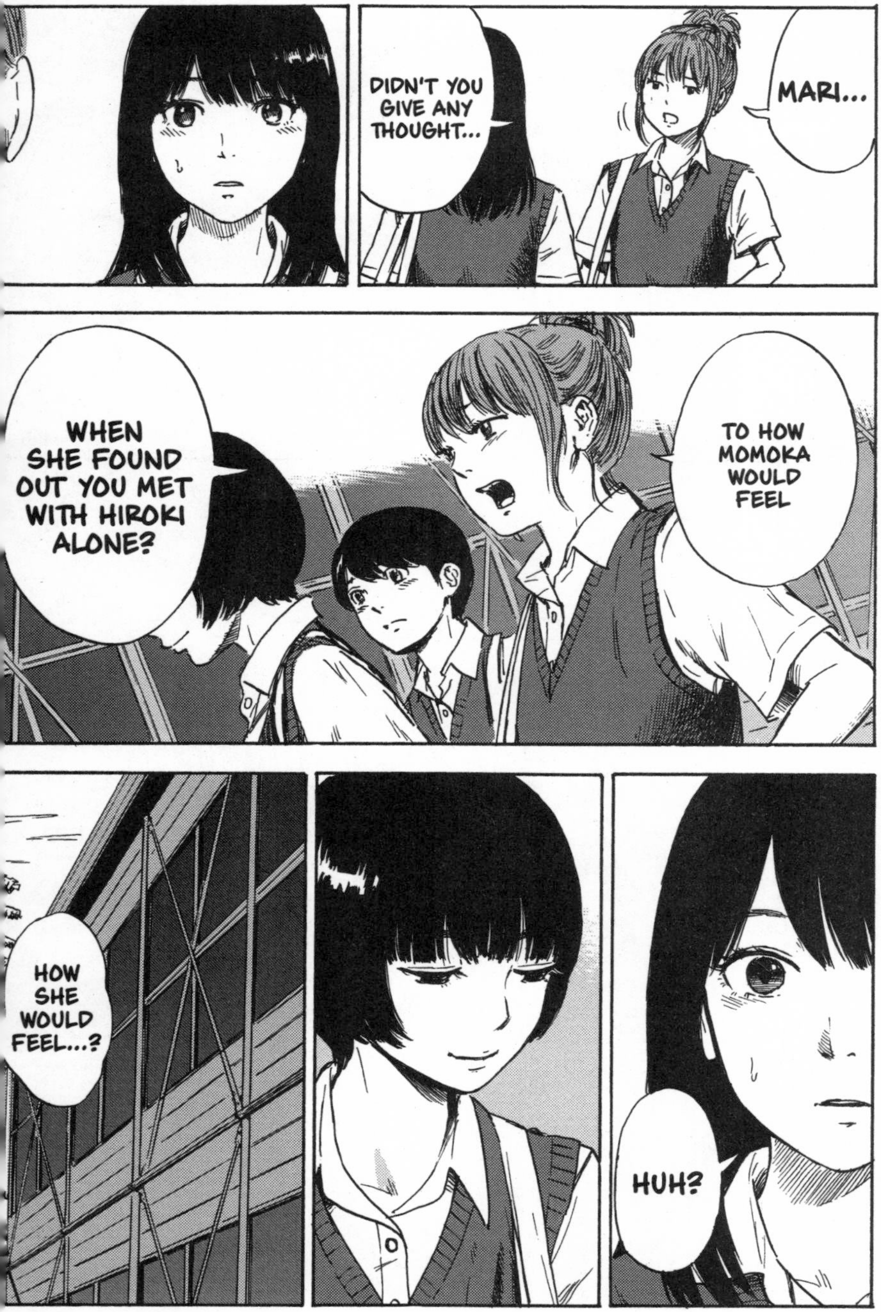
MARI...
DIDN'T YOU GIVE ANY THOUGHT...
TO HOW MOMOKA WOULD FEEL
WHEN SHE FOUND OUT YOU MET WITH HIROKI ALONE?
HUH?
HOW SHE WOULD FEEL...?

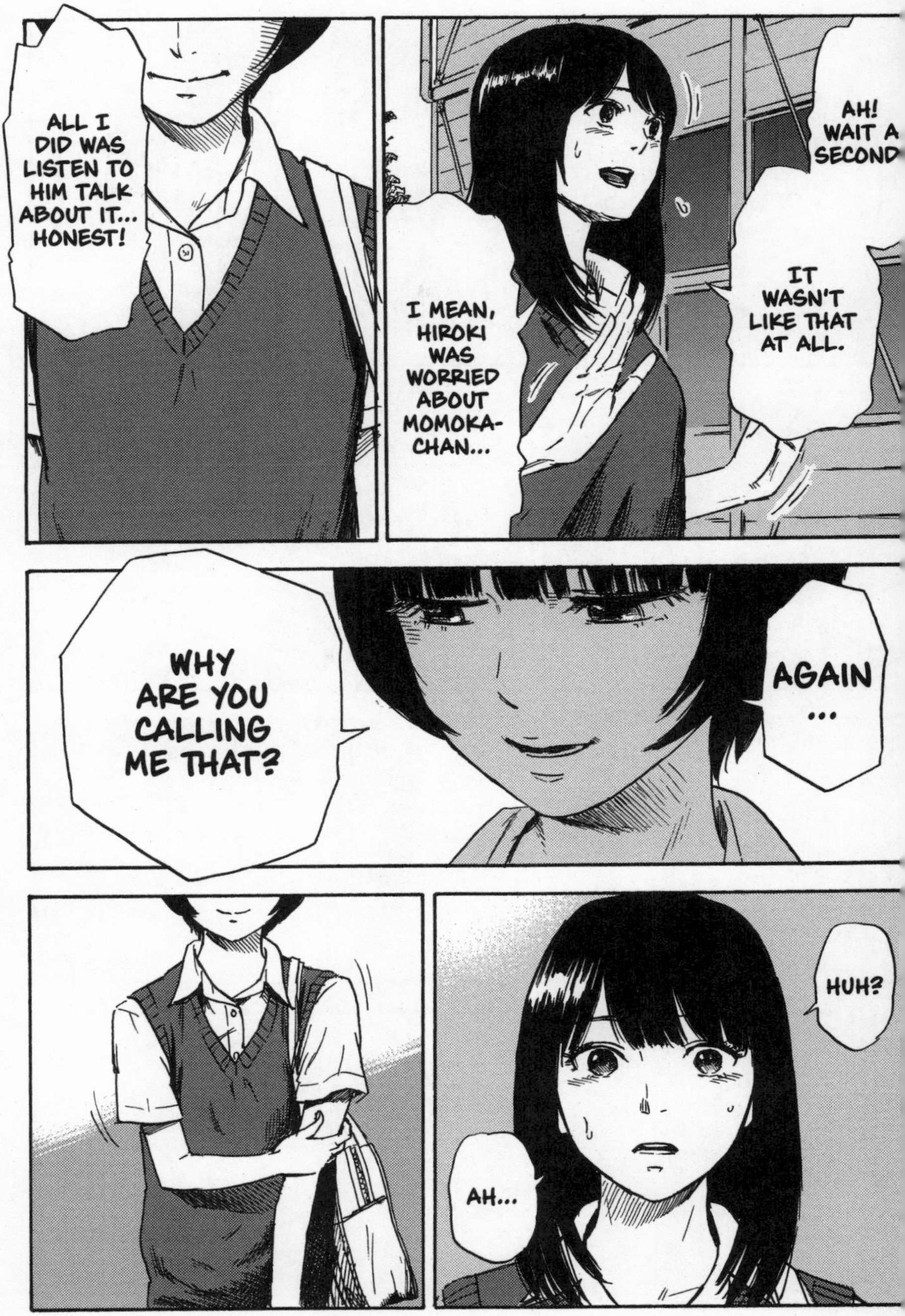
AH! WAIT A SECOND
IT WASN'T LIKE THAT AT ALL.
I MEAN, HIROKI WAS WORRIED ABOUT MOMOKA-CHAN...
ALL I DID WAS LISTEN TO HIM TALK ABOUT IT... HONEST!
AGAIN ...
WHY ARE YOU CALLING ME THAT?
HUH?
AH...

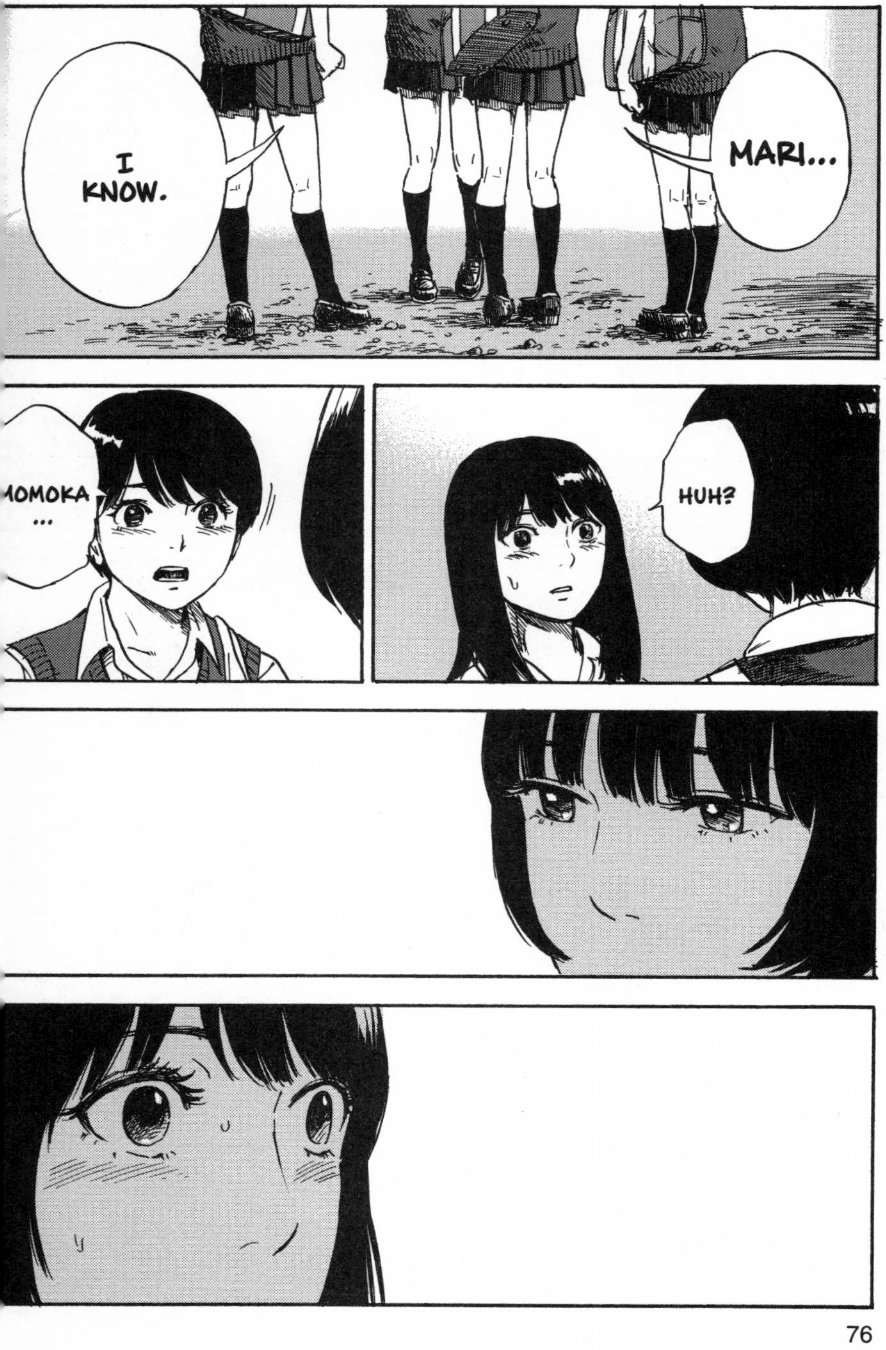
MARI...
I KNOW.
HUH?
MOMOKA ...

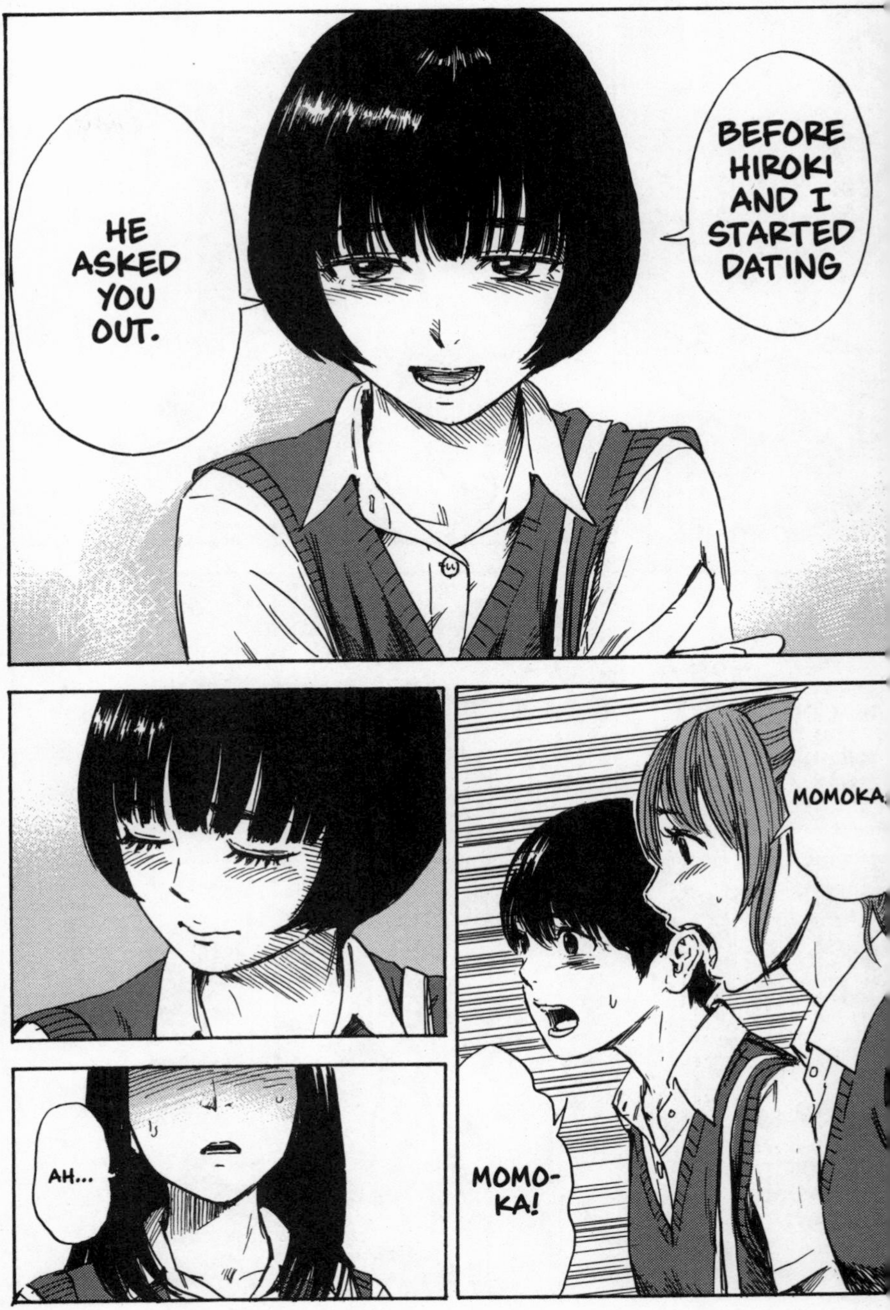
BEFORE HIROKI AND I STARTED DATING
HE ASKED YOU OUT.
MOMOKA.
MOMO-KA!
AH...

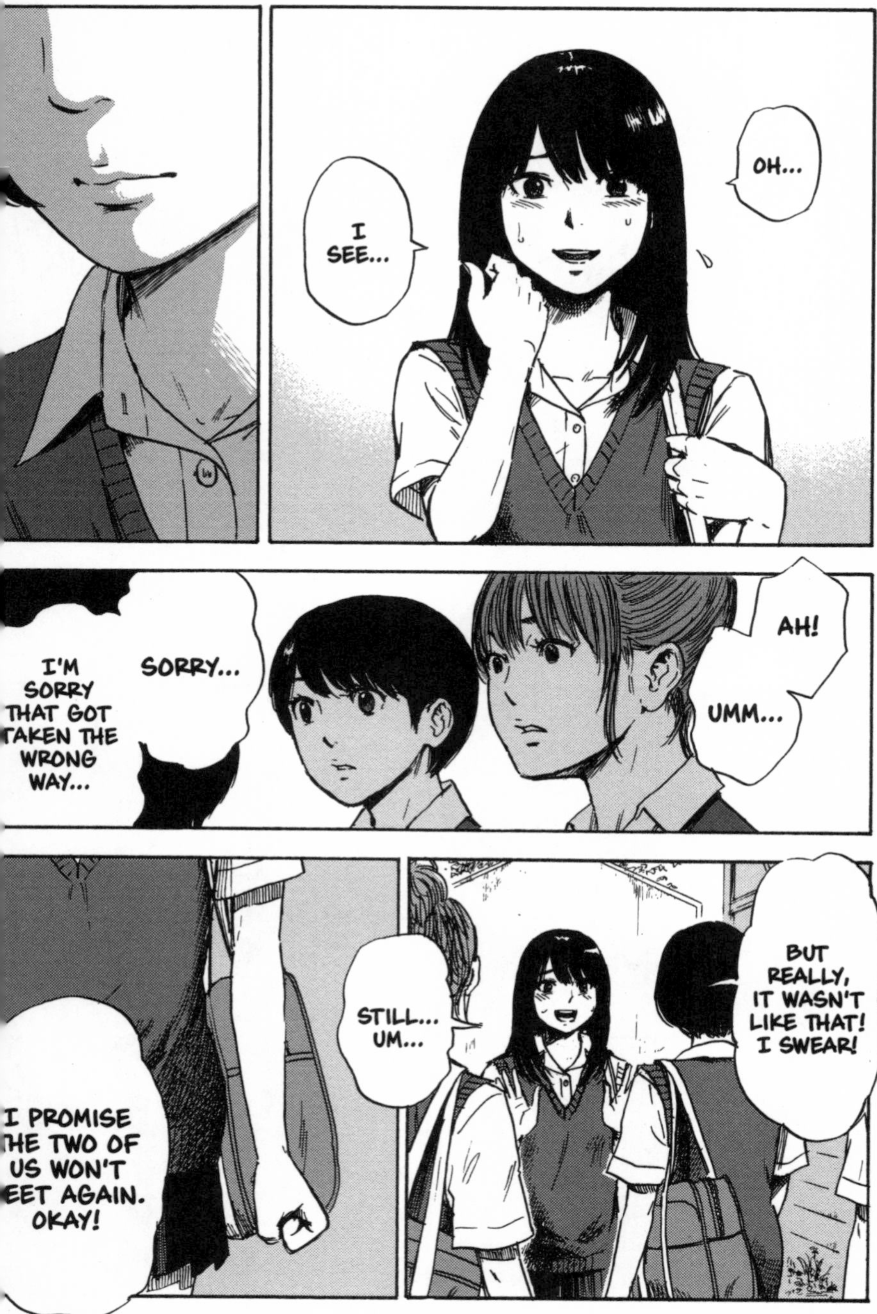

OH...
I SEE...
AH!
UMM...
SORRY...
I'M SORRY THAT GOT TAKEN THE WRONG WAY...
BUT REALLY, IT WASN'T LIKE THAT! I SWEAR!
STILL... UM...
I PROMISE THE TWO OF US WON'T EET AGAIN. OKAY!

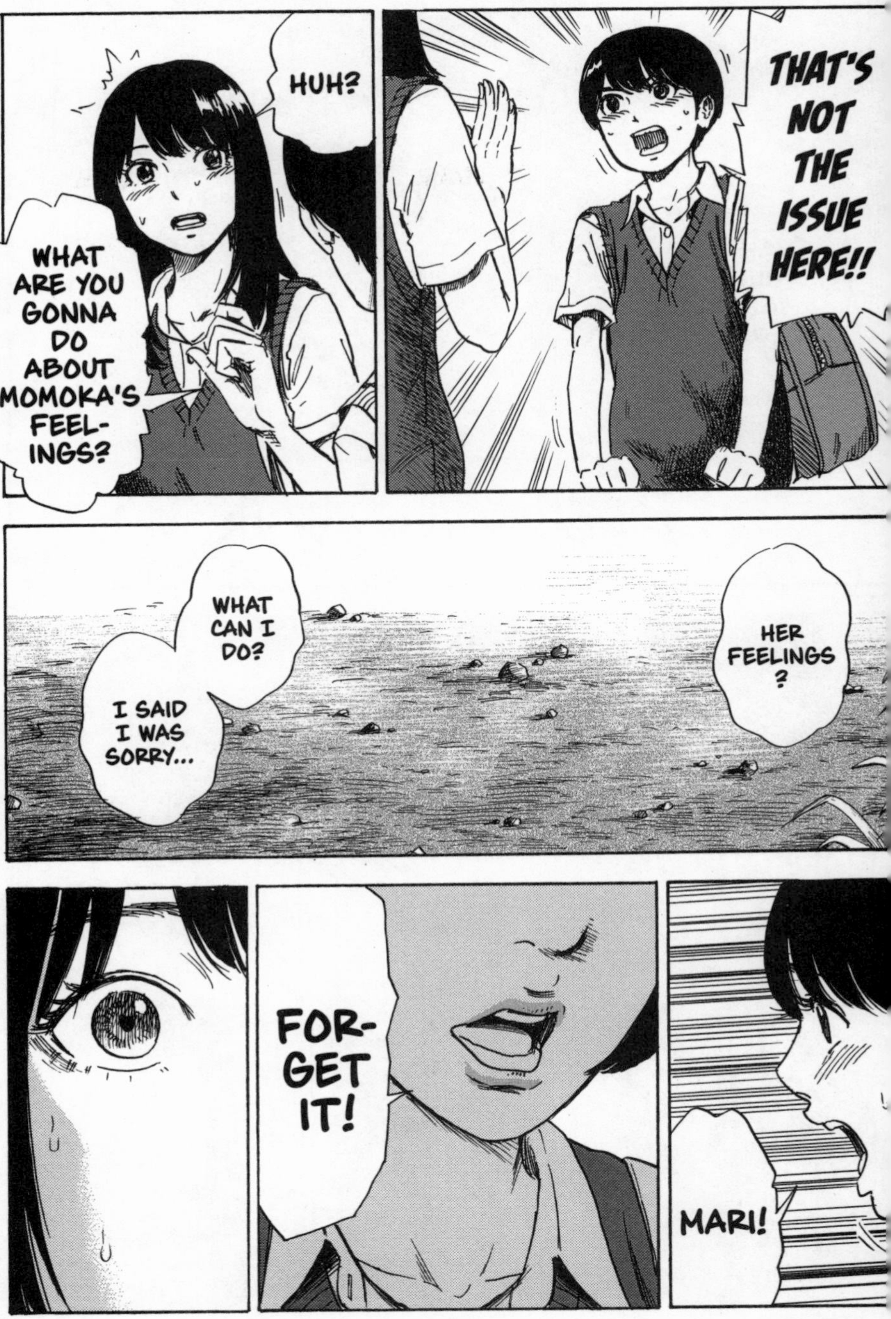
THAT'S NOT THE ISSUE HERE!!
HUH?
WHAT ARE YOU GONNA DO ABOUT MOMOKA'S FEEL-INGS?
HER FEELINGS?
WHAT CAN I DO?
I SAID I WAS SORRY...
MARI!
FOR-GET IT!

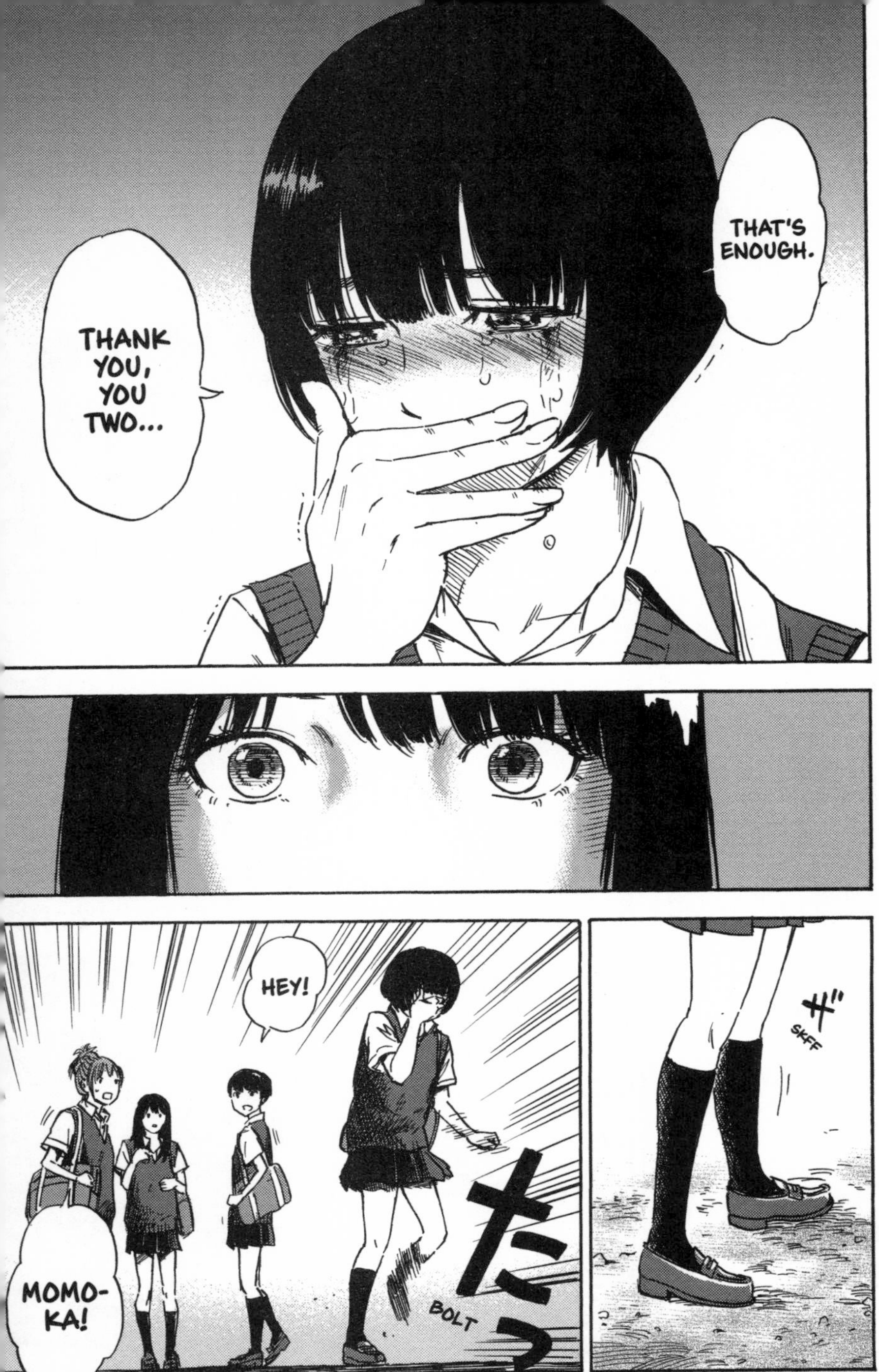
THAT'S ENOUGH.
THANK YOU, YOU TWO...
ザ
SKFF
HEY!
たっ
BOLT
MOMO-KA!

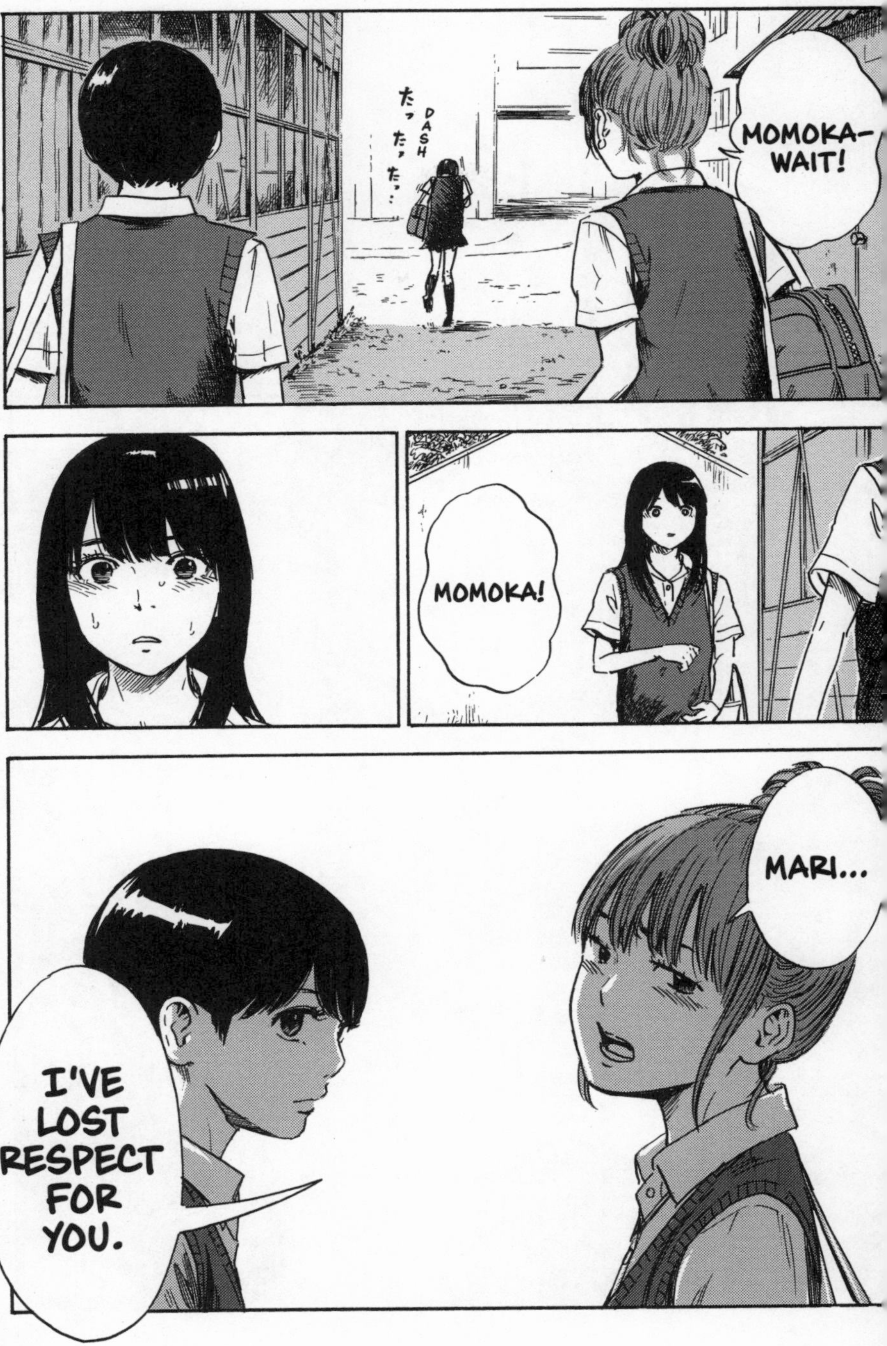
MOMOKA-WAIT!
たっ たっ たっ
DASH
MOMOKA!
MARI...
I'VE LOST RESPECT FOR YOU.

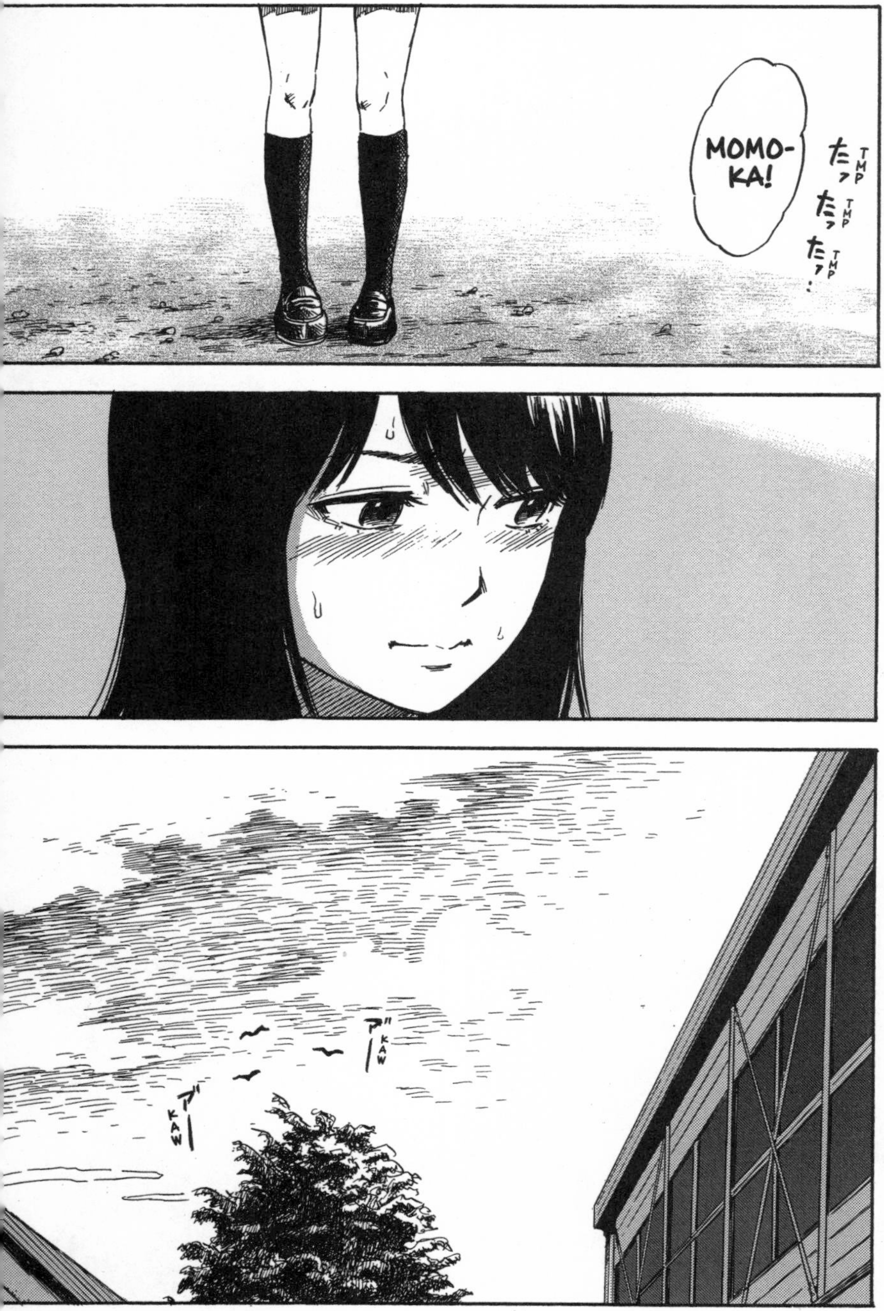
MOMO-KA!
たッ TMP
たッ TMP
たッ TMP
ア゛ー KAW
ア゛ー KAW

Chapter 22:
A Stagnating Atmosphere

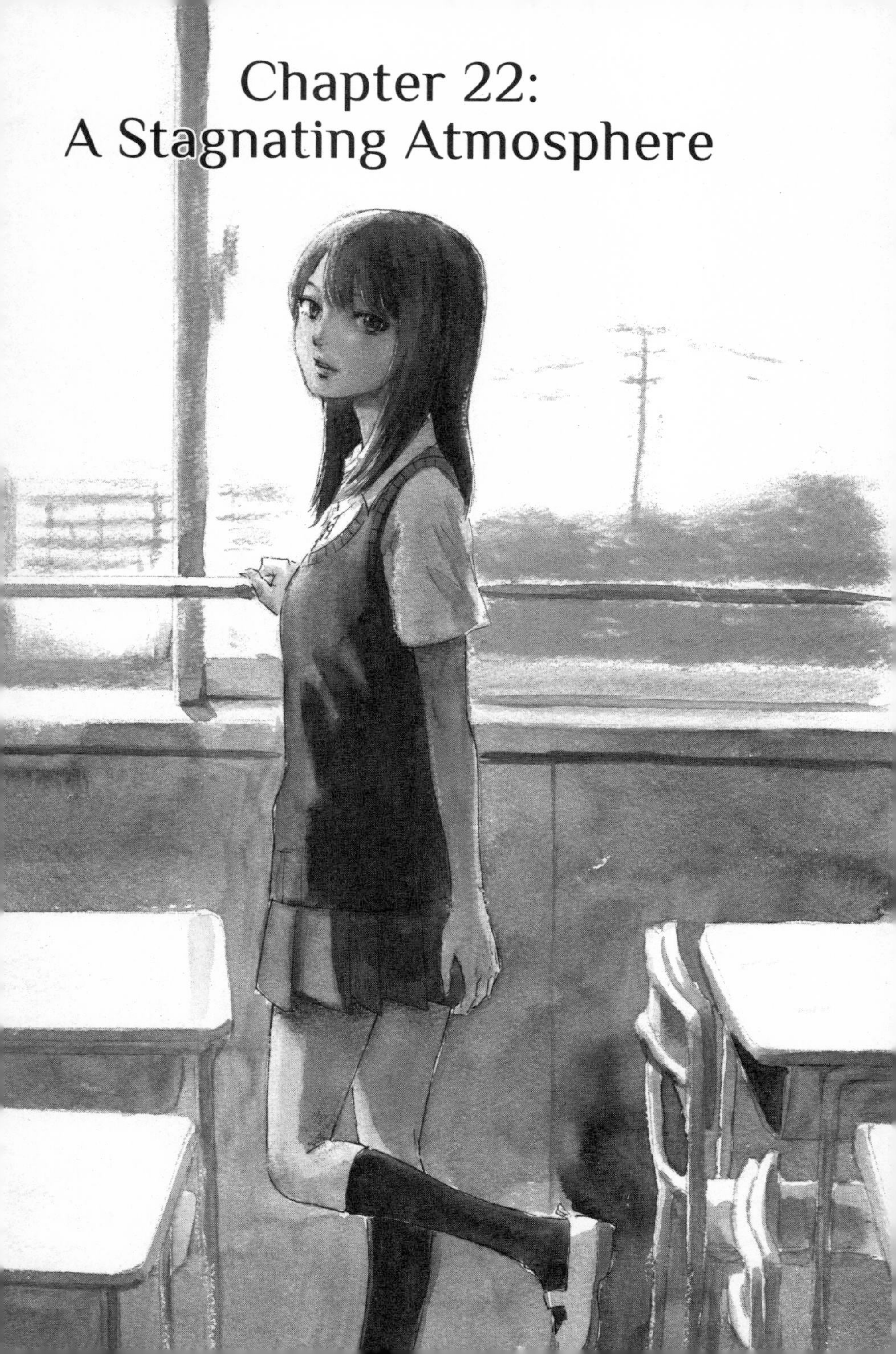

MEDICINE?
ONE WEEK LA-TER.
OKAY, FROM THE NEXT SECTION....
WHAT? WHAT?
YOSHI-ZAKI!
HERE.
UH... UM...
HUH?

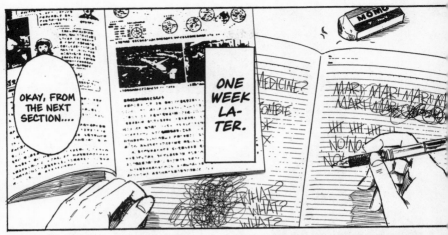

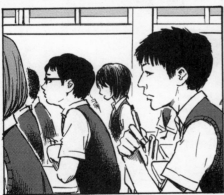

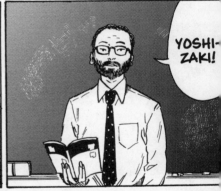

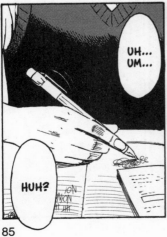

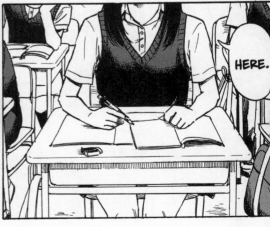

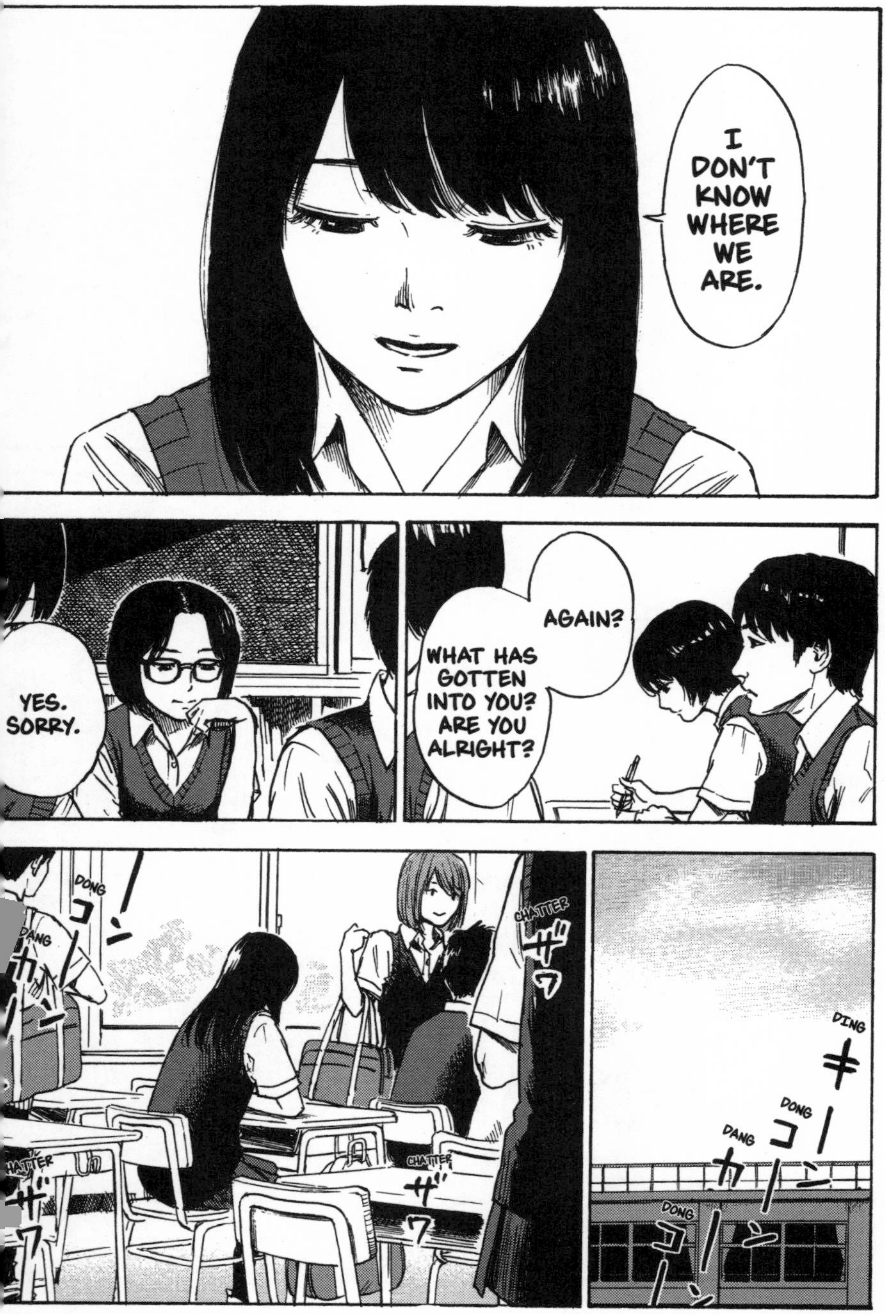
I DON'T KNOW WHERE WE ARE.
AGAIN?
WHAT HAS GOTTEN INTO YOU? ARE YOU ALRIGHT?
YES. SORRY.
DING キーン
DONG コーン
DANG カーン
DONG コーン
CHATTER ザワ
DONG コーン
DANG カーン
CHATTER ザワ
CHATTER ザワ

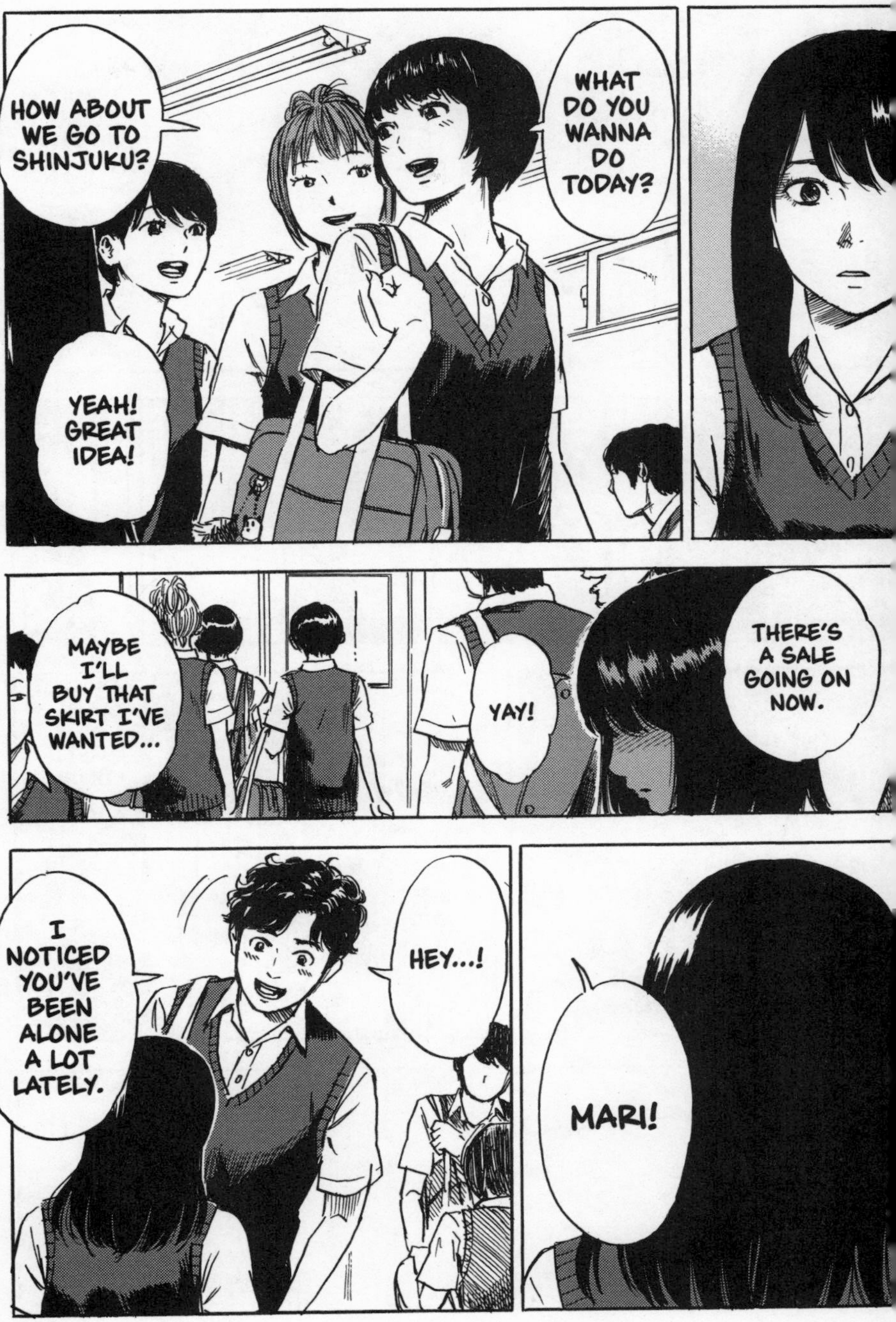
WHAT DO YOU WANNA DO TODAY?
HOW ABOUT WE GO TO SHINJUKU?
YEAH! GREAT IDEA!
THERE'S A SALE GOING ON NOW.
YAY!
MAYBE I'LL BUY THAT SKIRT I'VE WANTED...
MARI!
HEY...!
I NOTICED YOU'VE BEEN ALONE A LOT LATELY.

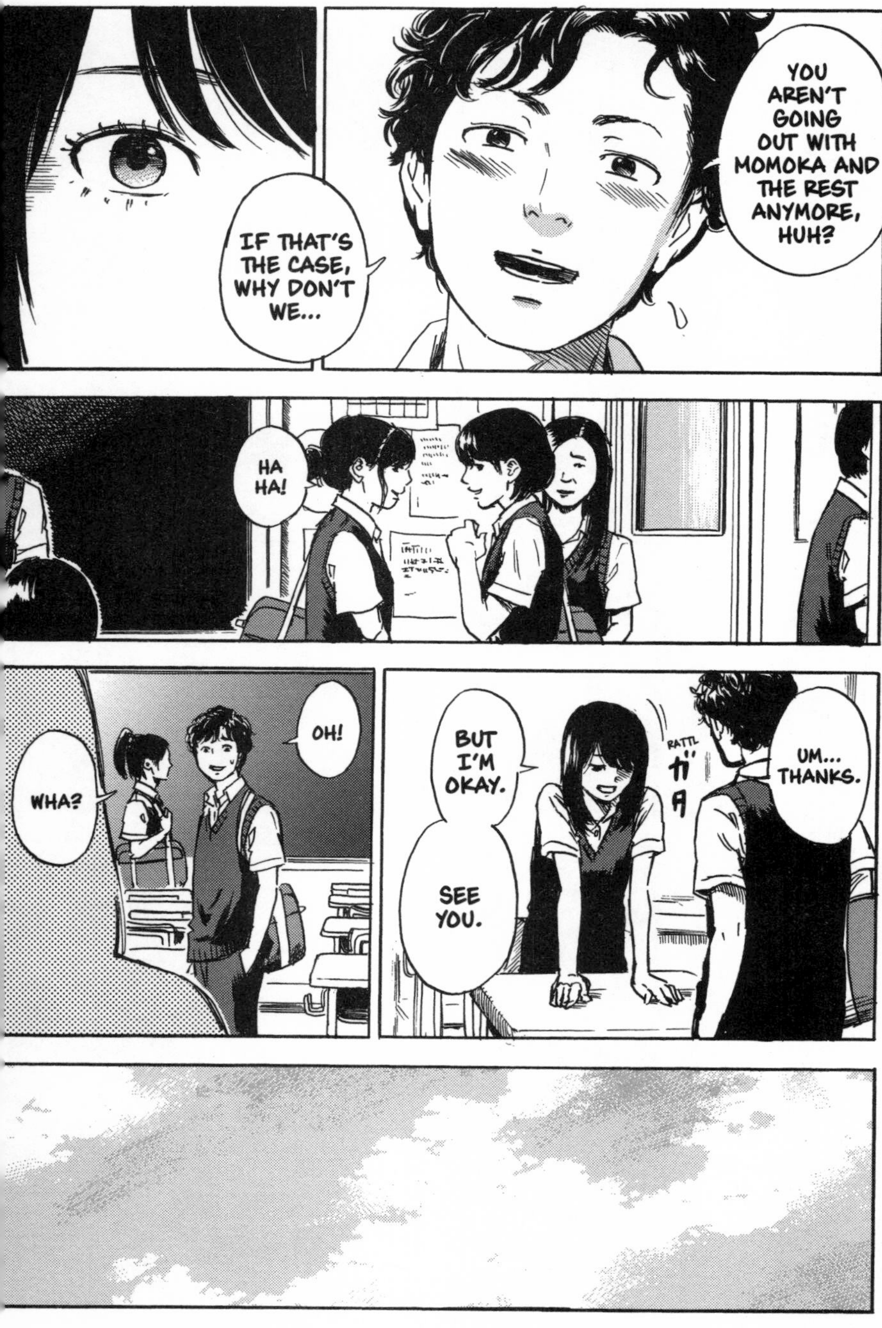
YOU AREN'T GOING OUT WITH MOMOKA AND THE REST ANYMORE, HUH?
IF THAT'S THE CASE, WHY DON'T WE...
HA HA!
UM... THANKS.
RATTL
ガタ
BUT I'M OKAY.
SEE YOU.
OH!
WHA?

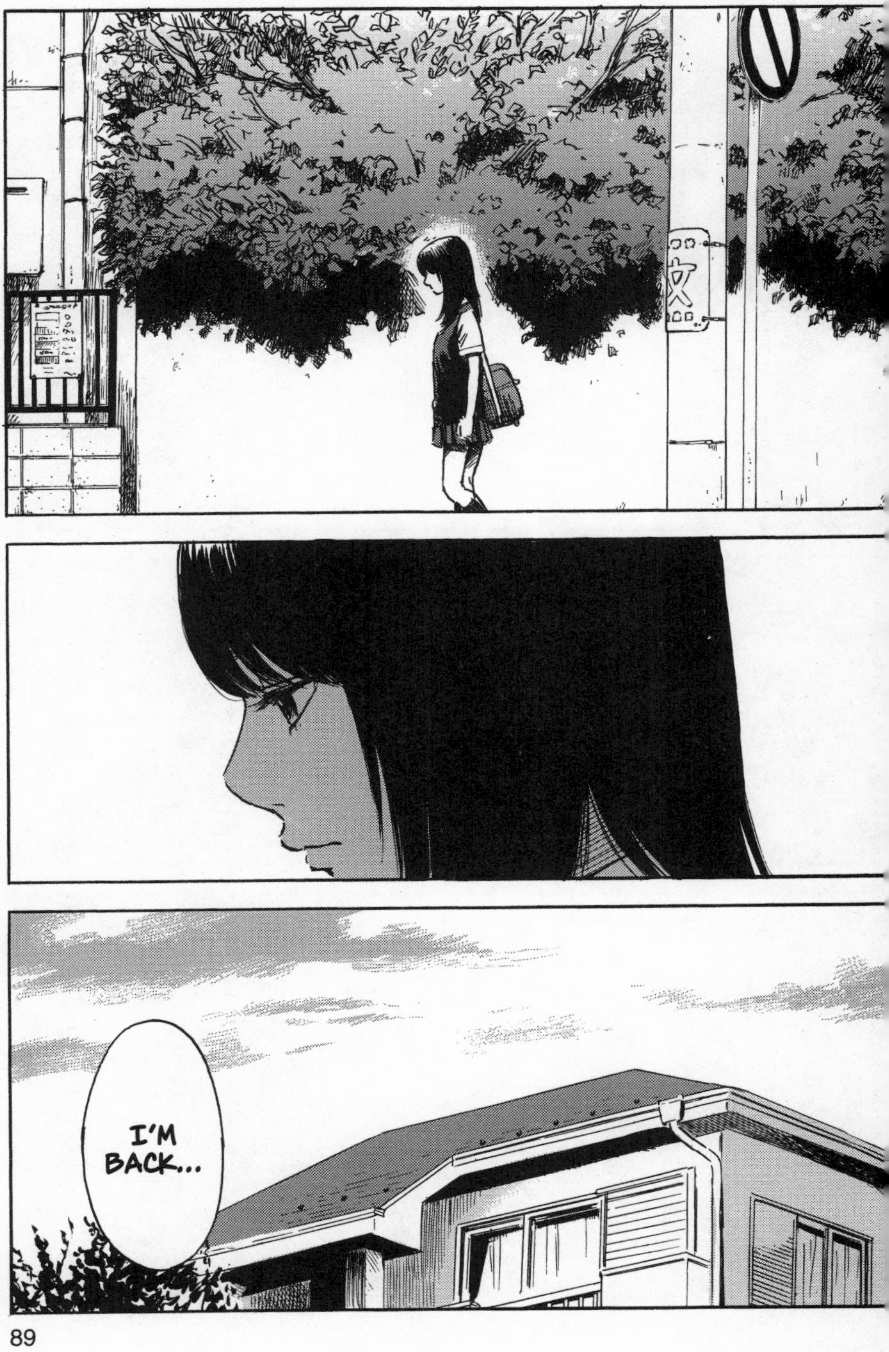
I'M BACK...

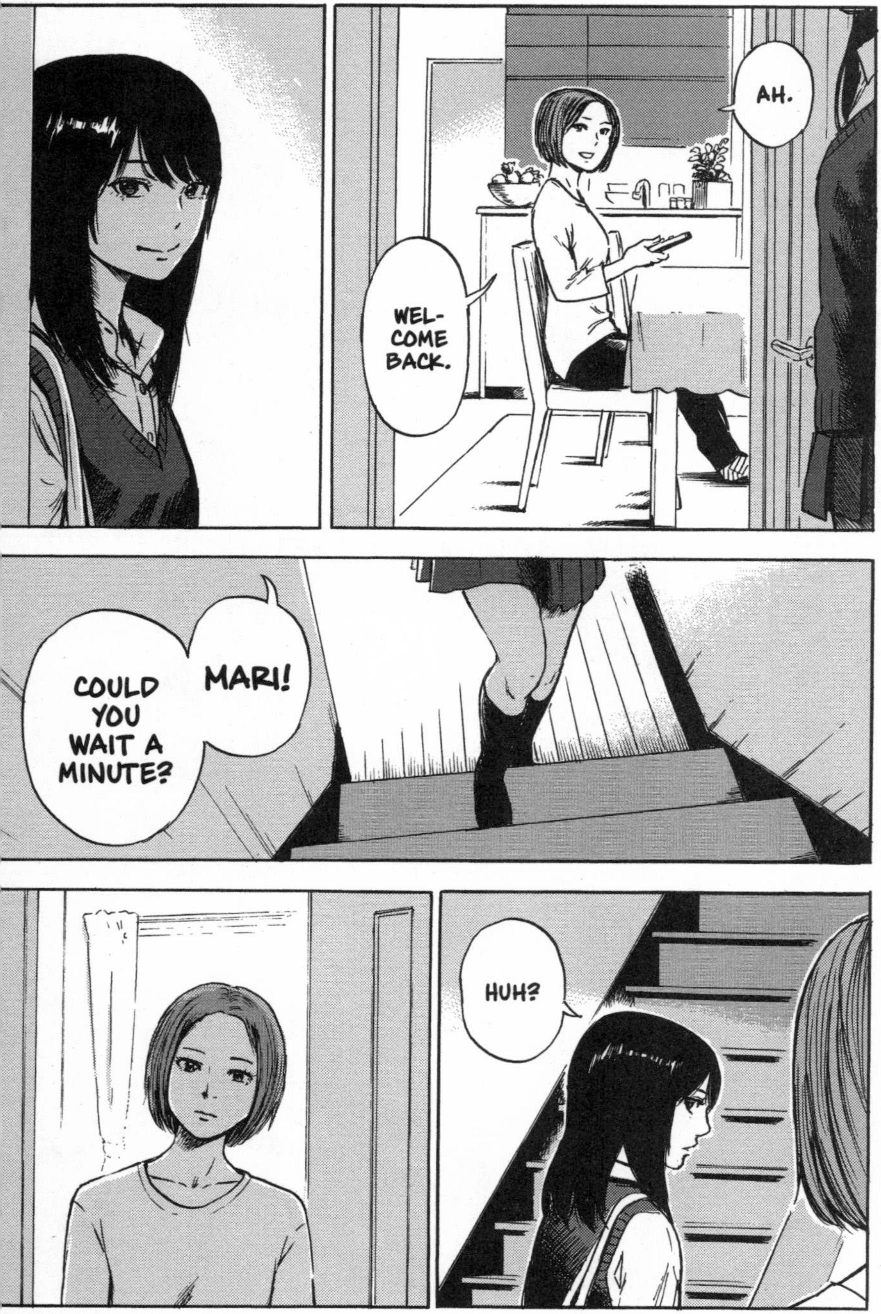
AH.
WEL-COME BACK.
MARI!
COULD YOU WAIT A MINUTE?
HUH?

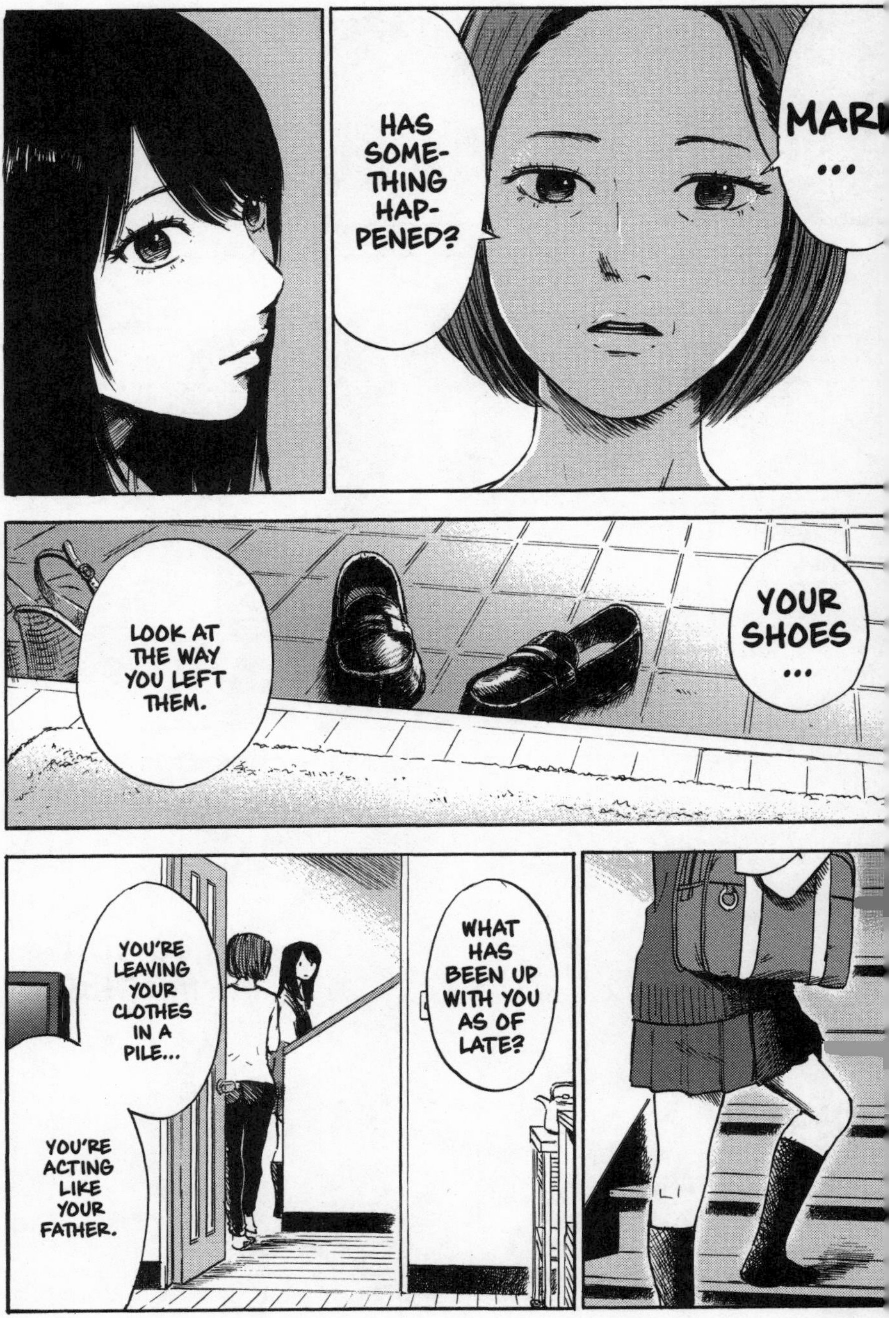
MAR ...
HAS SOME-THING HAP-PENED?
YOUR SHOES ...
LOOK AT THE WAY YOU LEFT THEM.
WHAT HAS BEEN UP WITH YOU AS OF LATE?
YOU'RE LEAVING YOUR CLOTHES IN A PILE...
YOU'RE ACTING LIKE YOUR FATHER.

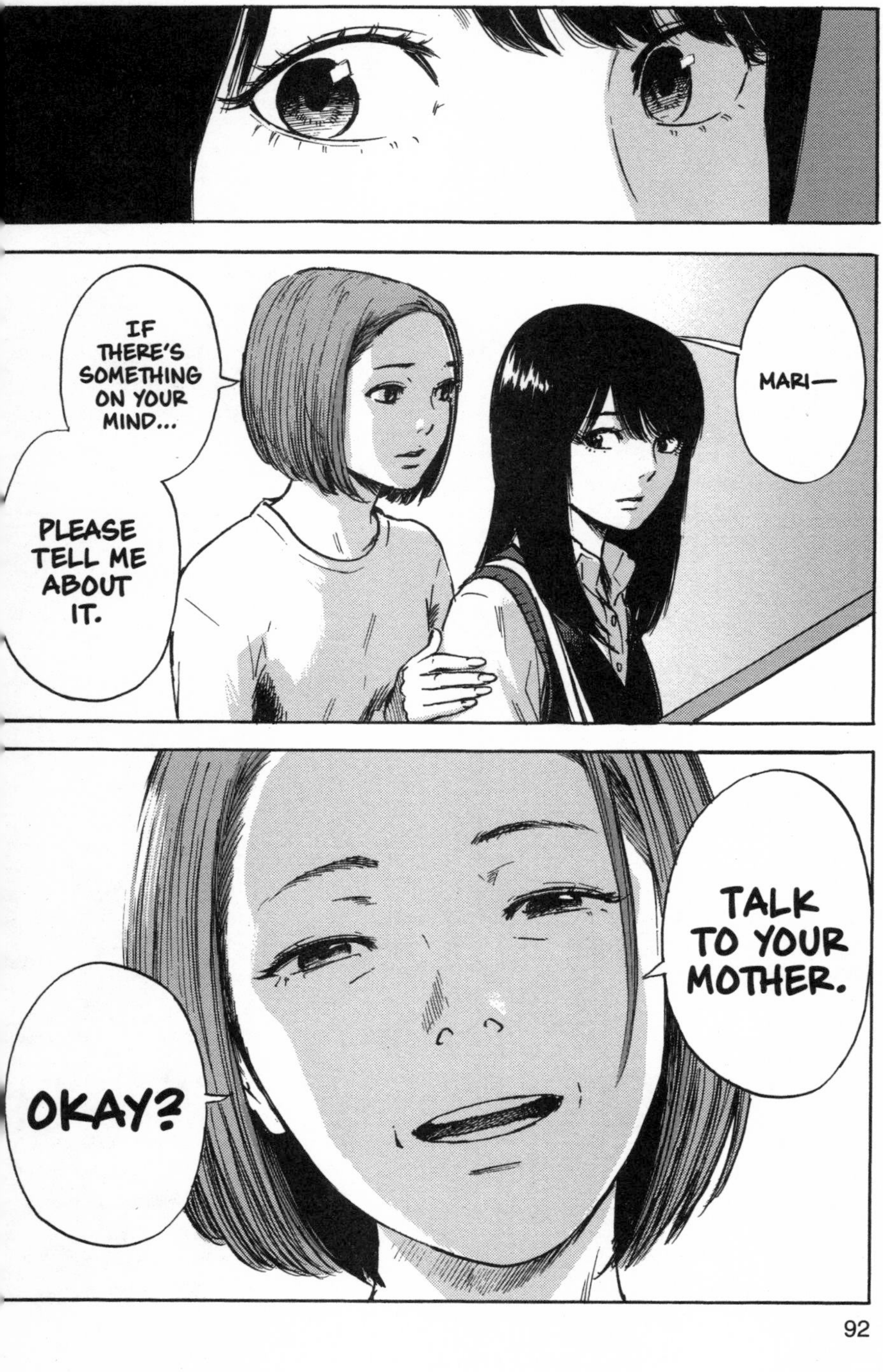
MARI—
IF THERE'S SOMETHING ON YOUR MIND...
PLEASE TELL ME ABOUT IT.
TALK TO YOUR MOTHER.
OKAY?

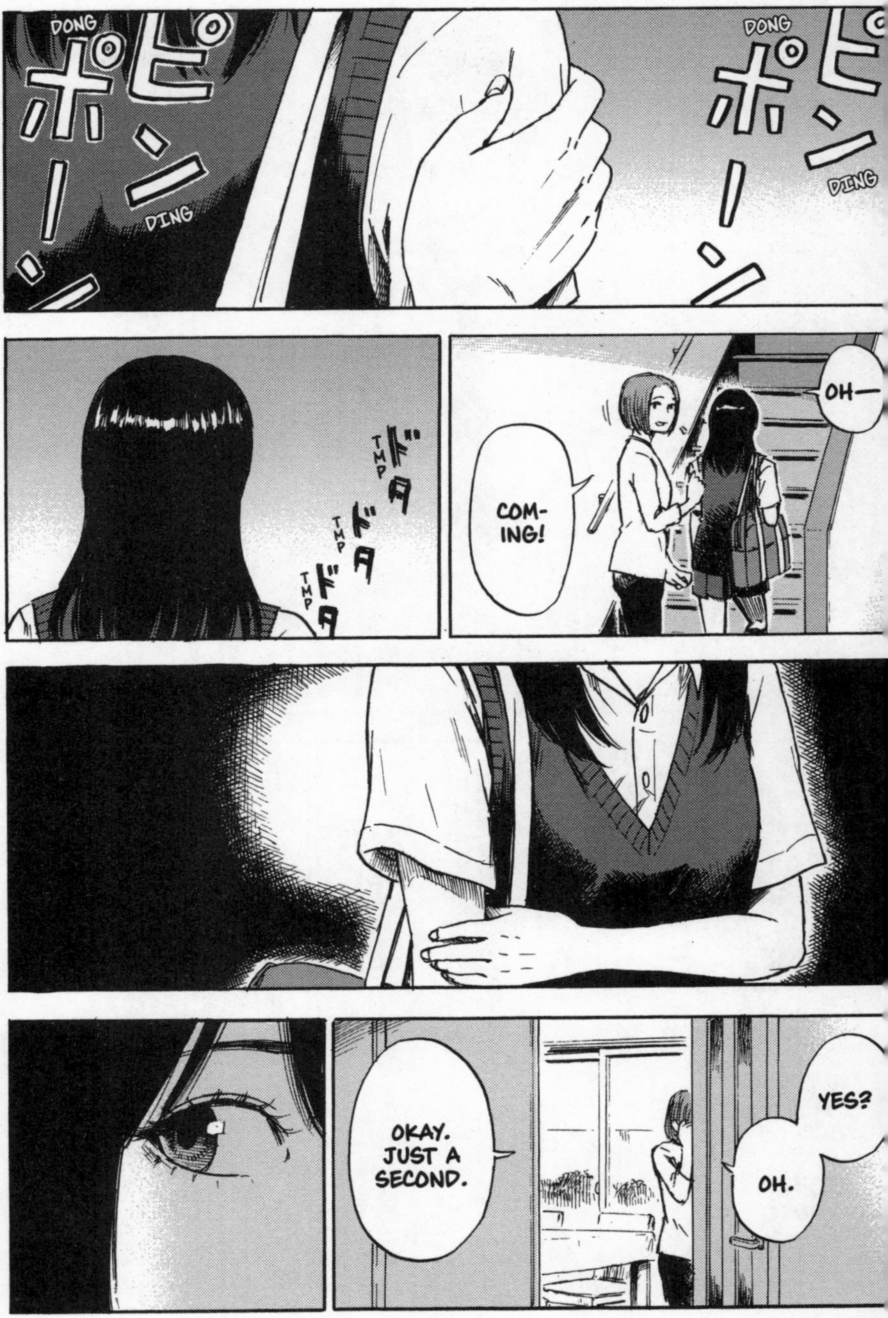
DONG
ピンポーン
DING
DONG
ピンポーン
DING
OH—
COM-ING!
TMP
ドタ
TMP
ドタ
TMP
ドタ
YES?
OH.
OKAY. JUST A SECOND.

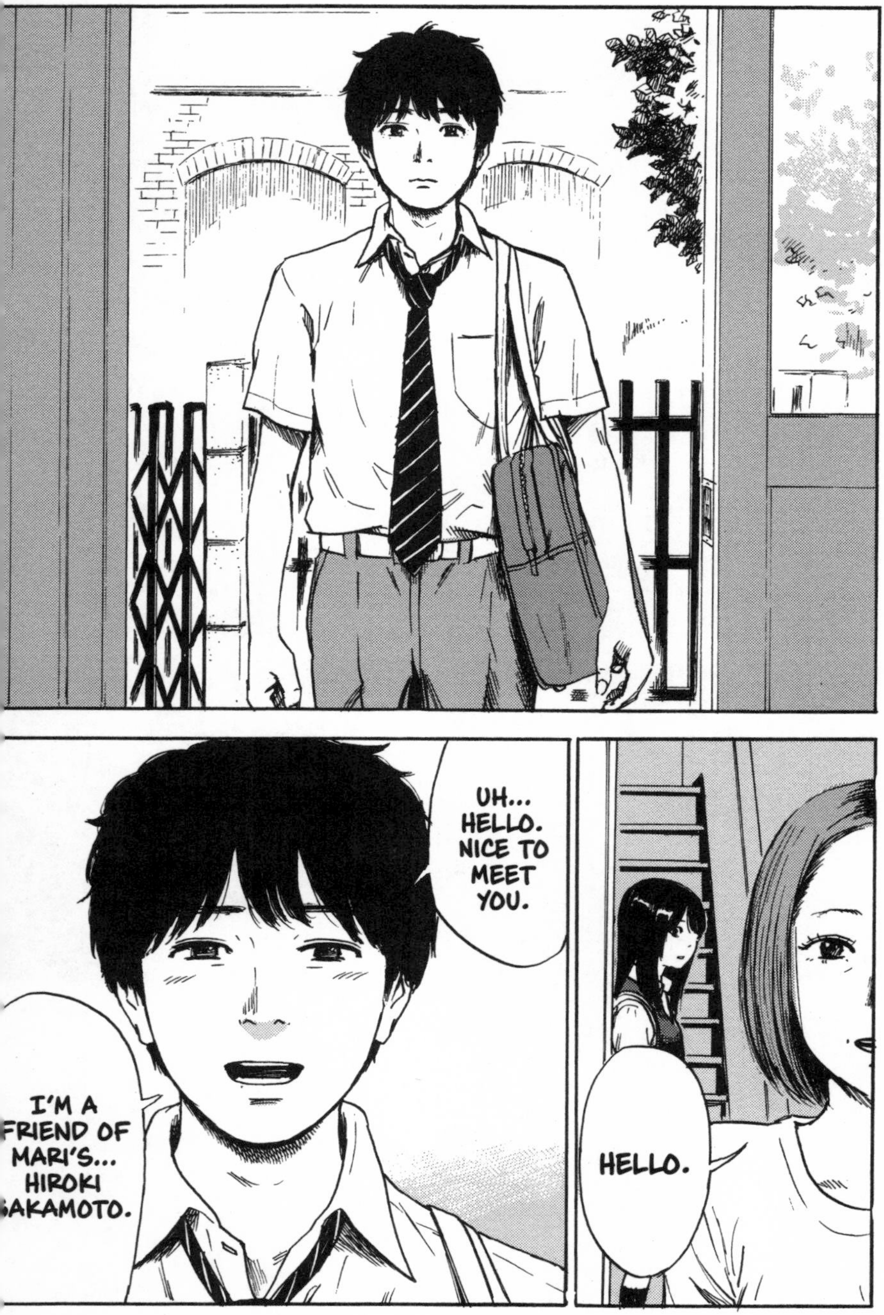
HELLO.
UH... HELLO. NICE TO MEET YOU.
I'M A FRIEND OF MARI'S... HIROKI SAKAMOTO.

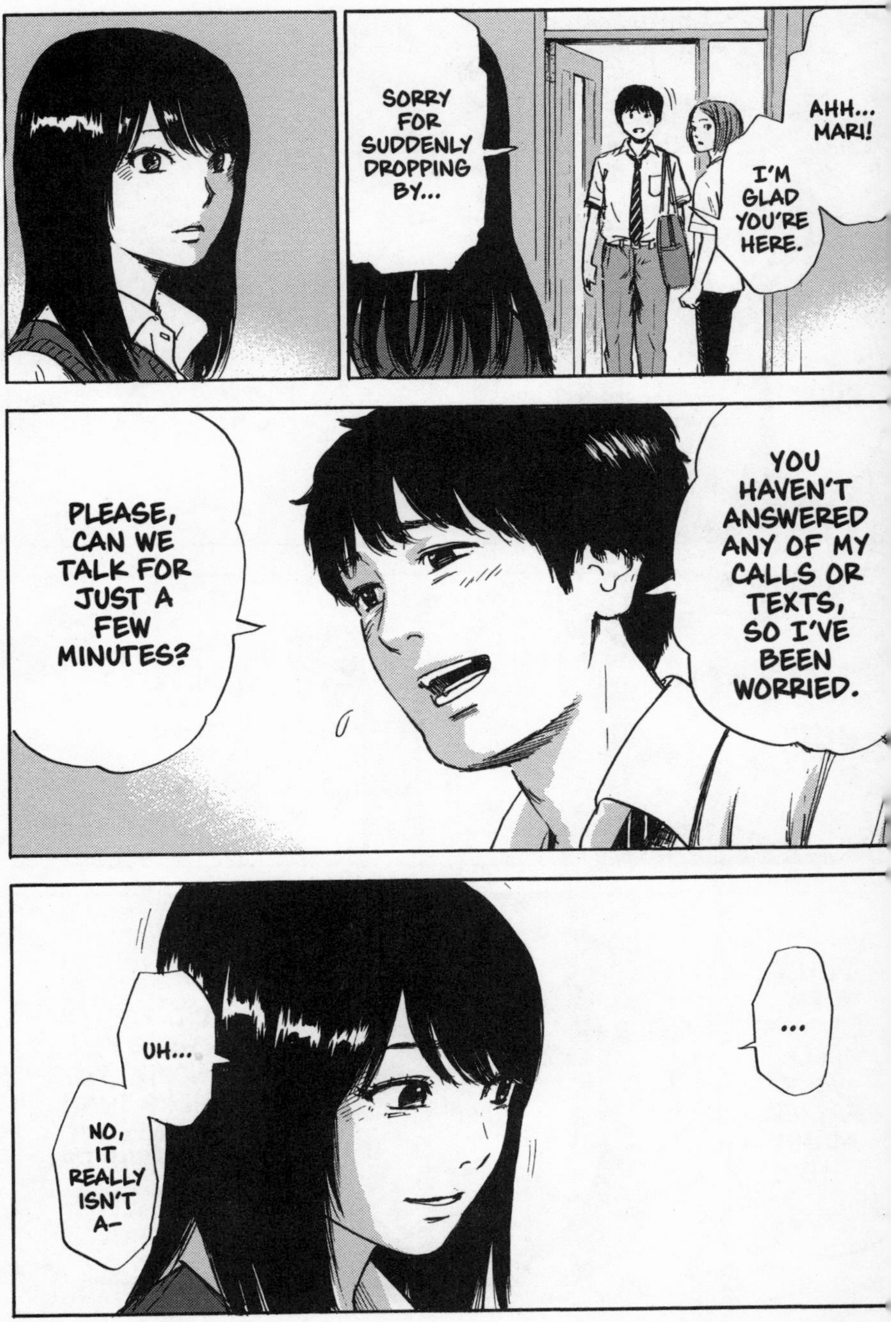
AHH... MARI!
I'M GLAD YOU'RE HERE.
SORRY FOR SUDDENLY DROPPING BY...
YOU HAVEN'T ANSWERED ANY OF MY CALLS OR TEXTS, SO I'VE BEEN WORRIED.
PLEASE, CAN WE TALK FOR JUST A FEW MINUTES?
...
UH...
NO, IT REALLY ISN'T A-

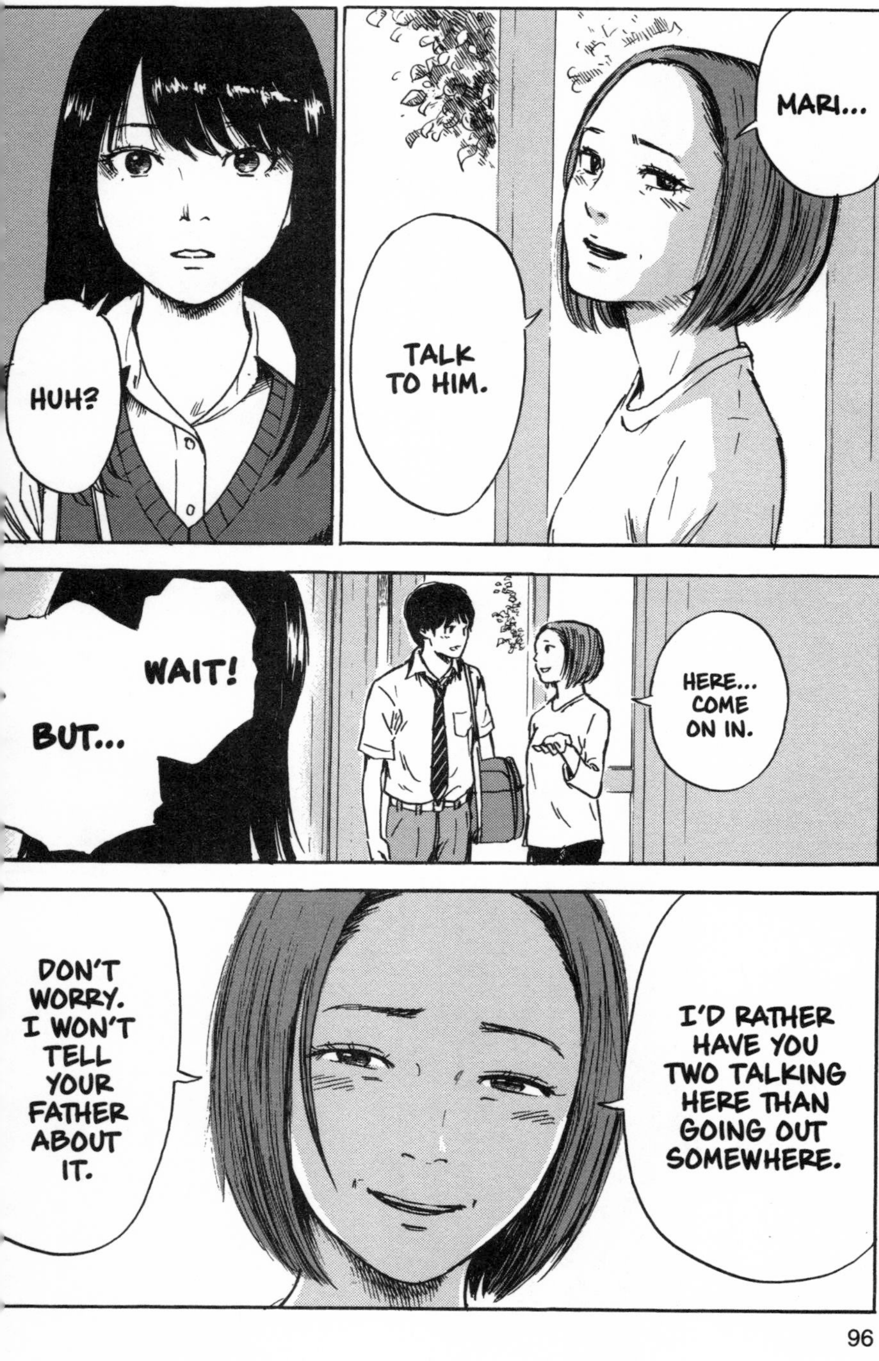
MARI...
TALK TO HIM.
HUH?
HERE... COME ON IN.
WAIT!
BUT...
I'D RATHER HAVE YOU TWO TALKING HERE THAN GOING OUT SOMEWHERE.
DON'T WORRY. I WON'T TELL YOUR FATHER ABOUT IT.

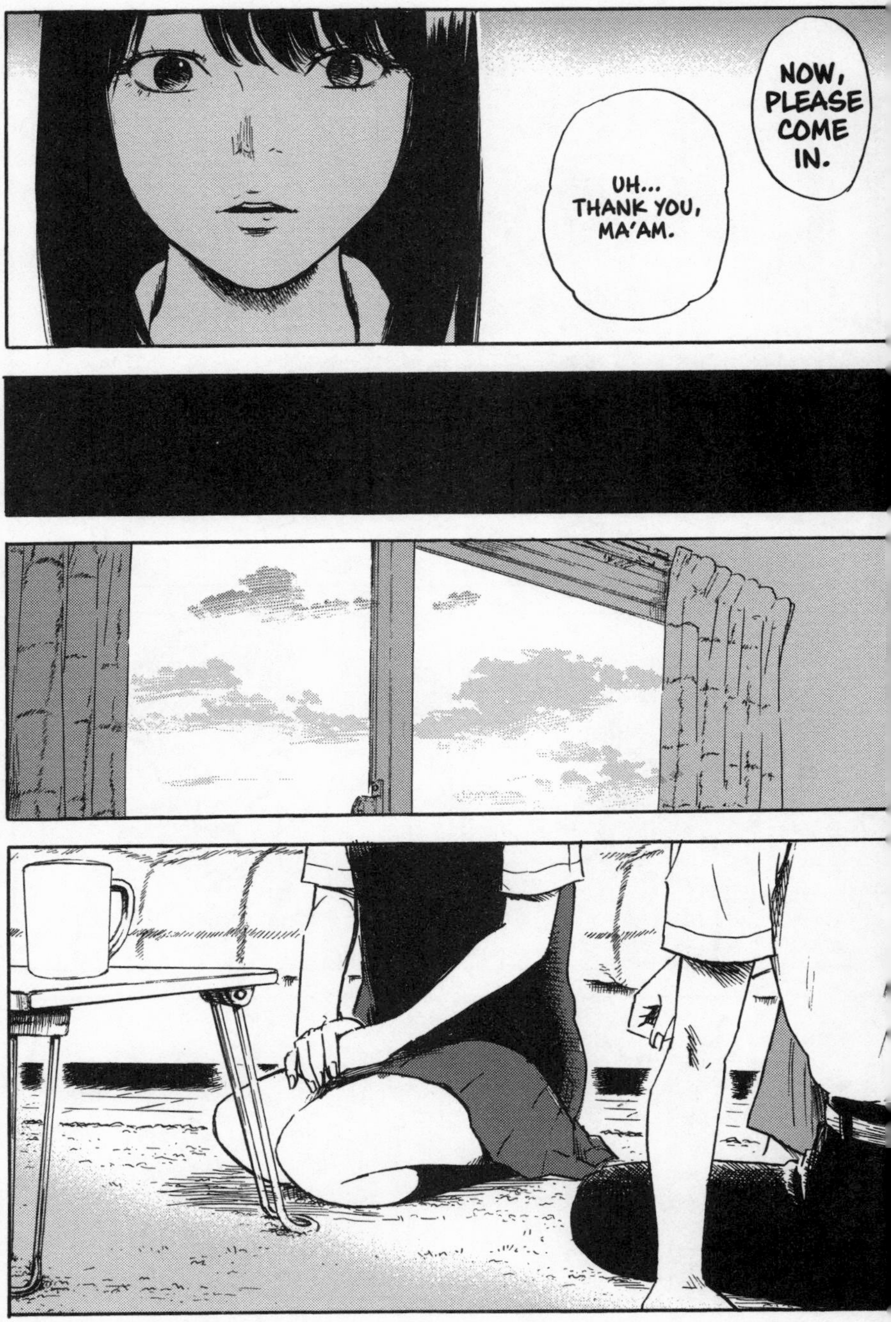
NOW, PLEASE COME IN.
UH... THANK YOU, MA'AM.

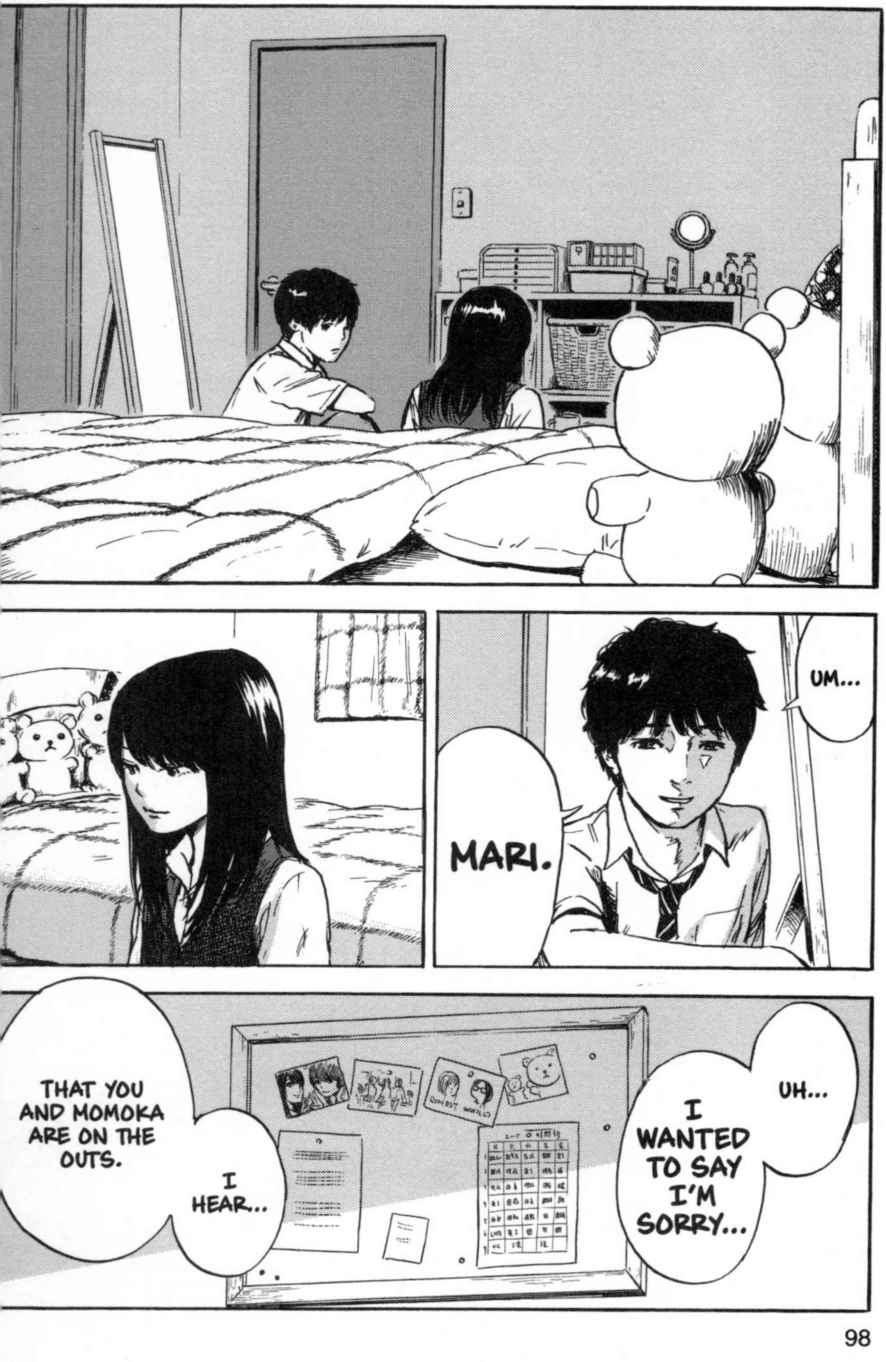
UM...
MARI.
UH...
I WANTED TO SAY I'M SORRY...
I HEAR...
THAT YOU AND MOMOKA ARE ON THE OUTS.

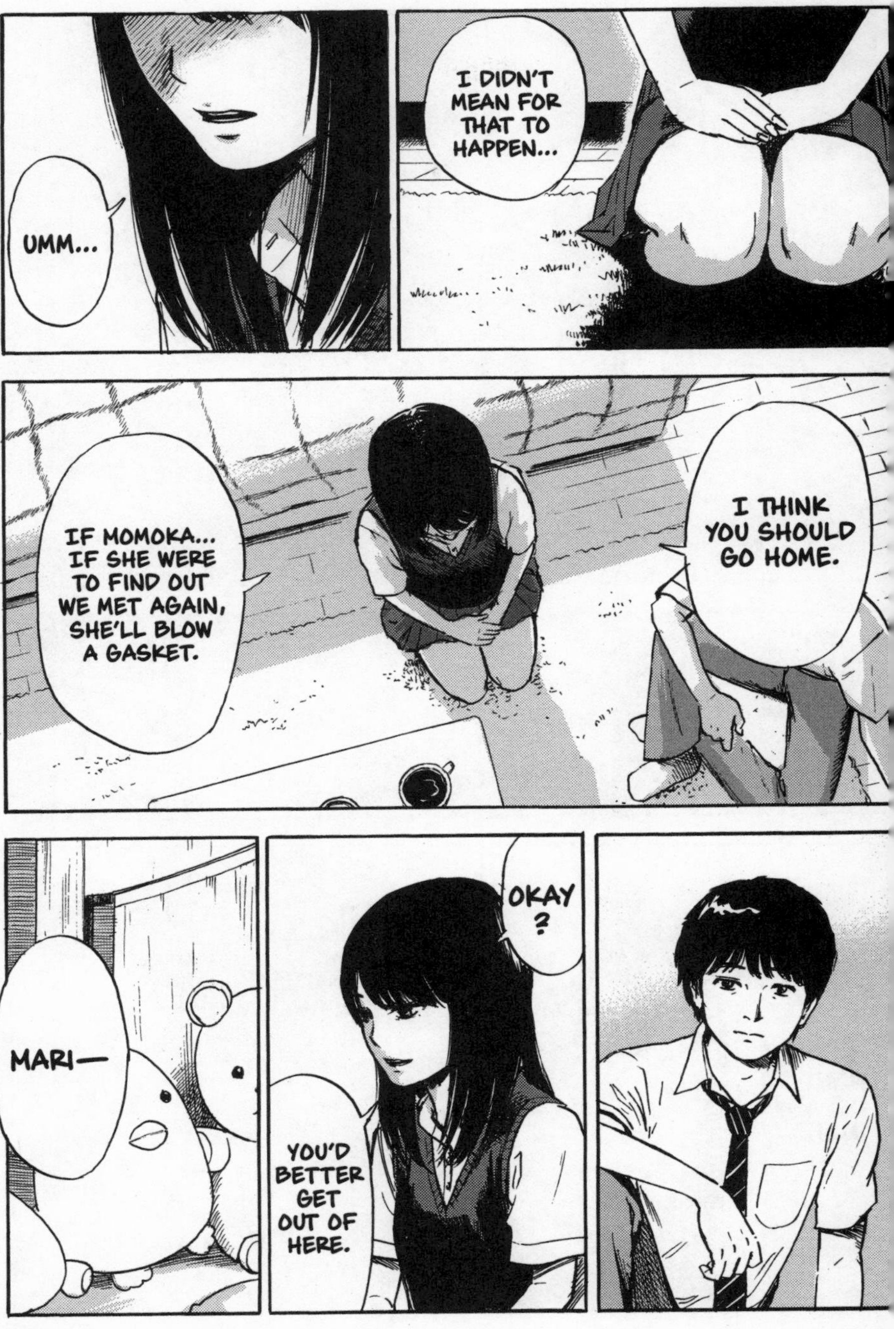

I DIDN'T MEAN FOR THAT TO HAPPEN...
UMM...
I THINK YOU SHOULD GO HOME.
IF MOMOKA... IF SHE WERE TO FIND OUT WE MET AGAIN, SHE'LL BLOW A GASKET.
OKAY?
YOU'D BETTER GET OUT OF HERE.
MARI—

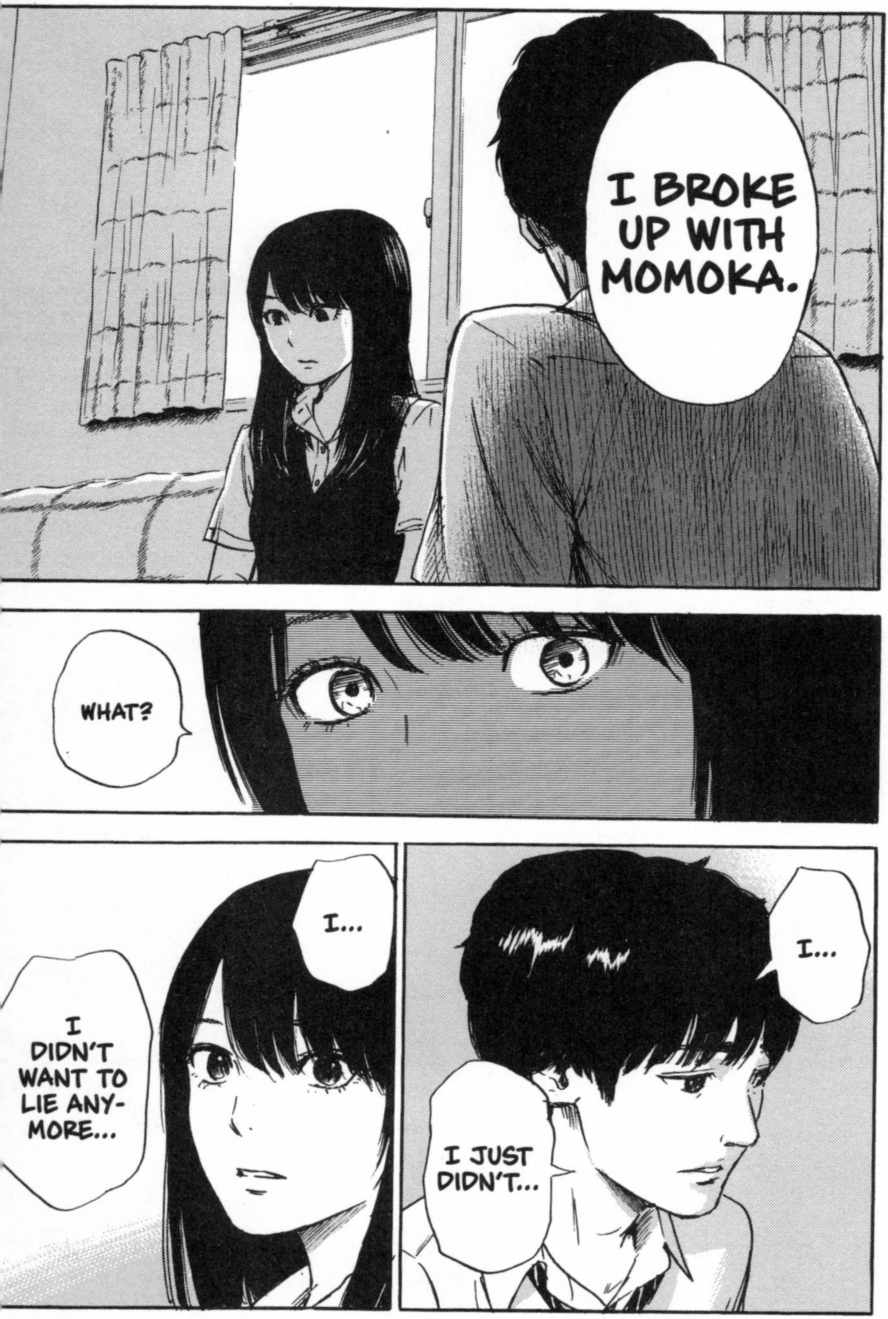
I BROKE UP WITH MOMOKA.
WHAT?
I...
I JUST DIDN'T...
I...
I DIDN'T WANT TO LIE ANY-MORE...

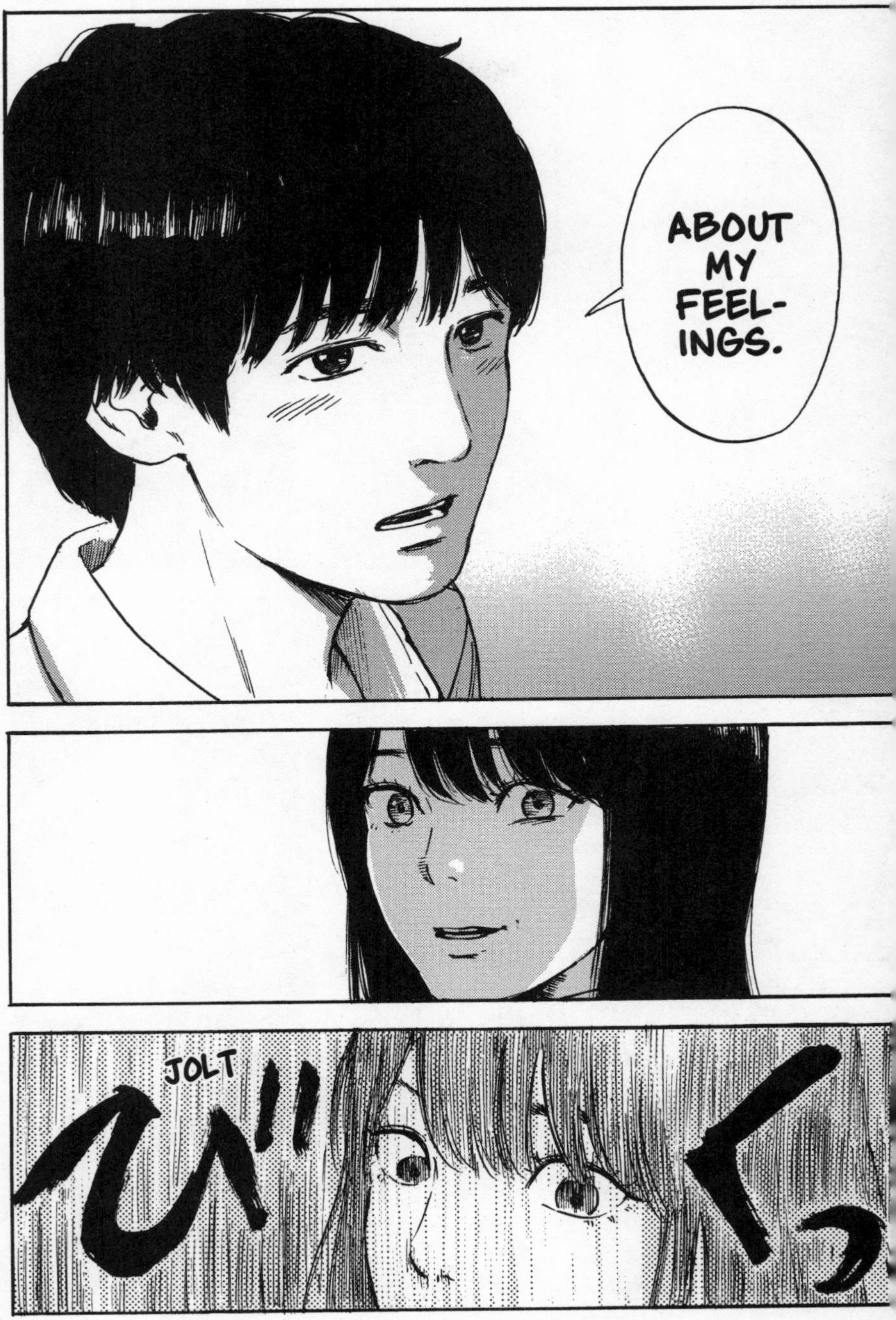
ABOUT MY FEEL- INGS.
JOLT
びくっ

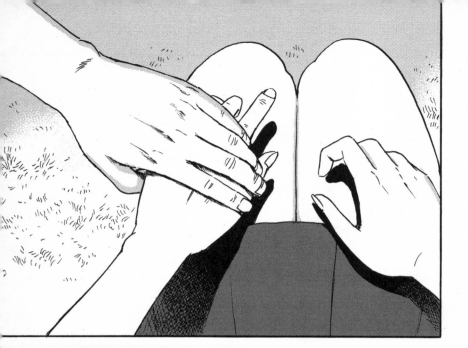

MARI...

SHUDDR

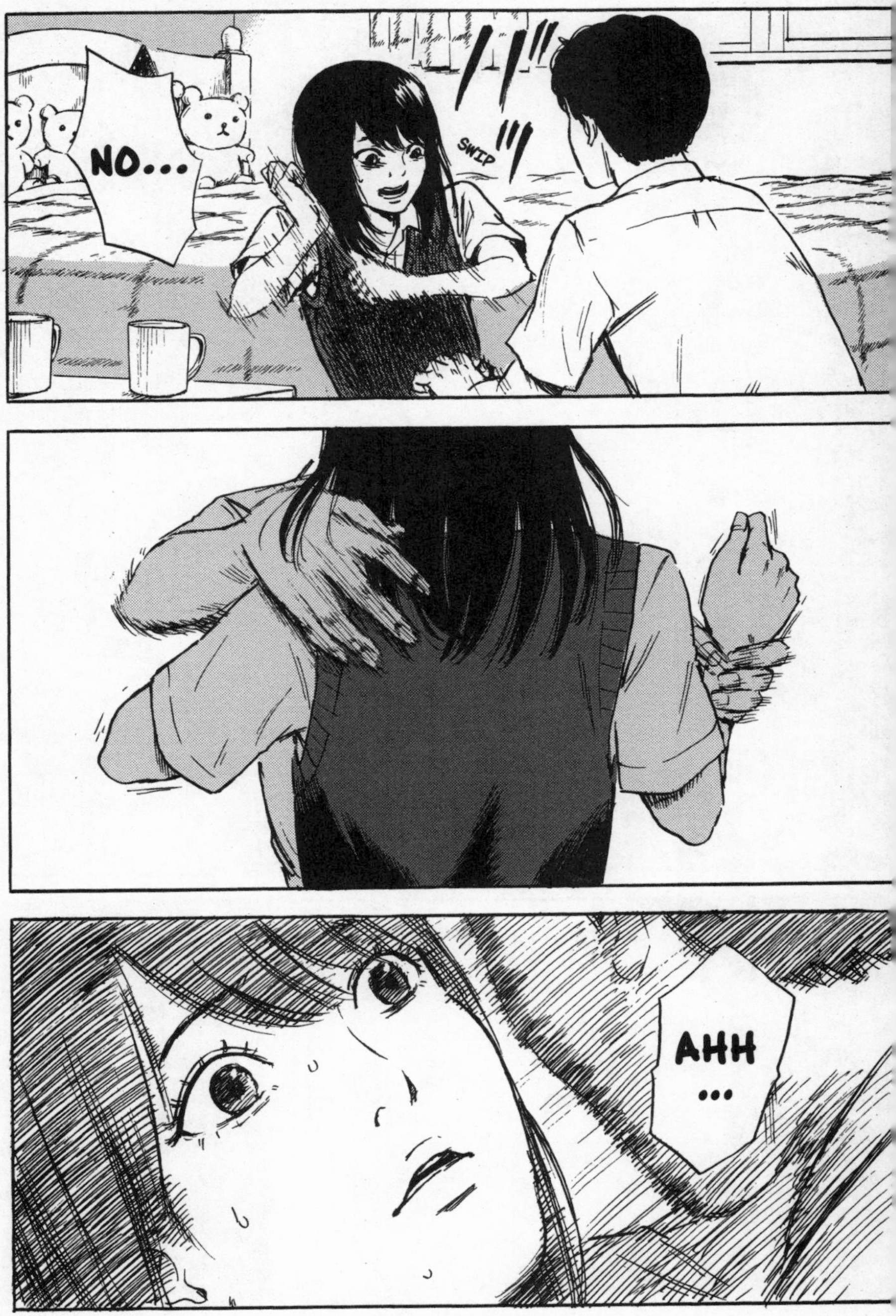
SWIP
NO...
AHH ...

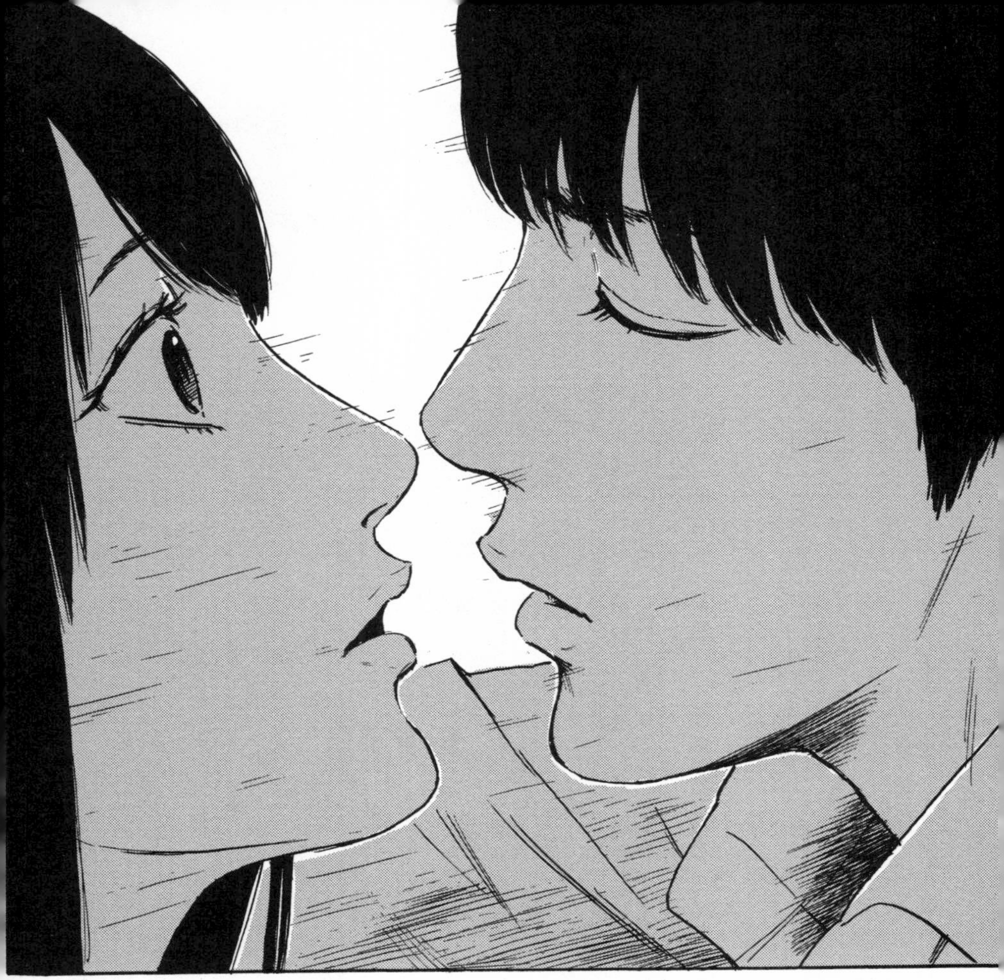

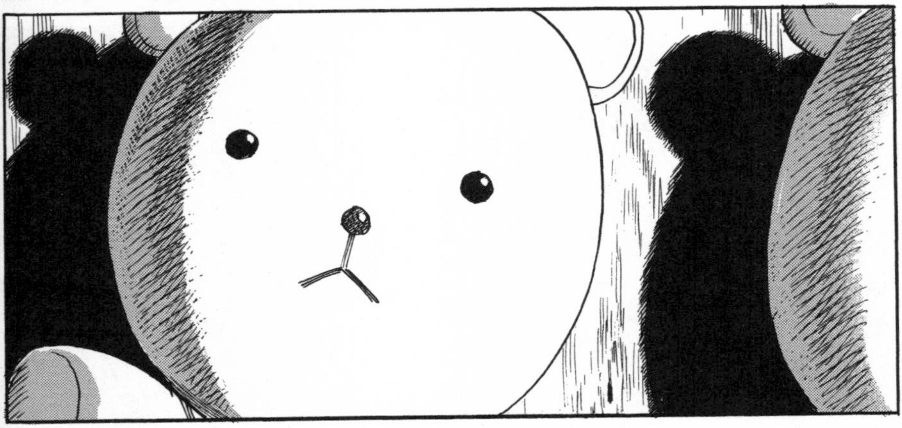

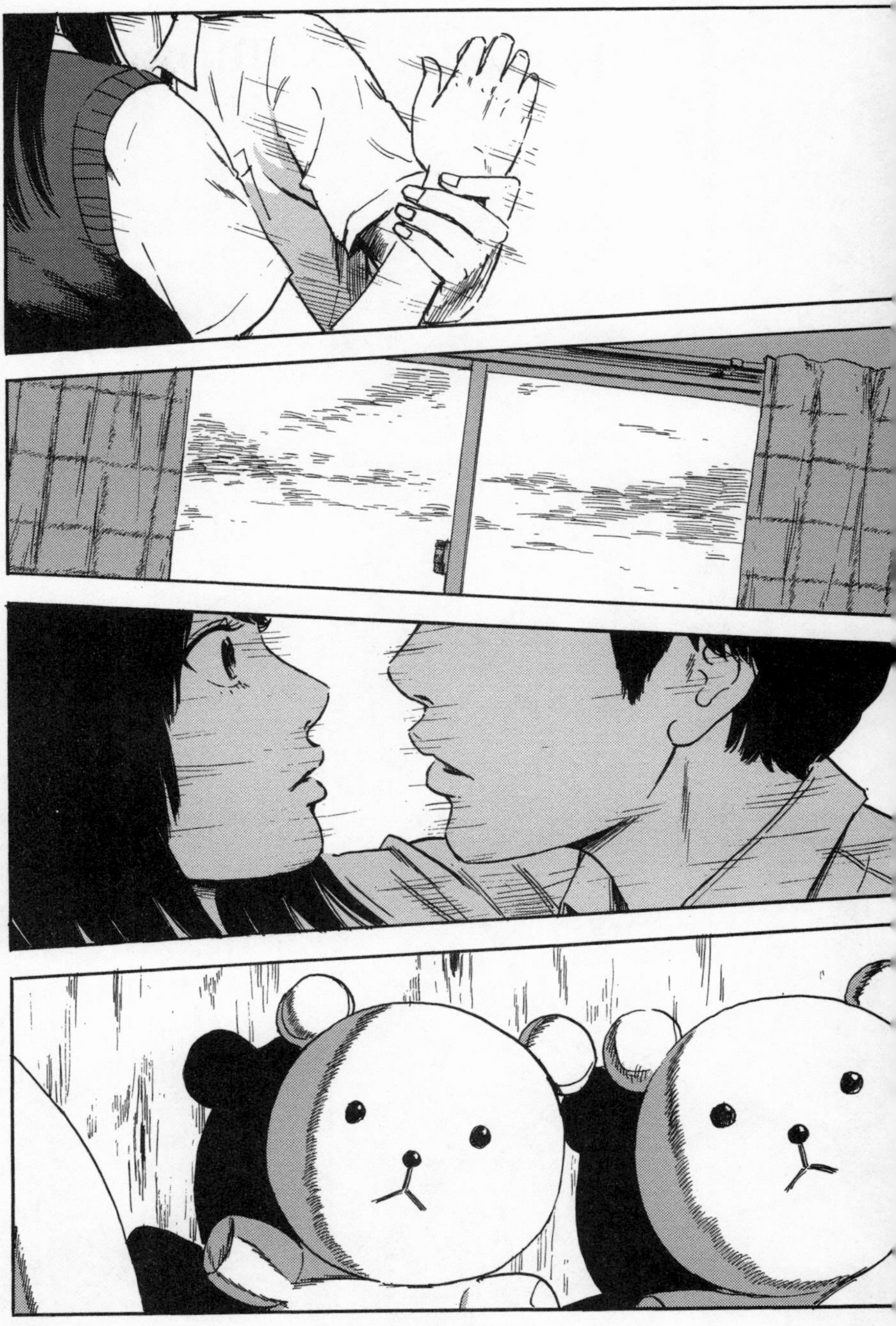

Chapter 23: Coming Out

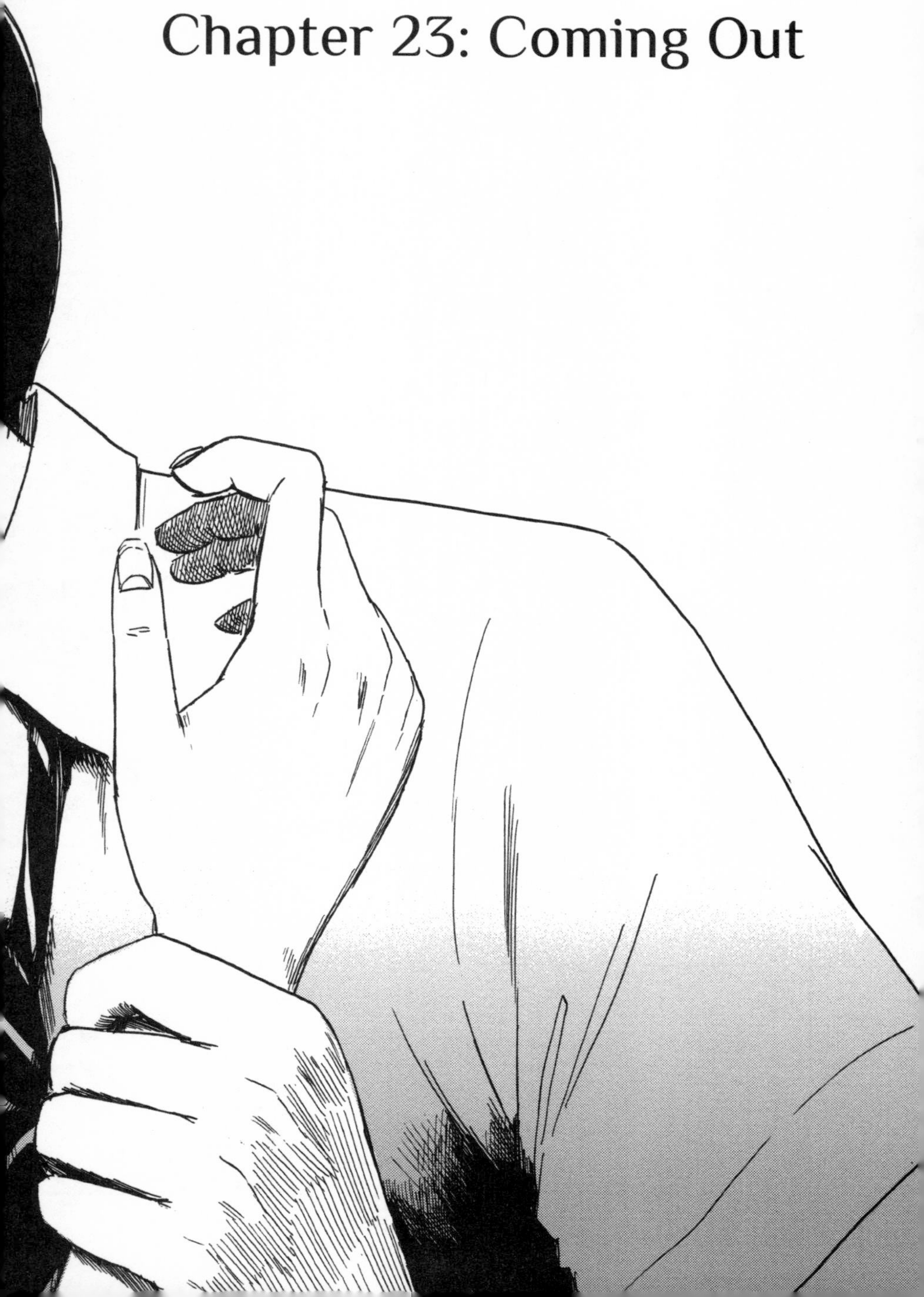

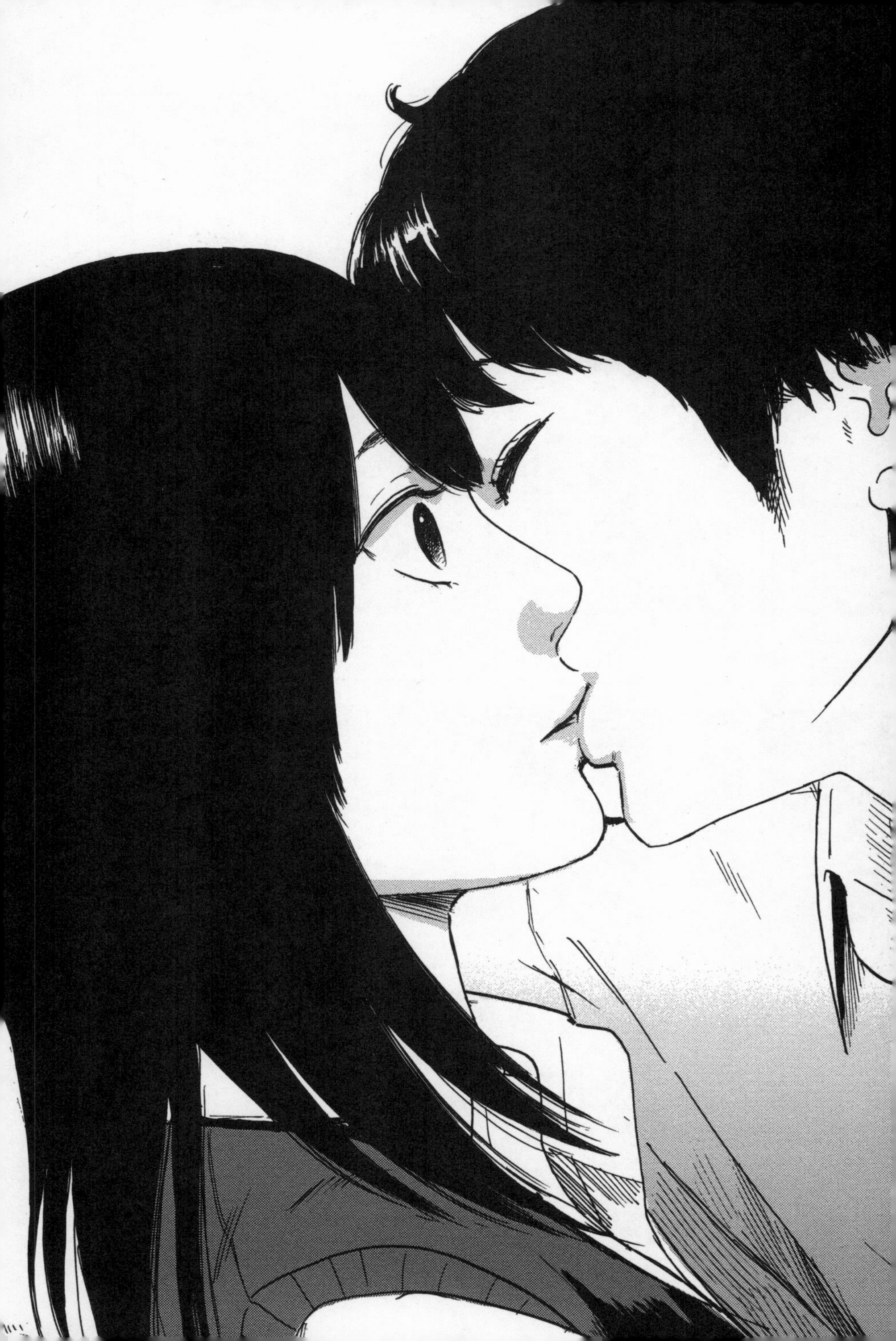

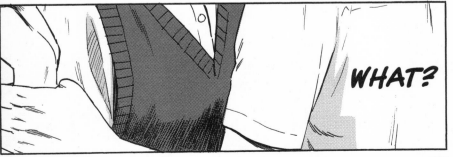

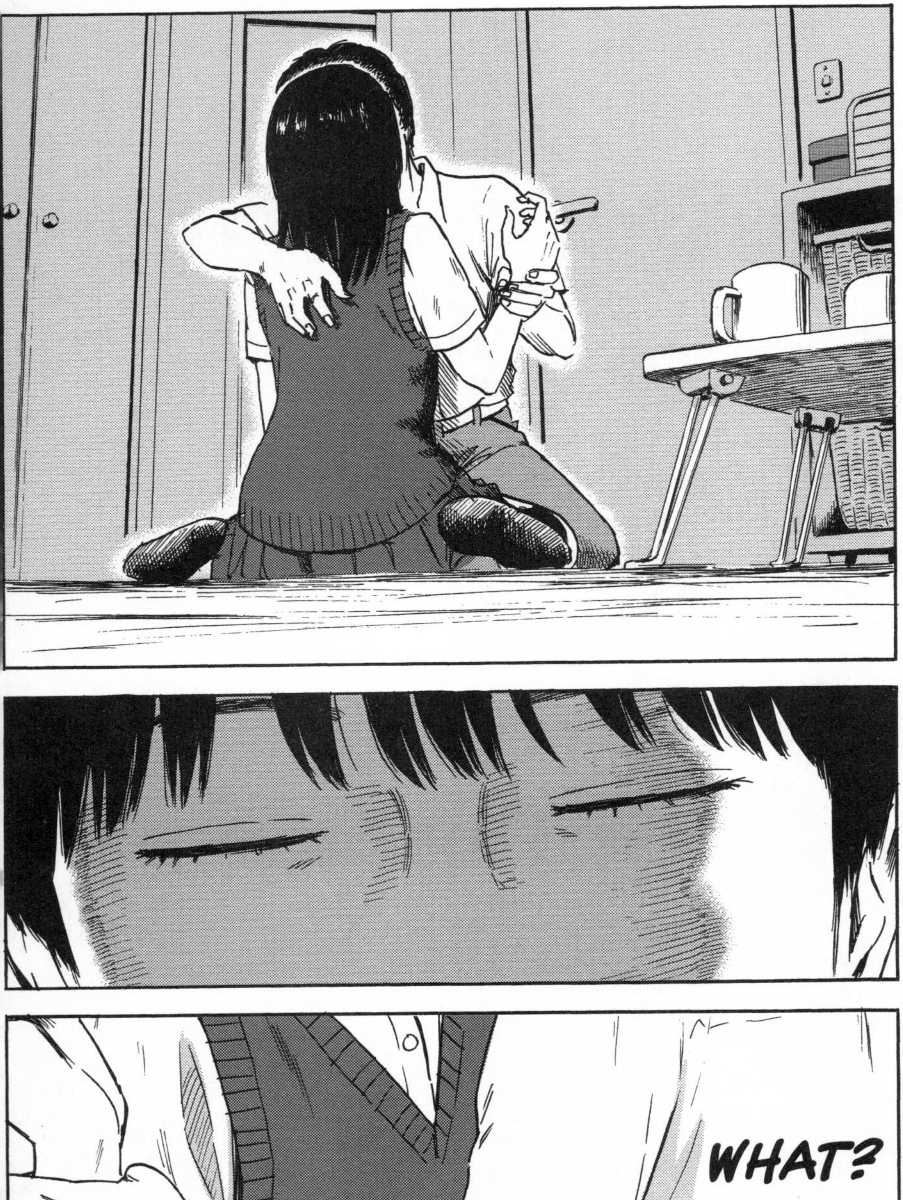
WHAT?

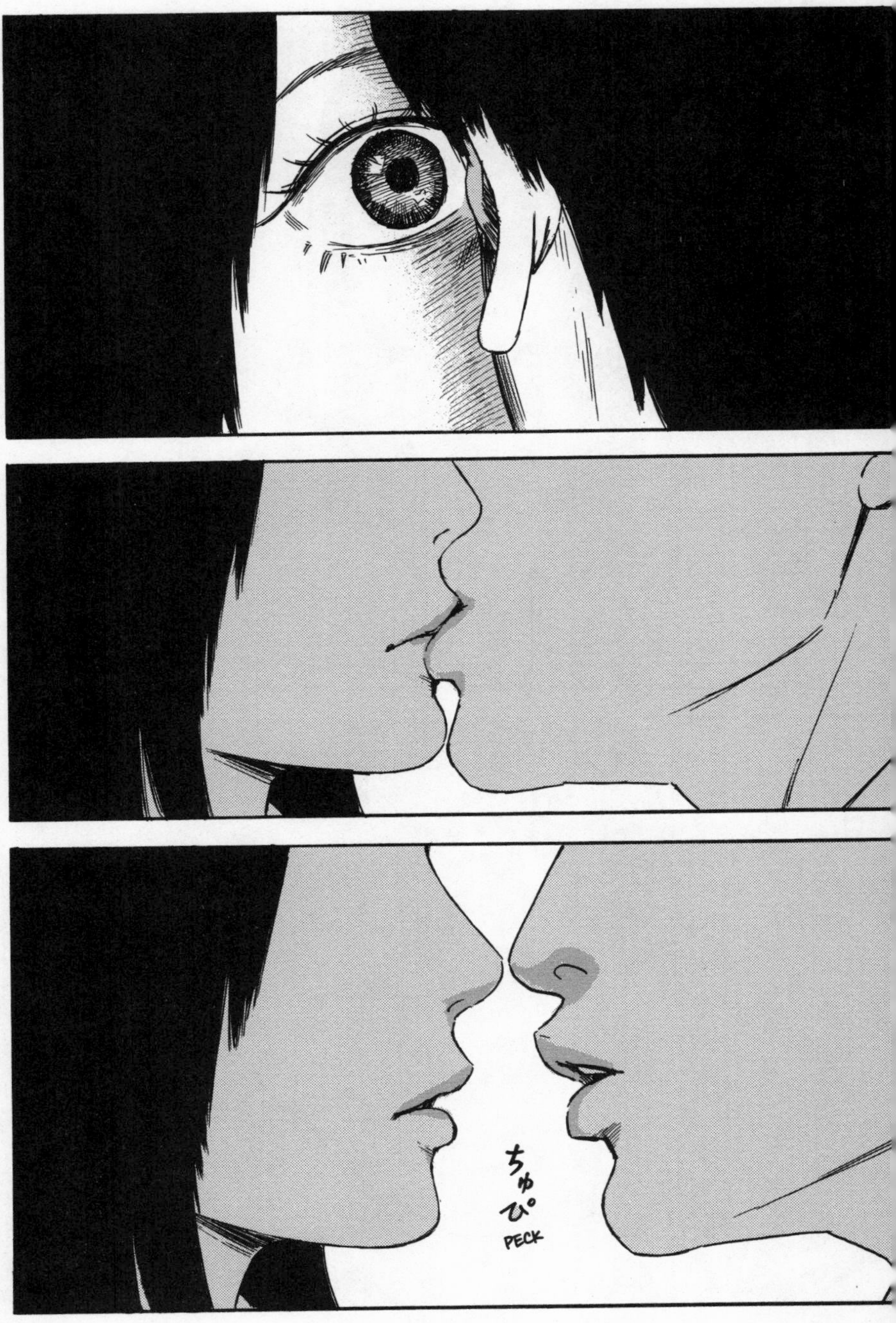
ちゅぴ
PECK

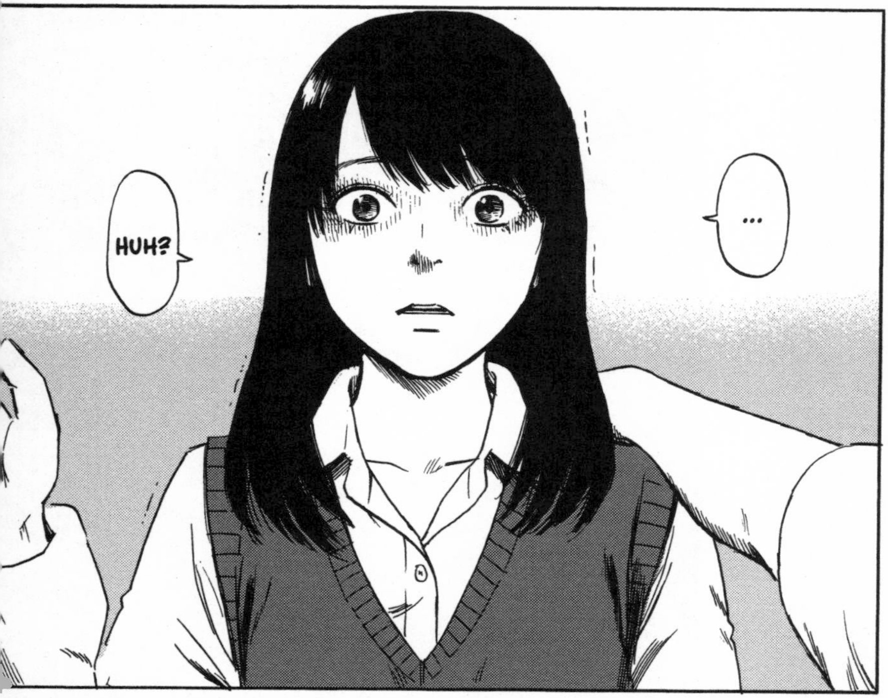
...
HUH?
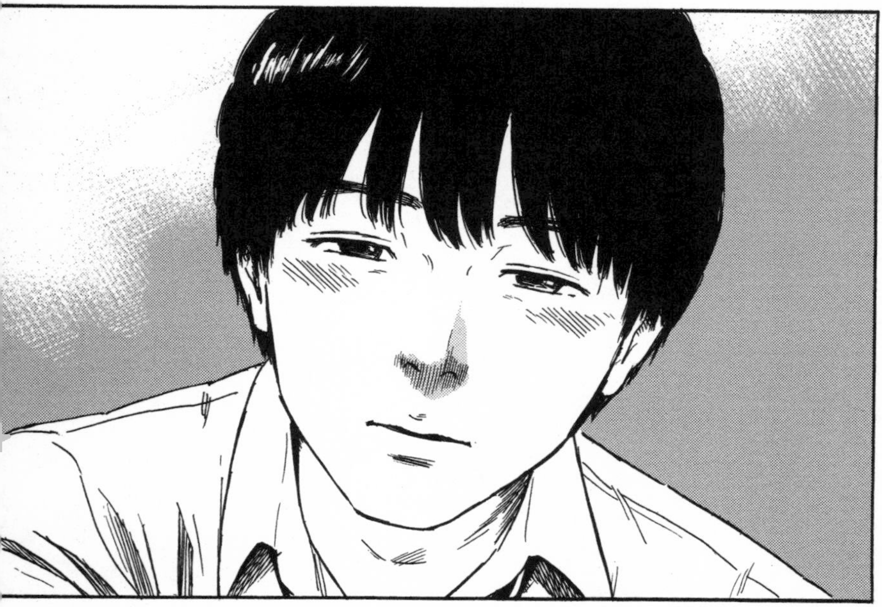

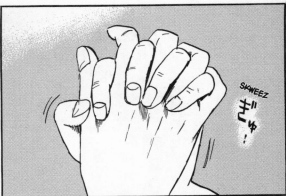

SKWEEZ

THAT...

FELT
GREAT
TO ME.

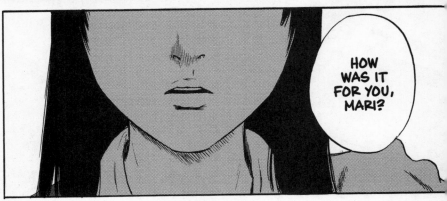

HOW
WAS IT
FOR YOU,
MARI?

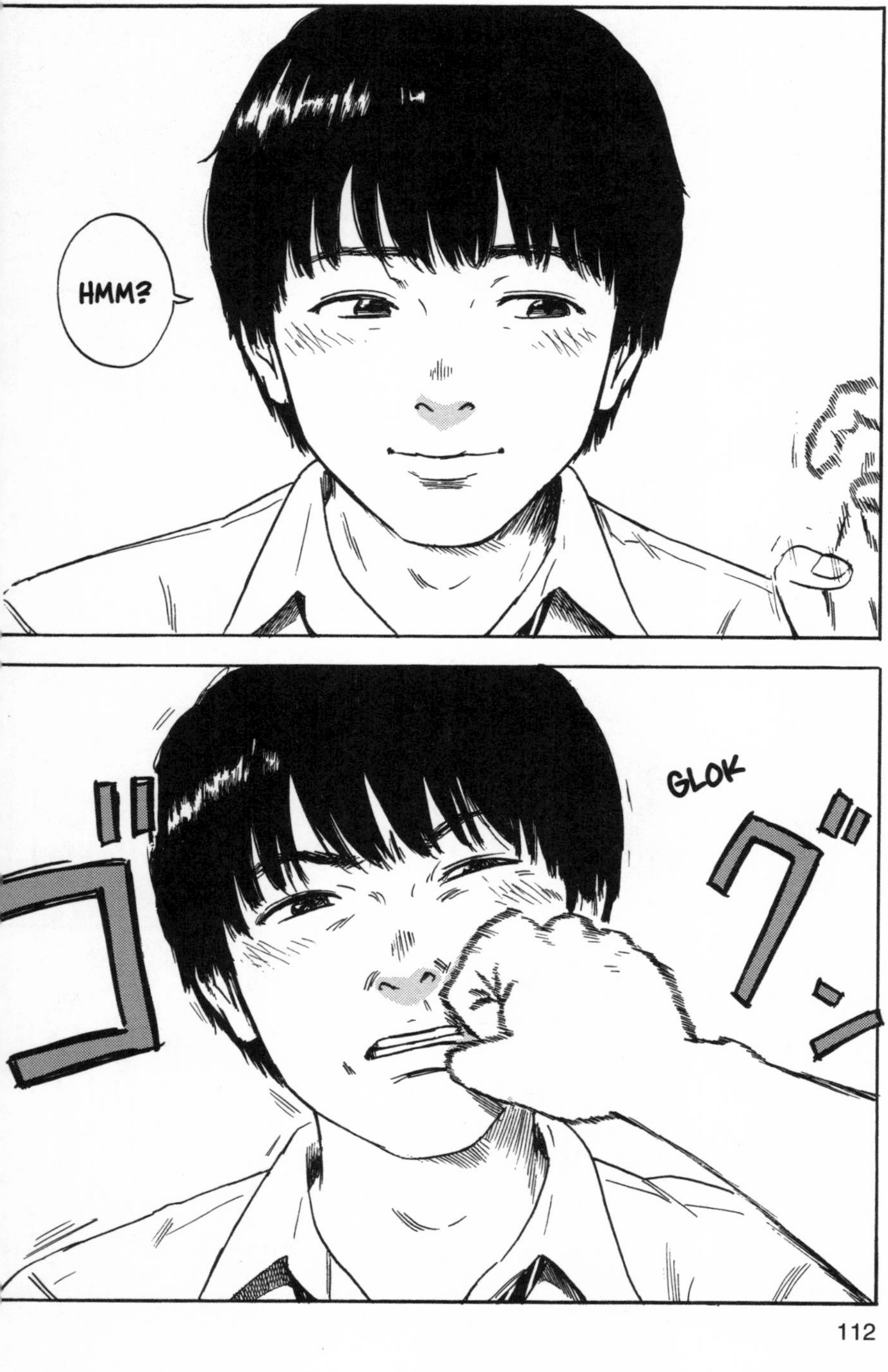
HMM?
GLOK

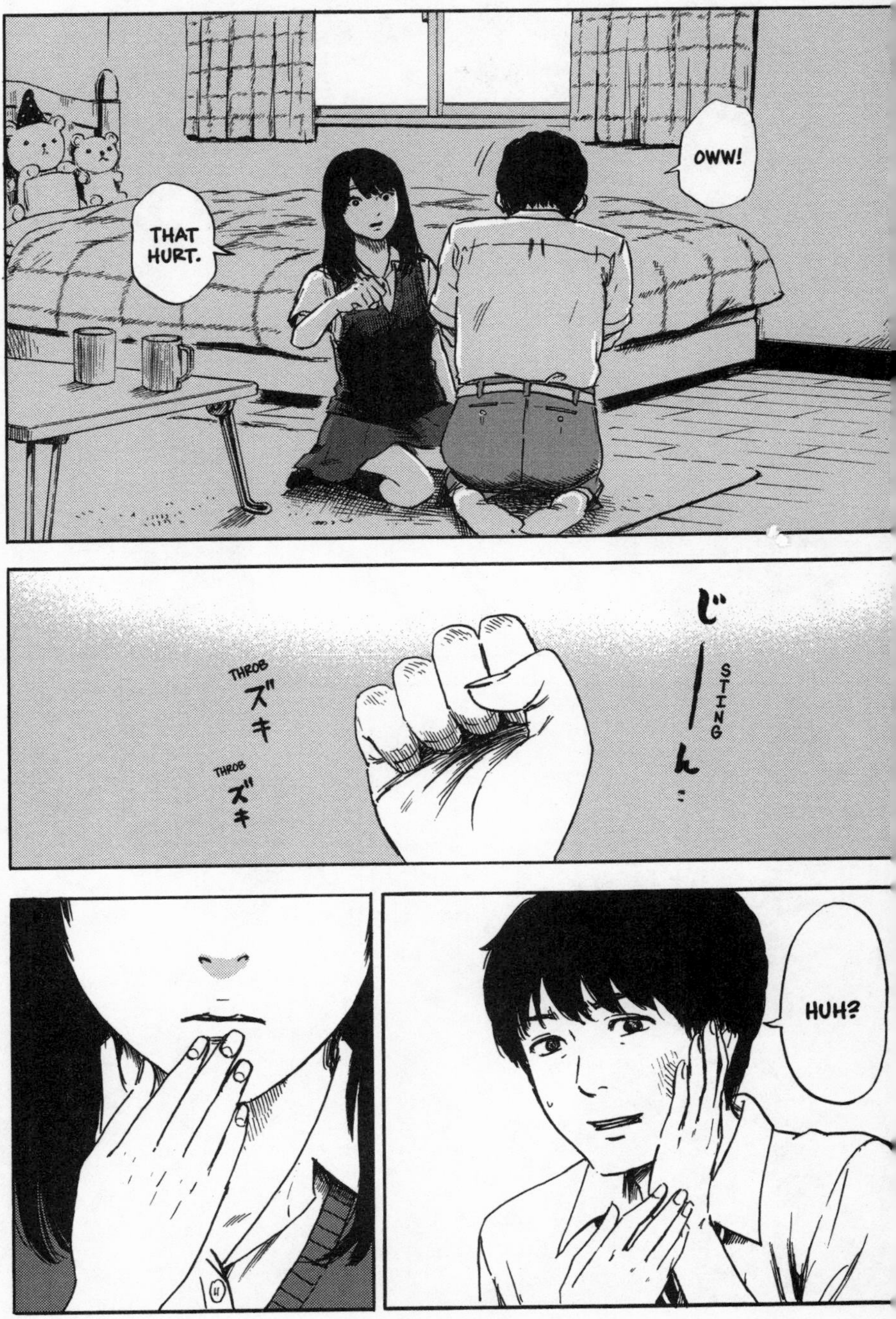
OWW!
THAT HURT.
じーん
STING
THROB
ズキ
THROB
ズキ
HUH?

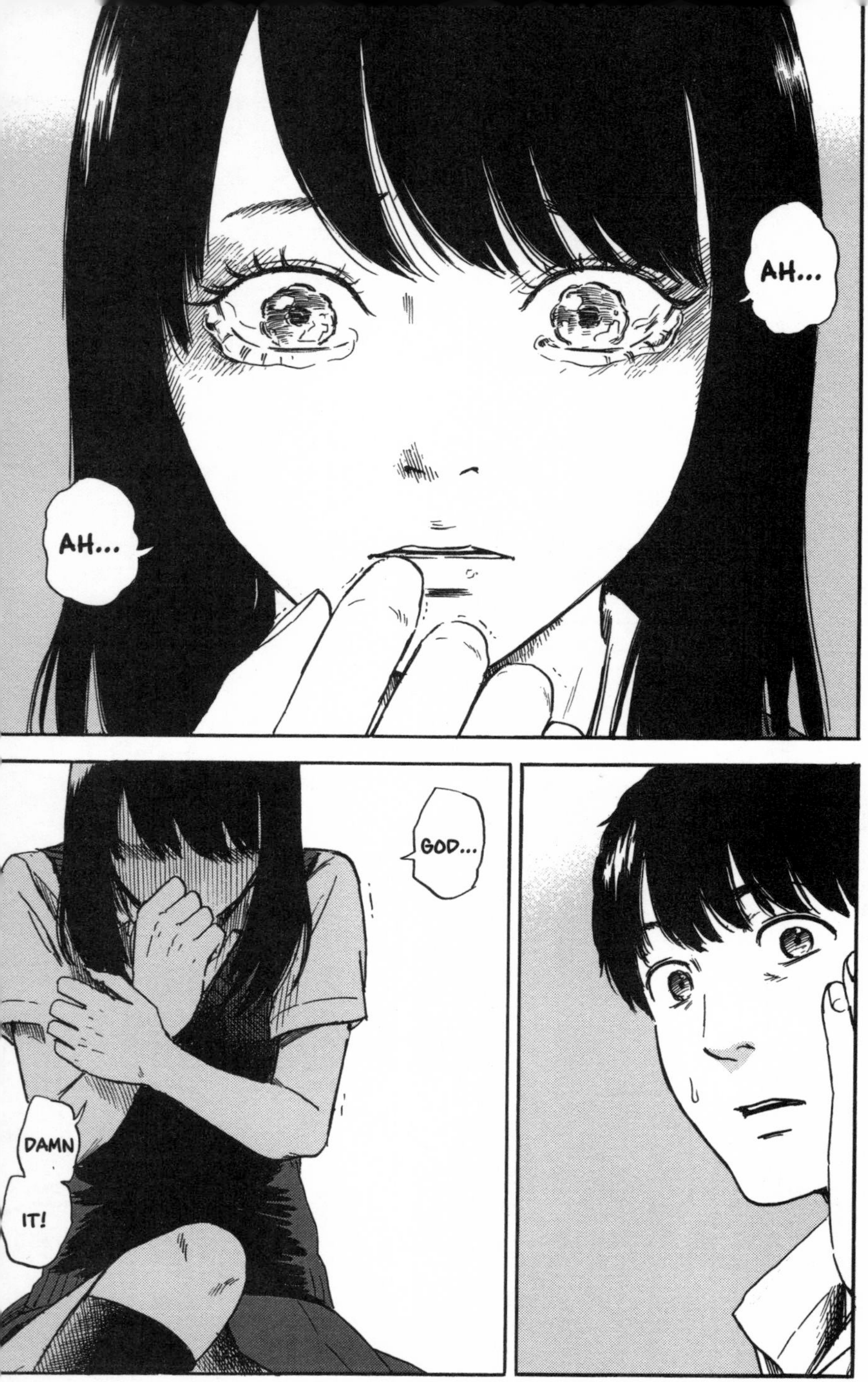
AH...
AH...
GOD...
DAMN IT!

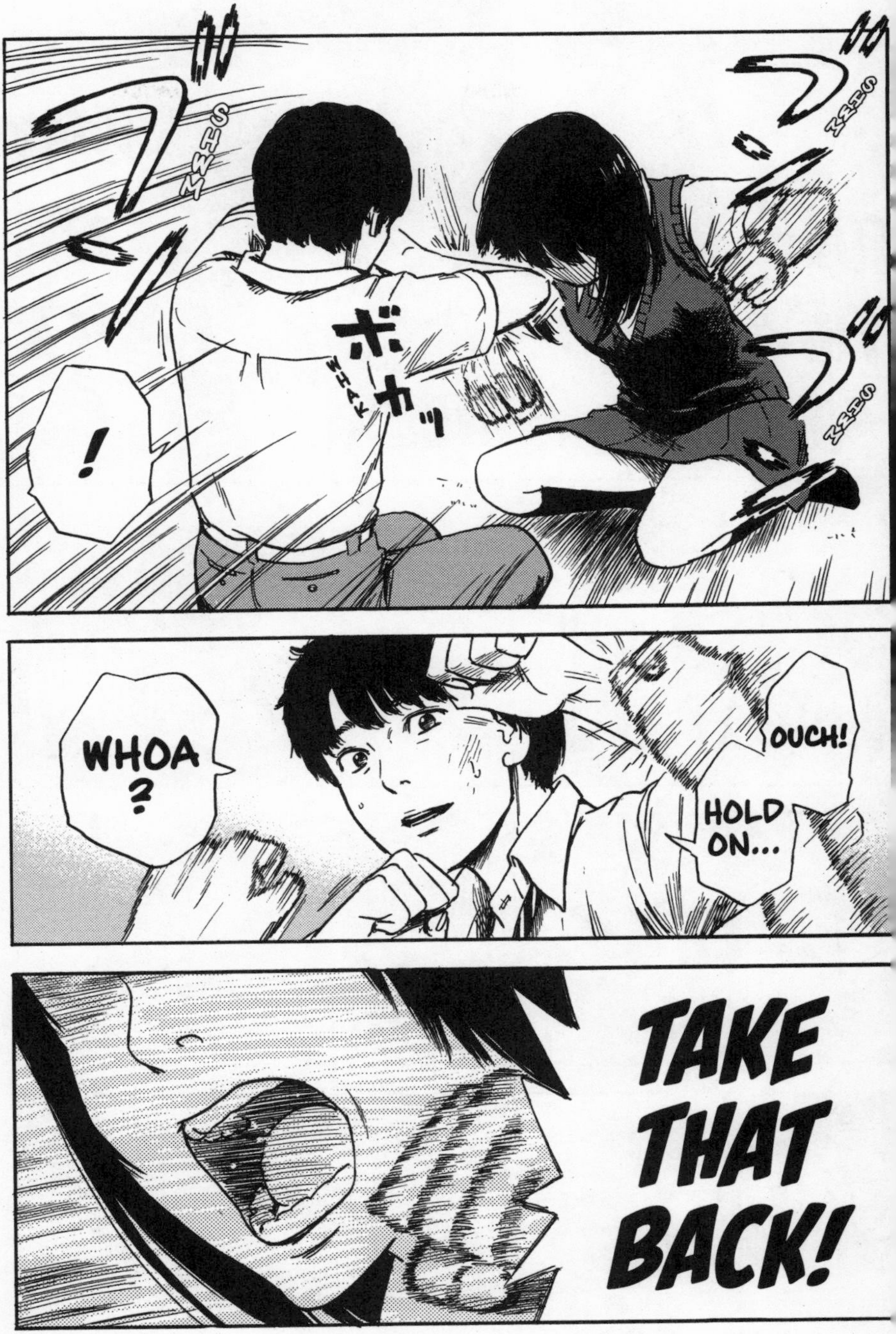
SHWM
ボカッ
WHAK
!
OUCH!
HOLD ON...
WHOA?
TAKE THAT BACK!

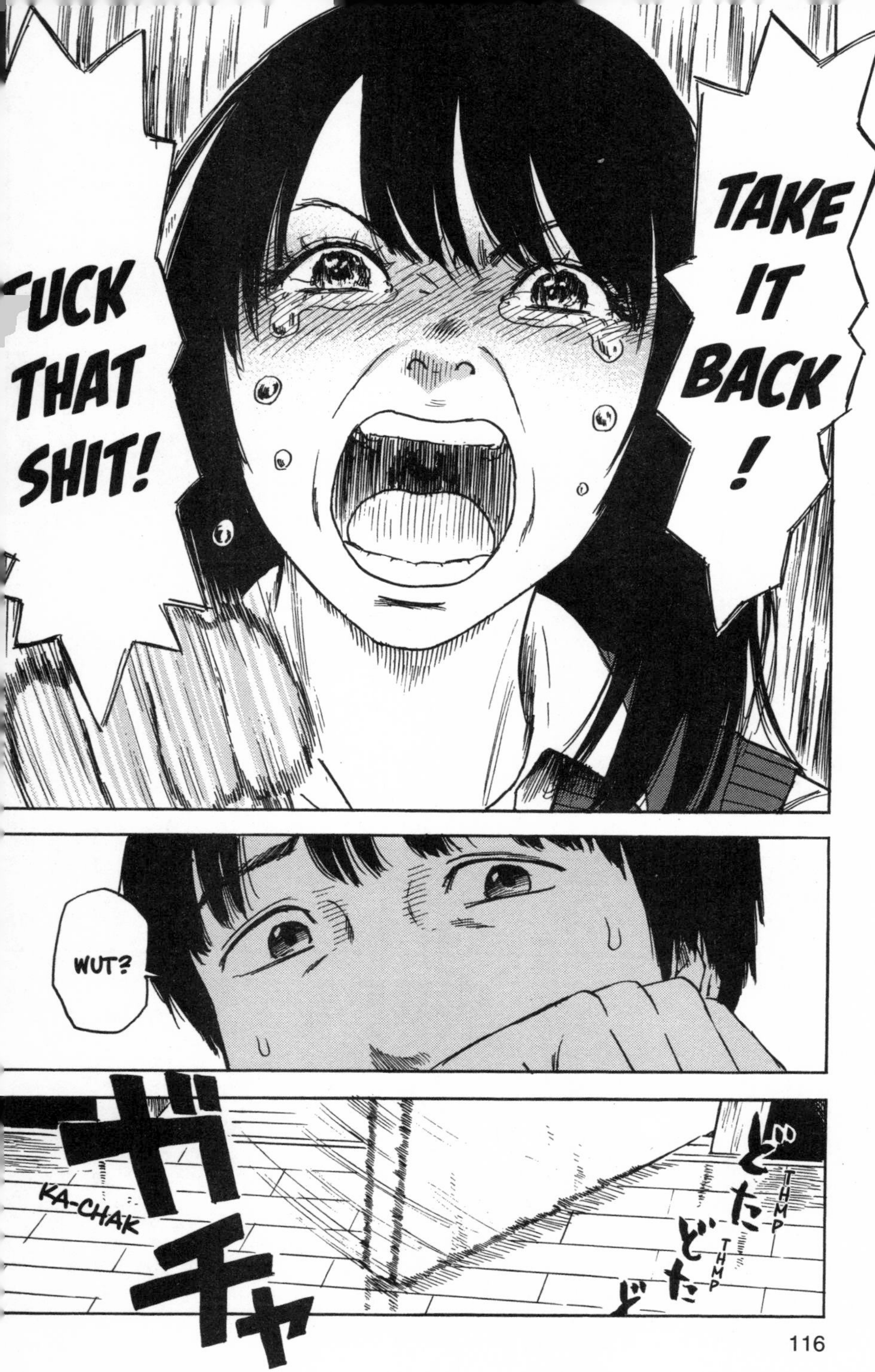
TAKE IT BACK!
FUCK THAT SHIT!
WUT?
どたどた
THMP THMP
ガチャ
KA-CHAK

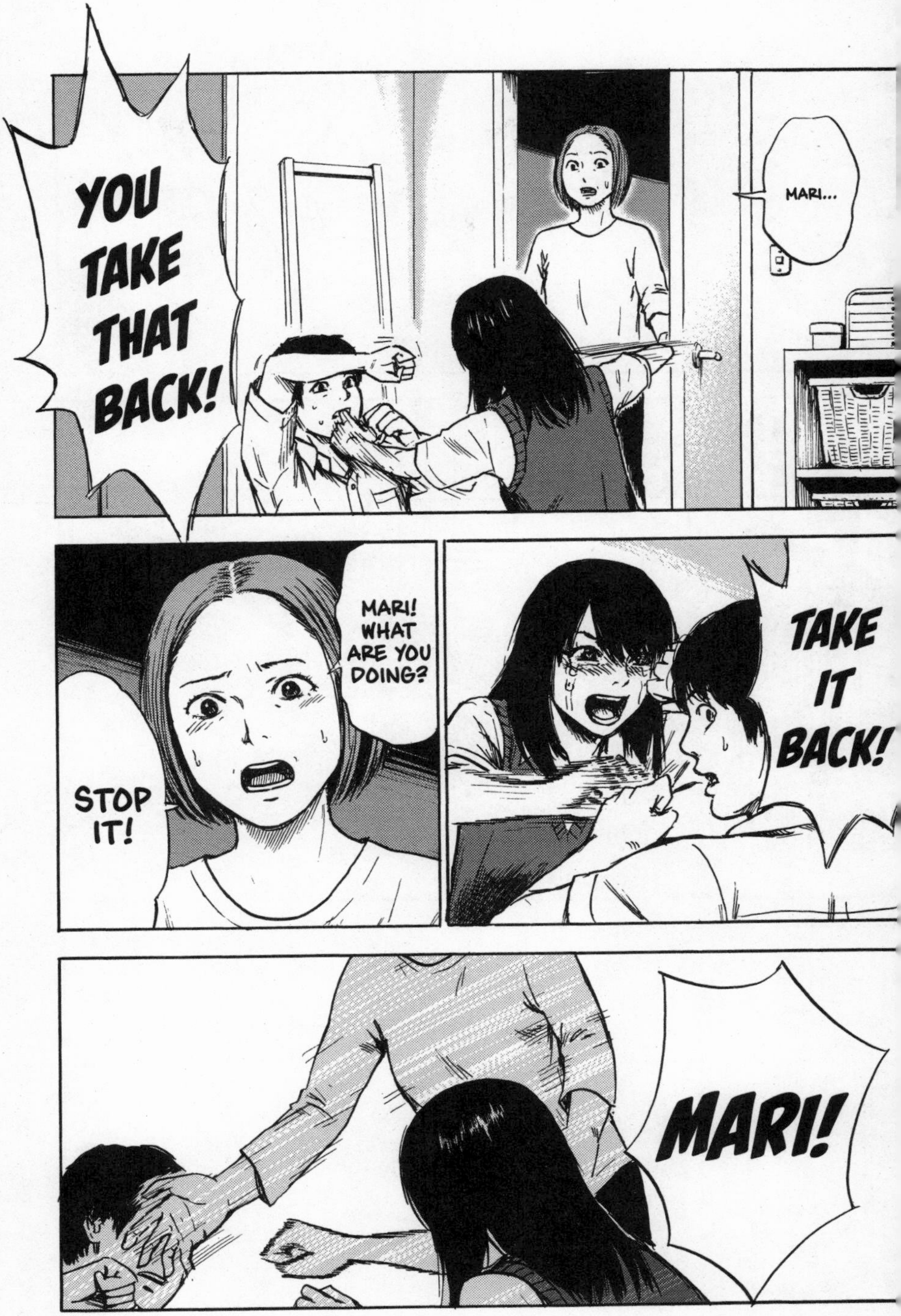

MARI...
YOU TAKE THAT BACK!
TAKE IT BACK!
MARI! WHAT ARE YOU DOING?
STOP IT!
MARI!

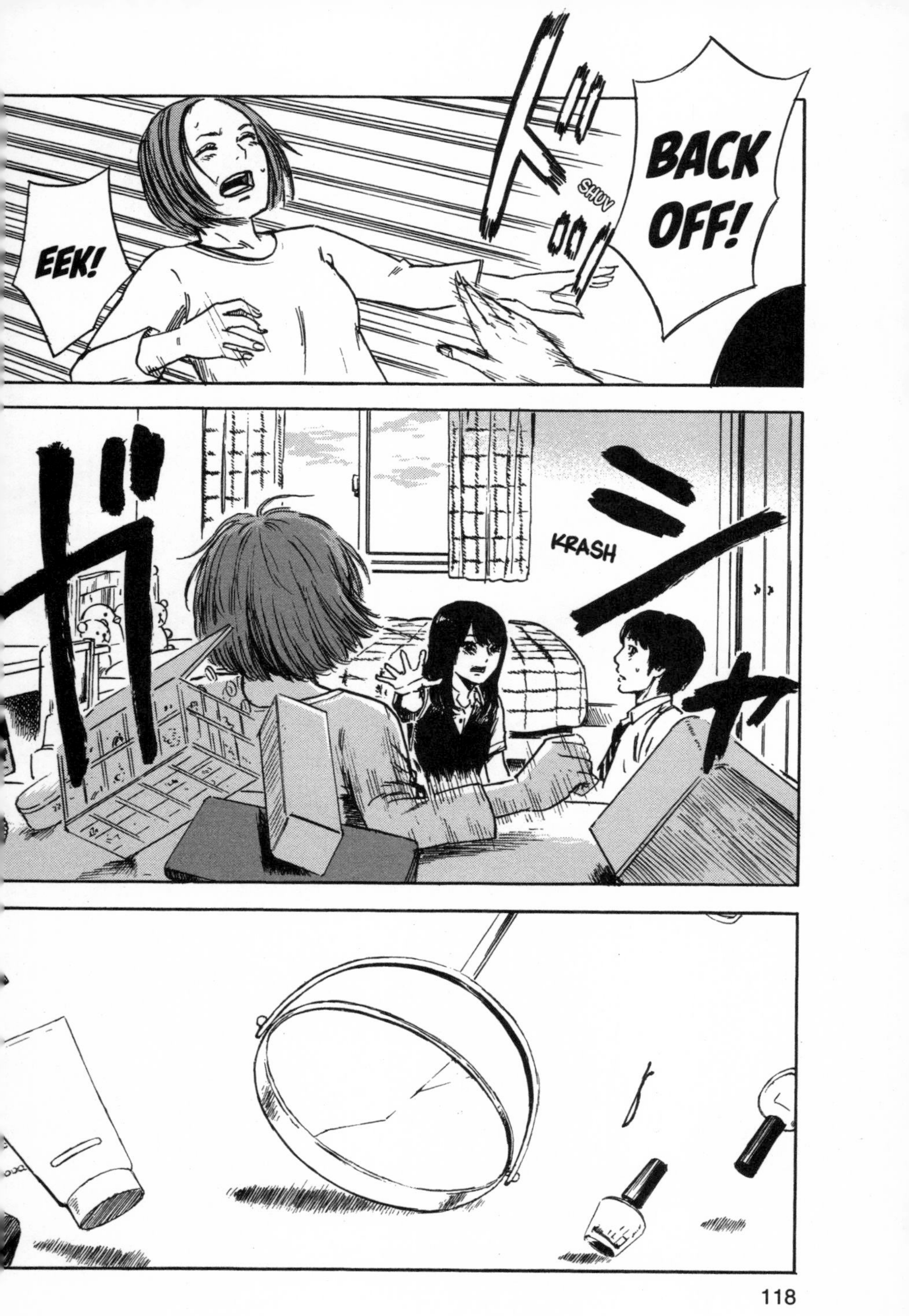
BACK OFF!
SHUV
EEK!
KRASH

OUCH...
ぺた
HALT

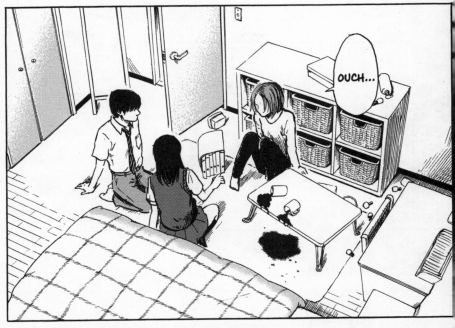

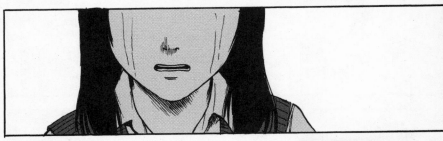

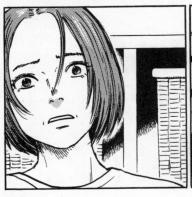

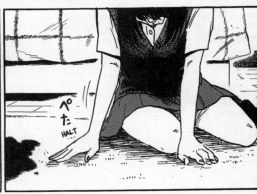

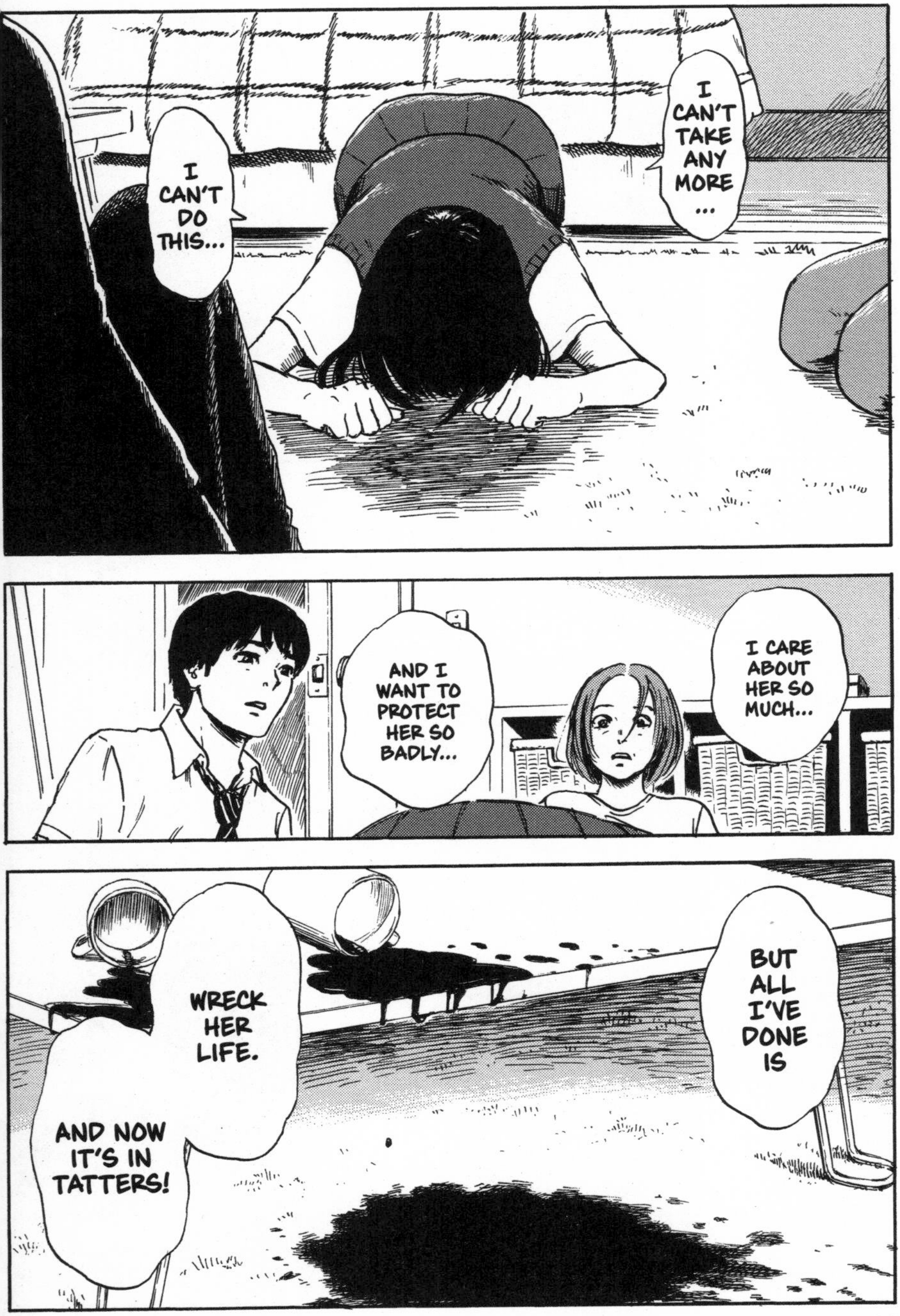
I CAN'T TAKE ANY MORE ...
I CAN'T DO THIS...
I CARE ABOUT HER SO MUCH...
AND I WANT TO PROTECT HER SO BADLY...
BUT ALL I'VE DONE IS
WRECK HER LIFE.
AND NOW IT'S IN TATTERS!

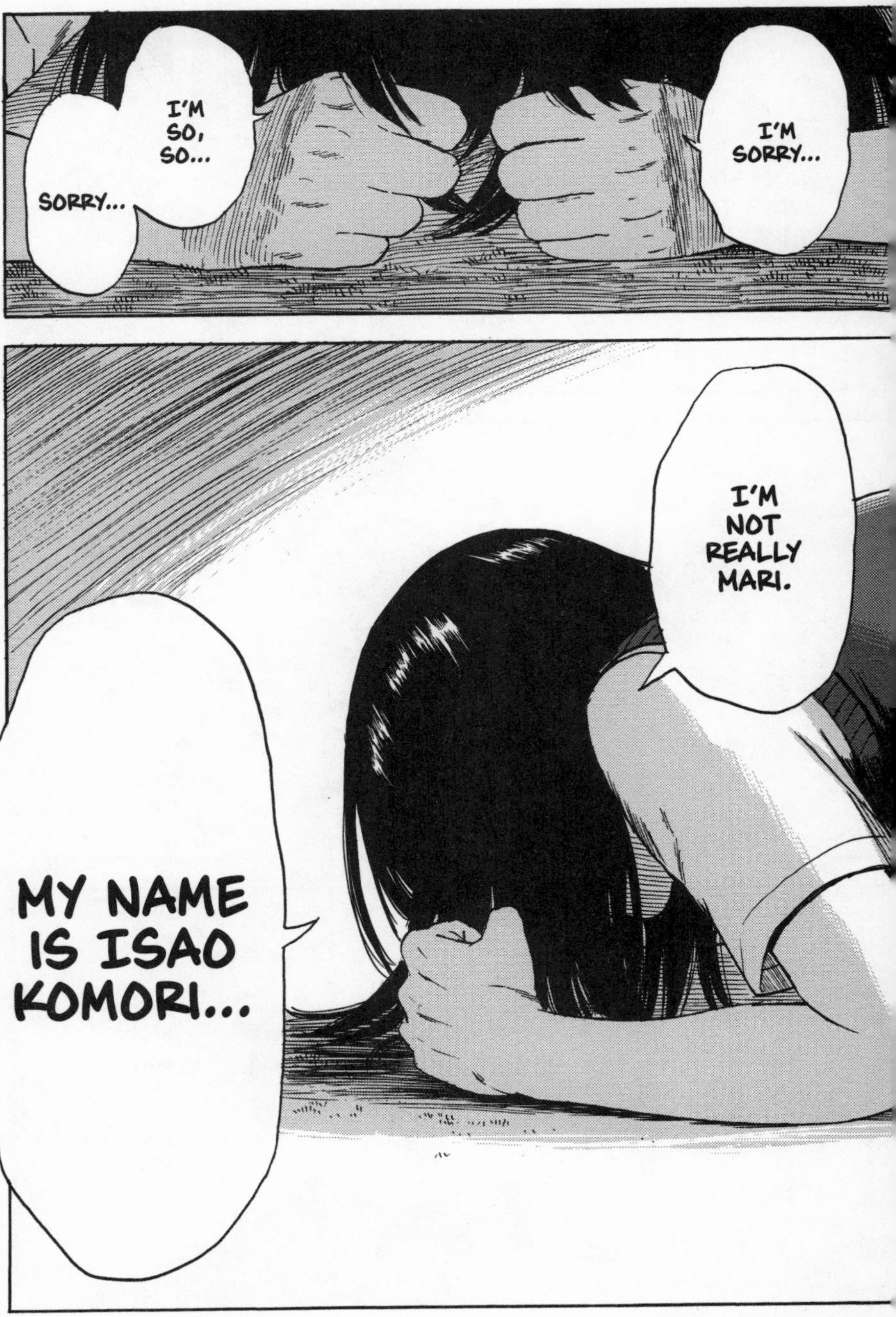
I'M SORRY...
I'M SO, SO...
SORRY...
I'M NOT REALLY MARI.
MY NAME IS ISAO KOMORI...

I NEVER... I NEVER WANTED THIS TO HAPPEN.
ALL I WANTED... WAS TO TALK HER.
I WANTED TO BE FRIENDS. I WANTED TO HEAR HER SAY SHE WAS IN LOVE WITH ME.
I WANTED HER TO KISS ME.
I WANTED TO HAVE SEX WITH HER.
I WANTED TO MARRY HER.
AND I WANTED HER TO RESCUE ME...
FROM THE ABYSS I WAS IN.

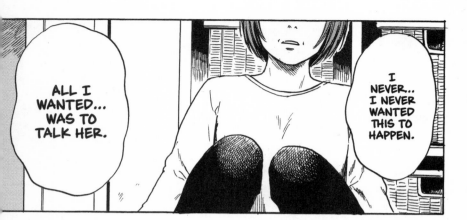

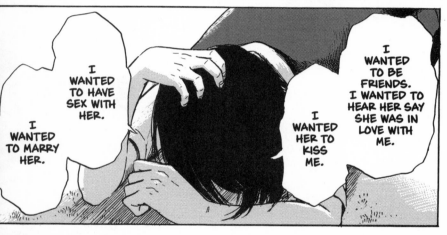

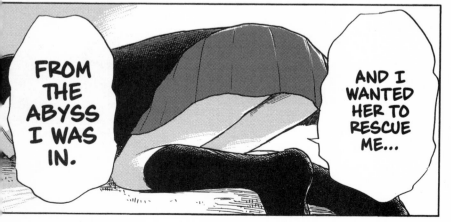

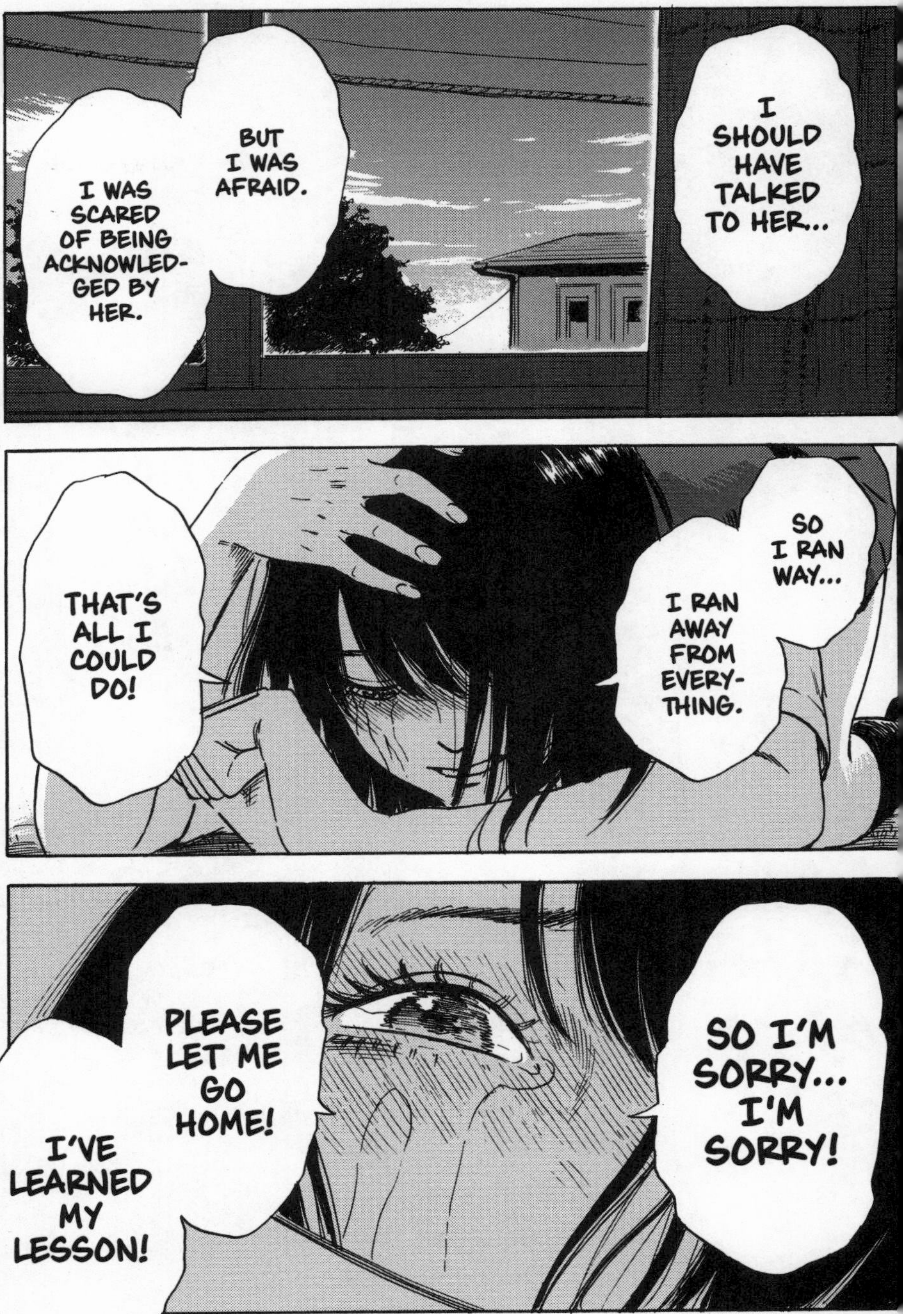
I SHOULD HAVE TALKED TO HER...
BUT I WAS AFRAID.
I WAS SCARED OF BEING ACKNOWLED-GED BY HER.
SO I RAN WAY...
I RAN AWAY FROM EVERY-THING.
THAT'S ALL I COULD DO!
SO I'M SORRY... I'M SORRY!
PLEASE LET ME GO HOME!
I'VE LEARNED MY LESSON!

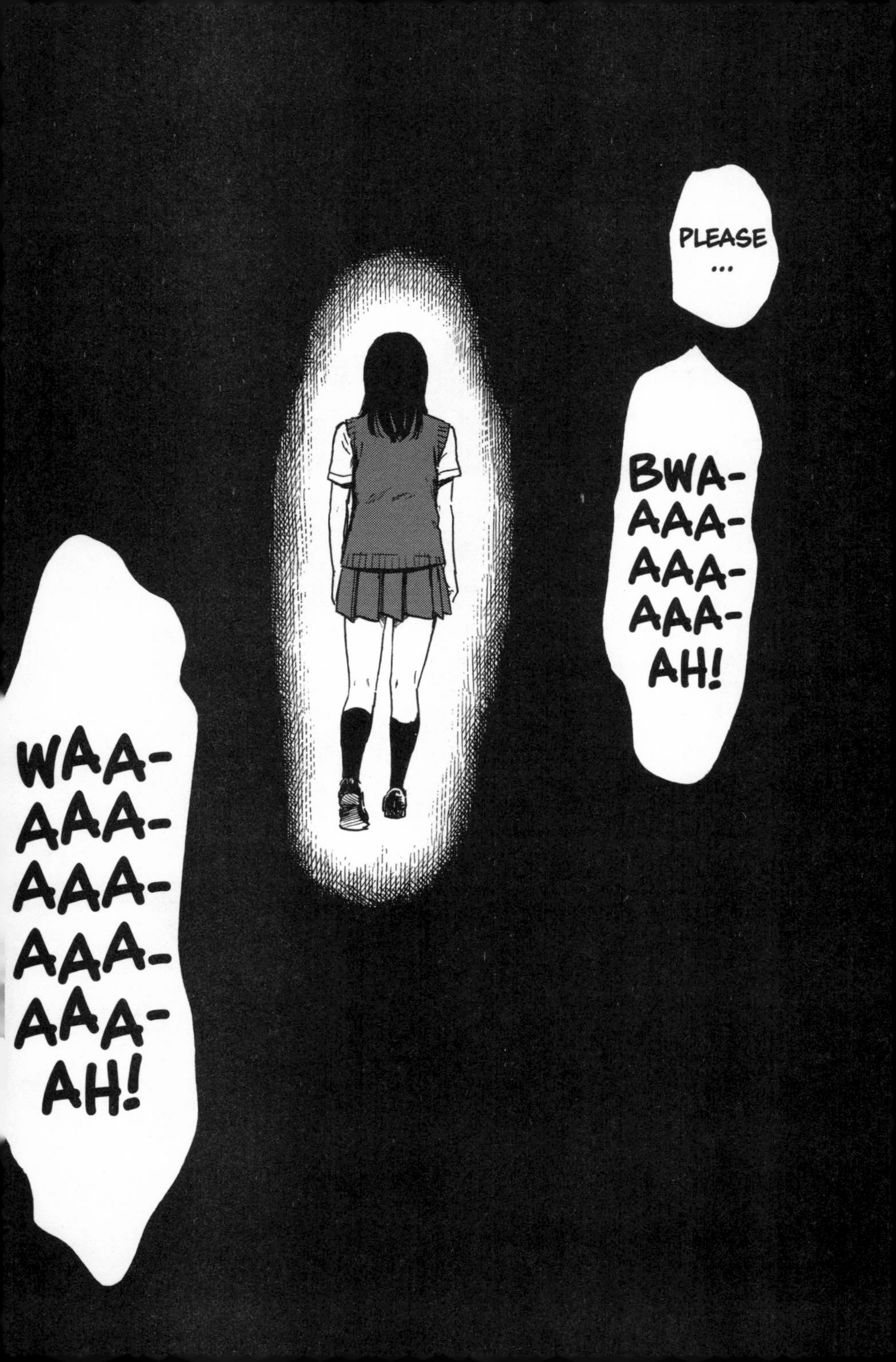
PLEASE ...
BWA-AAA-AAA-AAA-AH!
WAA-AAA-AAA-AAA-AAA-AH!

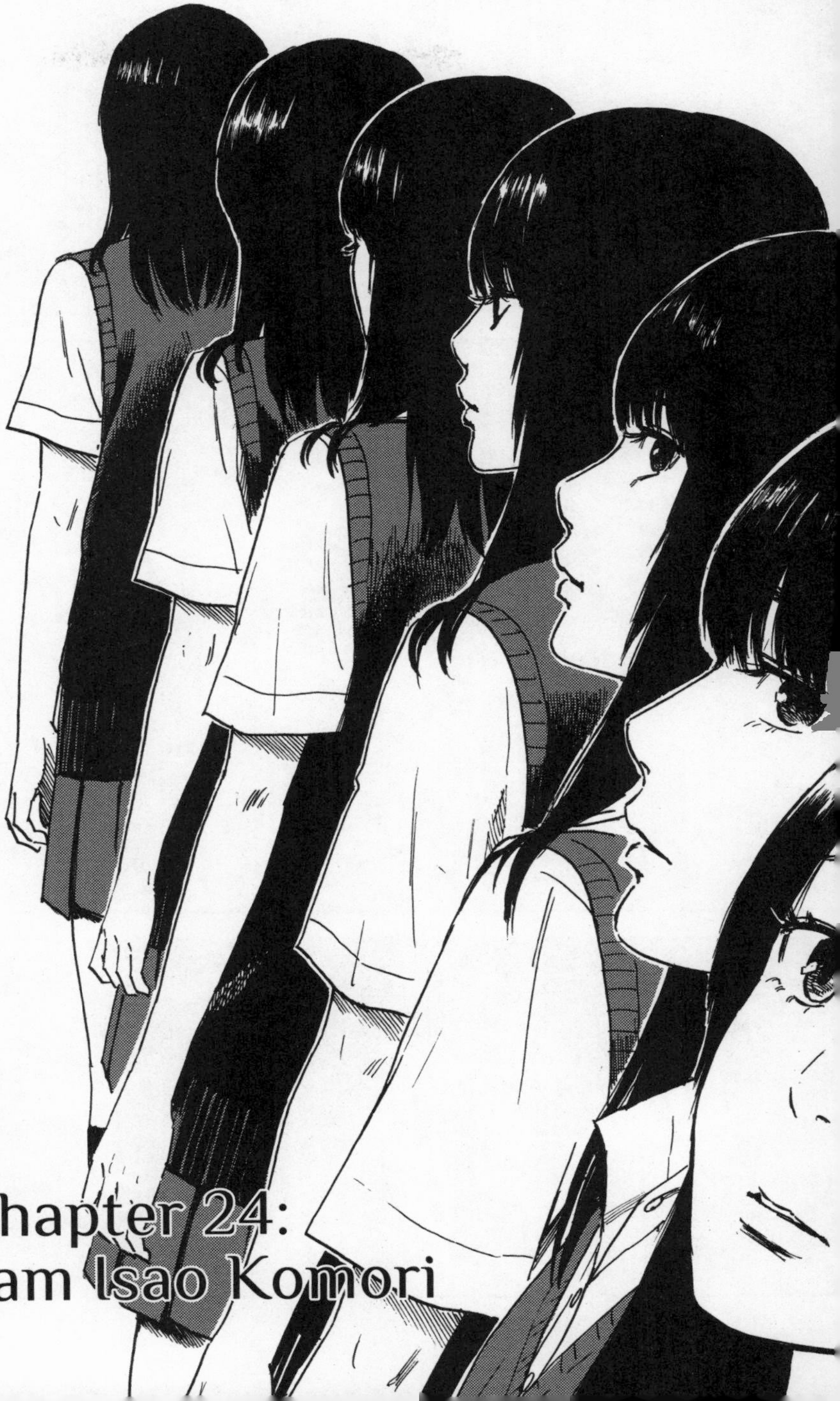
Chapter 24:
I am Isao Komori

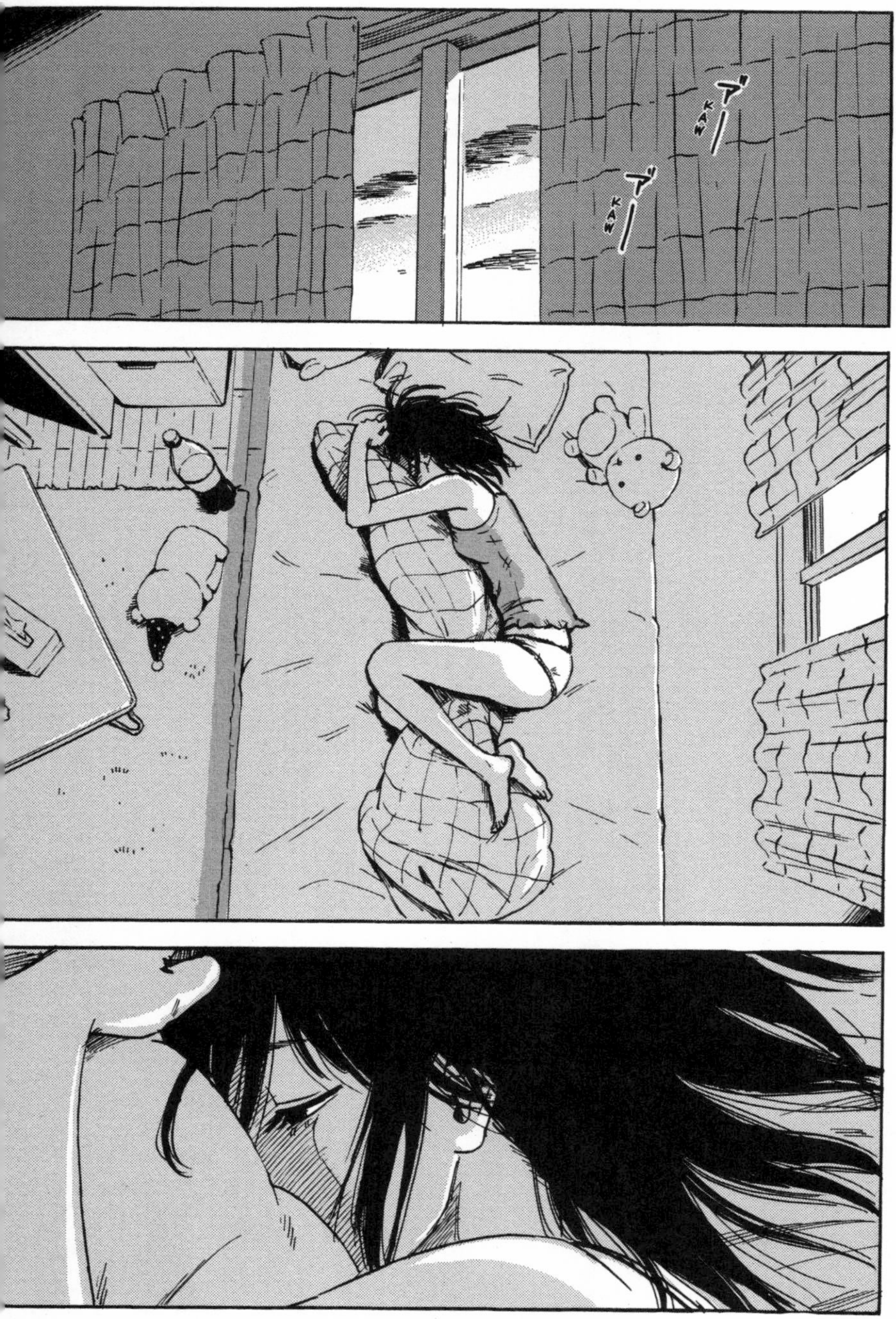
ア゙ー
KAW
ア゙ー
KAW

ゴク GULP
ゴク GULP
SIGH ...

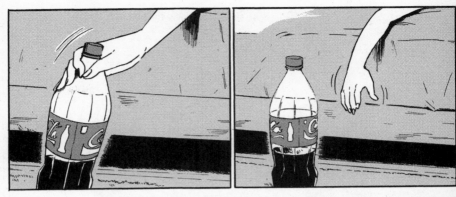

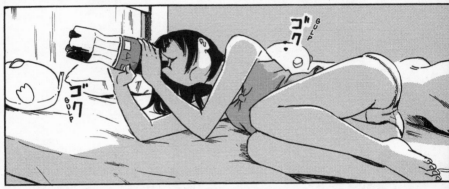

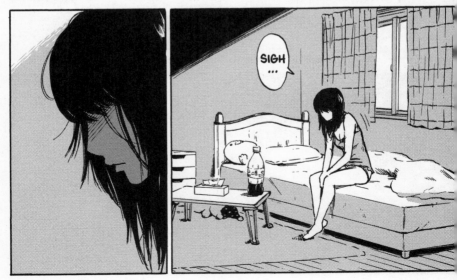

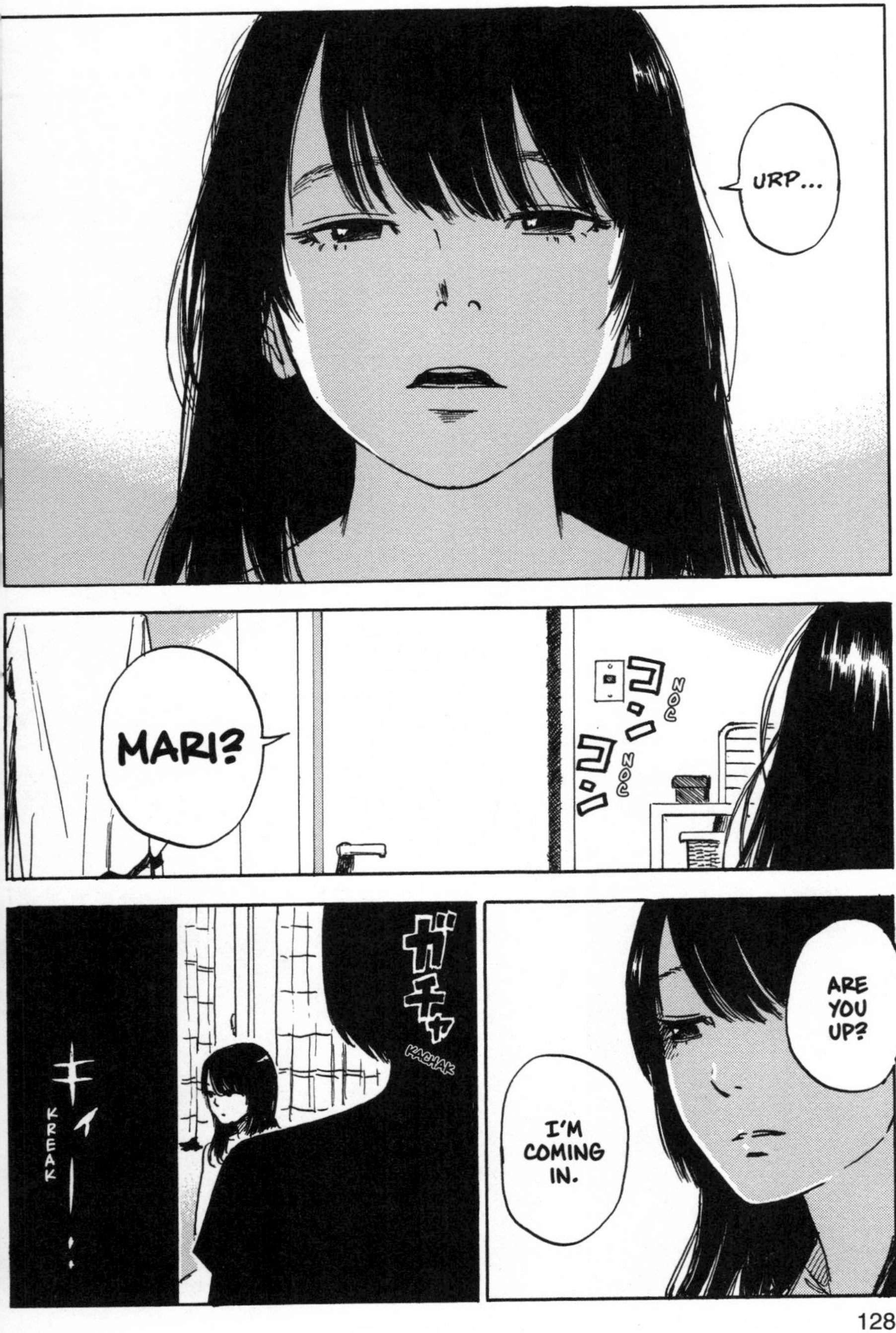
URP...
NOC NOC
MARI?
ARE YOU UP?
I'M COMING IN.
ガチャ
KACHAK
KREAK

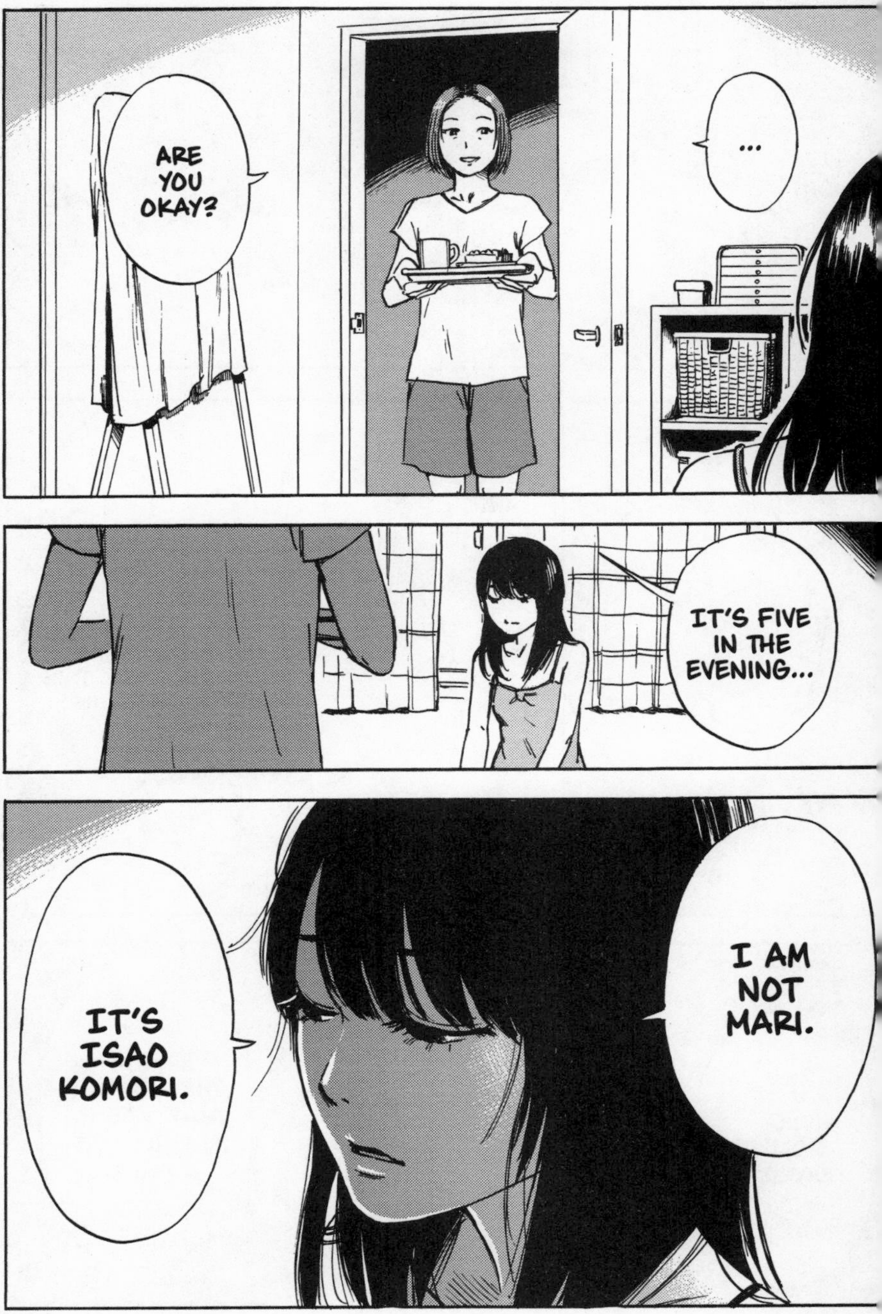
...
ARE YOU OKAY?
IT'S FIVE IN THE EVENING...
I AM NOT MARI.
IT'S ISAO KOMORI.

IT'S ALRIGHT ...
EAT THIS,
THEN TAKE THIS MEDICINE...
AND YOU'LL BE ALL BETTER SOON.
OKAY?
I TOLD YOUR FATHER THAT YOU'RE IN BED WITH A COLD.
SO DON'T WORRY.

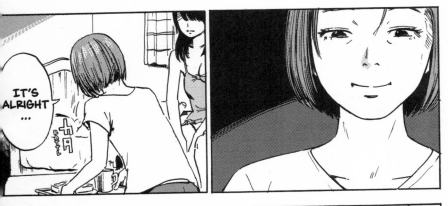

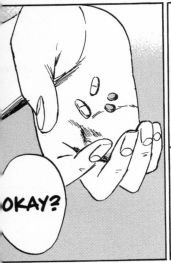

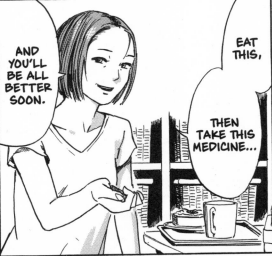

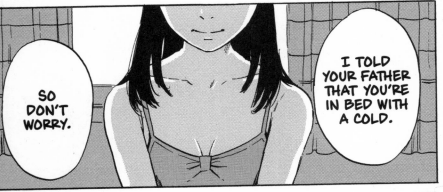

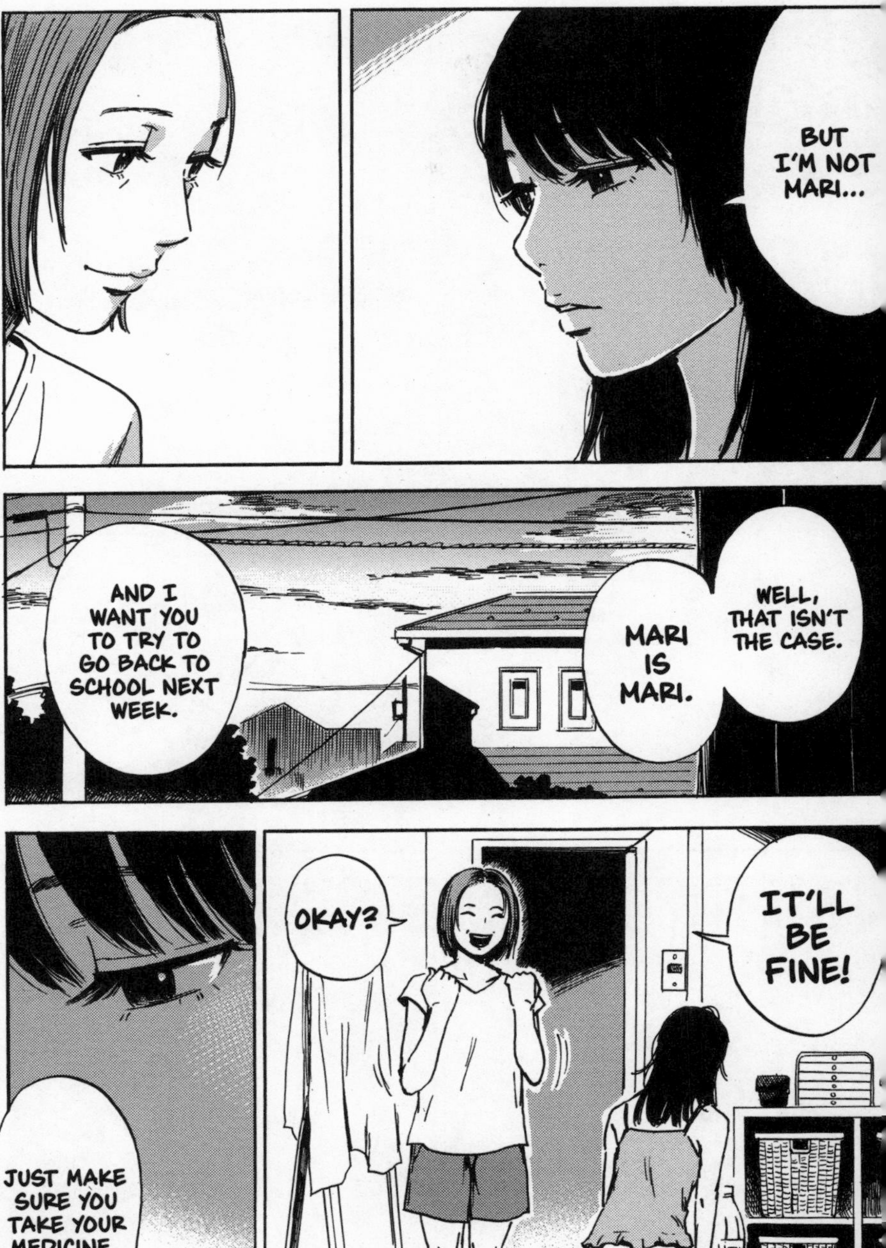
BUT I'M NOT MARI...
WELL, THAT ISN'T THE CASE.
MARI IS MARI.
AND I WANT YOU TO TRY TO GO BACK TO SCHOOL NEXT WEEK.
IT'LL BE FINE!
OKAY?
JUST MAKE SURE YOU TAKE YOUR MEDICINE.

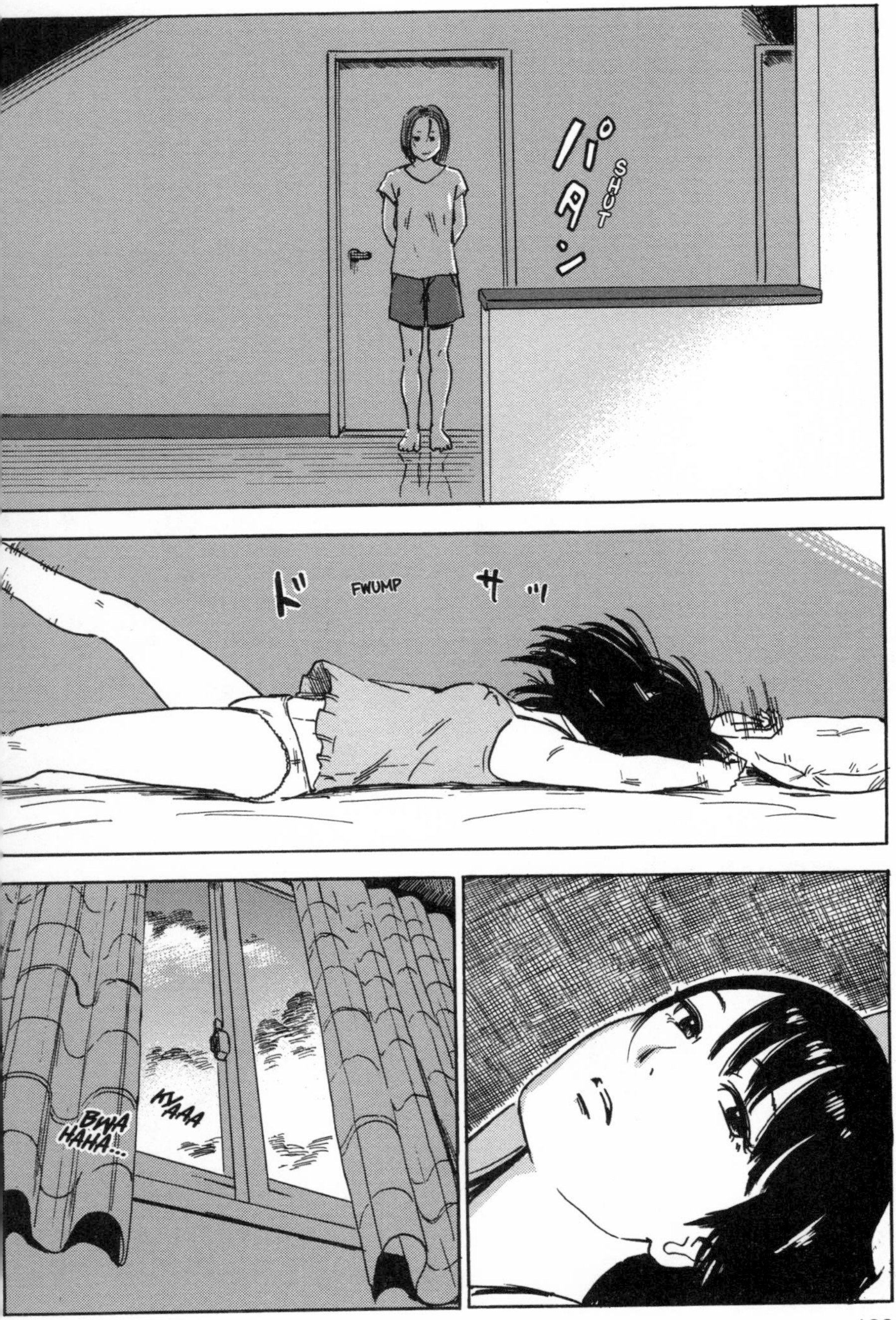
パタン
SHUT
ドサッ
FWUMP
KYAAA
BWA HAHA...

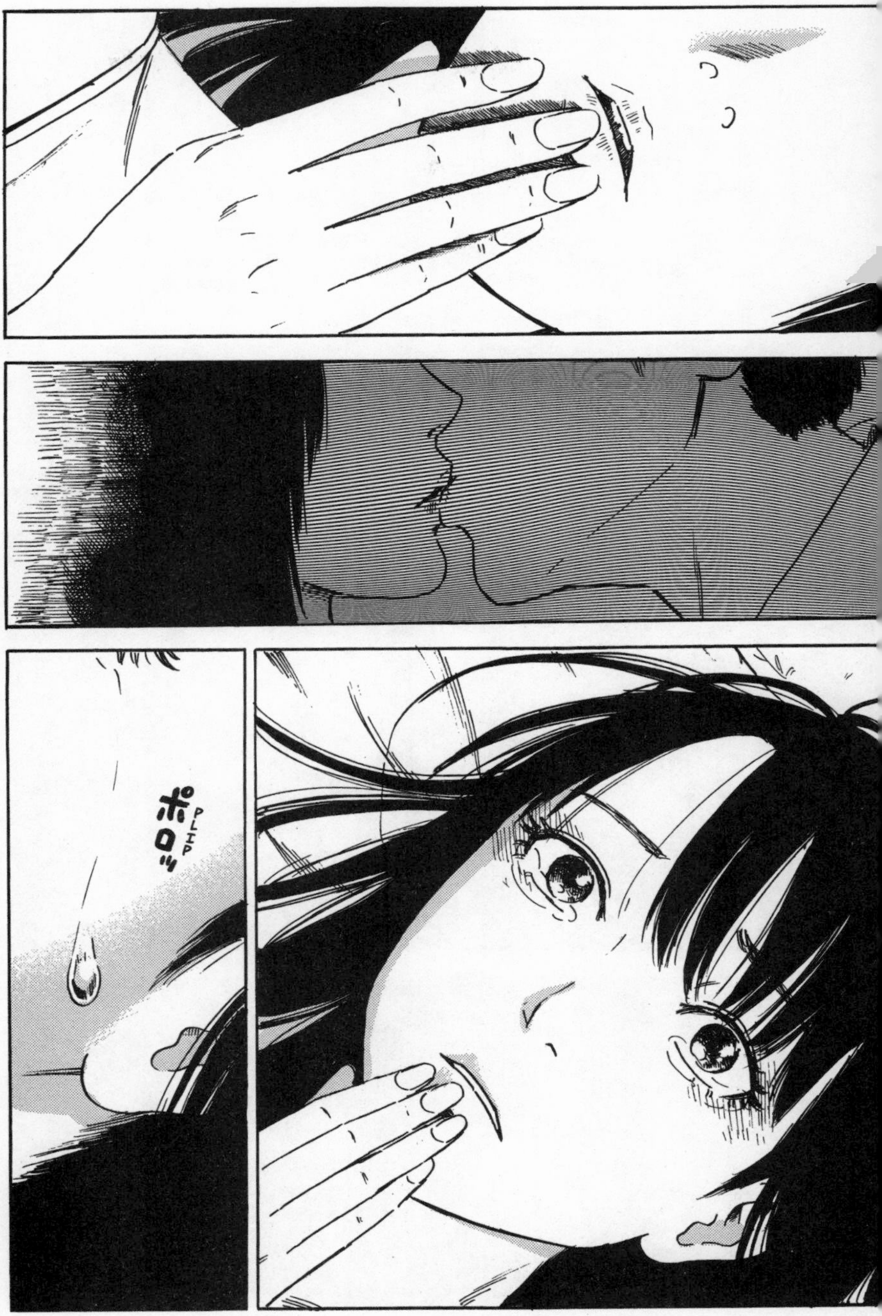
ポロッ
PLIP

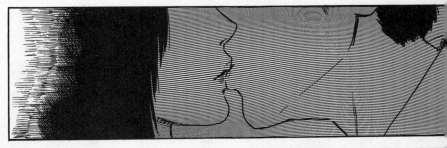

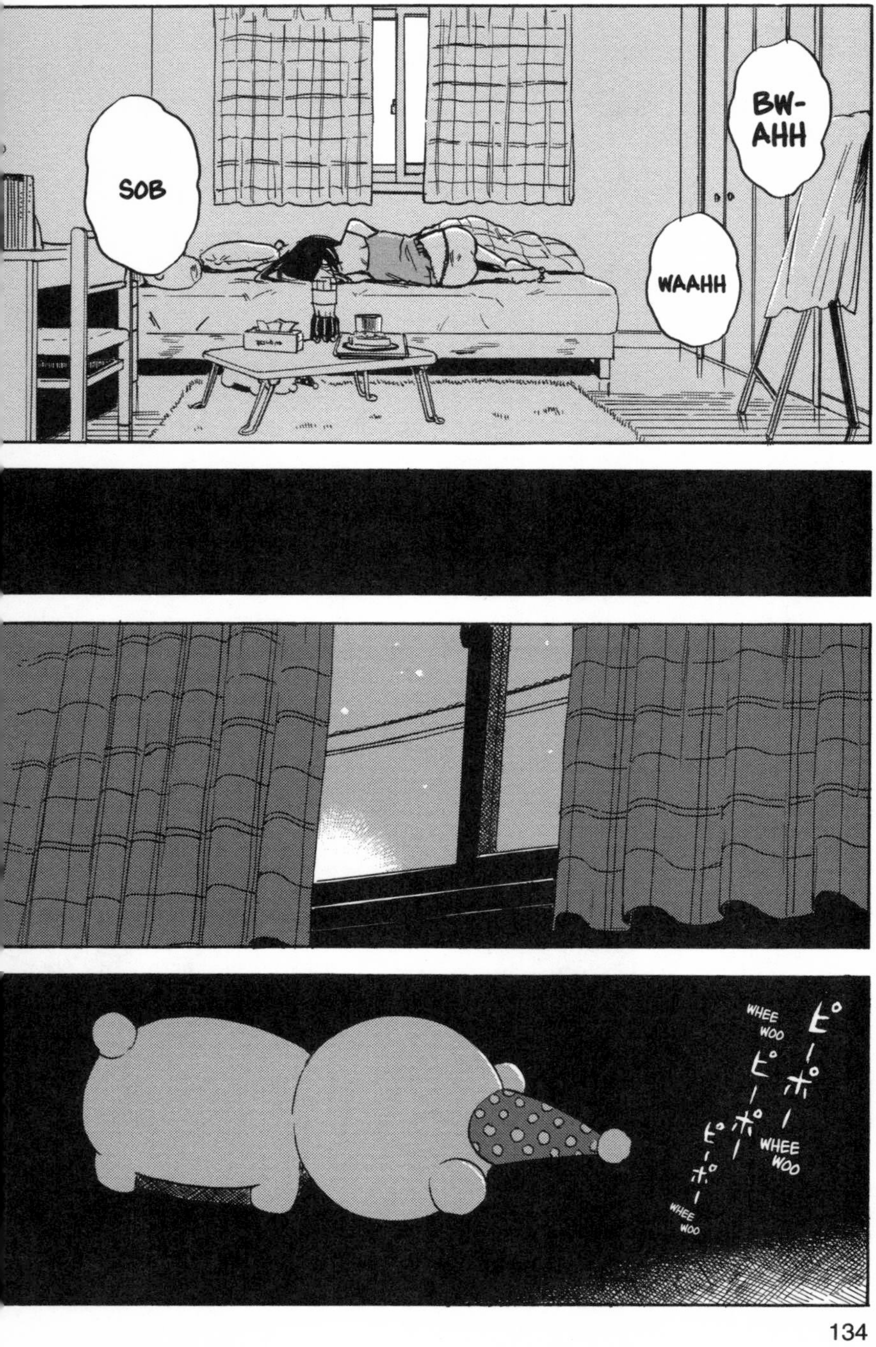
BW-AHH
WAAHH
SOB
ピーポー
WHEE WOO
ピーポー
WHEE WOO
ピーポー
WHEE WOO

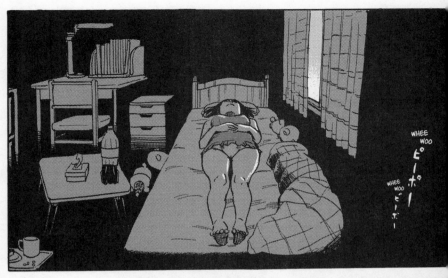

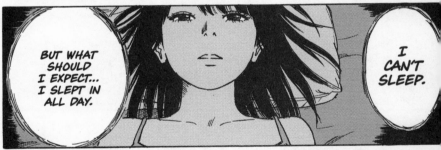

WHEE WOO
ピーポー
WHEE WOO
ピーポー
I CAN'T SLEEP.
BUT WHAT SHOULD I EXPECT... I SLEPT IN ALL DAY.
ムク
FWUM
シャラ
SHOOM

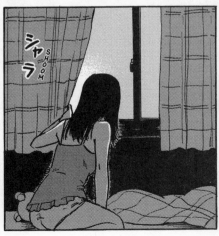

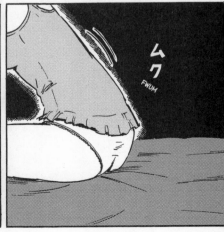

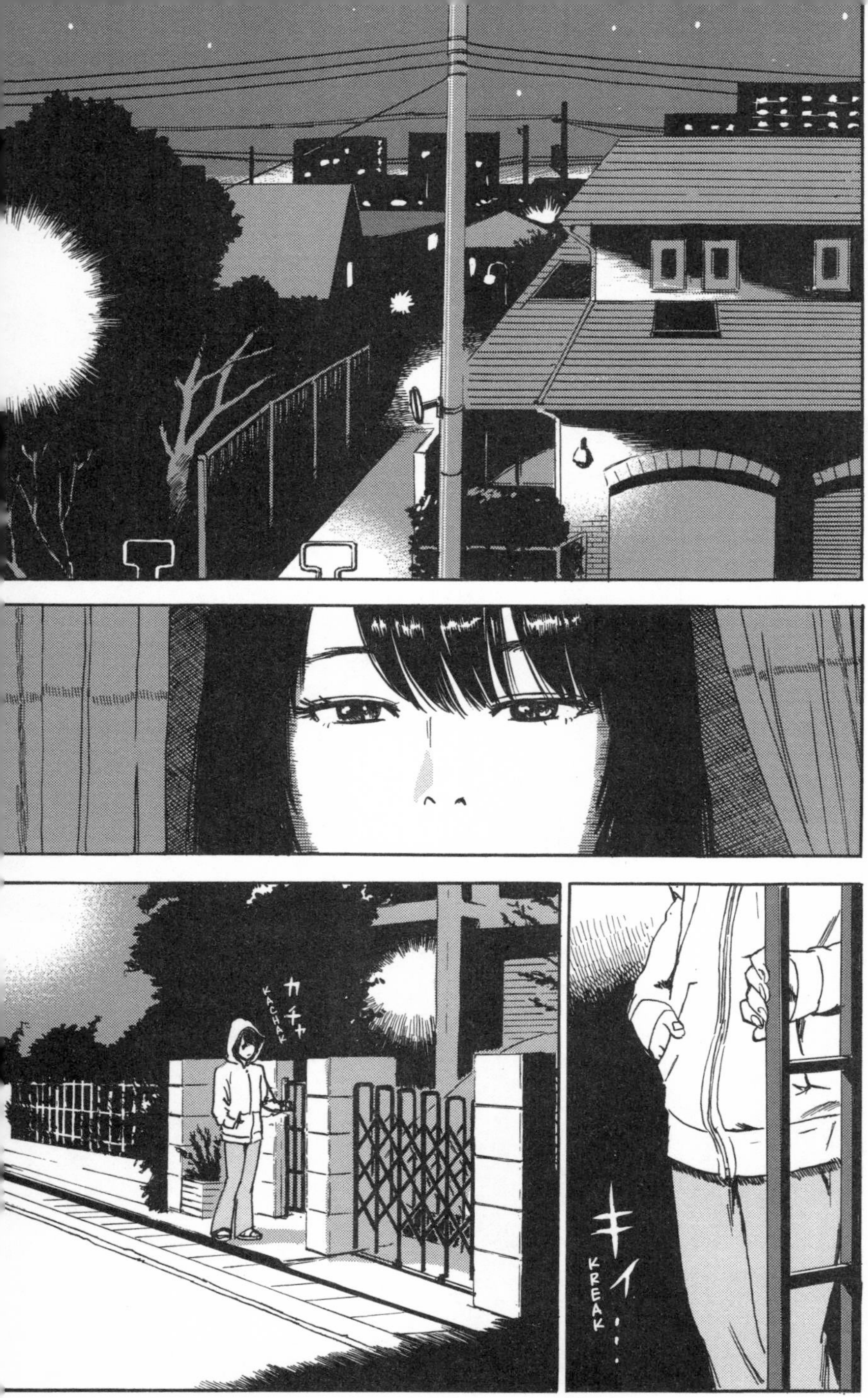
キイ
KREAK...
カチャ
KACHAK

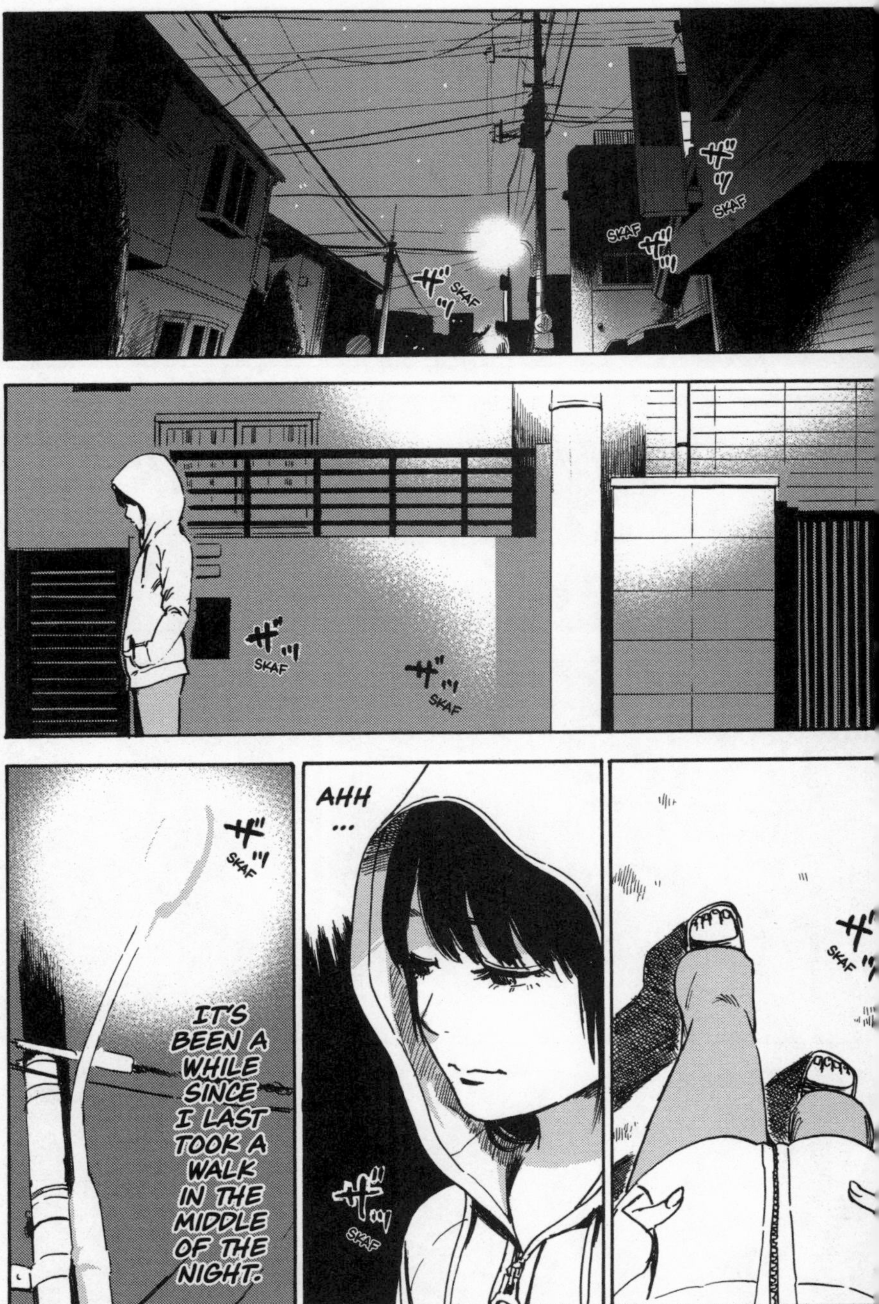
SKAF
SKAF
SKAF
SKAF
SKAF
SKAF
AHH ...
SKAF
SKAF
IT'S BEEN A WHILE SINCE I LAST TOOK A WALK IN THE MIDDLE OF THE NIGHT.

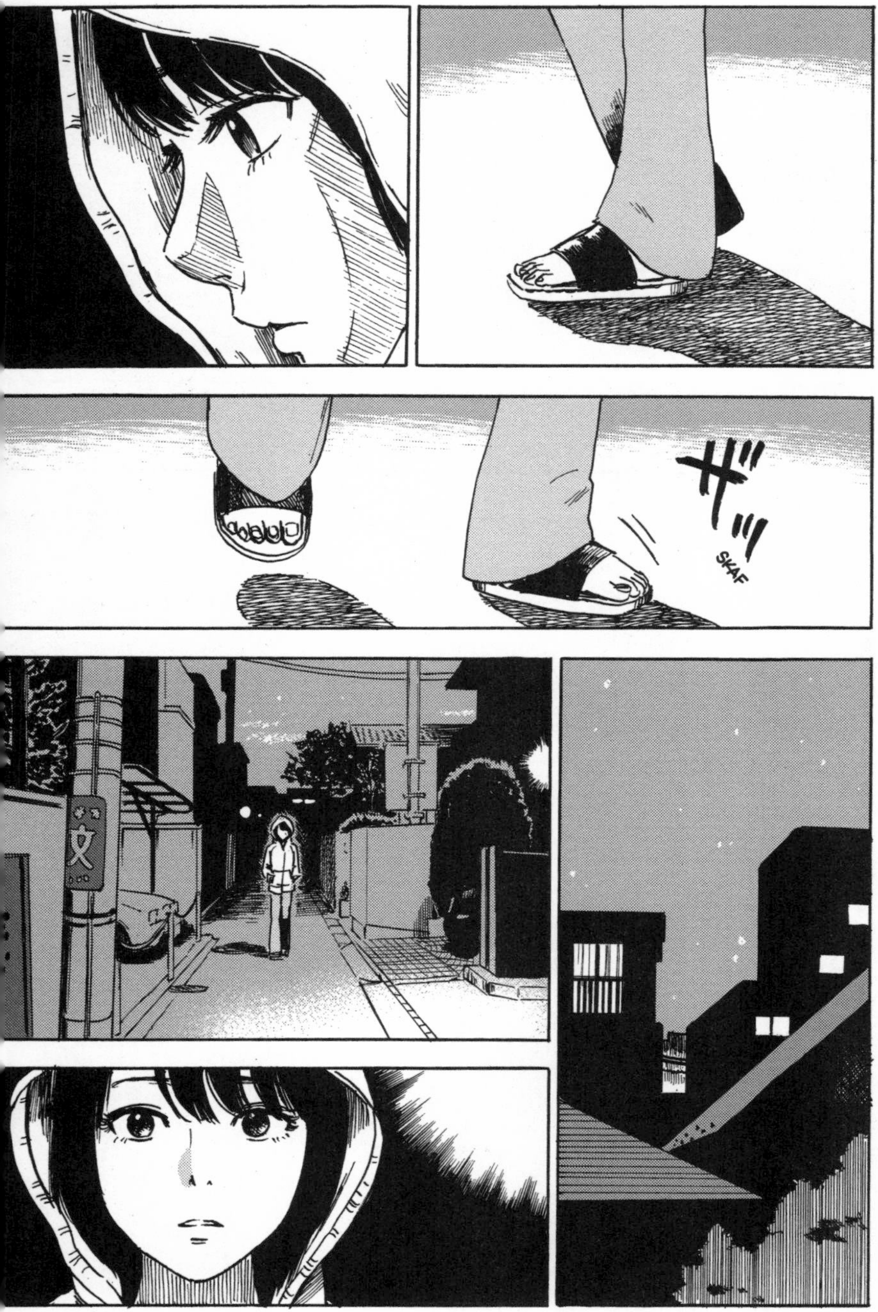
ザッ
SKAF
文

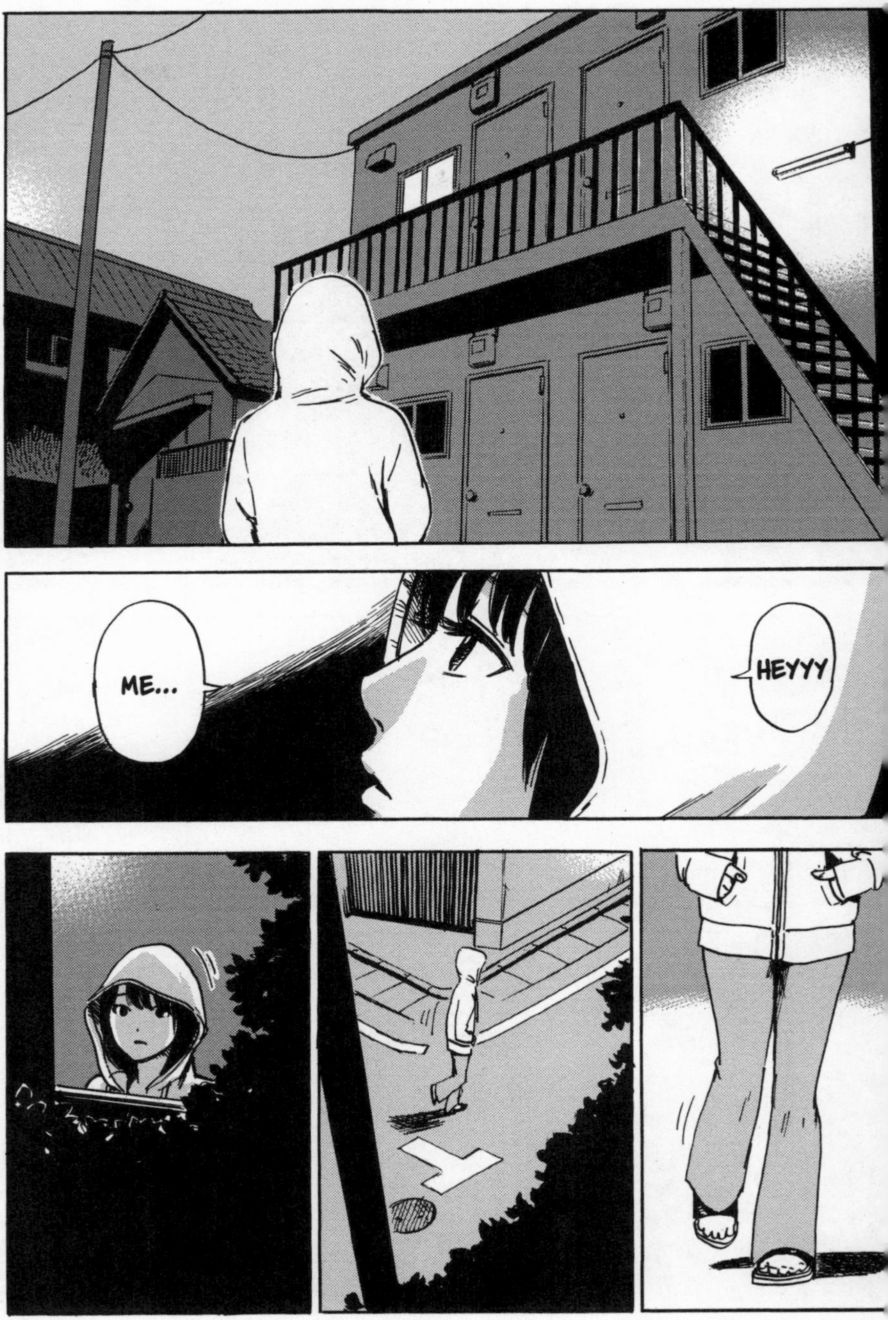
HEYYY
ME...

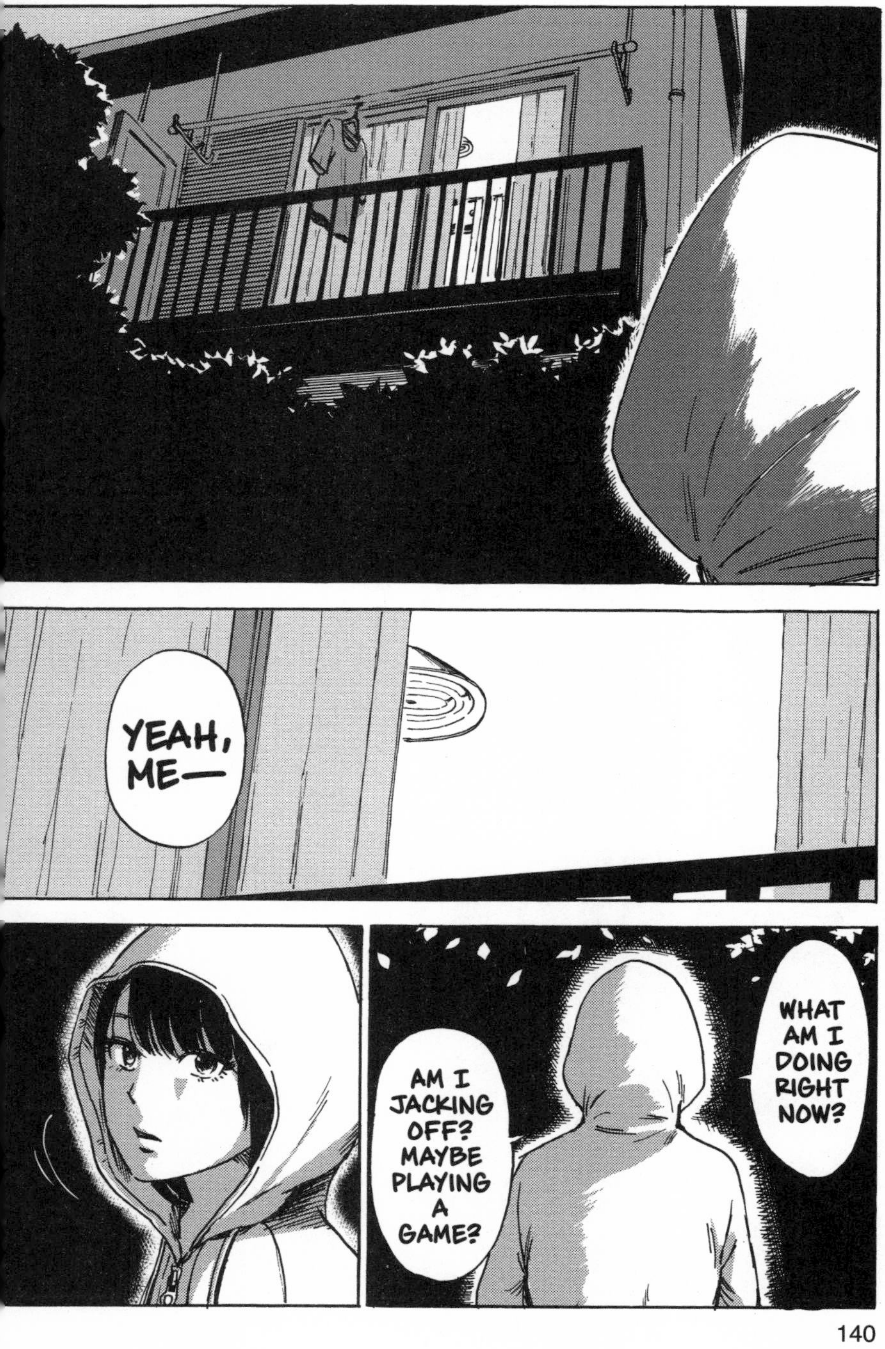
YEAH, ME—
WHAT AM I DOING RIGHT NOW?
AM I JACKING OFF? MAYBE PLAYING A GAME?

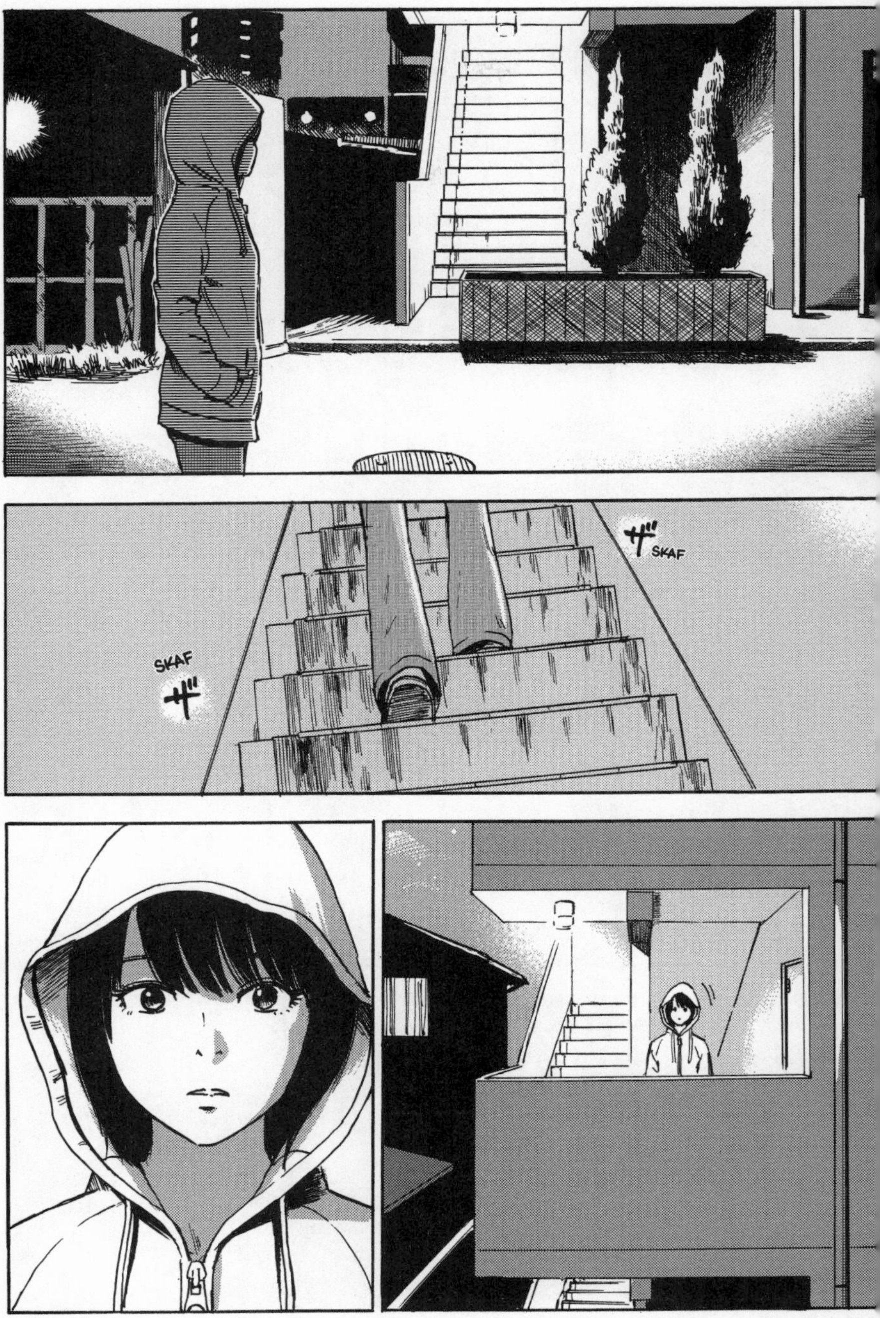
ザ
SKAF
SKAF
ザ

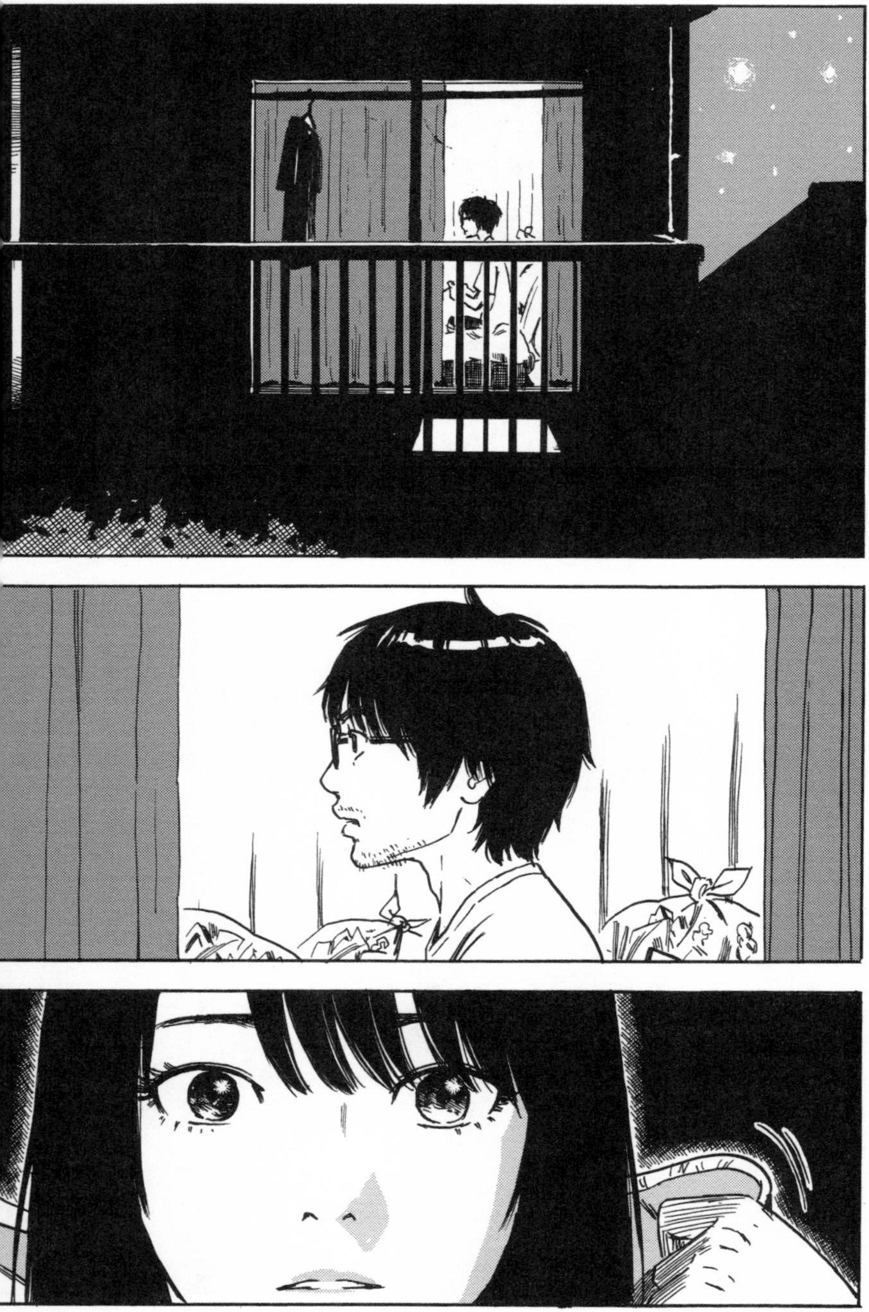

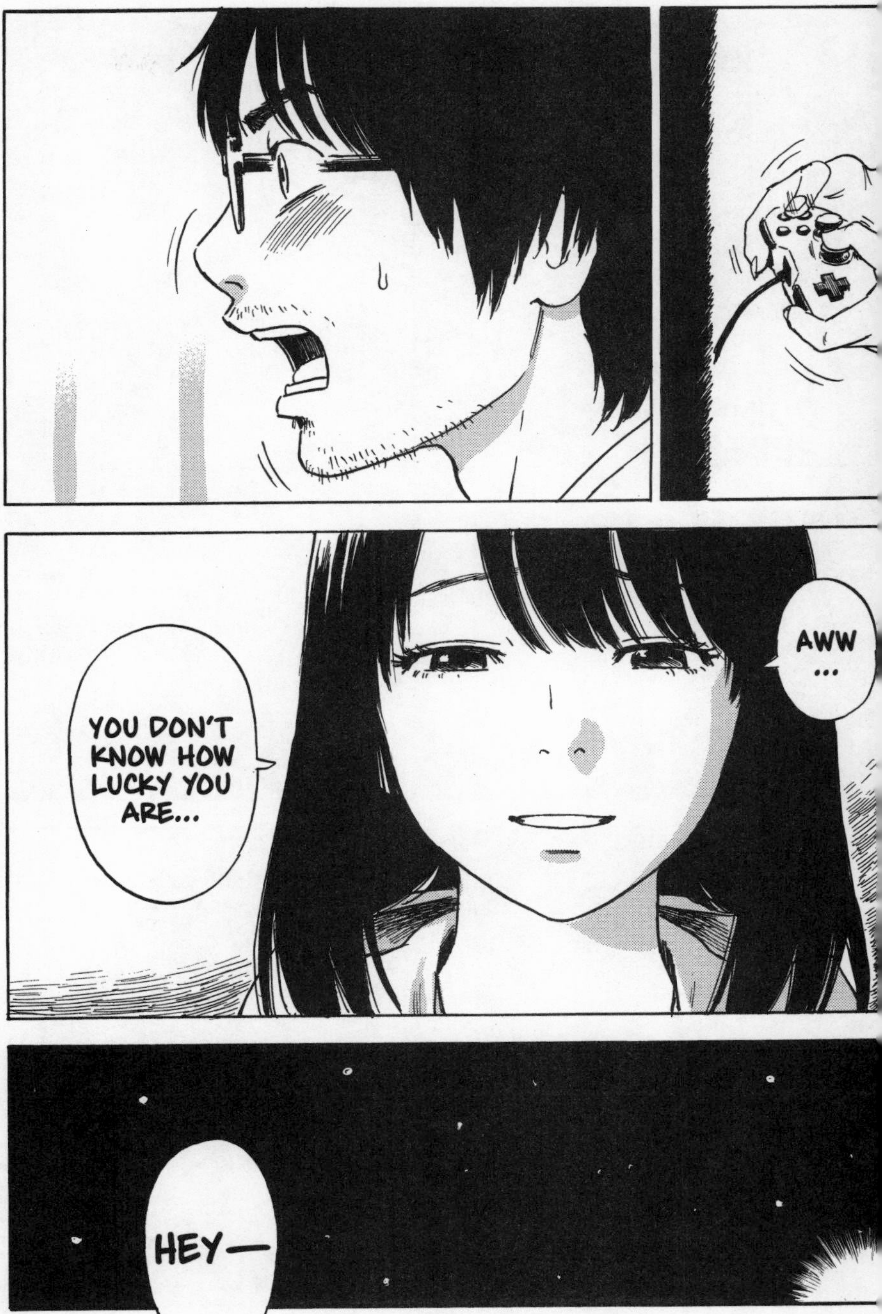
AWW...
YOU DON'T KNOW HOW LUCKY YOU ARE...
HEY—

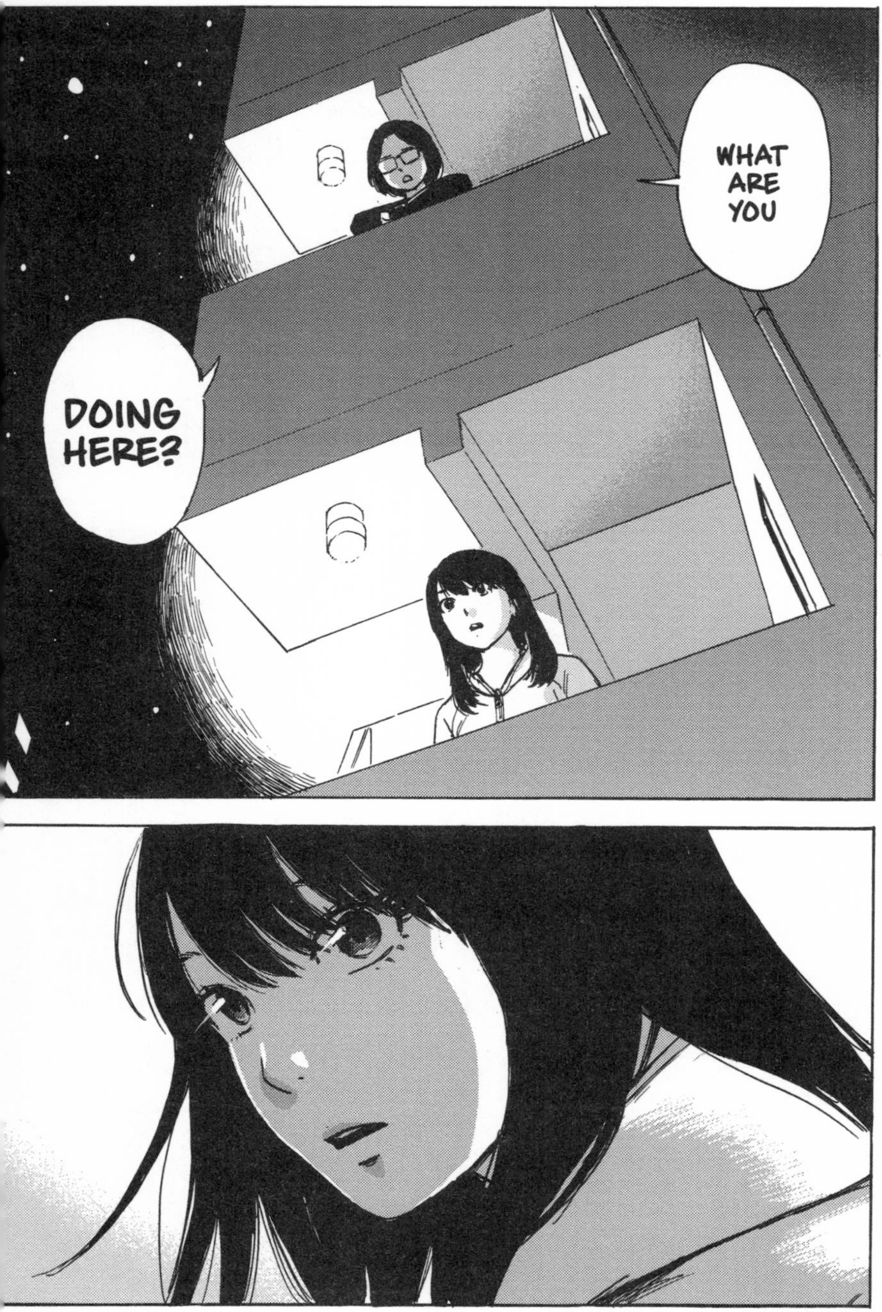
WHAT ARE YOU
DOING HERE?

Chapter 25: Mari's Message

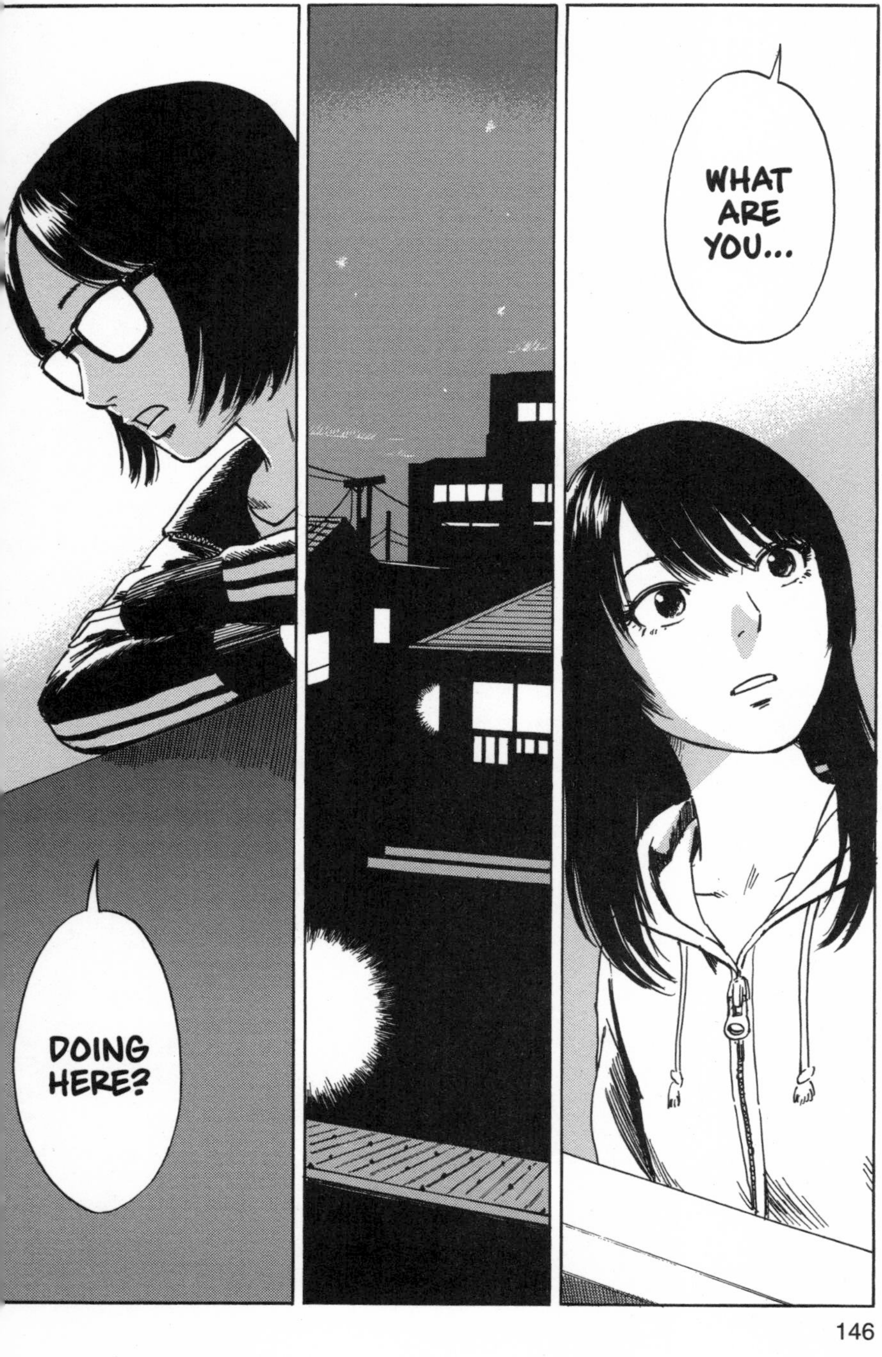
WHAT ARE YOU...
DOING HERE?

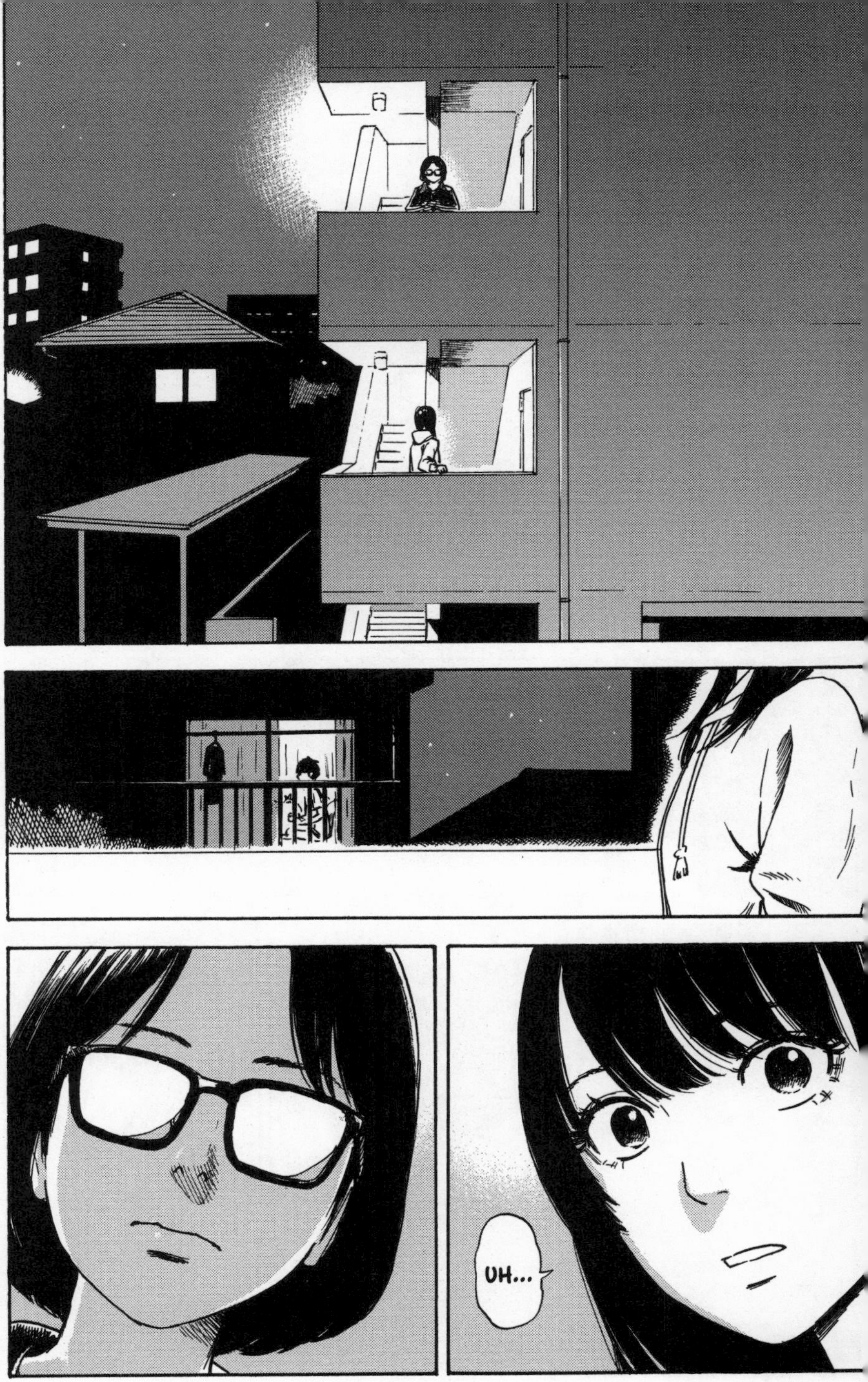
UH...

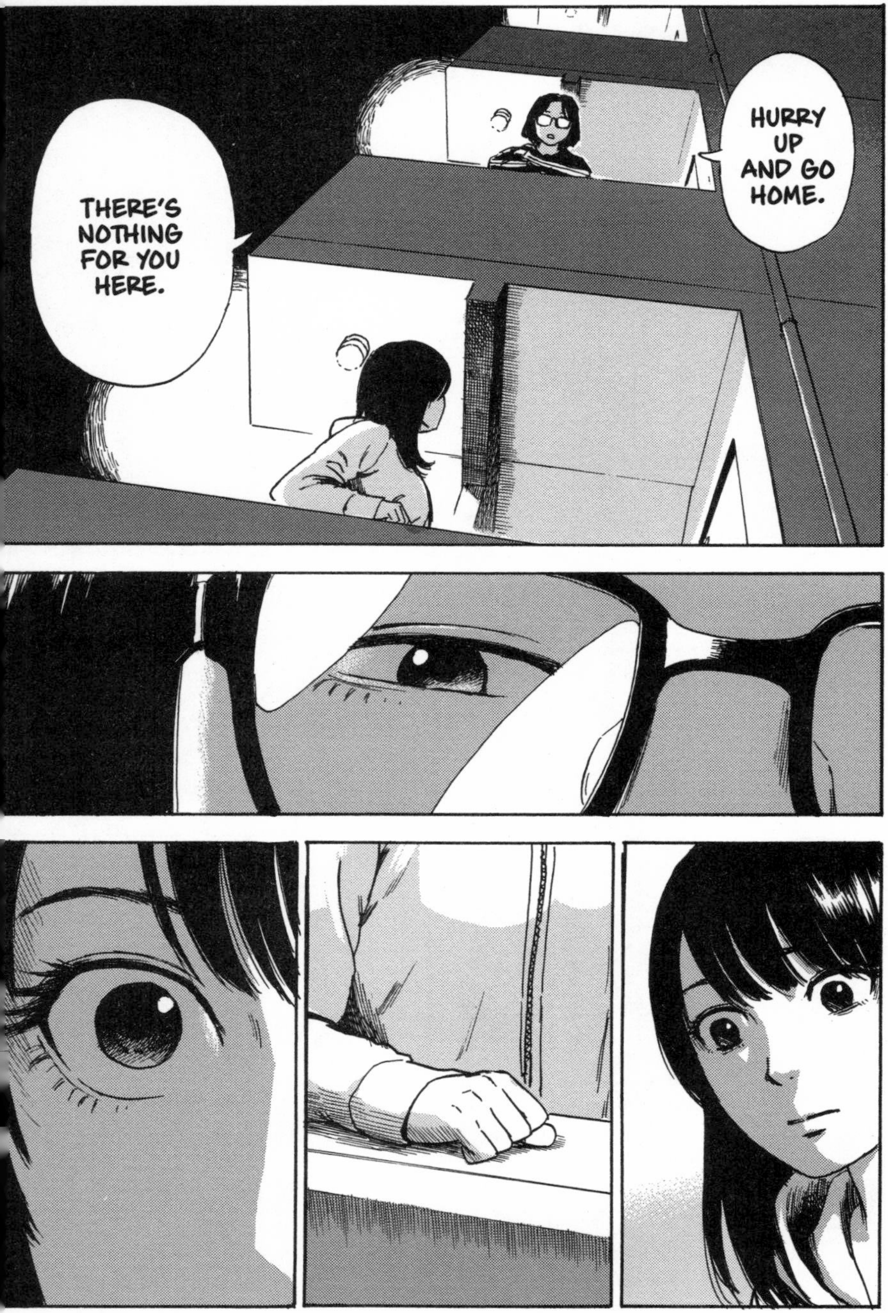
HURRY UP AND GO HOME.
THERE'S NOTHING FOR YOU HERE.

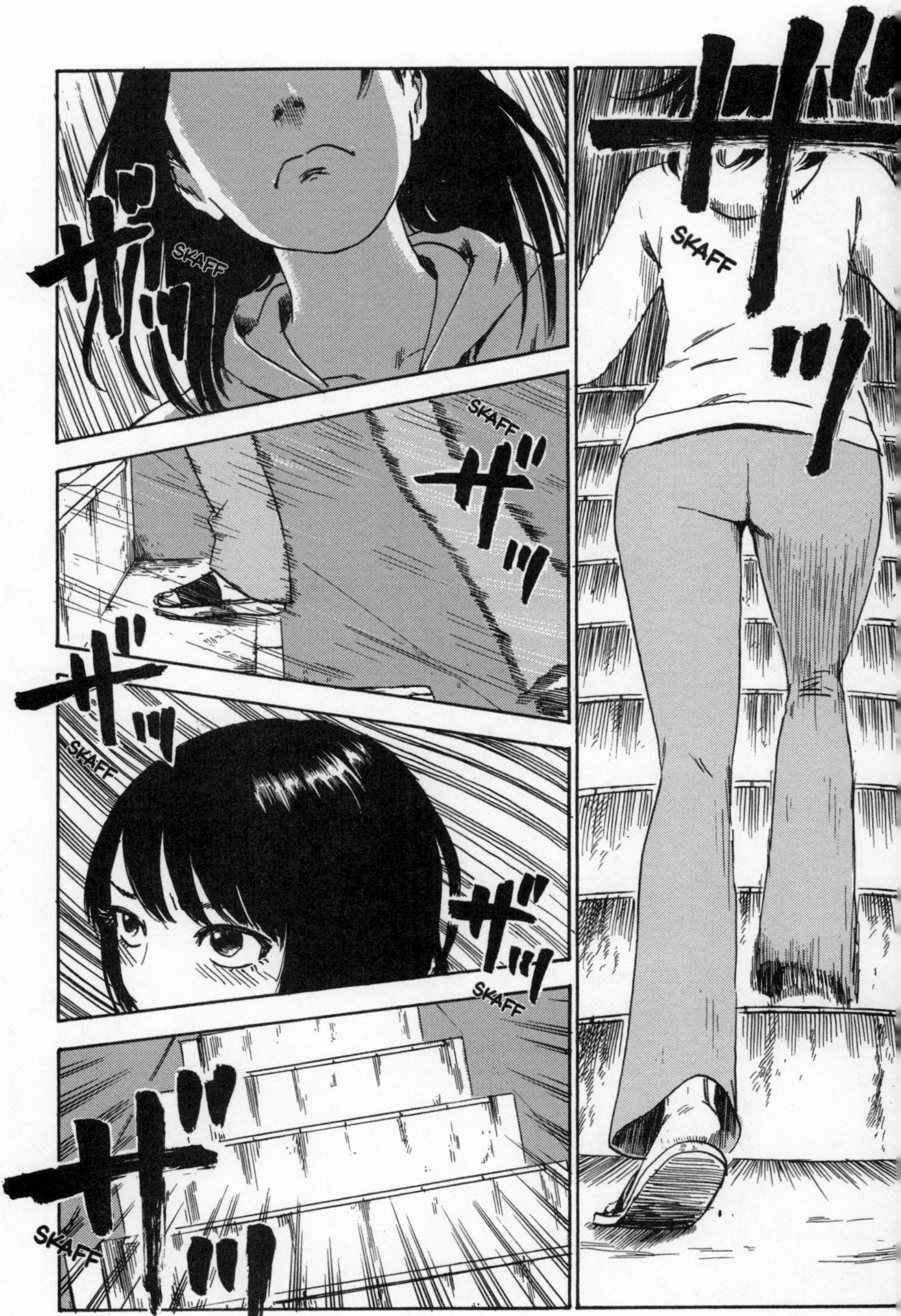

ザッ
SKAFF
ザッ
SKAFF
SKAFF
ザッ
ザッ
SKAFF
ザッ
SKAFF
ザッ
SKAFF

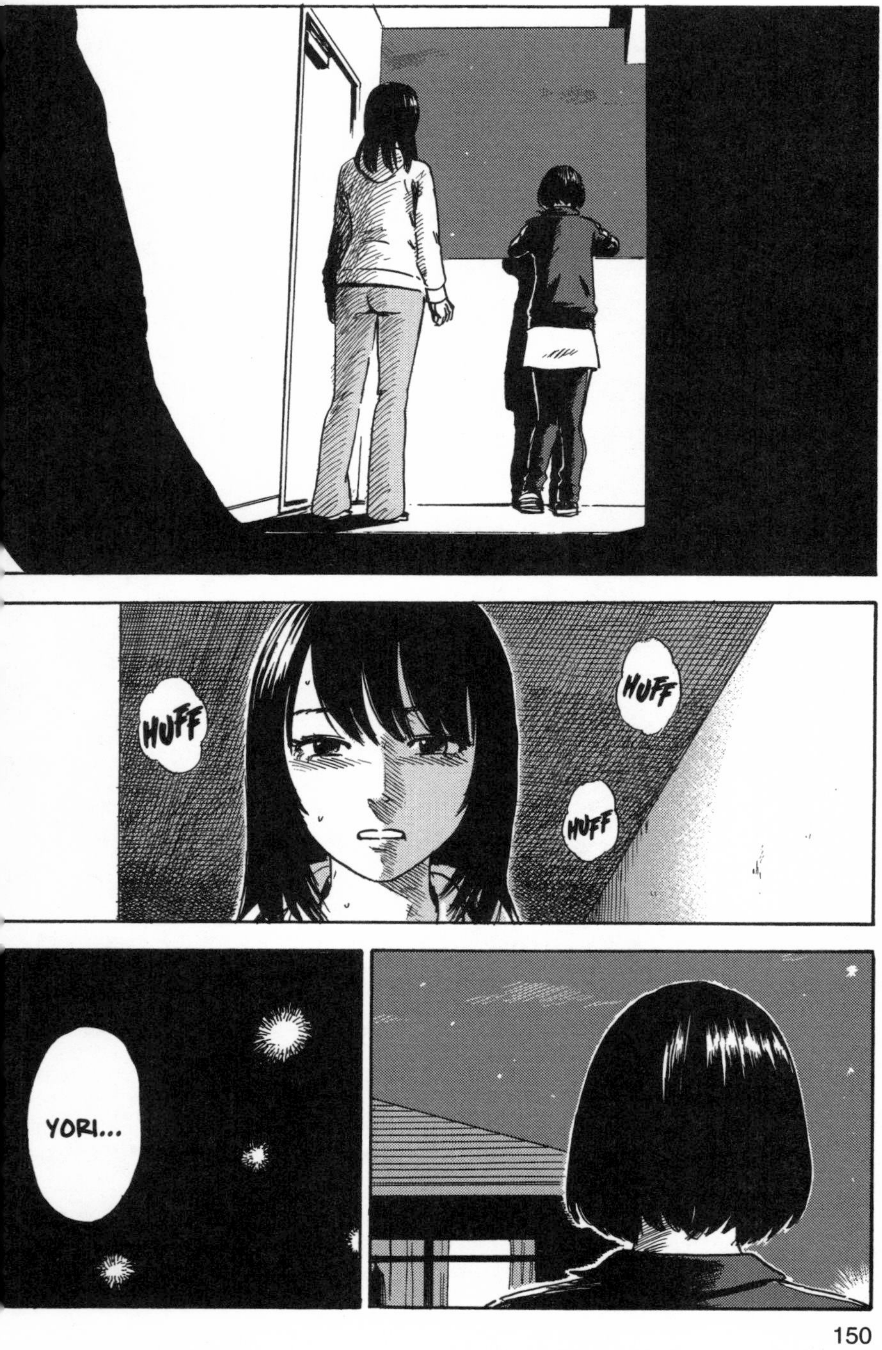
HUFF
HUFF
HUFF
YORI...

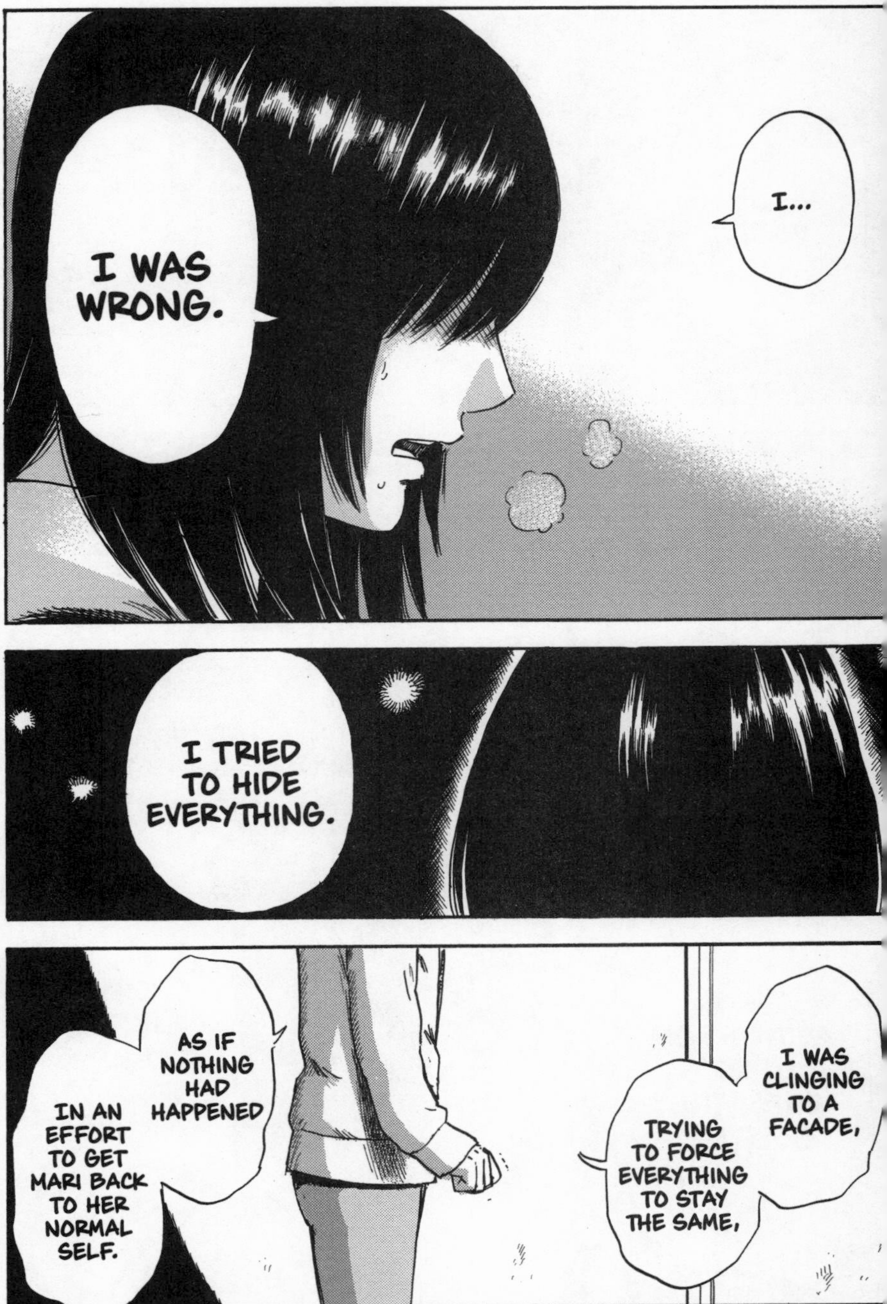
I...
I WAS WRONG.
I TRIED TO HIDE EVERYTHING.
I WAS CLINGING TO A FACADE,
TRYING TO FORCE EVERYTHING TO STAY THE SAME,
AS IF NOTHING HAD HAPPENED
IN AN EFFORT TO GET MARI BACK TO HER NORMAL SELF.

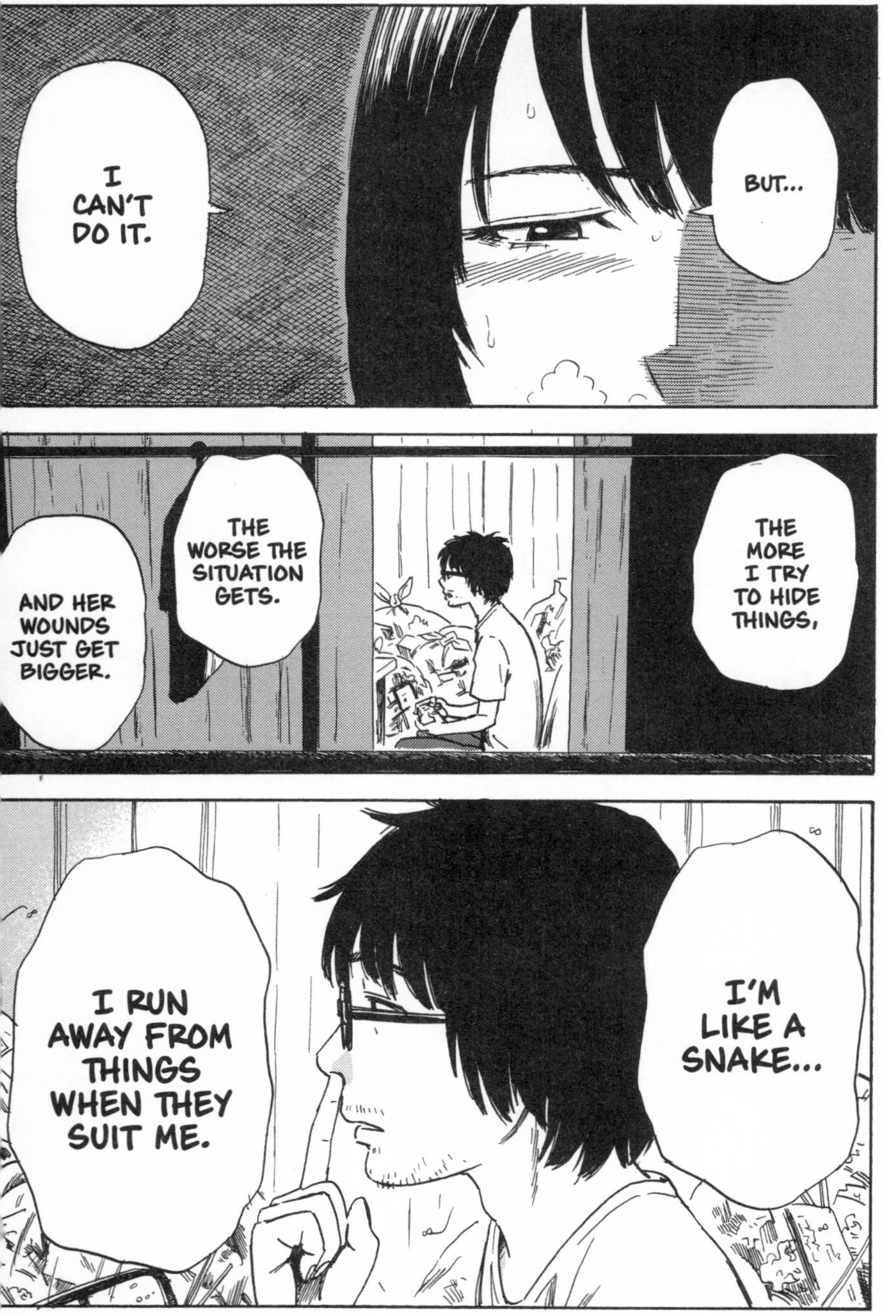
BUT...
I CAN'T DO IT.
THE MORE I TRY TO HIDE THINGS,
THE WORSE THE SITUATION GETS.
AND HER WOUNDS JUST GET BIGGER.
I'M LIKE A SNAKE...
I RUN AWAY FROM THINGS WHEN THEY SUIT ME.

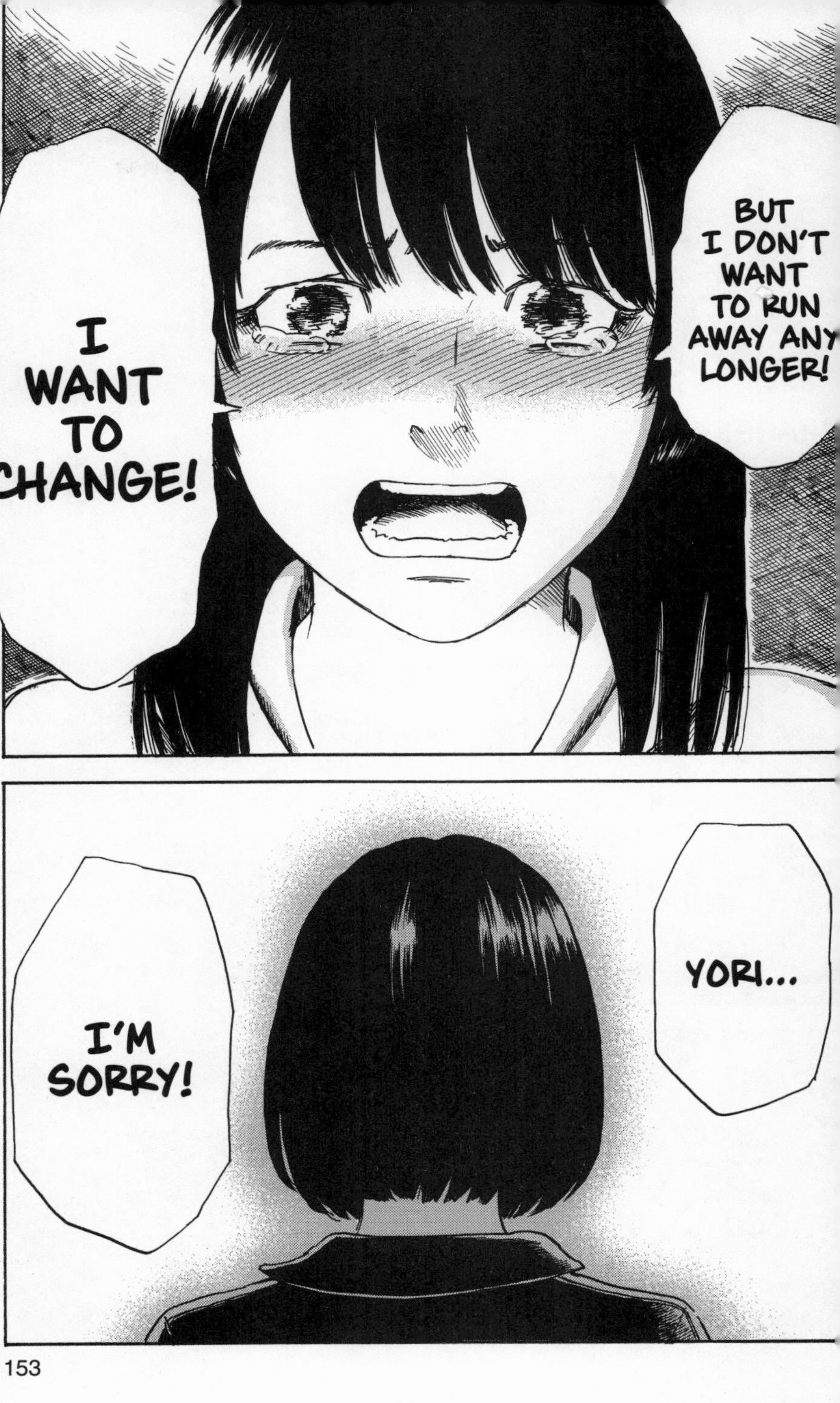
BUT I DON'T WANT TO RUN AWAY ANY LONGER!
I WANT TO CHANGE!
YORI...
I'M SORRY!

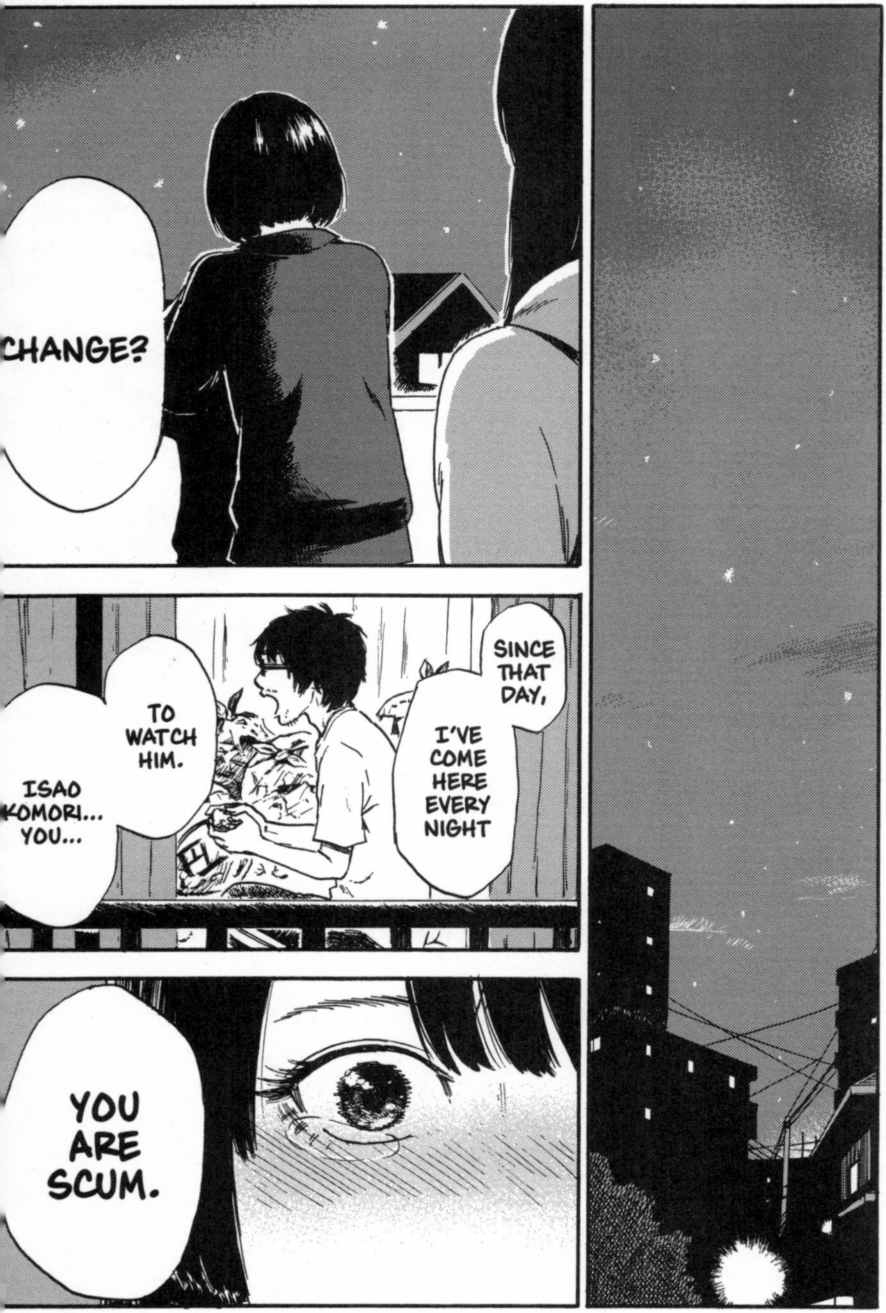
CHANGE?
SINCE THAT DAY,
I'VE COME HERE EVERY NIGHT
TO WATCH HIM.
ISAO KOMORI... YOU...
YOU ARE SCUM.

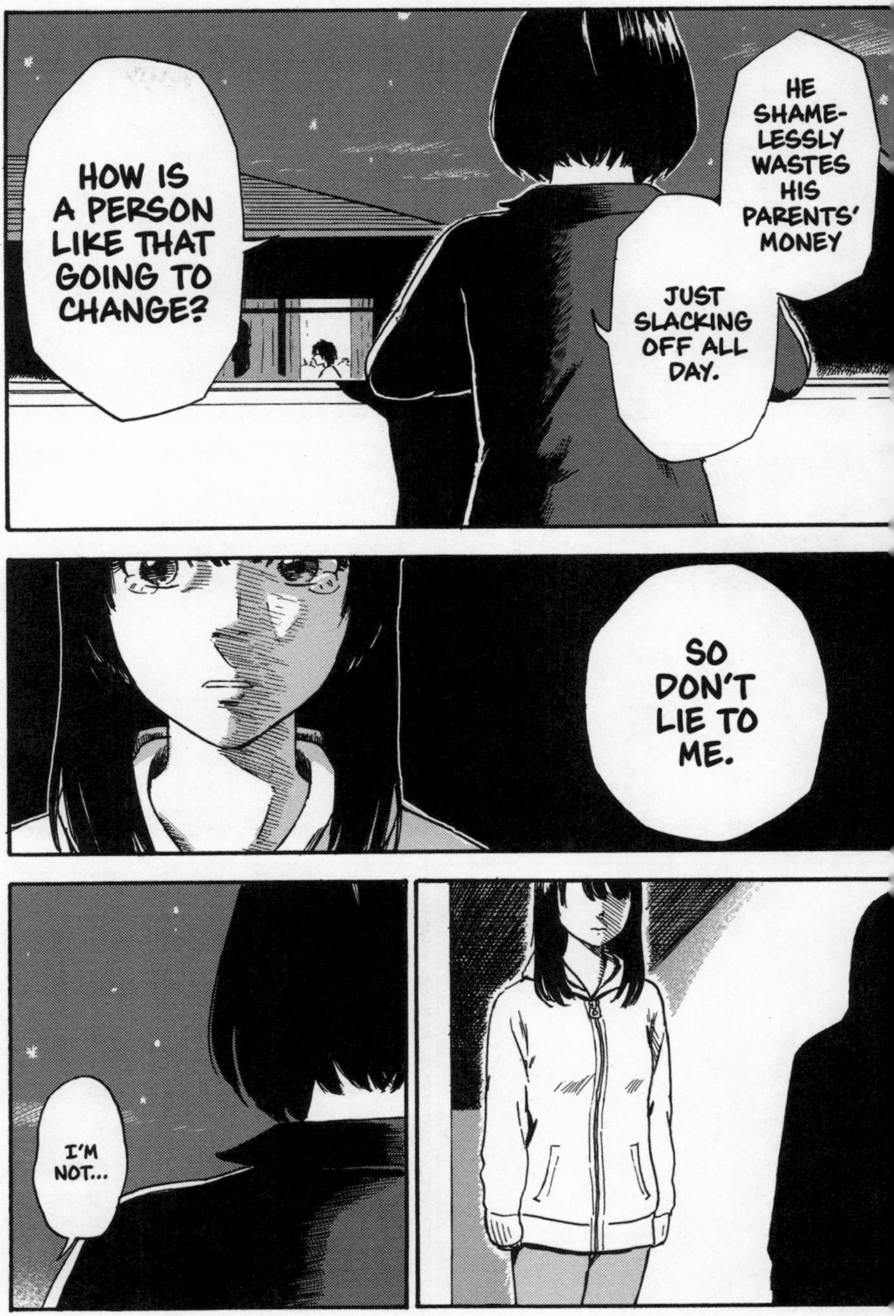
HE SHAME-LESSLY WASTES HIS PARENTS' MONEY
JUST SLACKING OFF ALL DAY.
HOW IS A PERSON LIKE THAT GOING TO CHANGE?
SO DON'T LIE TO ME.
I'M NOT...

JUST GO HOME.

WHY ARE YOU STANDING THERE?

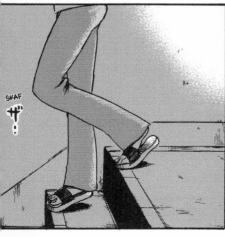

SKAF

I'M SORRY ...

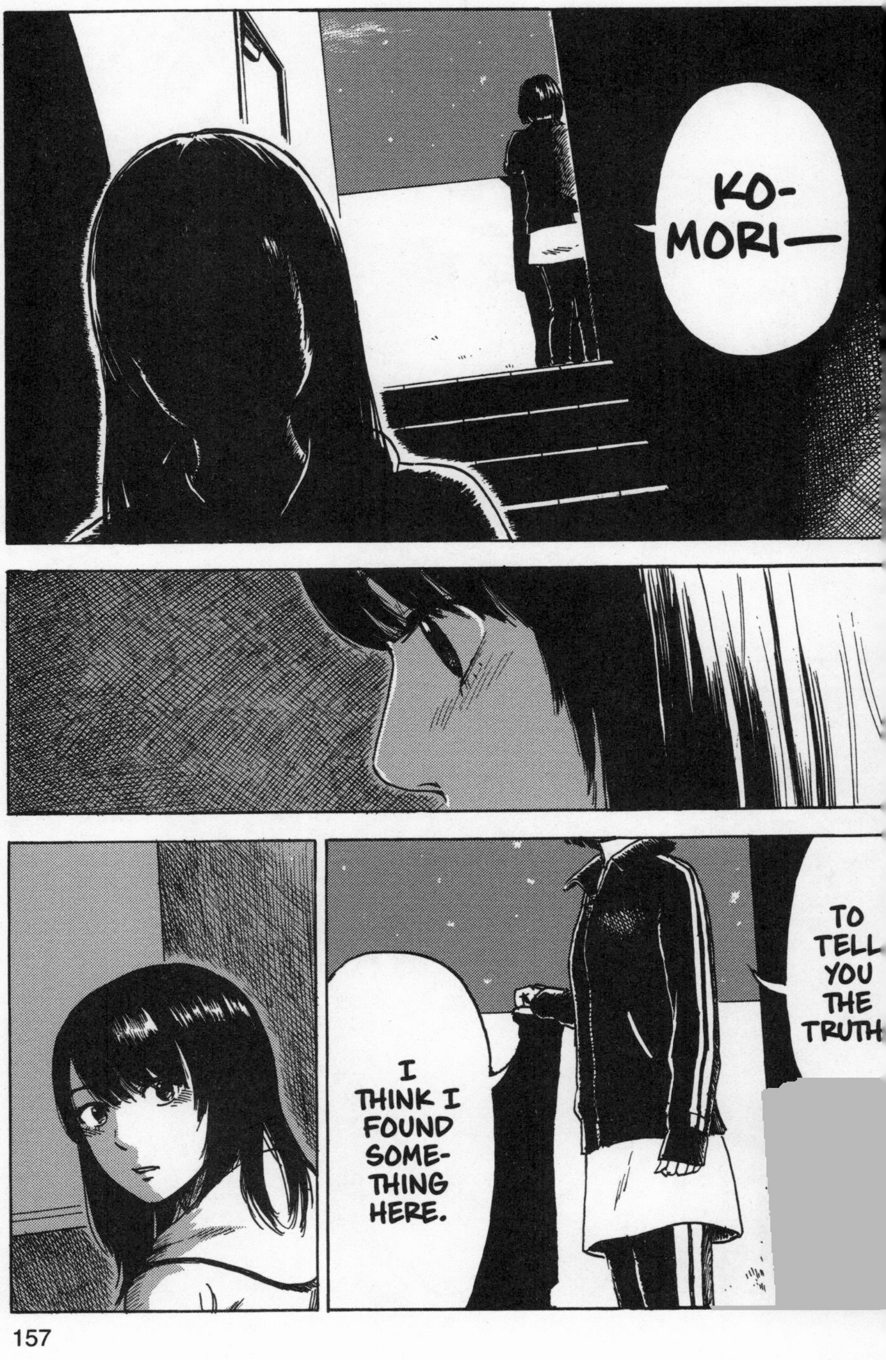
KO-MORI—
TO TELL YOU THE TRUTH
I THINK I FOUND SOME-THING HERE.

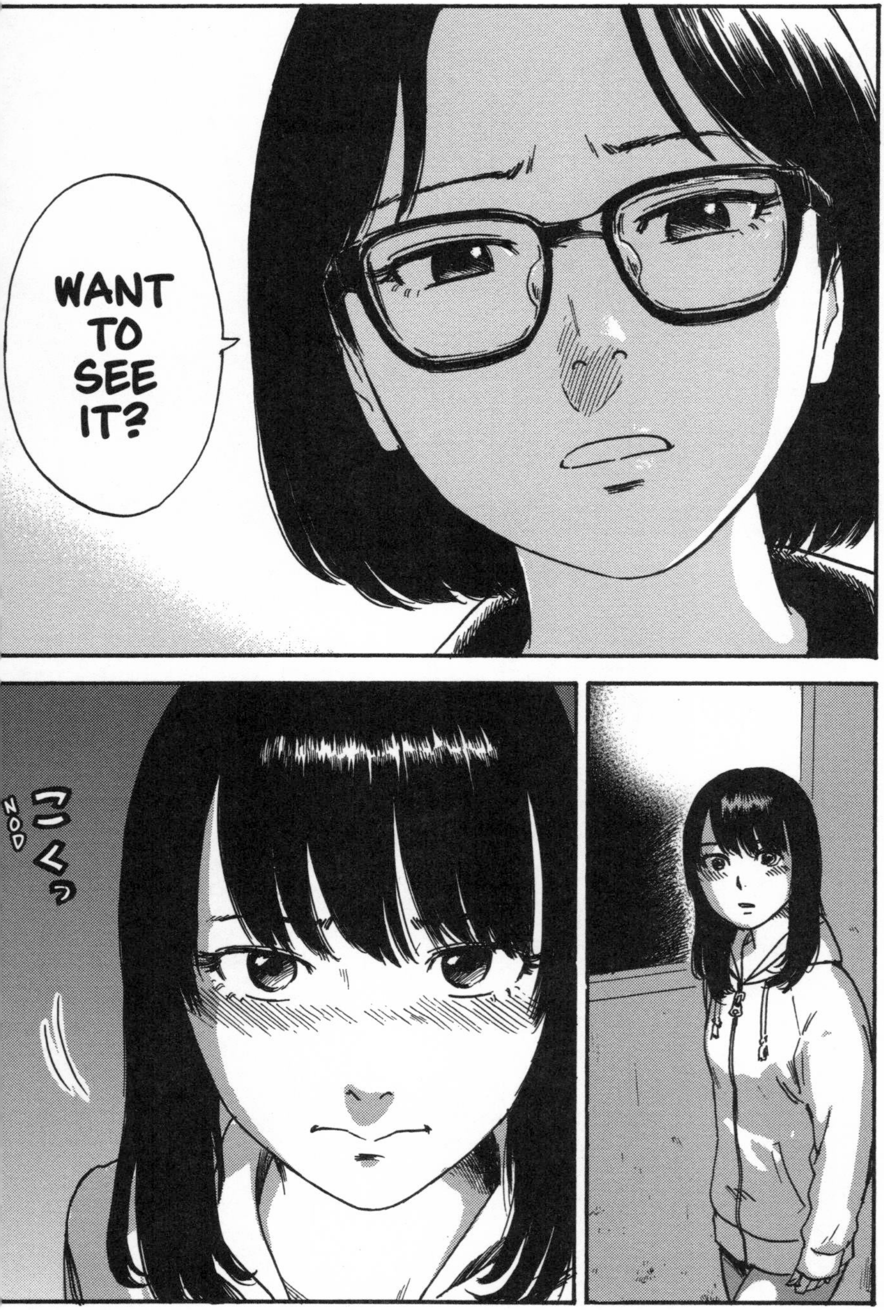
WANT TO SEE IT?
こくっ
NOD

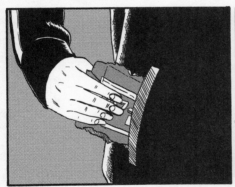

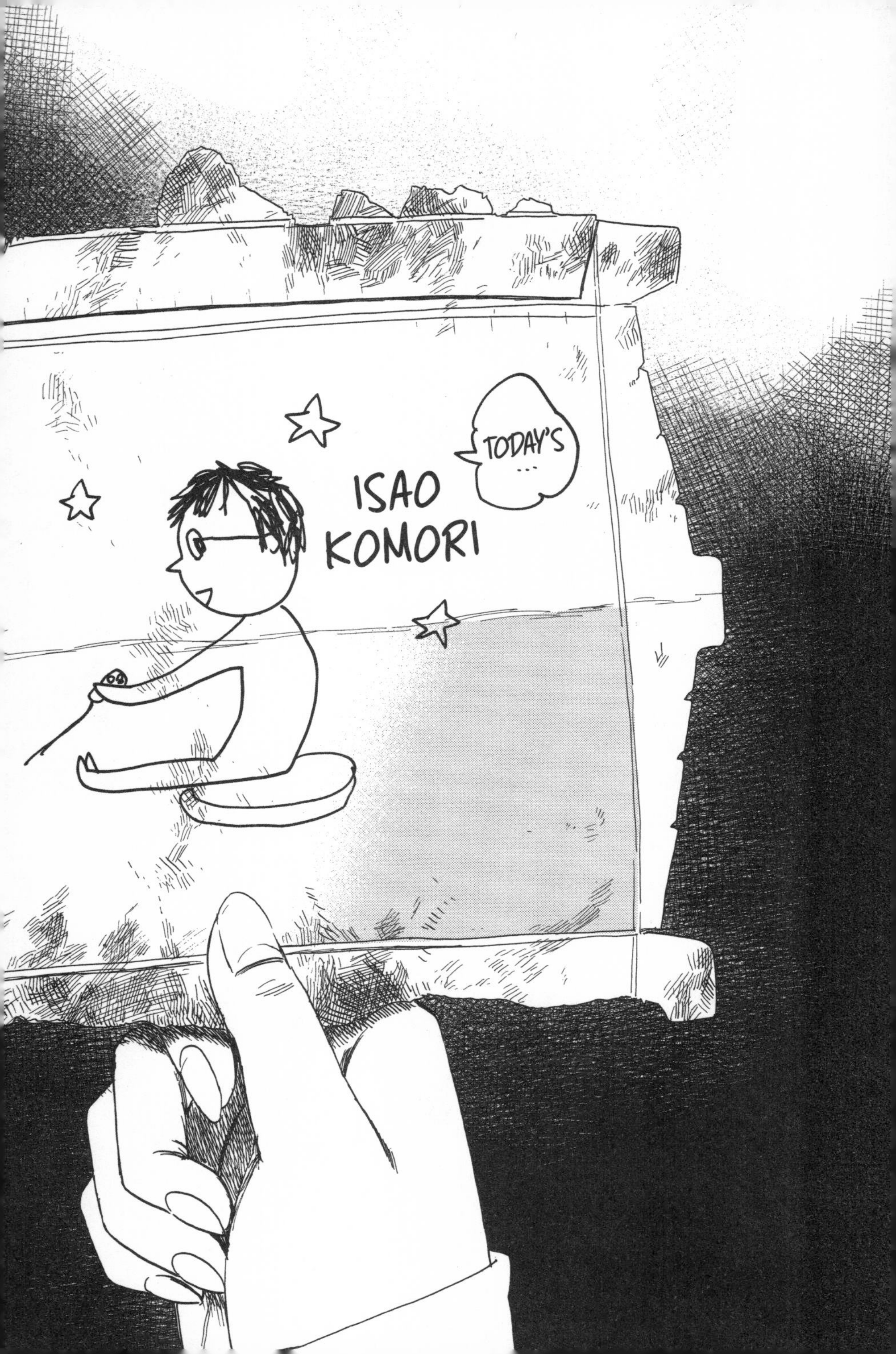
TODAY'S ...
ISAO KOMORI

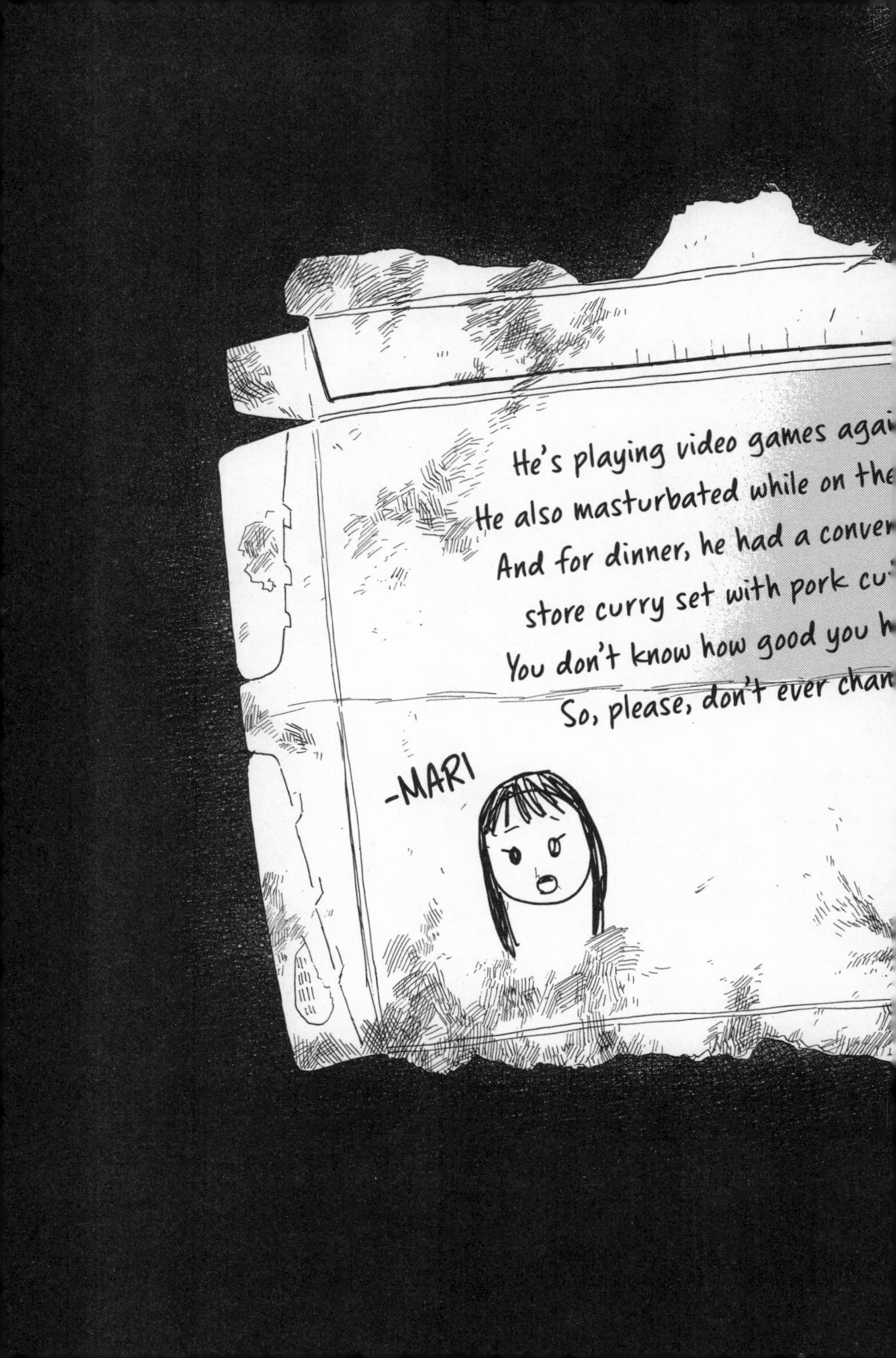
He's playing video games agai
He also masturbated while on the
And for dinner, he had a conver
store curry set with pork cu
You don't know how good you h
So, please, don't ever chan
-MARI

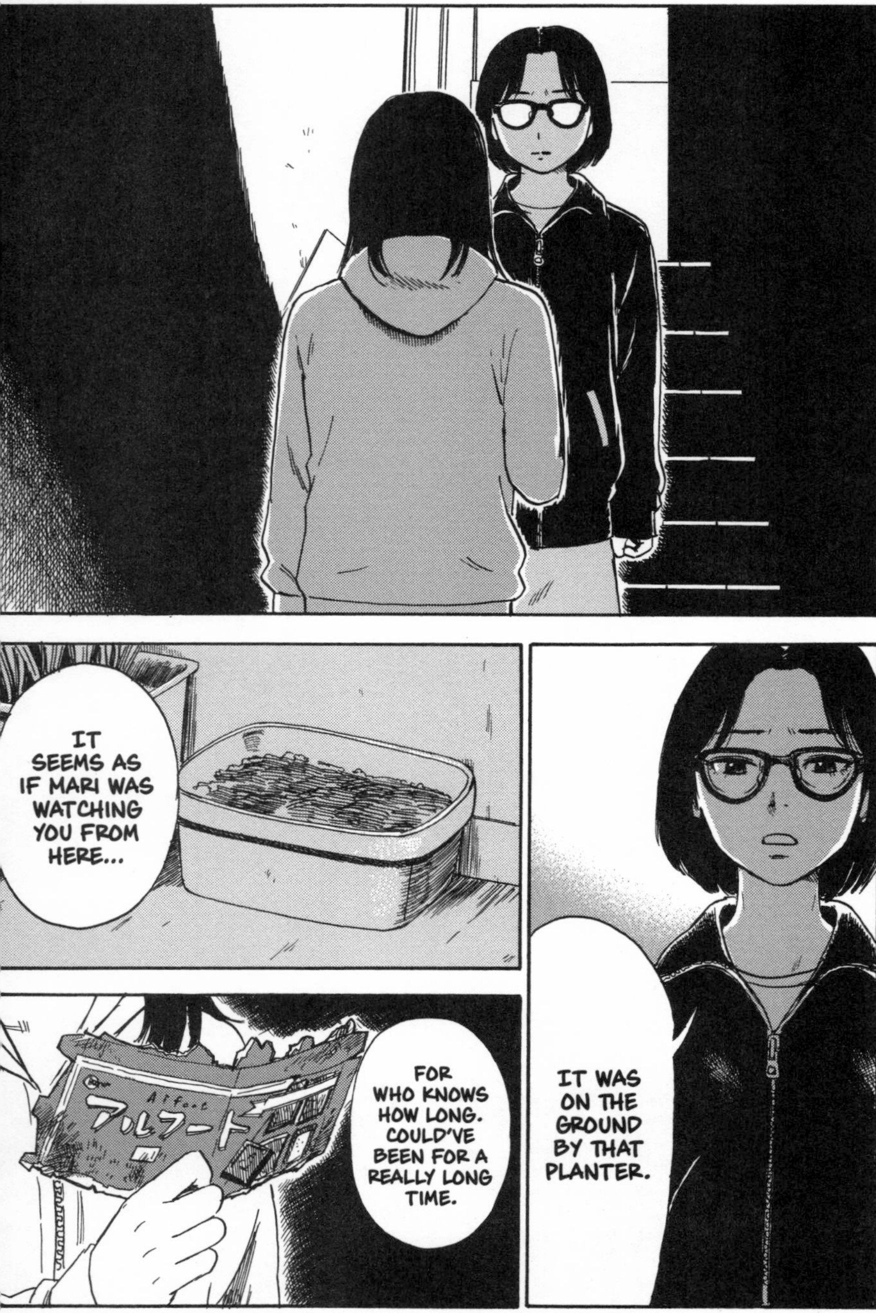
IT WAS ON THE GROUND BY THAT PLANTER.
IT SEEMS AS IF MARI WAS WATCHING YOU FROM HERE...
FOR WHO KNOWS HOW LONG. COULD'VE BEEN FOR A REALLY LONG TIME.

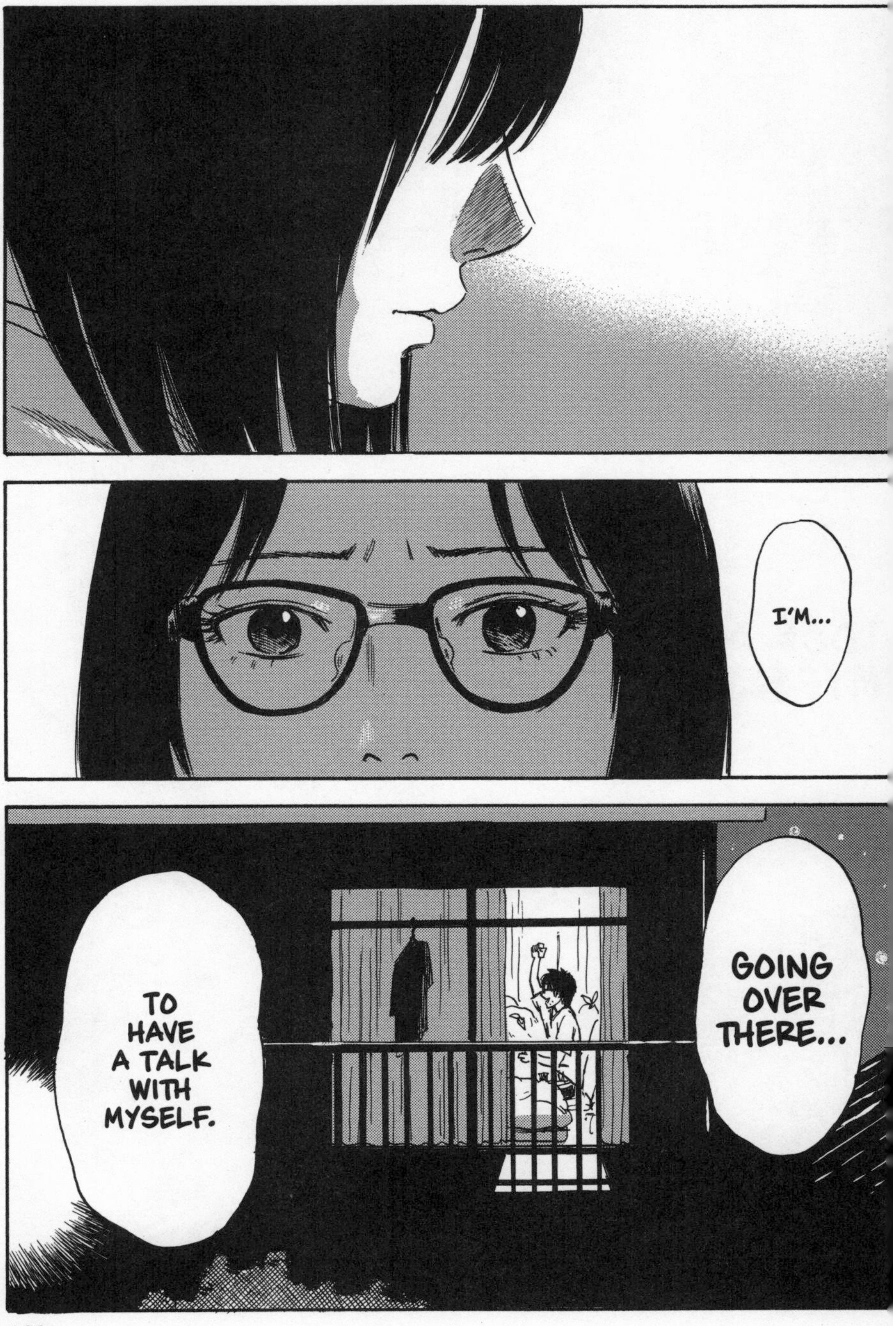
I'M...
GOING OVER THERE...
TO HAVE A TALK WITH MYSELF.

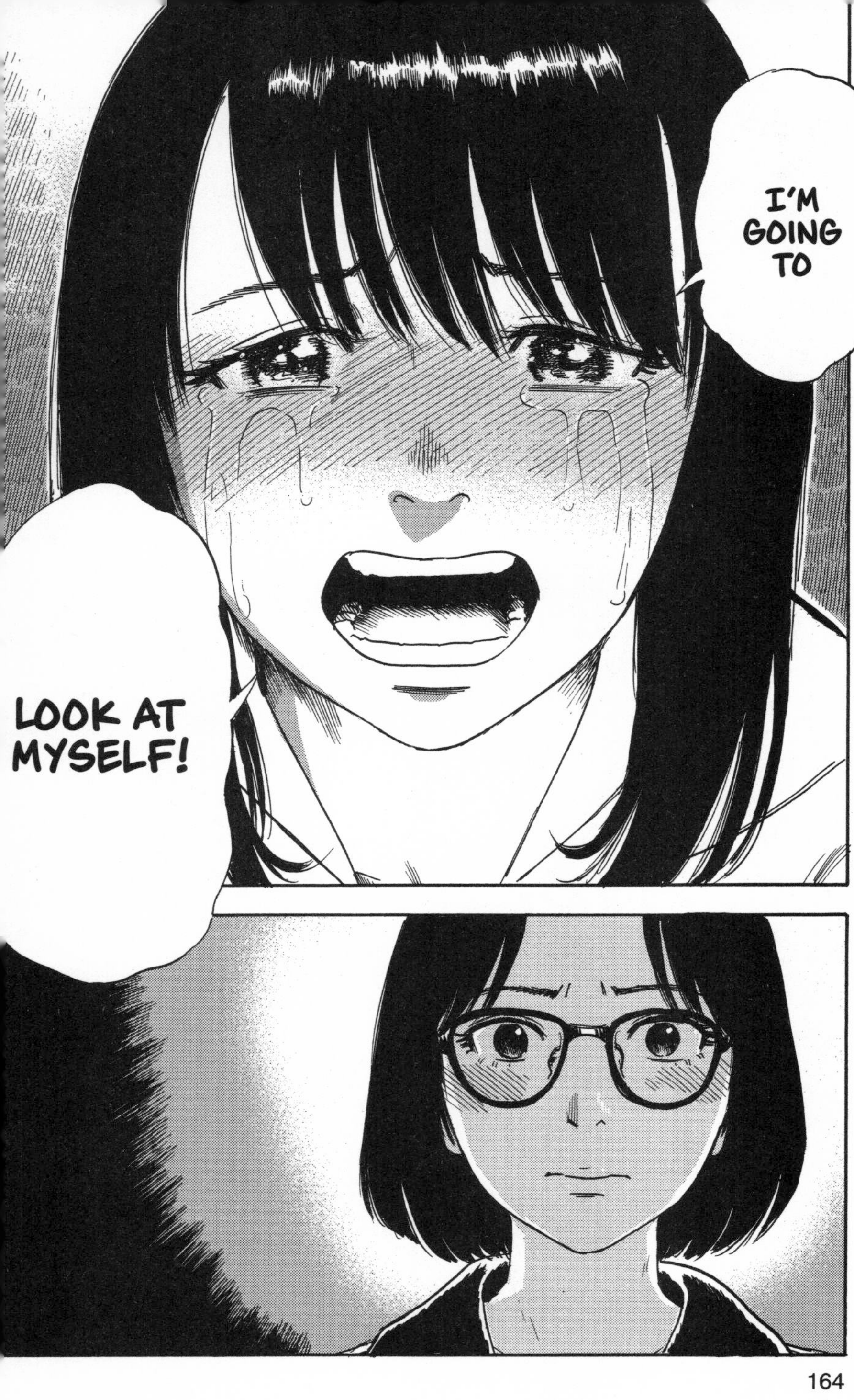
I'M GOING TO
LOOK AT MYSELF!

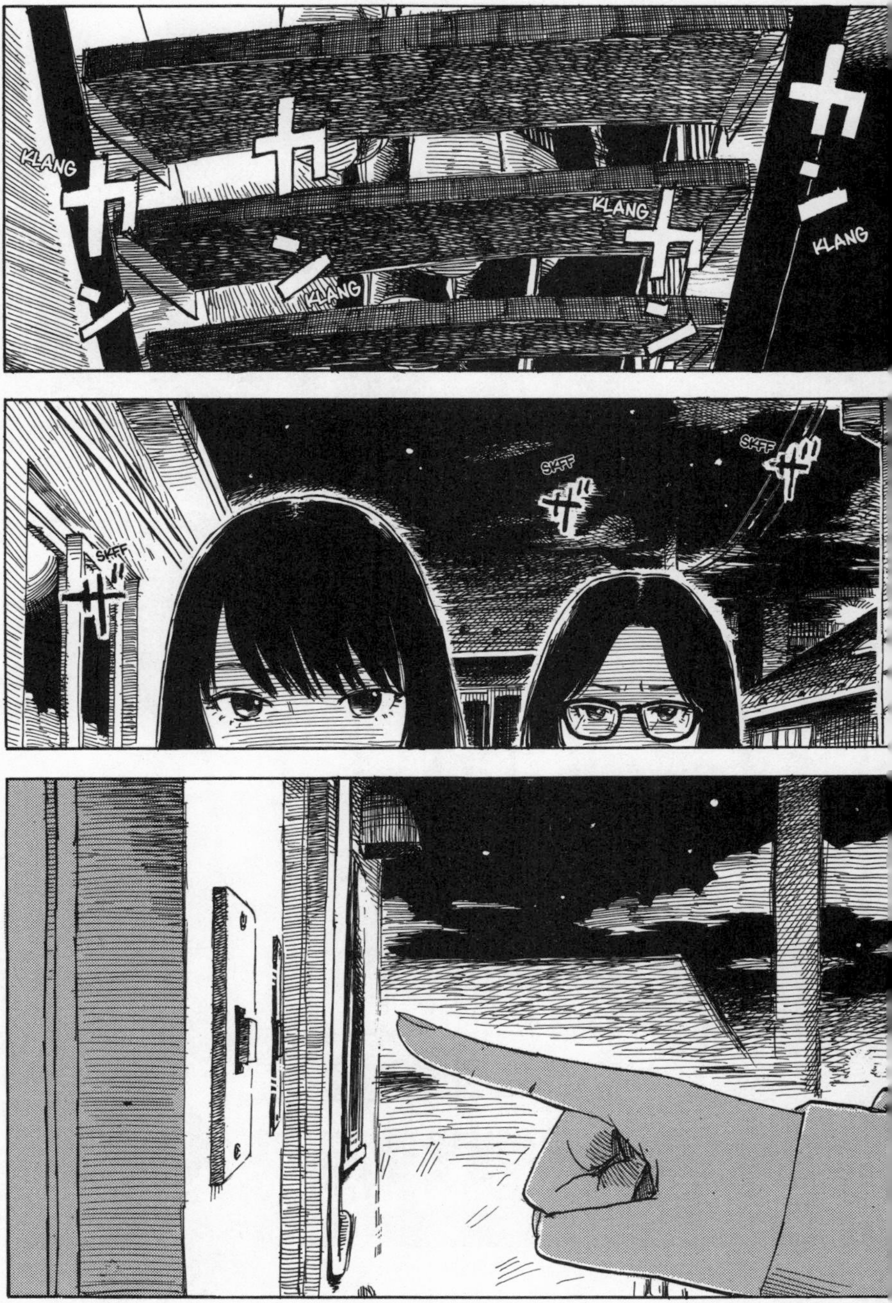
カーン
KLANG
カーン
KLANG
KLANG
カーン
KLANG
SKFF
SKFF
SKFF

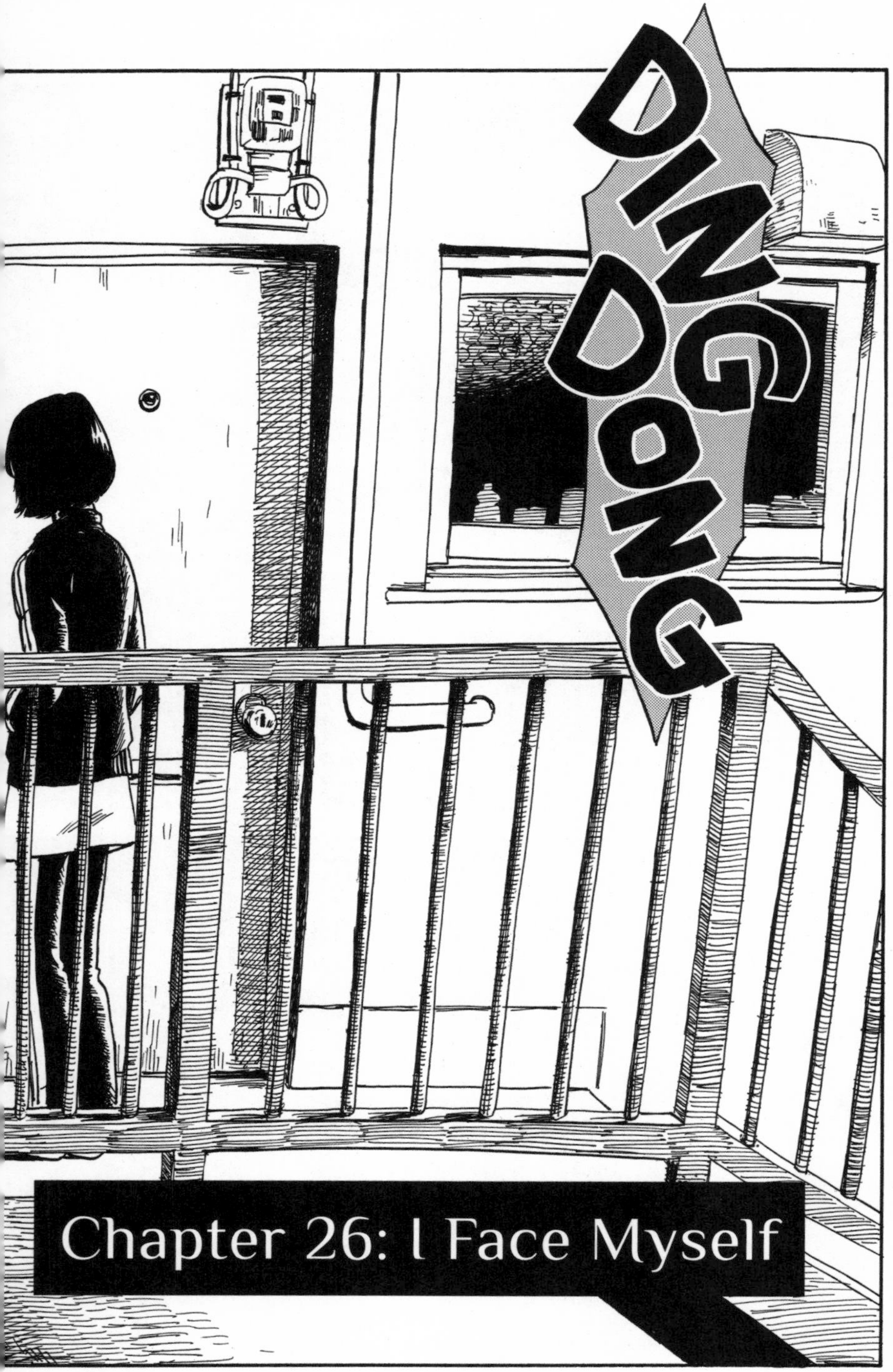
DING DONG
Chapter 26: I Face Myself

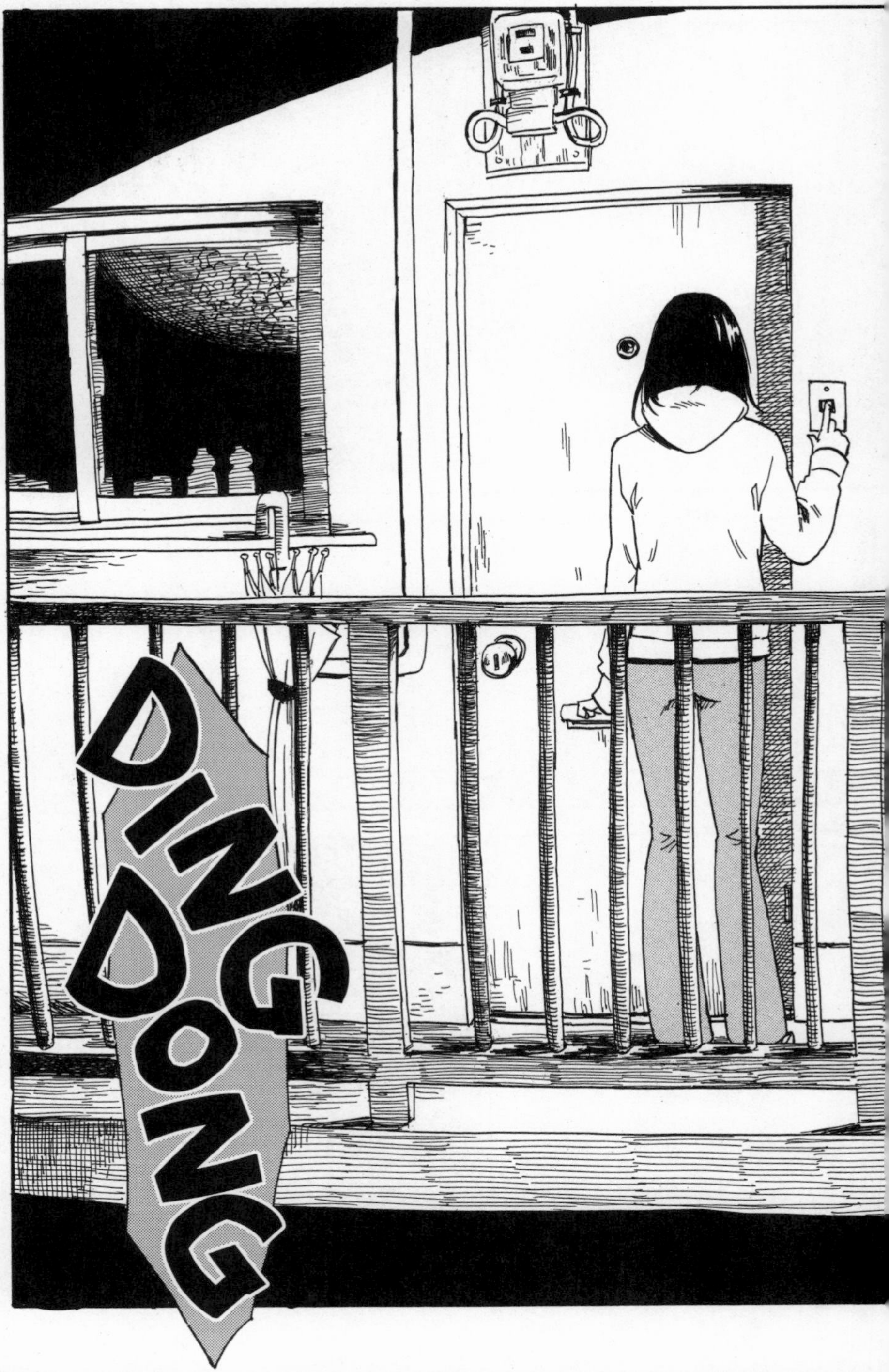
DING DONG

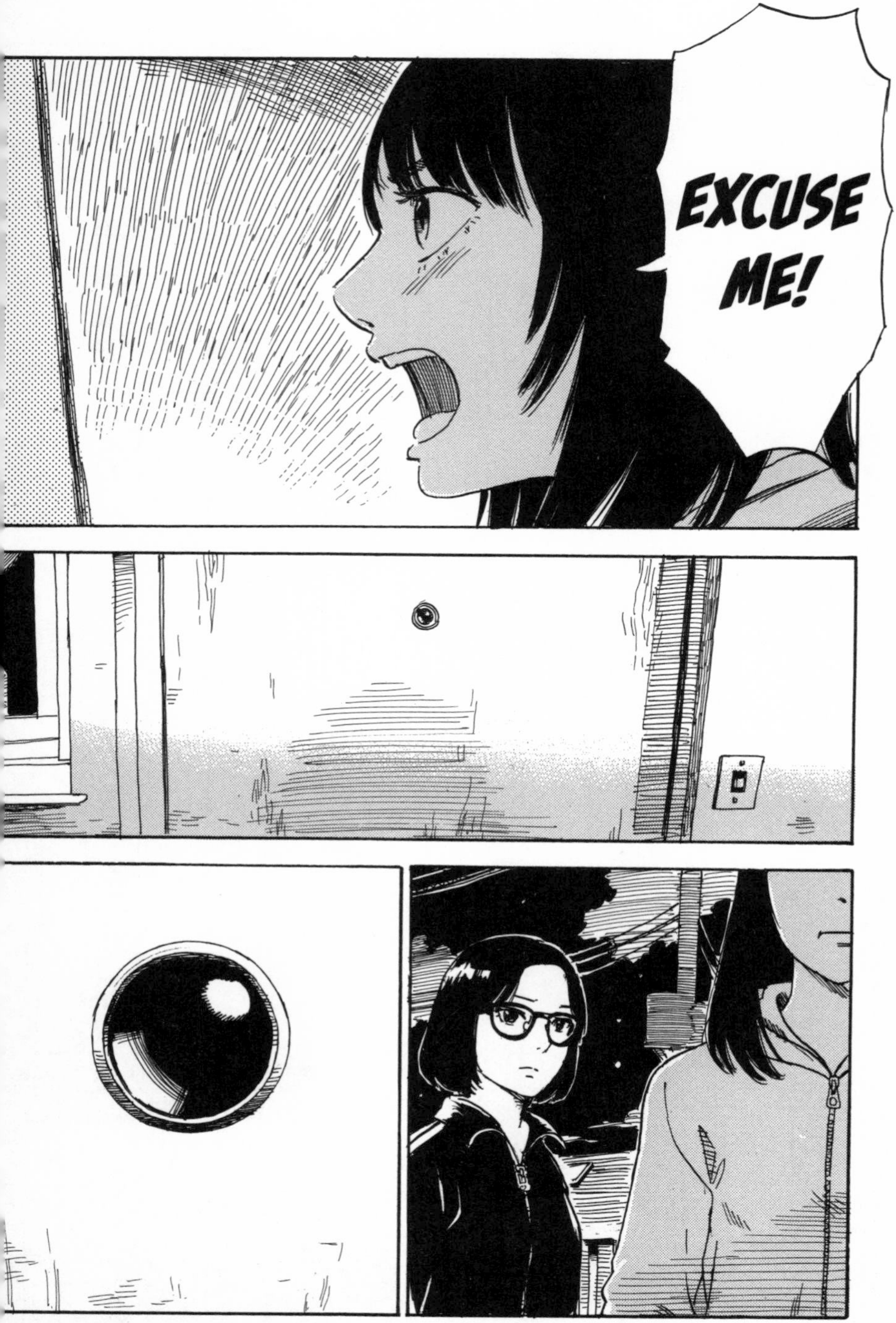
EXCUSE ME!

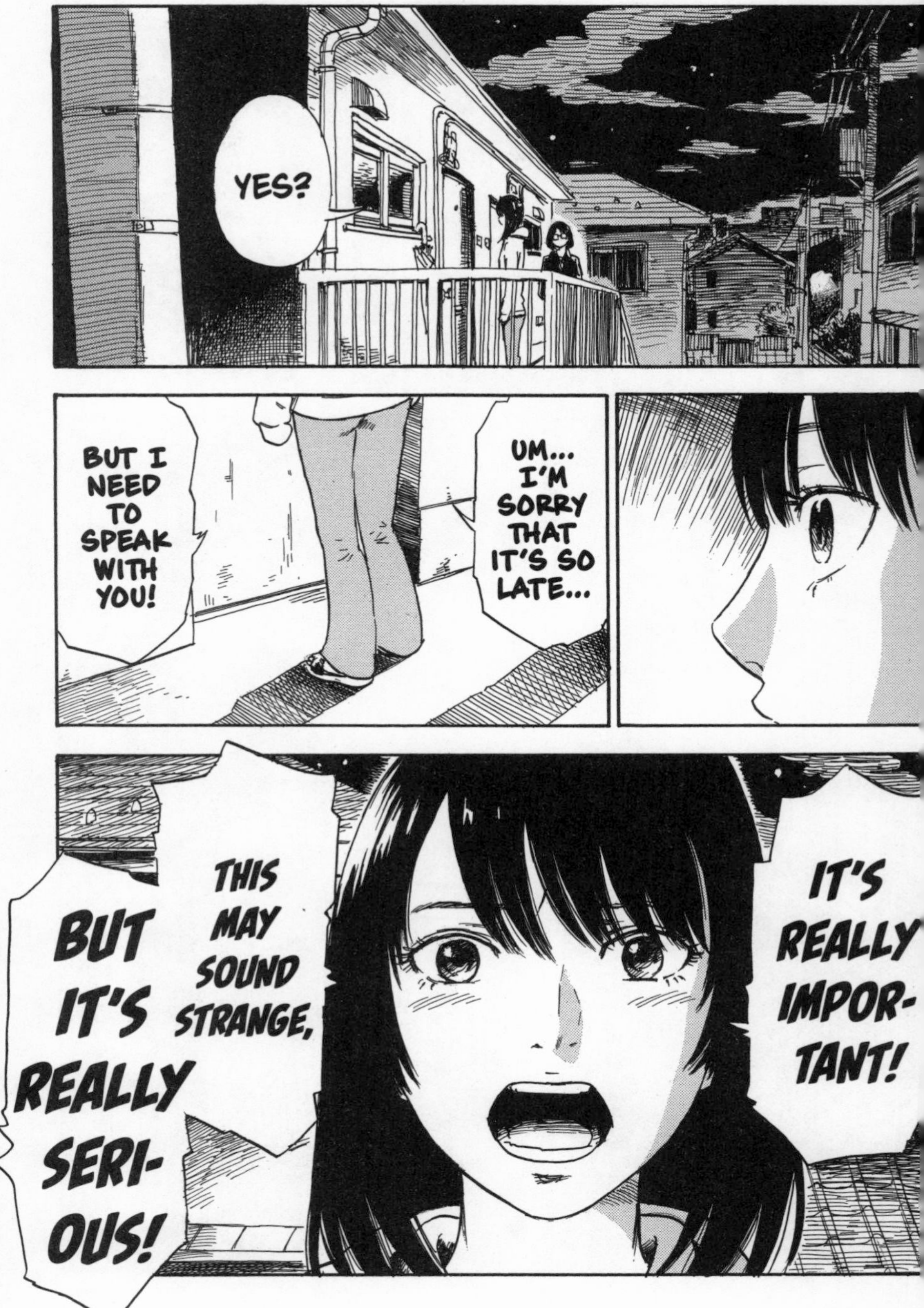
YES?
UM... I'M SORRY THAT IT'S SO LATE...
BUT I NEED TO SPEAK WITH YOU!
IT'S REALLY IMPOR-TANT!
THIS MAY SOUND STRANGE,
BUT IT'S REALLY SERI-OUS!

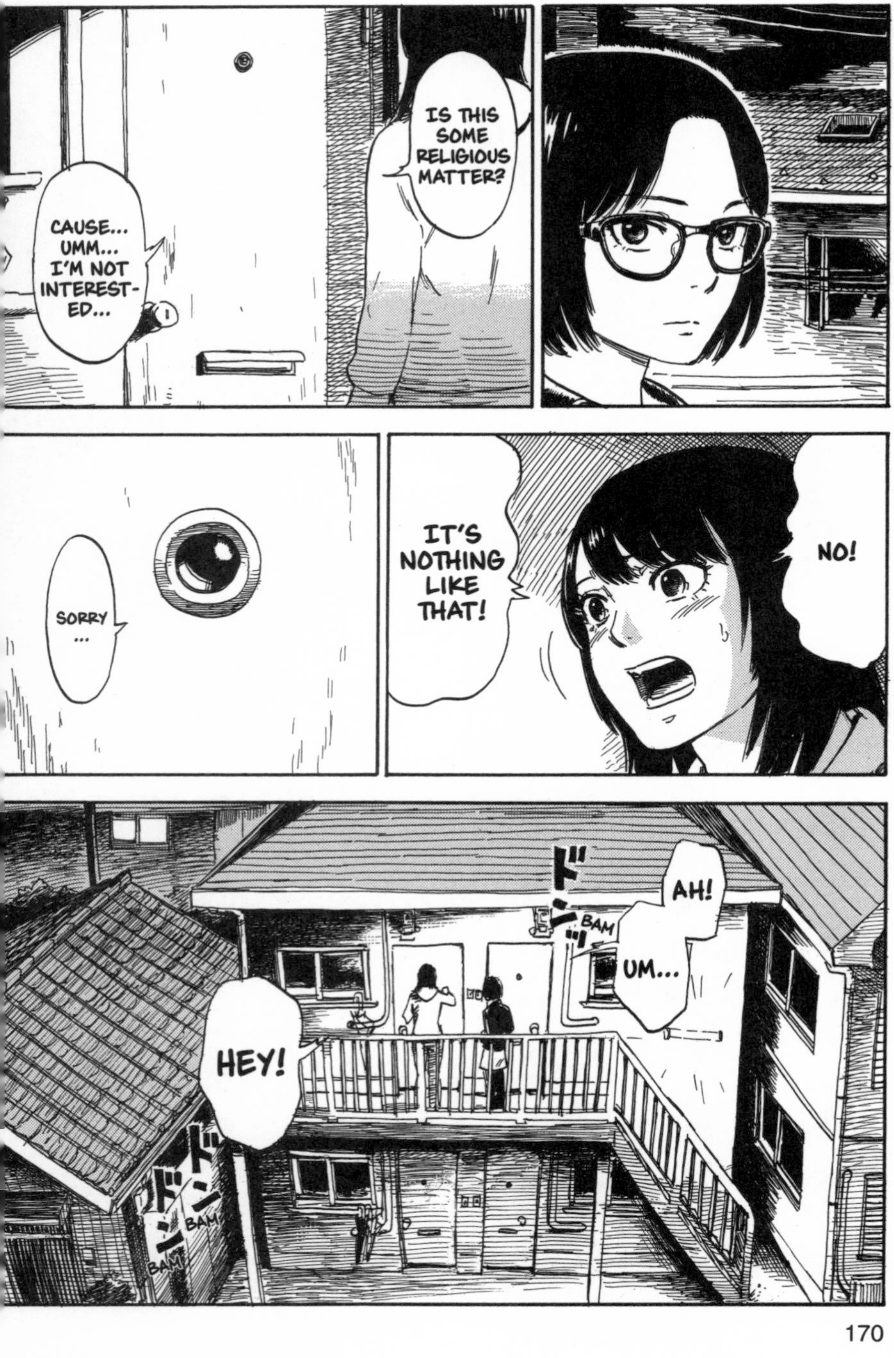
IS THIS SOME RELIGIOUS MATTER?
CAUSE... UMM... I'M NOT INTEREST-ED...
NO!
IT'S NOTHING LIKE THAT!
SORRY ...
AH!
BAM
UM...
HEY!
BAM
BAM

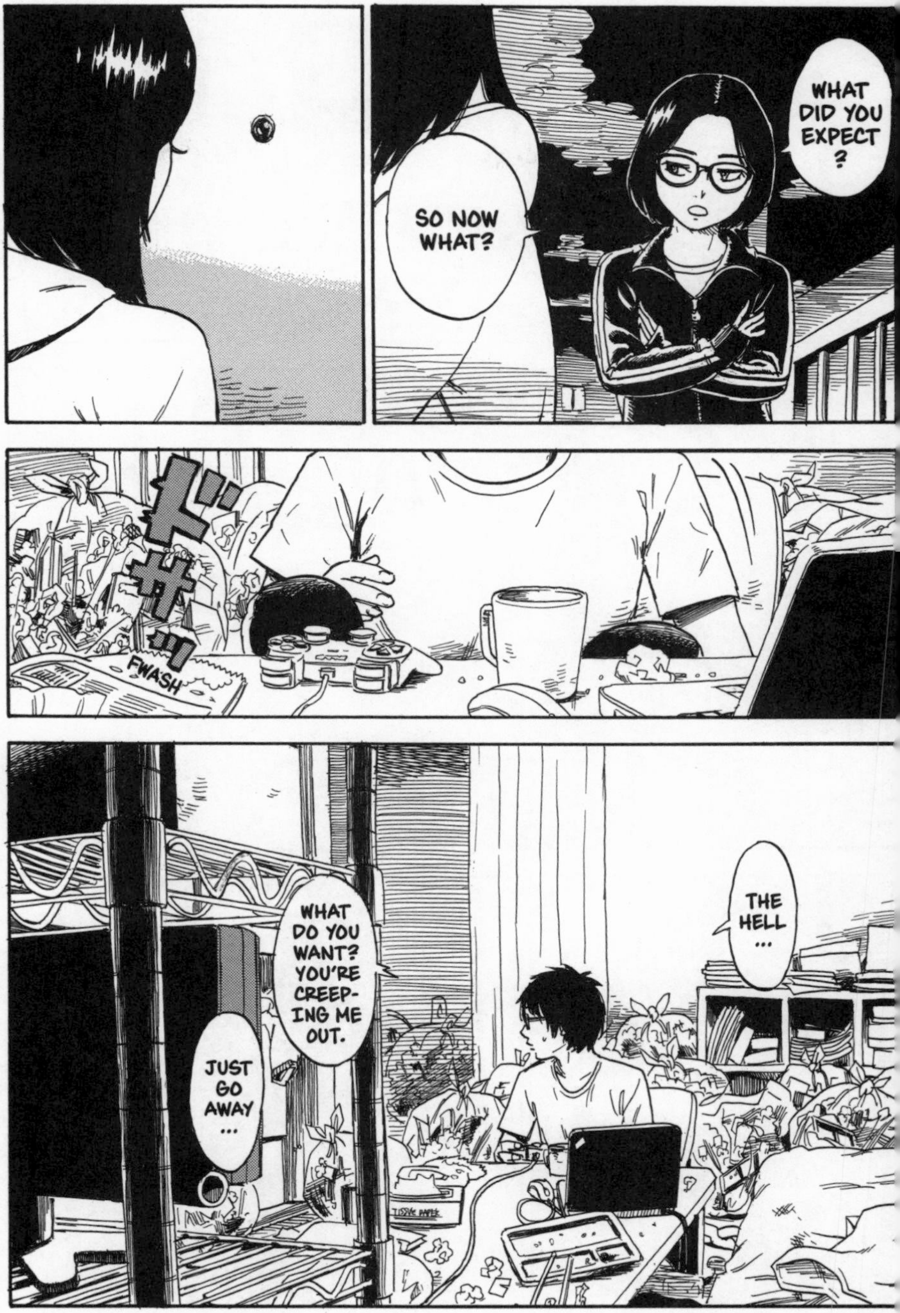
WHAT DID YOU EXPECT ?
SO NOW WHAT?
ドサッ
FWASH
THE HELL ...
WHAT DO YOU WANT? YOU'RE CREEP-ING ME OUT.
JUST GO AWAY ...

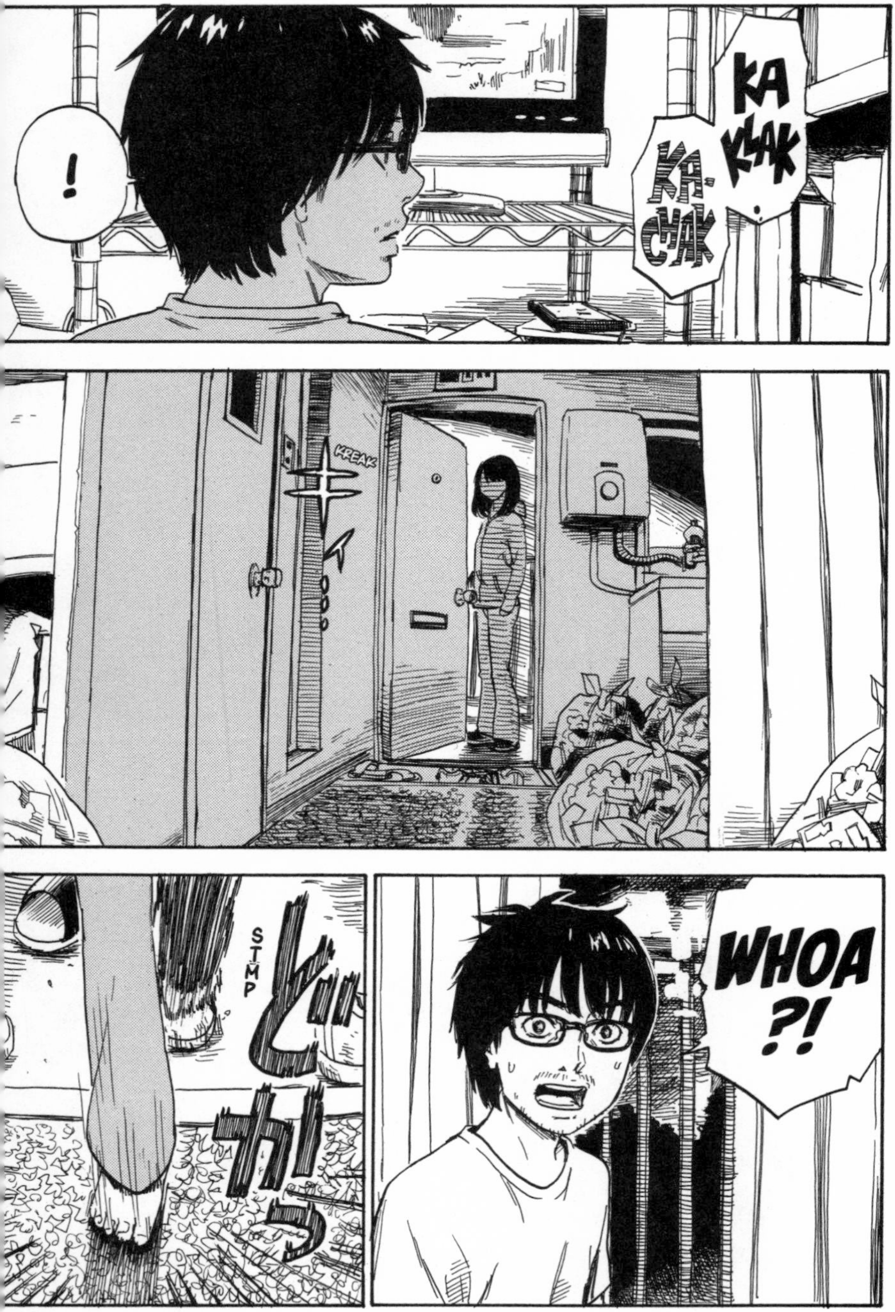
KA KLAK
KA-CHAK
!
KREAK
WHOA ?!
STMP

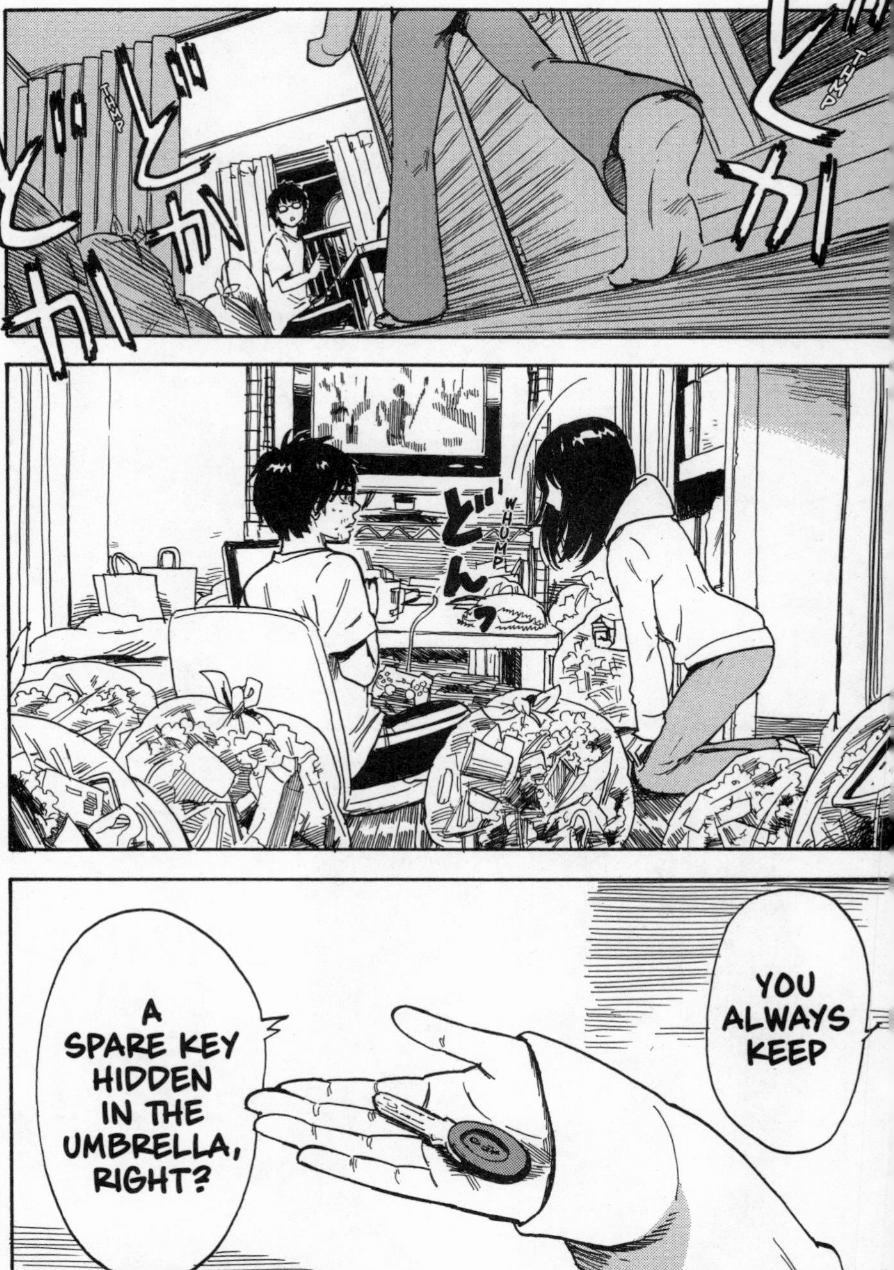
THMP
THMP
THMP
どん
WHUMP
YOU ALWAYS KEEP
A SPARE KEY HIDDEN IN THE UMBRELLA, RIGHT?

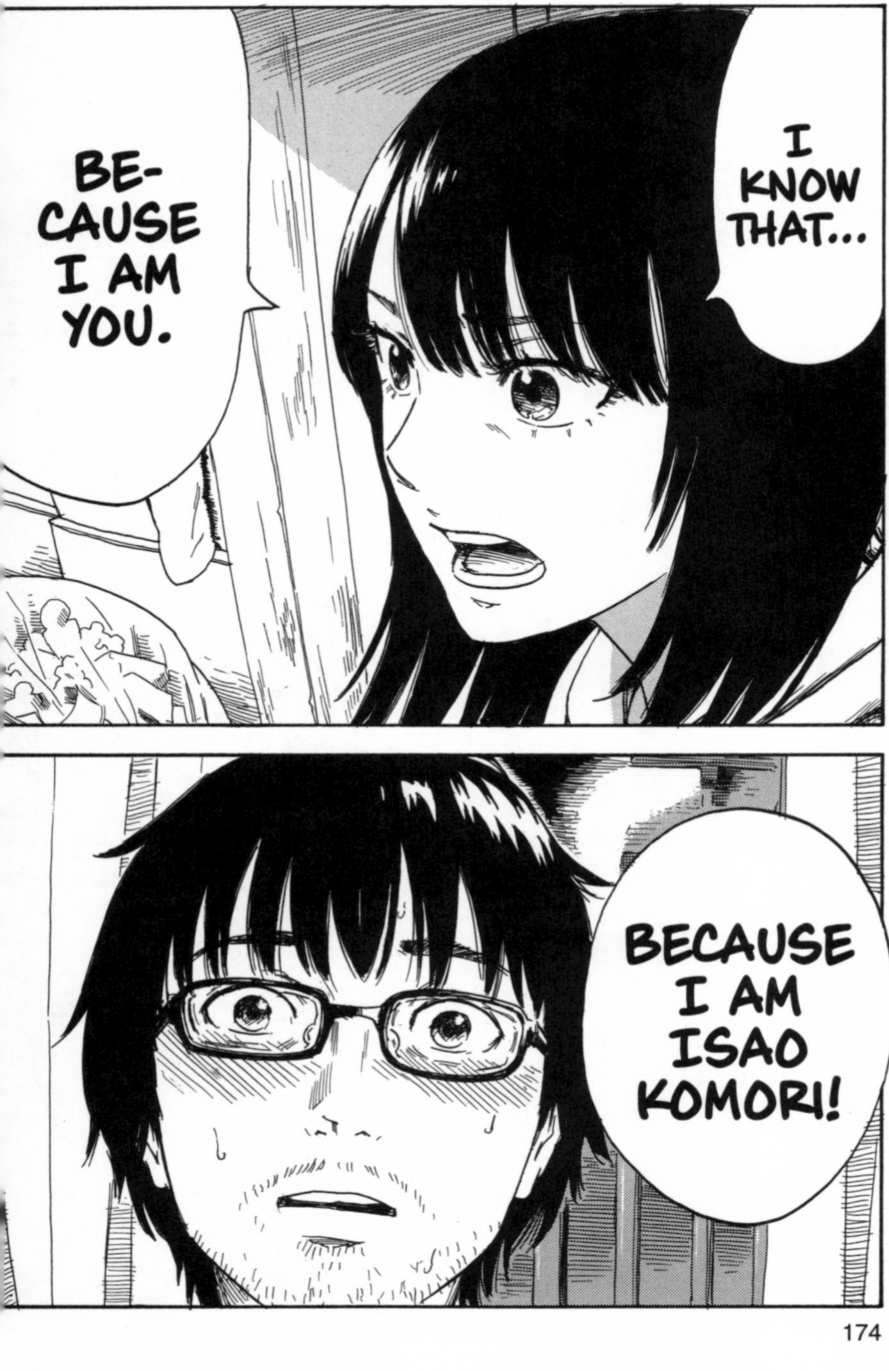
I KNOW THAT...
BE-CAUSE I AM YOU.
BECAUSE I AM ISAO KOMORI!

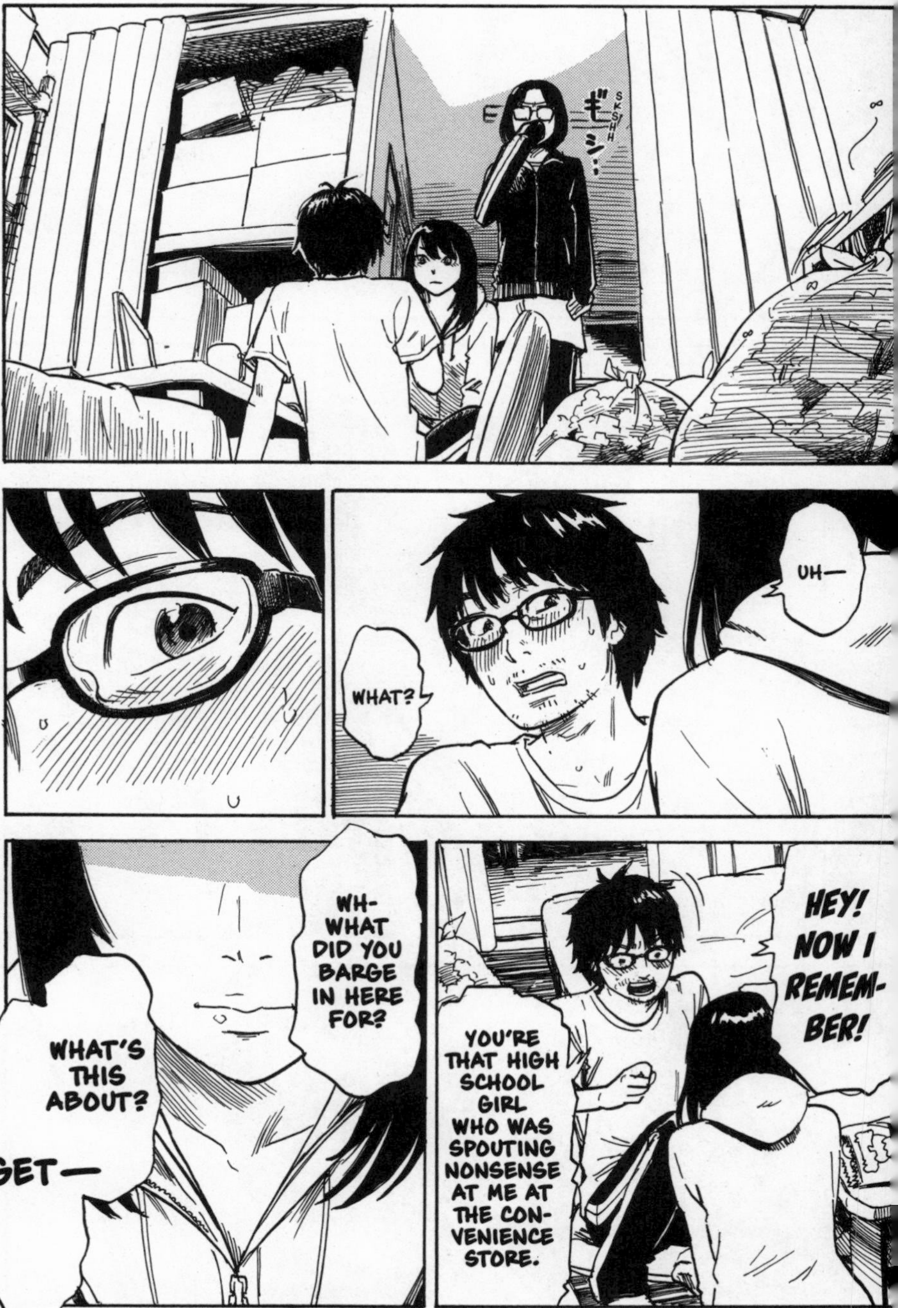
ギシ…
SKSHH
UH—
WHAT?
HEY! NOW I REMEMBER!
YOU'RE THAT HIGH SCHOOL GIRL WHO WAS SPOUTING NONSENSE AT ME AT THE CONVENIENCE STORE.
WH-WHAT DID YOU BARGE IN HERE FOR?
WHAT'S THIS ABOUT?
GET—

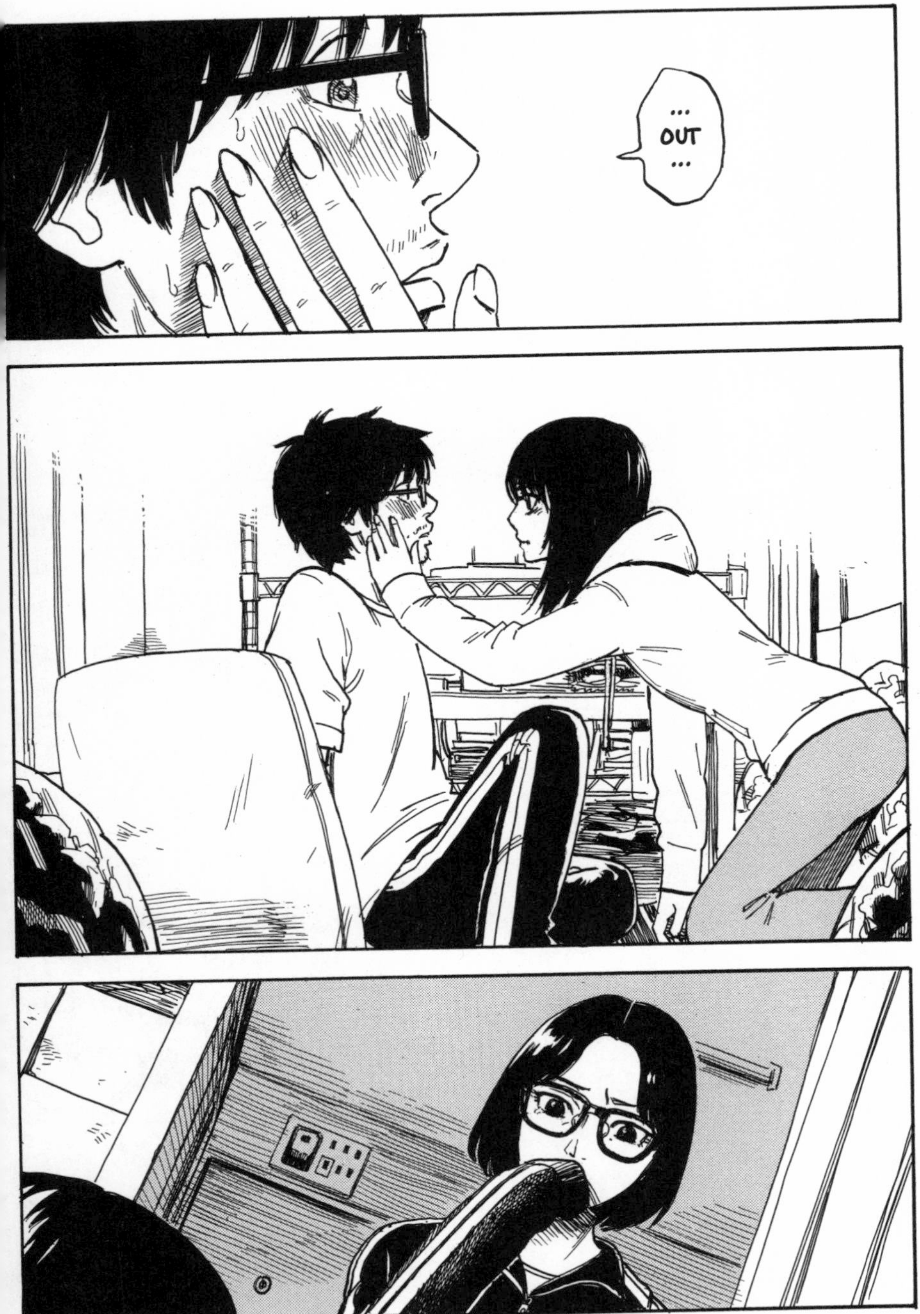
... OUT ...

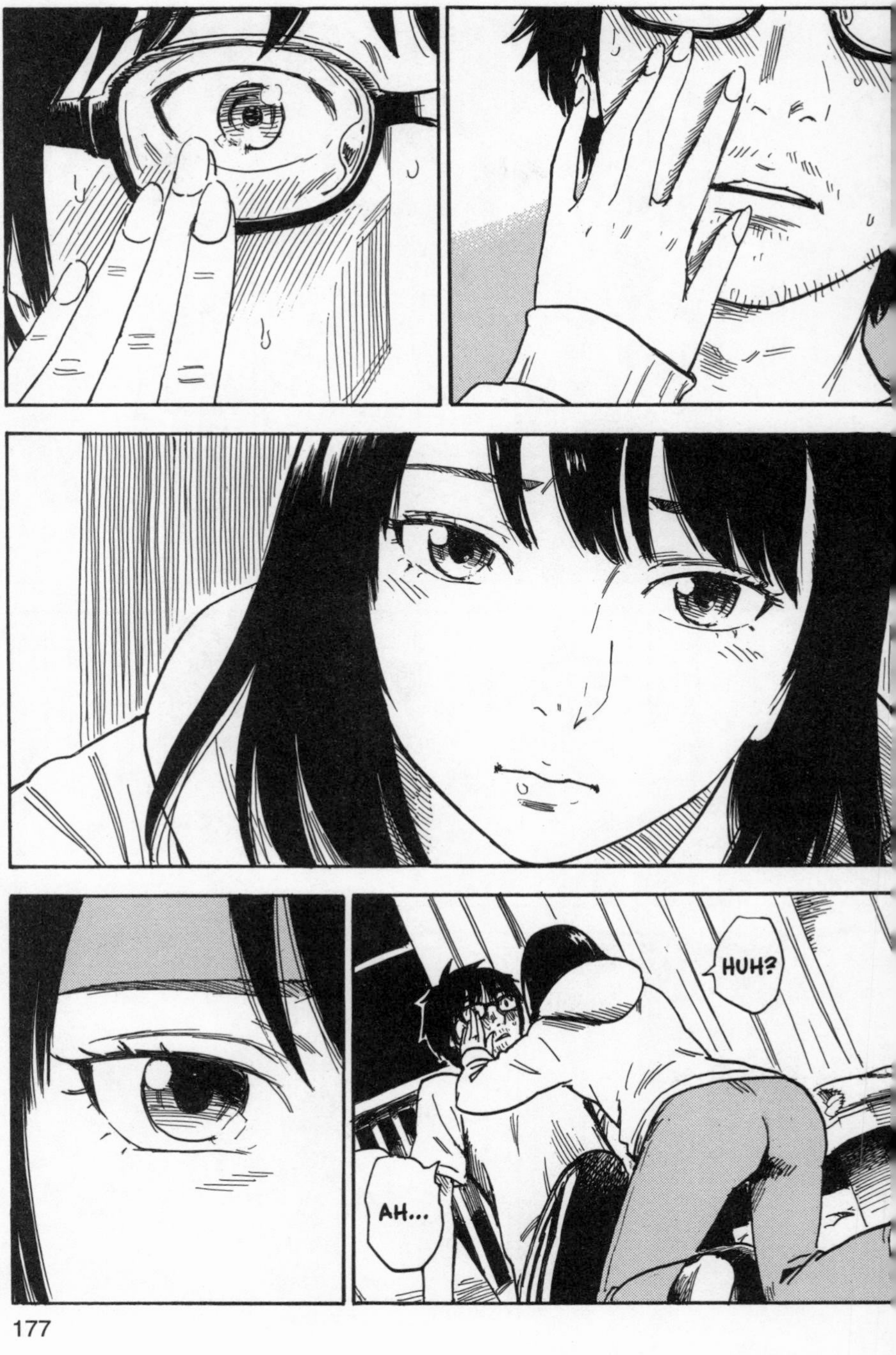
HUH?
AH...

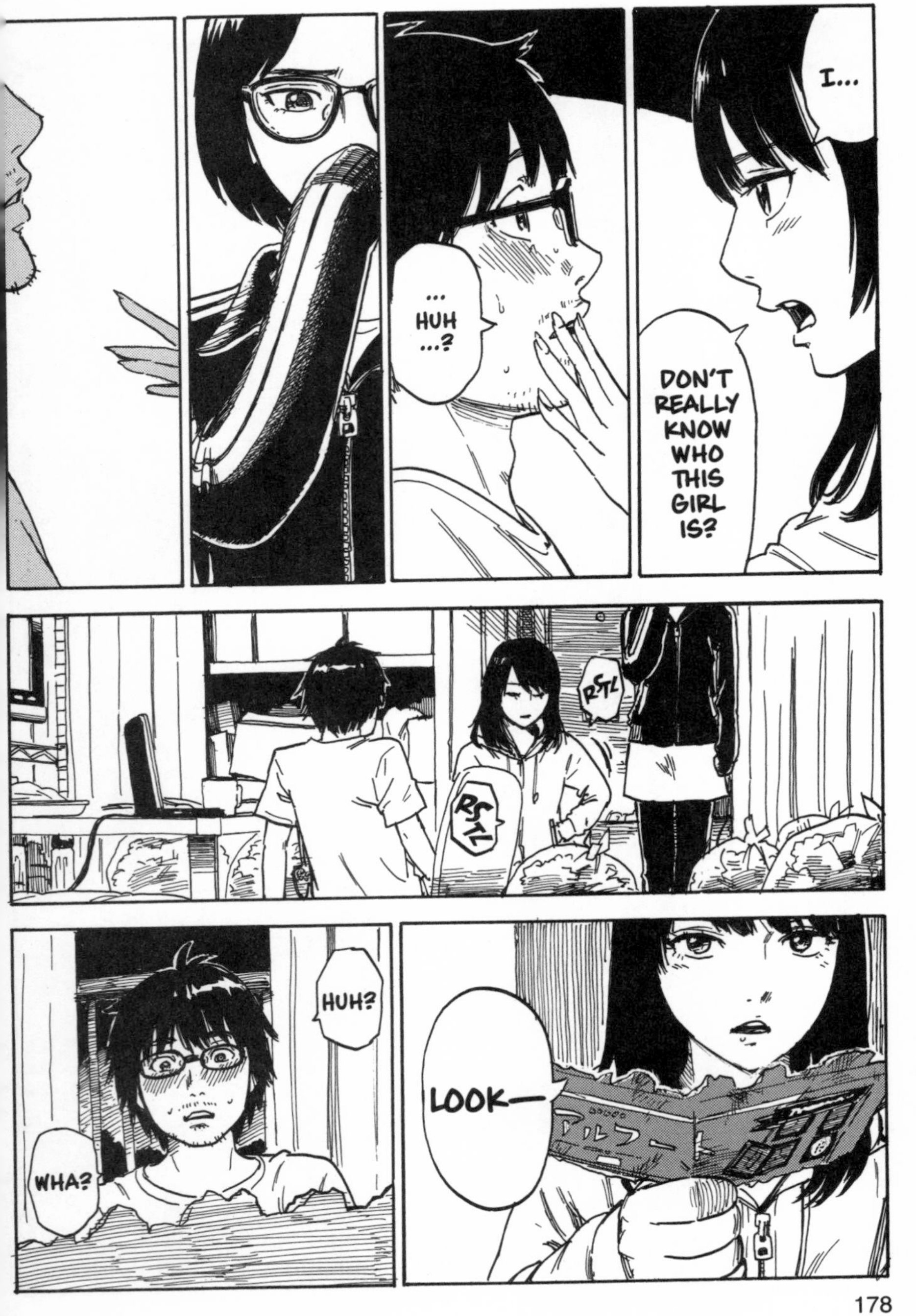
I...
DON'T REALLY KNOW WHO THIS GIRL IS?
... HUH ...?
RSTL
RSTL
LOOK—
HUH?
WHA?

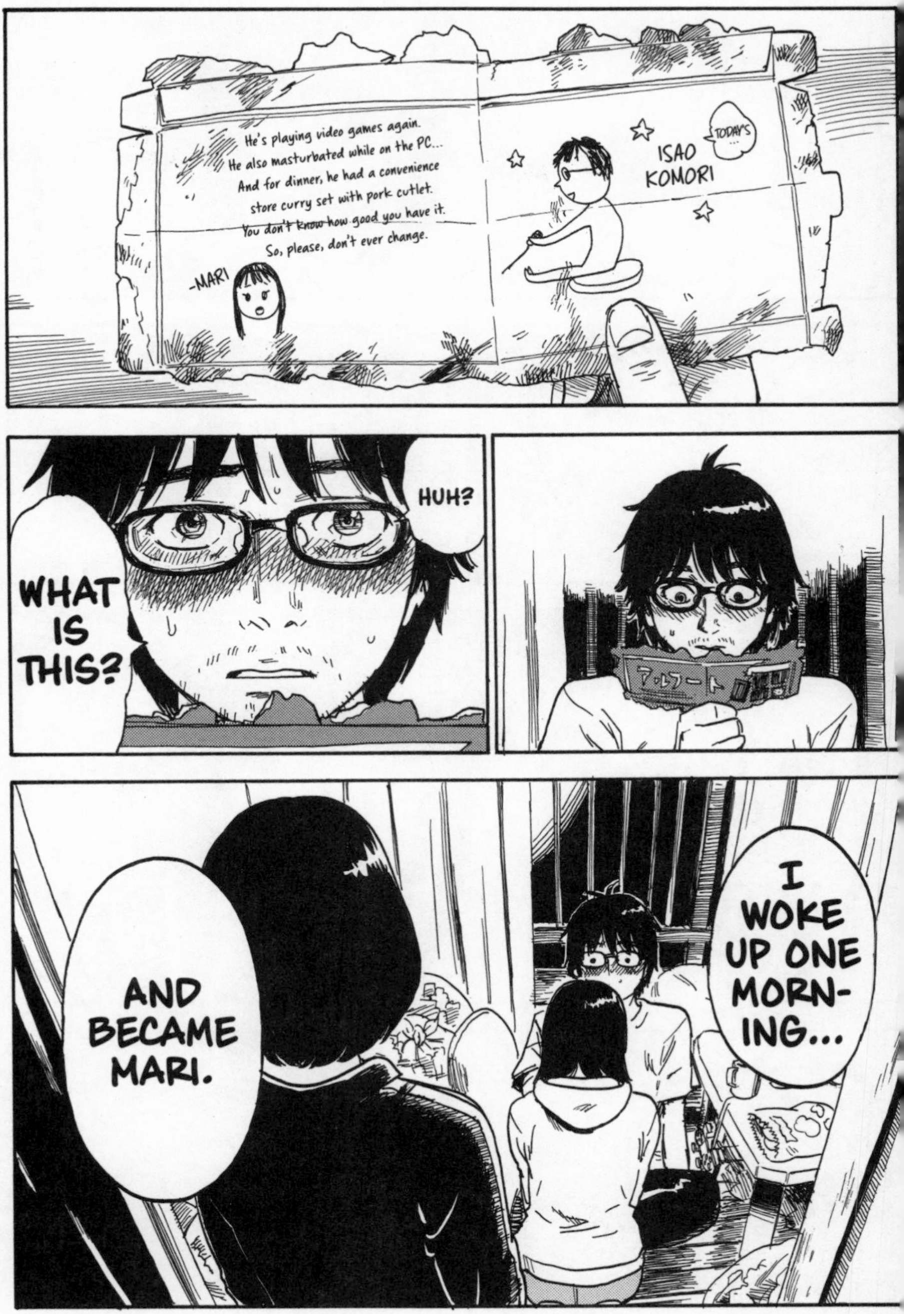
TODAY'S...
ISAO KOMORI
He's playing video games again.
He also masturbated while on the PC...
And for dinner, he had a convenience store curry set with pork cutlet.
You don't know how good you have it.
So, please, don't ever change.
-MARI
HUH?
WHAT IS THIS?
I WOKE UP ONE MORNING...
AND BECAME MARI.

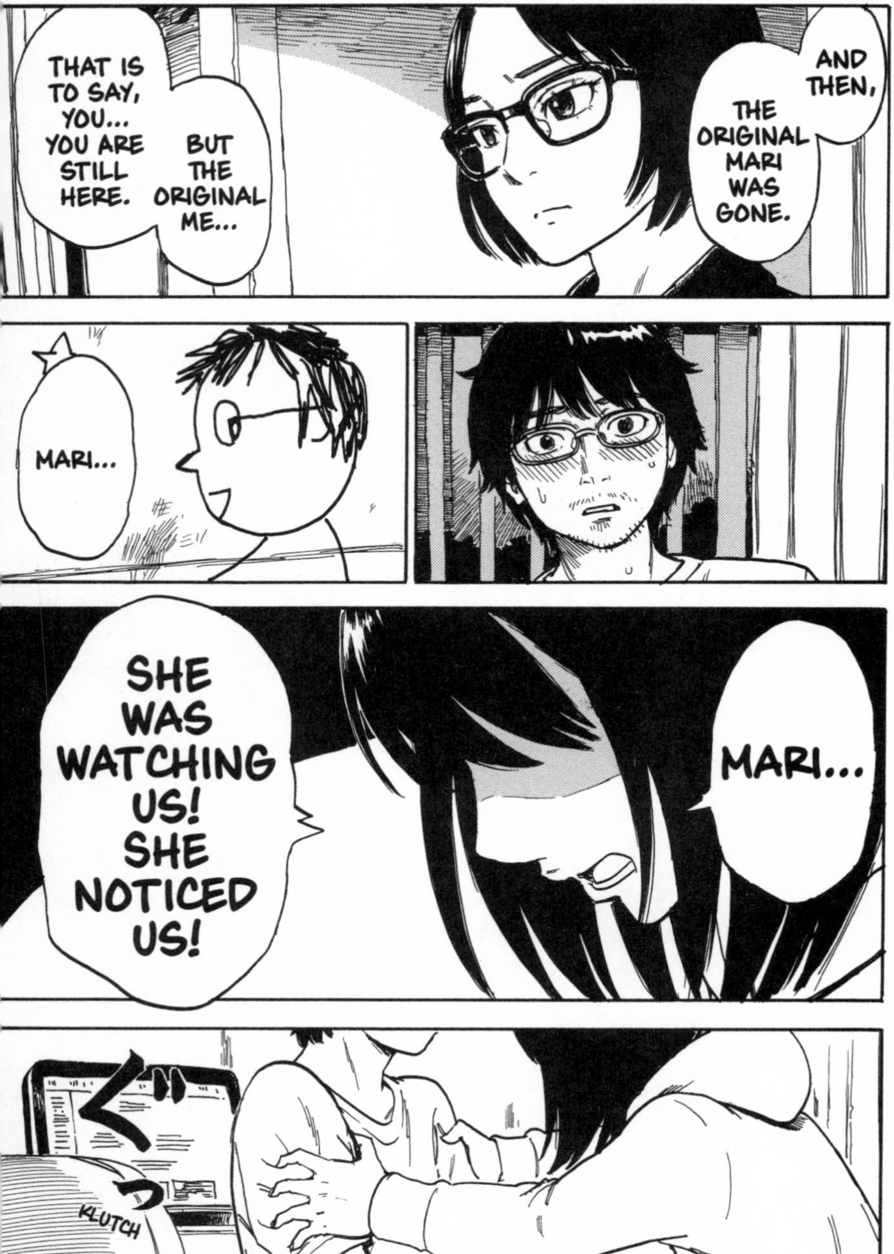

AND THEN, THE ORIGINAL MARI WAS GONE.
BUT THE ORIGINAL ME...
THAT IS TO SAY, YOU... YOU ARE STILL HERE.
MARI...
MARI...
SHE WAS WATCHING US! SHE NOTICED US!
ぐっ
KLUTCH

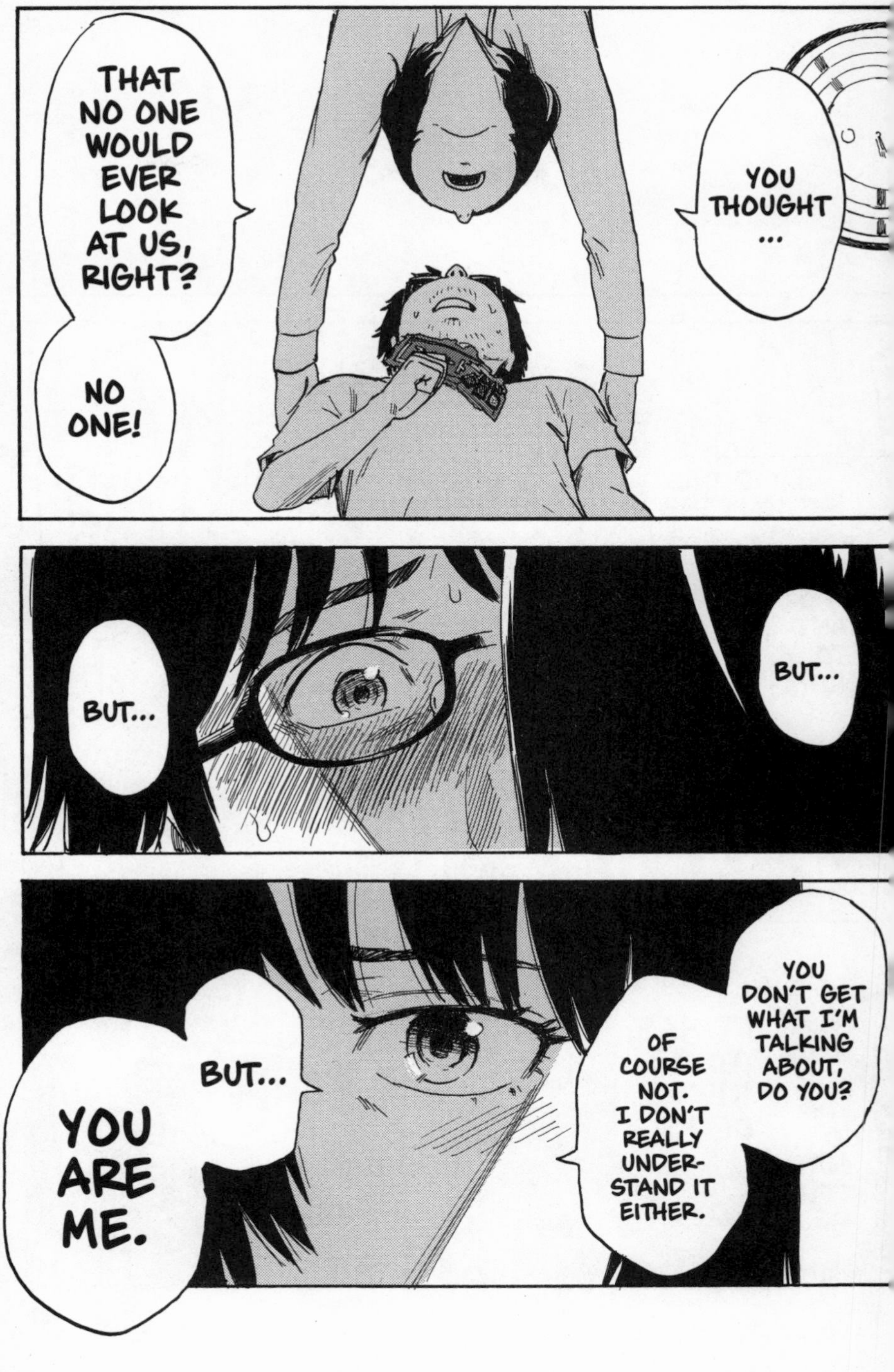
YOU THOUGHT ...
THAT NO ONE WOULD EVER LOOK AT US, RIGHT?
NO ONE!
BUT...
BUT...
YOU DON'T GET WHAT I'M TALKING ABOUT, DO YOU?
OF COURSE NOT. I DON'T REALLY UNDER-STAND IT EITHER.
BUT...
YOU ARE ME.

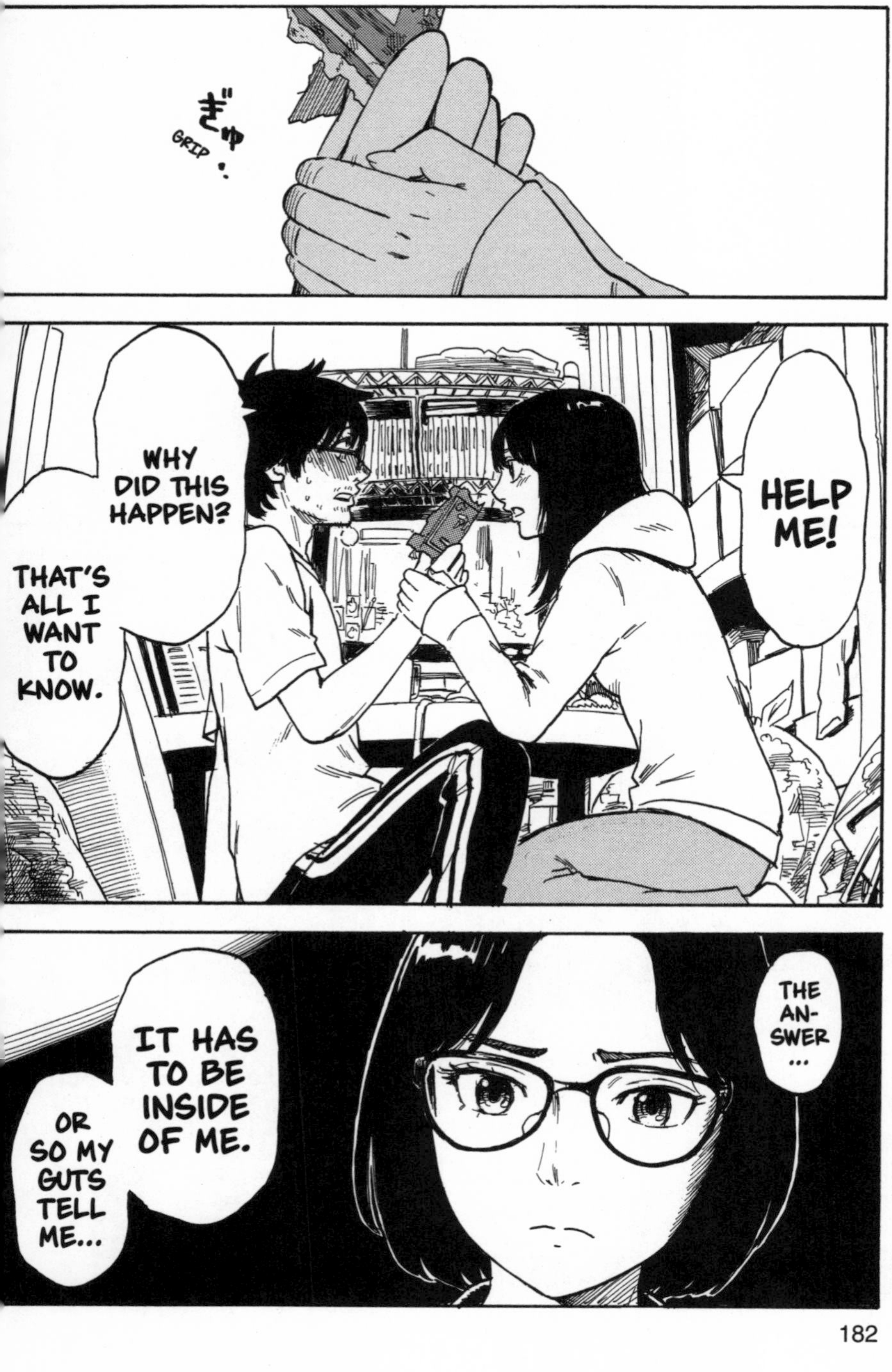
ぎゅ
GRIP
HELP ME!
WHY DID THIS HAPPEN?
THAT'S ALL I WANT TO KNOW.
THE AN-SWER...
IT HAS TO BE INSIDE OF ME.
OR SO MY GUTS TELL ME...

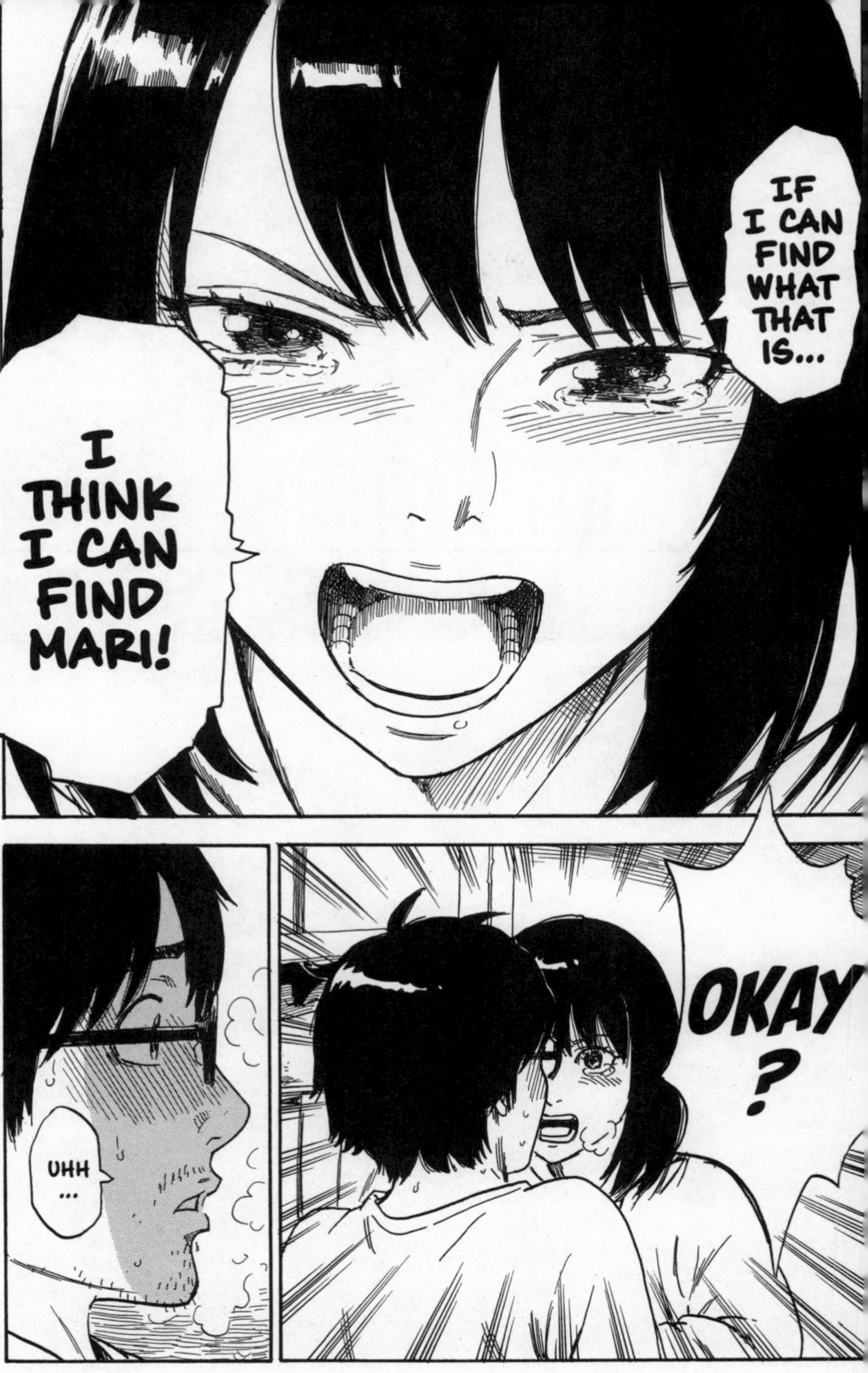
IF I CAN FIND WHAT THAT IS...
I THINK I CAN FIND MARI!
OKAY?
UHH ...

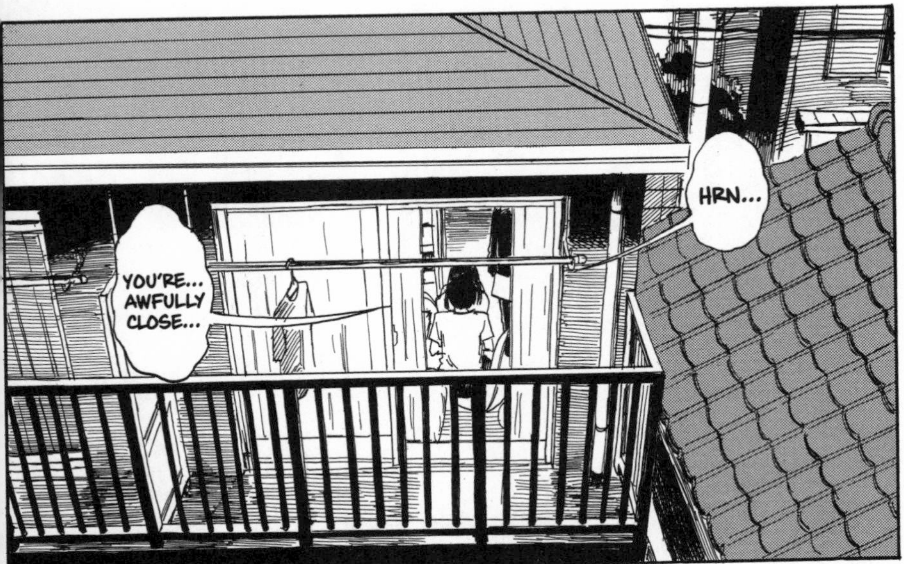
HRN...
YOU'RE... AWFULLY CLOSE...

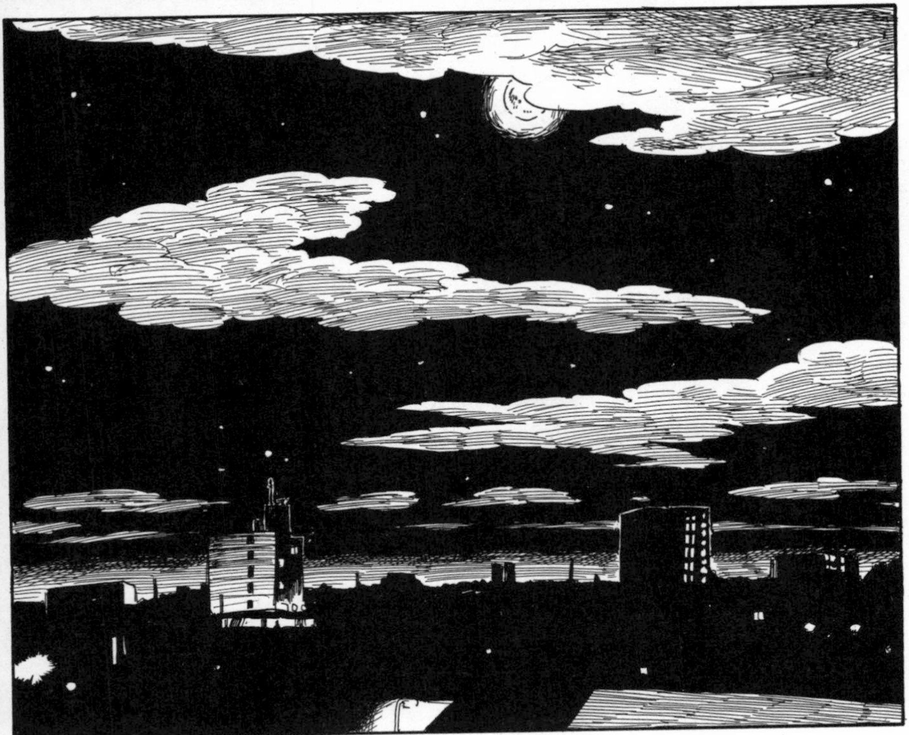

to be continued

Mari was looking at us...

Why did this happen?

The answer is inside of me.

If I could just find that out...

...I think we'll be able to meet Mari!

But, will we, with Yori, be able to find her?!

Inside Mari volume 4... Coming Soon!

IN SEARCH OF HOMETOWN EROS

~REPLACING THE AFTERWORD~

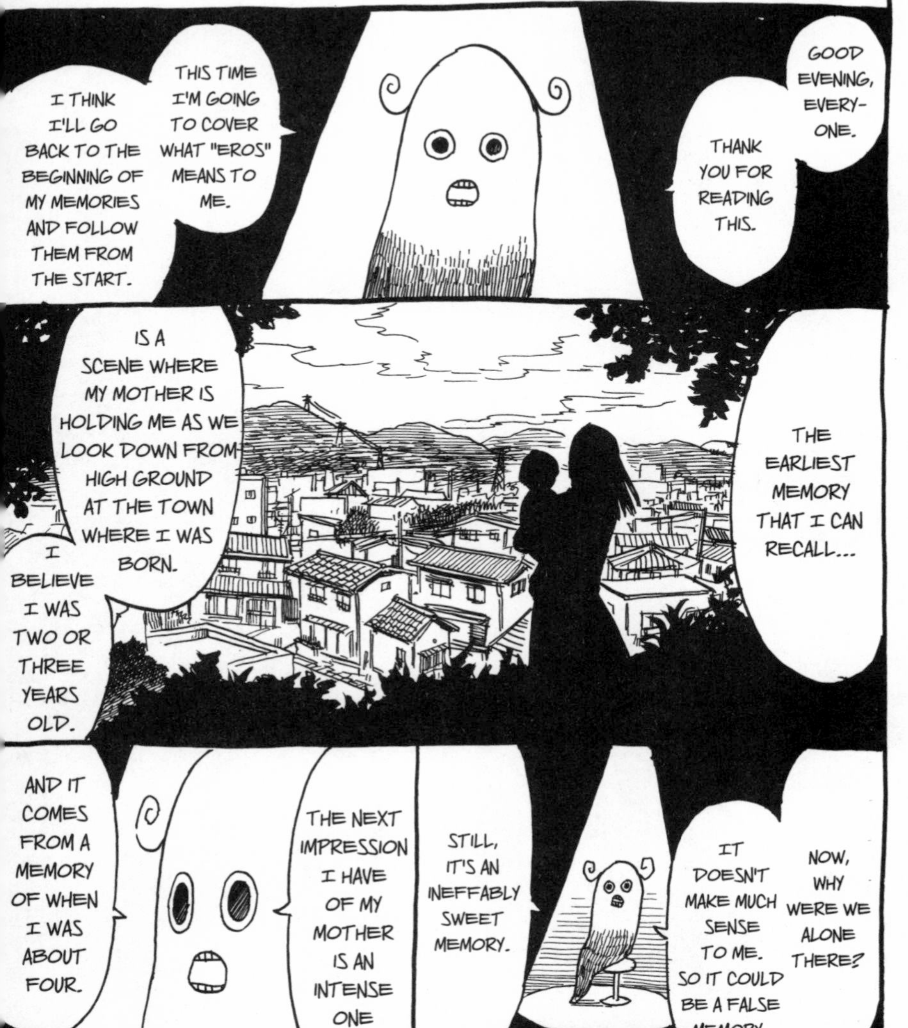
GOOD EVENING, EVERYONE.
THANK YOU FOR READING THIS.
THIS TIME I'M GOING TO COVER WHAT "EROS" MEANS TO ME.
I THINK I'LL GO BACK TO THE BEGINNING OF MY MEMORIES AND FOLLOW THEM FROM THE START.
THE EARLIEST MEMORY THAT I CAN RECALL...
IS A SCENE WHERE MY MOTHER IS HOLDING ME AS WE LOOK DOWN FROM HIGH GROUND AT THE TOWN WHERE I WAS BORN.
I BELIEVE I WAS TWO OR THREE YEARS OLD.
NOW, WHY WERE WE ALONE THERE?
IT DOESN'T MAKE MUCH SENSE TO ME. SO IT COULD BE A FALSE MEMORY.
STILL, IT'S AN INEFFABLY SWEET MEMORY.
THE NEXT IMPRESSION I HAVE OF MY MOTHER IS AN INTENSE ONE
AND IT COMES FROM A MEMORY OF WHEN I WAS ABOUT FOUR.

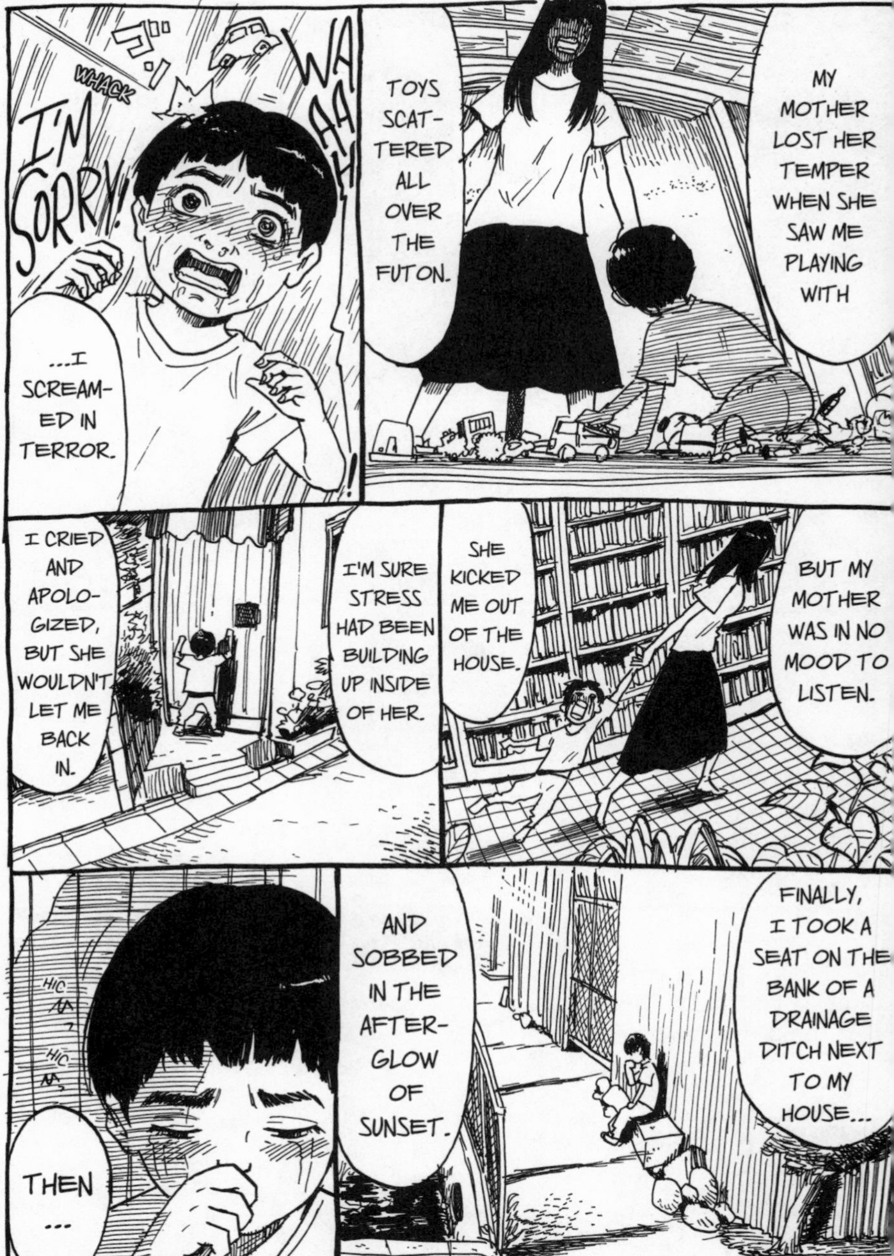
MY MOTHER LOST HER TEMPER WHEN SHE SAW ME PLAYING WITH
TOYS SCATTERED ALL OVER THE FUTON.
WHACK
I'M SORRY!
WAAAH!
...I SCREAMED IN TERROR.
BUT MY MOTHER WAS IN NO MOOD TO LISTEN.
SHE KICKED ME OUT OF THE HOUSE.
I'M SURE STRESS HAD BEEN BUILDING UP INSIDE OF HER.
I CRIED AND APOLOGIZED, BUT SHE WOULDN'T LET ME BACK IN.
FINALLY, I TOOK A SEAT ON THE BANK OF A DRAINAGE DITCH NEXT TO MY HOUSE...
AND SOBBED IN THE AFTERGLOW OF SUNSET.
HIC
HIC
THEN ...

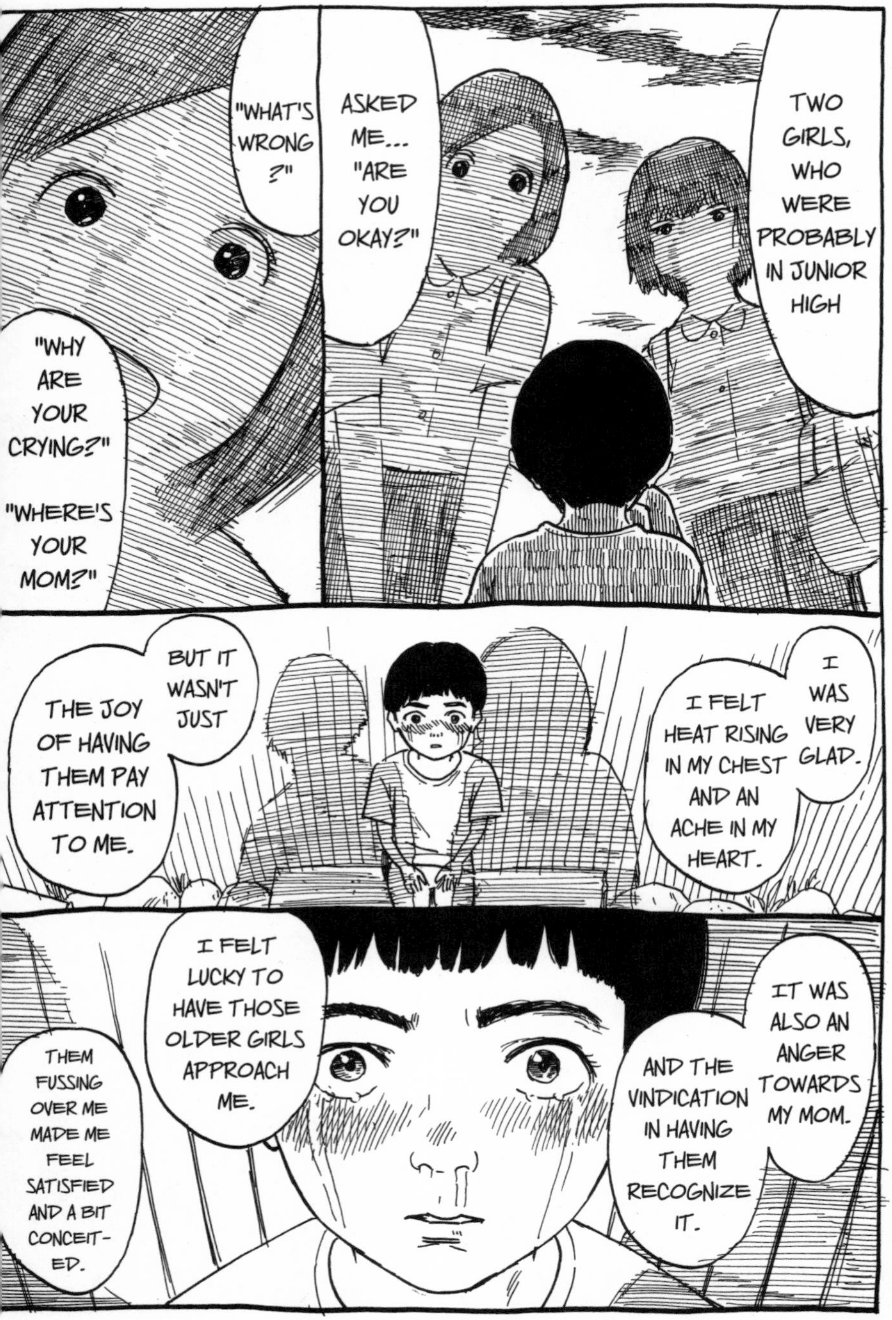
TWO GIRLS, WHO WERE PROBABLY IN JUNIOR HIGH
ASKED ME... "ARE YOU OKAY?"
"WHAT'S WRONG?"
"WHY ARE YOUR CRYING?"
"WHERE'S YOUR MOM?"
I WAS VERY GLAD.
I FELT HEAT RISING IN MY CHEST AND AN ACHE IN MY HEART.
BUT IT WASN'T JUST
THE JOY OF HAVING THEM PAY ATTENTION TO ME.
IT WAS ALSO AN ANGER TOWARDS MY MOM.
AND THE VINDICATION IN HAVING THEM RECOGNIZE IT.
I FELT LUCKY TO HAVE THOSE OLDER GIRLS APPROACH ME.
THEM FUSSING OVER ME MADE ME FEEL SATISFIED AND A BIT CONCEIT-ED.

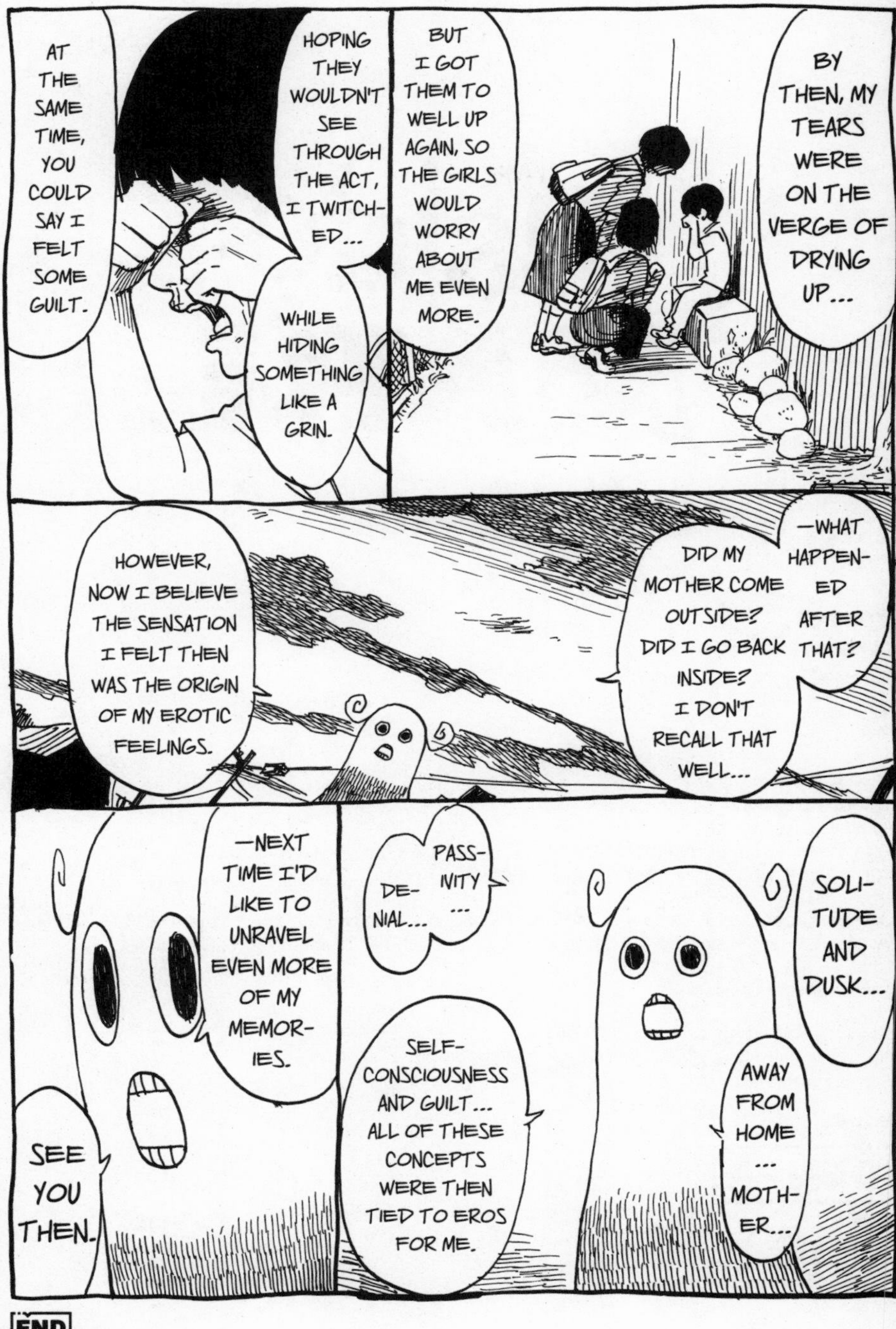
BY THEN, MY TEARS WERE ON THE VERGE OF DRYING UP...
BUT I GOT THEM TO WELL UP AGAIN, SO THE GIRLS WOULD WORRY ABOUT ME EVEN MORE.
HOPING THEY WOULDN'T SEE THROUGH THE ACT, I TWITCHED...
WHILE HIDING SOMETHING LIKE A GRIN.
AT THE SAME TIME, YOU COULD SAY I FELT SOME GUILT.
—WHAT HAPPENED AFTER THAT?
DID MY MOTHER COME OUTSIDE? DID I GO BACK INSIDE? I DON'T RECALL THAT WELL...
HOWEVER, NOW I BELIEVE THE SENSATION I FELT THEN WAS THE ORIGIN OF MY EROTIC FEELINGS.
SOLITUDE AND DUSK...
AWAY FROM HOME... MOTHER...
PASSIVITY...
DENIAL...
SELF-CONSCIOUSNESS AND GUILT... ALL OF THESE CONCEPTS WERE THEN TIED TO EROS FOR ME.
—NEXT TIME I'D LIKE TO UNRAVEL EVEN MORE OF MY MEMORIES.
SEE YOU THEN.

END

Volume 3

Translator:	Sheldon Drzka
Proofreading:	Ed Chavez
	Emily Martha Sorensen
Production:	Nicole Dochych
	Eduardo Manuel Chávez

First Published in Japan in 2014 by Futabasha Publishers Ltd., Tokyo.
Published in English by Denpa, LLC., Portland, Oregon, 2019.

Originally published in Japanese as *Boku wa Mari no Naka* by Futabasha Publishers Ltd., 2014.
Inside Mari first serialized in *Manga Action*, Futabasha Publishers Ltd., 2013-2014.

This is a work of fiction.

ISBN-13: 978-1-63442-904-7
Library of Congress Control Number: 2019933219
Printed in the USA

First Edition

Denpa, LLC.
625 NW 17th Ave
Portland, OR 97209
www.denpa.pub